SICKLY DODGER AND THE CITY OF ASSASSINS

OCCISOR CYCLE 1

LARS KONRAD MOORESMITH

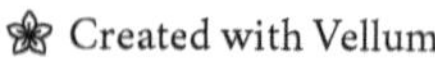 Created with Vellum

To my brother, mother, and father,
Gastronomes of story
Who taught me the same.

ACKNOWLEDGMENTS

No amount of praise or laurels would bury the mountain of debt I owe to everyone who read the intermediate drafts of this work. It should not be understated that without your indispensable advice, spot-on critique, and tireless support, *Sickly Dodger and the City of Assassins* would not have been possible. In no particular order, thanks to Liz, Austin, Orion, Mary, Dee Dee, Penny, Rosie, Olivia, Stacy, Kathleen, Fenn, Kathy and everyone else who offered insight and encouragement along the way.

Nor would the work be anything like as legible without the intense scrutiny and rigorous eyeballs of my editors, Elizabeth G. Wilmerding and Fenn MacDonald. For your cool heads and stoic respect of the English comma, thanks is not enough. Any errors are mine and mine alone. Thanks as well to Quinton, whose cover illustration was so exciting I had to finish writing the book. To Orion, Michaela, and Kara who were on the journey with me as I discovered the city of Hambridge hidden across the twisty, charming, and bizarre environs of Europe's hoariest metropolises, I salute you.

To my mother and father for their unfailing love and guidance and for introducing *The Hobbit* to a young boy, you have my eternal gratitude. I am profoundly lucky to be related to my brother, who keeps me honest, taught me how to use lock picks, and forced me to write a credible finale. To all my family, thank you.

CHAPTER 1

The River Ham begins its journey in the distant reaches of the Sternmetz Mountains, tumbling down lofty peaks in the direction gravity intended. It is not just a river. It is *The* River, the lifeblood of a dozen hamlets and villages that dot the gently sloping countryside following the meandering progress of The Ham. It flows past majestic forests, through deep ravines, coalesces in misty ponds, and widens and narrows with the changing terrain. It slakes the thirst of crops and beasts alike, a font of life for all. Finally, the River Ham reaches the big city where it is polluted, diluted, strained, filled with trash, and strangled of its natural resources.

But that's progress for you.

Mr. Stashcrumb walked his dogs through the grimy streets of Hambridge, pronounced Hame-bridge by locals with no sense of humor. It was indisputably the greatest city ever built, and anyone who said different would be set upon by a drunken mob of Hambridgers trying to sell them souvenirs.

The dogs nosed their way around an interesting pile of refuse, snuffling at moldy apple cores, empty fish-and-chips wrappers, and a steaming pile of anonymous excreta. The midmorning jumble of people, carts, and animals bustled and thronged. To an outsider the scene was business as usual. But Mr. Stashcrumb knew the little tells that marked the hidden knives people had begun to carry beneath their clothes. The Hambridge Watch stood on the street corners, cudgels at the ready. Two Kaldrian mercenaries escorting a merchant scanned the crowd with eyes as harsh as desert winds.

Mr. Stashcrumb gargled and spat onto the cobblestones, which began to sizzle. He fought his knitted cap more securely down over his ear hair, farted loudly, and made an obscene gesture at a passing merchant's carriage. That was the problem, these days. No one had any respect for the old ways. Too many carriages now, too many —

"Outta the way, gramps!" A young man in a patched jacket barged past.

Gramps! The nerve. Joints popping, Mr. Stashcrumb grabbed the butt of his cane and flicked the handle over the boy's shoulder. "Oi! You!"

The offender whipped around indignantly and spotted Mr. Stashcrumb at the other end of the cane. "Keep quiet, gramps," the boy hissed, reaching for a dagger inside the frayed jacket. "M'not playin' around." His hands were calloused. A scar puckered his upper lip. His eyes were cold and hard.

But the scowl turned to fear like butter going rancid as he saw the dogs. All six of them stood over three feet at the shoulder. They began to growl, advancing on him from all sides.

That was when the cane swung round and connected with a sensitive area at the joining of the young man's legs. As he sank to his knees, Mr. Stashcrumb growled, "I ain't a grampa, boyo. I prefer 'codger'." The young man tried to rise, saw the rows of gleaming canine teeth, and thought better of it.

"I believe you have summat o' mine." With surprising dexterity, Mr. Stashcrumb caught his money pouch as the young thief hurriedly threw it back to him. "Now, I ain't the kind to kick a man when 'e's down." The cane whistled in a deadly arc to crack against ribs. The boy yelped. "Not since me joints stiffened up, anyways." Mr. Stashcrumb coughed out a wizened chuckle.

The codger looked up. A small crowd had gathered, enjoying the spectacle. He glared at the nearest of them, who backed up, giving him and the dogs room. "Shove off, then," he muttered, and made his way up the street.

Hadn't always been this way. Back before there were so many merchants in this blasted city. Back before there were so many bleeding bankers, so many guilds and bureaucrats and alchemists and nobles and snot-dribbling arse-lickers. Back in his day . . . it hadn't been like this. It hadn't been . . .

There was something in the air. Under the melee that was Hambridge's normal fragrance of rotting fish, garbage, coal smoke, and piss, another odor writhed its way up his sinuses. It was subtle as cyanide and ugly as envy.

"Summat bad's coming, pups," he rasped. "I can feel it in me toes." His joints stiffened up when danger soured the air. This was the worst it had ever been. It was so bad he could even feel it in the toes that still remained attached to his feet.

Mr. Otto Blotter eased his bulk onto the new chair. He was happy in the knowledge that his honest, hard-working employees were, even at this hour, making him an enormous profit. His ponderous weight oozed through the chair, exploring its vast, red leather reaches. From a pocket on his smoking jacket he withdrew a cigar, as fat and expensive as himself. He ran it under his nose and sighed with anticipated pleasure.

With a practiced motion he clipped the end and lit it. He blew a noxious smoke ring toward the ceiling mosaic which had been imported specially from Khi Sian. A merry fire kept the chill of the early spring night off him. Years ago, before he had been quite so successful and so large, he would have rested his feet on the desk in front of him.

There was a knock at the door. Mr. Blotter frowned,

swiveling the chair to face the ash wood door. "Yes?" he asked coldly. He did not like to be interrupted while enjoying his cigars.

The door opened, revealing a small man wearing the clothes of a shop clerk – an apprentice to the company. "Pardon me, sir."

It was important to establish personal relationships with the employees. It improved workplace morale. "Yes . . ." He groped for the name. Something like, uh, "Eric." As often happens in such cases, Mr. Blotter registered only the boy's smile, and not its pained quality.

"Evening update for you, sir." The clerk consulted a sheaf of notes. "Mr. Haynickel says to remind you that the quarterly inspection by the Watch happens tomorrow. He says the, um, books are all set."

Mr. Blotter brightened at this, "Capital! You could learn a thing or two from the likes of Haynickel, m'boy. Man shows initiative! Ever participated in a quarterly before? No? Dreadful affairs, and there's no getting out of them for any of the guild masters or company executives. You ought to thank Caestos you're only a clerk, hah!"

The smile slid back into place, as smooth and glassy as ice. "Indeed sir. Next, the owner of Pier 27, Mrs. Fennel, is refusing to sell. She said, um, 'Not to come back till you increased your offer by a factor of ten.' Sorry, sir." Mr. Blotter rolled his eyes.

"I think it would be best if Ms. Fennel were to learn what kind of people she is dealing with here at the Ham River Traders. It would be such a shame if her home was broken into, don't you think?"

"I, ah, I see, sir. Lastly, there's the matter of the ongoing strike by the Handlers' and Stevedores' Union. They're still holding out for sick leave and special provision for workers with River Lung."

Gritting his teeth, barely able to enjoy his cigar, Mr. Blotter growled, "Collective bargaining, eh? More like collective delusion. A dockworker coughs and suddenly they claim River Lung. You'd think the city would be ringing the plague bells day and night if even half the cases were true. Bah! Have Haynickel hire a few more scabs, they'll break eventually. Well, if that's all? Marvelous. Off you go, then." The boy left, closing the door behind him. Mr. Blotter swiveled his chair the other way and puffed on the cigar.

"Simply magnificent," he sighed to himself, sequestered in his private fortress of luxury. The tiniest of drafts perturbed the hairs on the back of his neck. Mr. Blotter revolved back to face the door, he had sworn it was closed – ah, but the boy had neglected to shut the door after him. He took another pull on the cigar.

"Good evening, Mr. Blotter." A figure melted out of the shadows in the corner and crossed the room to lean easily against the desk. The cigar dropped from Mr. Blotter's fingers to land on the floor. "No need to get up."

"One of you!" Mr. Blotter gasped, and then choked on the smoke. He doubled over, shoulders shuddering. A black handkerchief found its way into his grasp, and Mr. Blotter wheezed into it. "Thank you," he croaked at last.

"No trouble," said the man. Through streaming eyes, Mr. Blotter peered up at the intruder. He had long black hair, a pale, handsome face with noble features, and cold, intelligent eyes. Mr. Blotter's hand not currently holding a handkerchief crept along the desk towards the tiny lever that would signal his private guards.

"What is this about? I have a right to know your client," Mr. Blotter wheezed, playing for time. A knife buried itself an inch deep in the wood of the desk, a hair's breadth from his wandering finger. Without taking those cold eyes off him, the assassin plucked his blade from the surface, and ran a cloth over it.

"No need for that, Mr. Blotter," he said conversationally. "But I'm afraid I can't answer you for a number of reasons. First, I'm still only a student assassin. I won't graduate for a few months yet."

"By Caestos, th-this isn't your red test?"

"No. Call it a personal project. More saliently, however, I am not being employed."

"Wh-what?" gasped the fat man, his heart racing. "Then you're not an assassin!"

"Oh yes, I am." The knife flashed. Mr. Blotter's wheezy breathing stopped. The assassin cleaned his blade with the handkerchief and tossed it into the fireplace. The knife returned to its sheath. He then strode out of the room, closing the door fastidiously behind him.

The cigar was still smoldering a hole in the rug. Someone else stepped out of the shadows. The Spy said, "Astonishing. He was right after all." And then she too was gone.

It was agreed afterward that Mr. Blotter's habit of smoking had finally gotten the better of him. Captain George Cassidy of the Hambridge City Watch personally investigated the fire which had started in an upstairs office of the Ham River Traders building. His statement highlighted the observation that the charred remains of the merchant appeared to have been reclining comfortably even as the man was engulfed in flame. The report concluded that, in Captain Cassidy's opinion, external forces had aided the victim's demise.

The report was summarily dismissed by his superiors at the Main Watch House.

The jimmied window slid upwards as delicately as a surgeon making the first incision. Gloved hands reached through, pulling a lithe figure forward into the darkened bedroom. Two booted feet sank into the shag rug as softly as snowflakes landing on a feather. They crossed the room, pausing only as their owner unhooked a razor thin wire tied to an alarm bell.

The intruder arrived at the moon-limned bed where a man lay, wrapped in blankets of wool and sleep. A smoky grey blade flourished into view over the dreamer's neck. With this barest of noises, the would-be victim turned over, brow furrowed.

The world held its breath. A snore escaped the target's lips. Above, the knife hovered.

Sickly Dodger paused a moment, shifted the angle of the knife, and made an experimental swing through the air, rather like a golfer readying a drive from the first tee. He frowned, examining the blade for an invisible speck of dust. He adjusted again, and took a second practice swipe. He closed his eyes, raised the knife and . . . stopped.

He stared down at the peaceful face of a middle-aged man, sighed, and sheathed the knife. His father would not have hesitated, he knew. The proctors from the Assassins' Guild grading his performance tonight would not be pleased. An assassin who couldn't kill was no assassin at all.

He ran a hand through his tousled black hair. "Shite. It's your lucky day, mate," he whispered, at last. His stomach back-flipped. He had always known deep down that he didn't have it in him.

The hairs on the back of Sickly's neck bowed under a slight change in air pressure. He turned just in time to see someone else dart through the window. Before he could move, this second prowler loped across the rug and slid a knife under the chin of the sleeping man. His eyes jerked open and he gave a startled gurgle as blood poured from the wound, choking his last cry. It was over in seconds and the killer withdrew the blade. Sickly's eyes widened in shock. "What the hells?"

The killer turned and removed the scarf that had wrapped her head. A curtain of wavy red hair fell to her shoulders, and Sickly's eyes widened.

"It's me, you idiot," said Eveline Lucrezia, Sickly's best friend from college.

"Vel? What have you done?" Sickly hissed, heart hammering.

"Obvious, innit? Now move!" Before he could protest further, Eveline grabbed him and yanked him toward the window.

Sickly looked back at the man, now horribly still. He

wrenched his arm out of Eveline's grasp and returned to the bedside. The body's mouth lolled open, tracks of blood oozing from its corners. "I'm sorry," Sickly whispered, and closed the man's stricken eyes.

"Sickly," Vel growled, and he followed her out the window and down the wall of the now-late Sir Denton Buckwood's townhouse.

Once safely on the ground, Sickly rounded on her.

"You had no right! He – that was my target!"

Eveline stared him down coolly. "What? You were going to do it, were you?"

Sickly's mind leapt to the image of blood spilling out over the man's neck, momentously black in the moonlight. His gorge rose at the thought, causing him to dry heave over the grass.

"You all right, then?" she asked, her voice softening for the first time.

He wiped the back of his glove over his lips. "No! That's the whole point of a red test! To see if you can really do it. Now what am I going to do?" he croaked.

"Now? Now you go back to Professor Clamnits and tell her you done it. Here's my knife, it's yours now. You'll get recommended for the Graduation Ritual and you'll participate. Most important, you never saw me. Got it?"

"But why, Vel?"

She glared at him. "You never saw me," she repeated, and disappeared into the night.

CHAPTER 2

The Dalton College for Men in Black was the preeminent school of assassination in the world. And contrary to its founder's wishes, it now produced both men *and* women in the business of inhuming their targets for money. Mr. Dalton, the founder of the great and prestigious institute, had not believed the profession suitable for ladies but had passed away quietly in the night, apparently suffocated by natural causes.

His successor made the necessary change to the enrollment requirements; on balance, she didn't have a problem with female assassins. After all, it didn't matter if the knife in your back was being held by a delicate but firm hand, or a large, brutal, and calloused one. Either way, you were still in trouble. And, of course, the men could get callouses if they worked really hard.

If there was one thing you could say about The Dalton College for Men in Black, it was that only the best graduated. Only the best and no one else. In fact, the college awarded only a single diploma each year because they still believed in the Old Ways. Each year the senior class competed for the title of 'Cum Sicario Undisputable' in a grand ceremony held in the best traditions of camaraderie, college pride, esprit de corpse, and leaving every one of your peers dead on the way to commencement.

Symbolically dead, in most cases. The rules of the Graduation Ritual decreed that any competitor found to use lethal force against their fellow man would be punished with a serious slap on the wrist. The college also retained a team of surgeons and nurses ready to reattach the dismembered limbs, suture the slashes, explant the arrows, and restart various bodily functions such as breathing. But, of course, accidents, and often intentional assassinations, did happen. It was a rare senior class that was not partially posthumous.

You couldn't hold it against the winner, Sickly thought, as his hands moved mechanically in a good imitation of clapping. Not when he, Sickly, had been lucky enough to survive his own death and join the ranks of the Occisor Cadre. The Occisor Cadre was organized by graduation year and comprised the large proportion of Dalton College attendees who did not graduate. It was still an honorable title, and represented years of training and sacrifice.

Beneath his black Cadre gown and the bandages, Sickly's wound twinged. The clapping went on and on as the weak Hambridge sun glimmered down on the assembly and this year's graduate.

Sable Levania certainly looked the part of assassin, with elegant medium length black curls framing a pale and noble face that worked perfectly with the black, tight-fit assassin's tunic and pants, black velvet cape, black doe-skin boots, black kid gloves, and, ultimately, the black.

But you couldn't hold his victory against him. Anyone bent on revenge would soon be found face down in the Ham, or worse, never found at all. Behind Sable's handsome features lay a chess grandmaster's icy intellect and reflexes sharper than an espresso-crazed fencer. In spite of the care offered by the surgeons of Hambridge's prestigious hospitals, they could only work miracles with people who were still loosely alive. Now that the Graduation Ritual was over, Sable wouldn't be forced to leave the doctors anything to work with.

Unlike most of his classmates, Sickly Dodger honestly didn't resent the man. Certainly not in light of recent events and failures on his part.

"Didn't you say your dad graduated from here, Sickly?" Sickly glanced to his right, meeting the watery brown eyes of Williams Kid, another burgeoning member of the Cadre. Sickly nodded. "If he was still alive, do you reckon he'd be disappointed in you?" Williams said snidely. Sickly raised an eyebrow. Williams, or Billys to those friends he hadn't alienated, had all the tact of a brick hurled through the sitting room window.

Sickly honestly had no idea what Henry Dodger would have said if he'd been alive to watch his only son fail to follow in his silent footsteps. He considered trying to explain the various metaphysical, philosophical, and emotional conundrums that barred him from guessing his father's judgment of the situation. As the attention of the crowd was drawn back to the stage, he settled for, "Shut up, Billys."

"Thank you, thank you, ladies and gentlemen," oozed the headmaster, Professor Hank Winderstint, his words coated in oil and dusted in sugar. Winderstint's black hair was slicked back over his skull, revealing high cheekbones and a rather sallow visage. But all these features were secondary to the gleaming smile which dominated his face, displaying a single crooked front tooth.

Professor Winderstint had been headmaster for one semester, after taking over from Professor Ignacius who had mysteriously "resigned." The Dalton College traditionally had at least one new headmaster a year thanks to little academic disputes amongst the faculty. Sickly was ready to bet money, if not a lot, that Winderstint would be resigning soon, if only because his vocal quality would have offended an alley cat.

"As I was saying, this young man is a shining example of the traits we at the Dalton College look for in our graduates. In these changing times, it is the responsibility, nay, the *duty* of the next generation to assert their will on the future. To bring every one of us forward with them. There are, as ever, forces seeking to degrade this great city, to disempower the noble class, to corrupt our statesmen and bring down our guilds. Forces both external and internal.

"But what made this city, this great city, was the commitment to hard work, responsibility, and the courage to do what needs to be done. Under the gaze of Father Caestos we prospered. Now, if we are to face the coming struggles, we need to return to the values that built Hambridge into the greatest city the world has ever seen. Values that stood strong in the face of foreign influences and unchecked migrants.

"And who better to lead us into the future than this young man you see before you? I see a man who will uphold the balance of power. The privilege of the noble class. Who will defend the merchants so that trade enriches everyone in this great city. From Lord Reiker down to the lowest dockworker. Who will —"

A woman one row ahead of Sickly snorted derisively. His friend, Jamie Webb, leaned over to her neighbor and whispered in outrage, "Can you believe this tripe? Defend the bloody merchants? Or the nobles? As if they'd share a bent penny!"

The other woman was Eveline Lucrezia. She tilted her head and murmured back, "I know, luv. But look at that lot out there in the audience. Silver spooners, every one of them, innit. They're lapping it up."

"They've got no idea. I doubt half of them have even been down to the docks except in a coach-and-bleeding-four!"

"What, and sully our boots?" hissed Sickly's other neighbor, Hamilton Traplek. Jamie and Eveline turned to glare at him. He smirked in response and then dismissed them with an imperious tilt of his head.

Winderstint was still droning on in that awful voice. "This man embodies the true assassin that this institution strives to produce. Ruthless, efficient, and ready to execute a contract to the letter. Nyeh heh. Heh." The audience tittered. "Now, ladies and gentlemen, I give to you . . . Sable Levania!" More applause.

The graduate stepped to the podium. "Thank you, Professor Winderstint." He paused and the room hushed. Every eye was upon the assassin. He spoke softly, almost dispassionately. "Drasilla's wheel turns, as the expression runs. I'm sure that the coming years will bring about great change indeed. Those who adapt will survive. We must all strive to adapt." He paused again. The crowd shifted, unsure of his intent. "To my classmates: The past years have tested and taught us much. About our tools. About our trade. And most importantly about ourselves. Why we do what we do.

"But the hardest test is the next step we take. Where will we go from here? How will we drive change? What new future will we carve? Do not mistake me. The road ahead is full of danger. Always beware the gleaming trap that has lured in so many before us.

"Though our college days have come to a close, I look forward to the day I see each one of you again." His eyes swept the other fourth-years. Sickly shivered. Finally, Sable turned once again to address the crowd, "I thank you for your time."

The man gave a slight bow and walked off the stage. Scattered applause rippled uneasily in his wake.

"That took bloody ages, dinnit?" said Jamie Webb, making her way through the hubbub of people clogging the Dalton College's main lawn.

"Too right," agreed Billys as he accompanied Sickly and Jamie "'Sable this' and 'Sable that' and 'Oh, what a lovely graduate' and piss all."

"You've got to admit, he looks the part, don't he?" Jamie said.

Billys scoffed. "Psshh, yeah. Right down to his sodding perfect gloves. How does he keep them so clean? We ought to prank him by stealing them and dipping them in the Ham. I bet that would knock the smirk off his face."

"Probably best you didn't, Billys. Where's Vel?" Sickly asked, "I thought she was with you. And has anyone seen Terry?"

Jamie jerked a thumb back toward the crowd, "Back there. You know how he is in crowds. And Eveline's in the loo."

It was not long before the hulking form of Terry Andrews appeared, bobbing through the press of people. Even at this distance they could hear him apologetically rumbling 'Pardon' and 'Excuse me, please'. As Sickly's oldest college friend finally eased through the mob, Sickly was struck as always by the man's mountainous stature.

"Sorry 'bout dat," he rumbled.

"No worries, dear," Jamie said. "Let's get clear of this lot." Sickly followed the tall woman with long dark braids towards a venerable oak tree. It had stood tall and proud against years, storms, and the lewd graffiti of generations of students. Jamie ran a brown hand up and down the trunk, bidding farewell to her favorite studying spot. "I reckon I'll miss this place."

"My, my, look who it is." A woman in graduation gown approached them. She had bronze skin and beautiful features delicately enhanced by makeup, but her smile was a little too wide to be sincere. "Hamilton, Doyle, come look what I've found." Jamie and Billys had both reached for weapons hidden beneath their gowns. They did not relax as Hamilton Traplek, tall and fair, and Doyle Gaspard, stocky and pallid, closed in.

"Joanna Martinez, what a surprise," Sickly said automatically. Joanna's sugary smile widened further as she swept her eyes over the little group.

"Sickly Dodger! And Jamie Webb. How did you enjoy the ceremony?"

"I thought it was a bit stuffy," Jamie said offhandedly, "You know, with that stick up everyone's arse."

"Oh, that's a shame," Joanna pouted, her face framed by a wavy curtain of black hair. "Maybe if we'd been in a bawdyhouse you would have felt more at home. Maybe your family could even have attended."

"Now, Joanna, I'm sure they were enriching themselves doing an honest day's labor," Hamilton said, pretending to admonish his friend while smirking openly at Jamie. Doyle snorted derisively.

"Right, which is more than you've ever done, Traplek."

"What can we do for you?" Sickly asked, in a futile attempt to steer the conversation out of the roiling straits of open hostility and into the calmer waters of frigid civility.

Joanna Martinez was the daughter of Annette Martinez, the head of the Merchant Consortium and the wealthiest woman in Hambridge. Joanna and her cronies, both noble born themselves, gazed at Sickly and his friends with the air of three cats overlooking a nest of baby birds.

Joanna tapped a finger against her square jaw. "Oh, you can't do anything for us, Mr. Dodger, really. I only wanted to say goodbye before the class goes its separate ways."

"I see," Sickly said, trying to ignore her rudeness. "And what's next for you? What line of work are you going into?"

Joanna gave him the pristine smile of a doll. "I'll be working for the Merchant Consortium. They hand-selected Hamilton as well."

"So what you're saying, right, is the Consortium hires based on nepotism and pity," Jamie observed. Hamilton glared.

"What about you, Jamie?" Joanna purred. Jamie froze for the briefest moment. "Oh, what a *shame* that no one has recognized your obvious talents. Even after you made the top ten in the Graduation Ritual." Jamie flinched and Joanna grinned in triumph. "All the people with taste must be looking elsewhere. Ah well, I'm sure someone will hire a person of your . . . background." On cue, Hamilton and Doyle smirked. "You'll get those loans paid off in no time, I'm sure. What about yourself, Mr. Dodger? Has anyone found a use for someone like you?"

Sickly merely raised an eyebrow, but Jamie rushed to his defense. "What do you mean by that?"

"Only that Mr. Dodger is so . . . unique."

There was a snicker of nasal laughter from Billys, whose pinched, pink face was contorted with mirth.

"What?" Billys asked, "Joanna's right, Sickly. You get sick all the time, and your face doesn't move. You're a bit of a freak." Sickly had to admit his friend was partly right. If the Ten Gods played games with the lives of humans, then they had seen fit to bless Sickly with a perfect poker face. In truth, it was physically beyond him to smile, smirk, frown, or perform any one of the bewildering facial maneuvers that everyone else took for granted. The most he could do was raise his eyebrows, which he did now, at Billys.

"Shut up, Billys," Jamie snapped. He stuck his tongue out at her.

"A freak. I couldn't have put it better myself," Joanna exclaimed, her smile turning really nasty. "Maybe you could join a circus, Dodger."

"I like da circus. Dey have lotsa animals." They turned to Terry, whose normally ruddy face went even redder at the attention.

"Andrews could join up too. Perhaps in the service department. Playing the role of, oh I don't know? The stage?" Doyle added.

It was at that moment that Eveline finally caught up with them. Their three antagonists tensed slightly, and adopted wary stances. "Oh, it's you lot," she said. "Why don't you move along?"

"Well, well, Lucrezia, it looks as though your little —"

"Joanna, you will leave. Now." Eveline's liquid tones suddenly became as hard and sharp as ice.

Joanna opened and shut her mouth once.

"Come on, then," Hamilton said to the others, and the three of them flounced off, down the sweeping lawn.

"What were those vultures up to?" Vel asked offhandedly. With a grace the envy of any dancer, she swung herself onto a curled branch that had bowed so low it brushed the top of the grass.

Sickly couldn't emote, but he did have to force himself to stop glancing at her face every few moments, hoping to meet her green eyes. He had long ago convinced himself that being friends was all he needed, that he didn't actually want anything else. Sometimes he almost believed this.

"Just looking to launch a last round of barbs while they still can, I think," he replied.

Sickly looked round at the other faces. Billys was picking his nose. Terry smiled to himself, still thinking about the circus. But Jamie had her head downcast. "Jamie, you all right?"

The young woman straightened and brushed her braids over her shoulder. She put on a smile, "Yeah, I'm grand."

"What did they say to you?" Vel asked sharply.

"Oh, the usual," Jamie said, with an attempt at airiness. "Shaming us commoners for paying our own way through school." Vel's expression darkened.

"Jamie," Vel started, "Being born into a golden crib makes you soft, and drinking –"

"And drinking from a fancy goblet gives you lead poisoning. I know, Vel." Jamie said shortly. "Just leave it alone, all right?" Vel pursed her lips.

CHAPTER 3

There was a mansion. Not the gaudy manor of an ostentatious ingénue, but the really old kind. It had huge, wrought iron gates and massive, dead black trees like the skeletons of forgotten gods. Inside, there was old oak furniture, mahogany paneling, deep red velvet, brass fixtures, peeling wallpaper, and elephantine stairways. It was a labyrinth of passages and rooms that would require several days' food and water to navigate from bedroom to privy.

There should have been an army of butlers and batmen and ladies in waiting to attend on the owners. But no, it was nearly empty. Nearly, but for the several dozen hopeful assassins vying for life and fortune in the Dalton College Graduation Ritual.

Sickly hung at the intersection between two walls, suspended nearly twenty feet in the air above a long, carpeted hall. He blended perfectly with the dark molding behind his head, allowing him to watch the area as safely as possible.

There had been very few screams. After all, assassins preferred to kill silently. But this hush was almost worse. It gave Sickly's imagination too much to work with.

He hadn't moved in an hour, feet slowly going numb on the austere bust that supported him. But at least he was alive. If he was lucky, no one would find him, and the last two assassins would finish each other off. He might survive. He might even graduate.

On the whole, Sickly Dodger was not a lucky man.

An assassin burst down the hallway, charging off up the passage. Sickly's heart pounded for a few seconds before he calmed it with a few measured breaths. He had not been seen. Before Sickly knew what was going on, and surely before the young man below him did, a second figure appeared in hot pursuit. It fired a small, handheld crossbow at the running man, hitting him in the calf. He fell with a grunt of pain.

The shooter drew a knife and was on the downed man in seconds. Sickly saw the man roll aside and draw a blade of his own. They grappled with each other, and blood, shiny as fresh paint, spattered the carpet. Sickly wanted to crawl down the wall and flee before someone discovered him. But his hands were sore from hanging on to the wall, and his legs shook as he began the descent.

He had almost reached the top of the door frame when there was a thud and Sickly saw the victor stand, wipe her knife clean and turn. Sickly swore, dropped and rolled, the thick carpeting catching him as he landed. As he fell he drew from the folds of his black clothes a knife. It was ready for combat as soon as he regained his feet. "Come off it, Sickly," the woman said, tiredly.

"Vel?" His heart skipped a beat. If he was going to die, it wouldn't be so bad to be killed by her.

"Yeah. It's all right, innit. I'm not going to kill you unless we're the last two, ok? We're friends."

"That's very comforting." Sickly's face was level. "But how do you know you'd win?"

She gave him a pitying look. "Come on Sickly, I've been in school with you for four years. I know how you fight. And anyway, if you'd wanted to kill me you would have drawn those throwing knives and picked me off while I was finishing Denner over there. And finally, there's that whole thing where you don't kill people."

"Oh."

"Hullo, you two." Jamie Webb had just rounded the corner. Eveline raised her knife and dropped into a crouch, but Sickly shook his head. "How are you dears doing?" Jamie asked politely.

"Surviving," they said together, and Vel smiled at Sickly. Sickly looked back.

"I marked 'Yesterday Sam' and Roderick Gablehaus but only just escaped ambush from Sable. He's teamed up with Ulrich Munz, of course. They're killing anything that moves," Jamie said to fill the silence.

"I saw Terry go down, but the doctors got to him quick I think. Haven't seen Billys anywhere," Vel supplied, sheathing her knife.

"Sable finished him with a punching dagger," Jamie said indifferently.

"Just us then, innit?" Vel said.

"Yep. Do you want to make a go of it together? I bet we'd have a chance of giving Sable some exercise," Jamie said, flashing a smile, white against her skin and the gloom of the mansion.

Before anyone could answer, two assassins appeared at the end of the hall, and charged. Sickly turned and raised his weapon in a fluid motion but was too slow to deflect the incoming knife. The small blade caught him in the left arm, and he felt a sharp, stinging pain. He realized only vaguely that if he hadn't turned as quickly, he would have been dead right there. He recognized Ulrich Munz charging at him. Ergo, the other ambusher was Sable Levania, and they were dead already. It was only a matter of time.

Sickly leapt backwards, holding his knife protectively in front him. Ulrich grinned hugely. "Failing to live up to your surname, Dodger. I'd consider it a personal favor if you made this interesting for me."

"I'll do my best." Sickly stealthily drew his throwing knife from its sheath on his left shoulder on the pretext of feeling his wounded arm.

"Remarkably decent of you, my good man." Ulrich charged again, not the typical bull-like rush you might expect from someone who was nearly as large as Terry. Instead of the head forward, bellowing dash, Ulrich moved like a snake using graceful side to side motions that belied his power.

Sickly hurled his melee knife clumsily with his left hand. Ulrich dodged easily, laughing, but stopped when Sickly threw the concealed knife with his right hand, and the steel blossomed out of Ulrich's shoulder. "Bickering blintzes that stings!" Ulrich cursed. "But a good feint," he allowed as Sickly dodged past.

"I try," Sickly confessed as he pulled another knife out of a hidden sheath. His last one.

Ulrich smiled at Sickly. His teeth were bone white. One of his hands was balled into a fist. The other drew a short sword from a hip scabbard, and Ulrich swung it towards Sickly. Sickly blocked using both hands, groaning as his left arm seared with pain. During the split second when he closed his eyes, Ulrich stepped inside Sickly's guard, too fast for him to retreat. Ulrich raised his curled hand, opened it, and puffed on a small pile of powder in his palm.

It billowed up in a foul red cloud, catching in Sickly's eyes and burning worse than the pain in his arm. Sickly knew what was coming. He leapt back again, swinging with his knife and trying to wipe away the dust with his left hand. He felt an awful pain in his back and blacked out.

"Hello? Sickly? Are you still with us, or should I have you carted off to Mr. Gizzard for autopsy?" Sickly shook himself out of his memories.

"That won't be necessary, Billys," he said. It was lucky that it hadn't been necessary after the test, either.

Rain pounded the café's windows as the little group, now official members of the Occisor Cadre, searched eagerly for the bottoms of their cups. Sickly sipped a water.

Across the table Eveline continued to try to improve Jamie's spirits. "Jamie, luv, just because we didn't graduate doesn't mean we didn't learn how to assassinate people. We'll get contracts, just you wait."

"We're part of the largest Occisor Cadre on record, dear. The last two years' cohorts were large too. The assassination market is getting . . . saturated. Clients can be more choosy."

"Then it's good we made it into the top ten, luv! They'll want the best, and that means us. Professor Rector recommended me to Lord Salsa. He's already approached me with a contract against one of the members of the Bakers' Guild. You should talk to Professor Scucheon, see if she can set you up with a patron."

"I tried. She said she'd look into it, but I haven't heard from her in weeks," Jamie said.

"Dat sounds nice, Ev'line," Terry rumbled after a few seconds. Terry usually needed a running start before he could speak about anything. "I'm thinkin' 'bout gettin' hired by da Merchants' Guild."

"Terry dear, what do you mean 'thinking about getting hired'?" Jamie asked, in spite of herself. "It's them who decide whether or not to accept you."

"No, dey accept me."

"Why?"

"Cos' I ask nicely." No one could be sure if this was intended to be funny.

"I've gotten a couple of offers, but I might do freelance," Billys said. "That way I could pick and choose my own work."

"Ugh, Billys, you're going to be a gold dagger?" Jamie sneered.

"A what?" Sickly asked, confused.

"An assassin who just takes the highest paying contracts, no matter who the target is," Jamie explained.

"What about it?" Billys retorted, aggressively. Jamie rolled her eyes.

"You could do two jobs at once, Billys," Eveline said, snidely.

"What do you mean?"

Vel sighed. Billys never understood jokes on his pluralized name anyway.

"So what 'bout you, Sickly?" Terry asked, turning like a glacier.

"I don't know," Sickly started. Ever since that night when Vel had killed his first ever target, he had been dreading this question. He felt trapped by it, unable to see past the monolithic fact of his own inability to perform the one job he had been trained to do. But there was no beating around it. He had made up his mind. He wouldn't kill.

"I was thinking about . . . walking dogs." Eveline burst out laughing, Jamie smiled in spite of herself, and Billys' scowling face broke into a grin. Sickly's face was completely straight. It was easy to do since he couldn't have made a crooked one if he'd tried. "For rich old ladies with poodles or something."

"Is that an innuendo?" Billys asked, still laughing. Vel gave him a glare that would have scarred a more sensitive person for life.

"Sickly, dear, that's a summer job," Jamie tried.

"I reckon dogs need to be walked all year round," Sickly replied.

"Well, if it makes you happy," she said, in the tones of a mother worrying after an underachieving son majoring in philosophy.

"But . . . dog walking?" Eveline asked, her tone of voice suggesting that if he had displayed an interest in making giant rubber squid puppets, she could not have been more aghast.

"I hear it pays well if you know the right person and the right dog." Sickly said a little defensively.

Vel's confusion and mirth turned suddenly cold. She glared at him, making him squirm slightly in his seat. "You've just earned a Dalton College education. You participated in the Graduation Ritual. And you want to walk dogs for a living?"

As uncomfortable as he was, Sickly stared her down flatly.

"Yeah, I guess I do." If she had just left well enough alone, he could have failed the red test honorably and carried on with his life.

"Sounds nice ta me. I like doggies," Terry said. "Good luck, Sickly."

"Thanks, big guy."

CHAPTER 4

The blustery and rain drenched Hambridge spring evolved into a muggy but short Hambridge summer. Sun broiled the Ham's usual sludge into a brown crust; the world's largest oven baking a toxic soufflé. The river's odor permeated nearly every square foot for miles, save the top of Tumult Hill, exciting the city's entrepreneurs to invent new perfumes, smelling salts, and air fresheners shaped like Reiker's Bridge. The miasma was only truly dissipated by the onset of autumn's cooler weather and increased rain, leading the same entrepreneurs to drop whatever they were holding in favor of scarves, cloaks, and alchemical heating wafers.

The Spy sat in the back room of The Uppers, one of Hambridge's grubbiest taverns. She wore a sensible gray dress and work boots, her hair pulled into a simple bun. She did not look like a spy. Real spies often don't.

The man across from her wore a beery smile displaying a feast of rotten teeth. She returned it with a saccharine smile of her own. "So who was it that resigned from the Merchant's Council this week?" she asked.

"Misster Carstein, for one. An' fer another . . ." His expression clouded for a moment. He stared myopically through the alcoholic haze of his vision. "Who're you again?"

"I am Ms. Floren. I'm going to be a secretary on the Merchant's Council, remember?" She smiled again. The man, who for the purposes of an informal meeting in a seedy tavern was called Mr. Acorn, grinned.

"Tha's right, tha's right. I remember-ember-ber." He chuckled. "An' fer another there was that bloke Greenman. He resigned too."

"Fascinating," the Spy said, sounding absolutely entranced. "Who replaced them?"

"That fellow Callolay, no, Calloway, replaced Carstein. And Greenman's poshition was taken over by . . . er . . . Lonsk. Can't say as I've 'eard of either of 'em. Shifty eyes they had, too."

"And do you know why they resigned?" she asked, in a hushed whisper. He leaned forward, his breath foul with many tankards of beer.

"They say it was assass'nation. Word on the street's that you should watch out fer . . . fer a man called Sable." Mr. Acorn looked momentarily sober, his hand suddenly steadier as he passed two fingers over his right eye to ward off Merafey's malevolent gaze. He took a long swig. The Spy smiled her winsome smile, and the man brightened. "Hey, pretty lady, why don't we go back to my plashe for a while, eh?" He tried to wink, but had lost control of his eyelids.

"Oh, but you haven't finished your beer!"

He peered into the depths of the mug, utterly dismayed. "Yer right," he said in the tones of one being led to a profound philosophical conclusion. He drained the last of the glass and slumped forward onto the table. The Spy rose, leafed through Mr. Acorn's coin pouch, paid for the drinks, and left.

Mr. Acorn, when he awoke, remembered nothing.

. . .

Sickly sat at his table and nibbled a piece of unbuttered toast because dairy made him ill. Really, he reflected, his father could not have picked a more suitable name.

The story went that Henry Dodger had felt unbearably queasy after waiting for his son to be born. When a nurse had kindly asked him what they wanted the baby's name to be, he had thought she was asking how he felt. There was no way to know now if it was true or not, but Sickly hadn't really blamed his father until school. After the first day Sickly had come home leaking water from his eyes because so many of the other children had laughed at him.

The rented flat was as bare bones as he could afford on a dog-walker's earning. It offered nothing in the way of amenities and even less in the way of comfort, especially now that a faint hint of the Traveler's autumn chill leaked in under the rickety door. Though he had been living here for more than a season, it still felt too cozy a word to call the place home. Sickly shivered and examined the four pieces of that morning's post.

Word of his small business had begun to get around. The first two were job offers from a Mr. Stashcrumb and a Ms. Tonita respectively. Next came an envelope of creamy, rich paper and the imposing grey seal of the Guild of Barristers. Inside was an even creamier, richer page printed with the momentous letter-head of Kharnassi and Rolls. Sickly's eyes glazed a bit as they grappled with the jungle of legal adverbs and redundancies. As far as he could make out, the Dodger family retainers were informing him politely that despite him being the only living heir to the Dodger estate, the lawyers still held iron control over the purse strings. Their objection was on the grounds that his dog-walking business fell outside the spirit of his father's will. Until he started taking Assassins' Guild sanctioned work, he was on his own.

Looking around his bare flat, and the four whole pieces of furniture he owned, he shrugged. He was doing all right, wasn't he? He could sort it out later.

The fourth package was a small box wrapped in black paper. Sickly frowned and went over to the large chest at the foot of his bed. He produced from it a pair of tools which looked a bit like ink pens crossed with small, precise knives. With them he returned to the table and set to work opening the box. His caution was well deserved but not put to the test, as it opened without setting off any poison gasses, concealed needles, or alchemist's fire.

Sickly shrugged. He wasn't very important in assassin hierarchy, so it was unlikely anyone would try to kill him. But he had learned a few tricks from the Dalton College, and old habits died hard. Unlike careless assassins.

Inside was a folded piece of parchment and a small pouch. He pulled the parchment out and read:

To the son of Henry Dodger,

I write to you as an old friend of your father. For reasons I will not include in so free a correspondence, I cannot tell you my name or where to find me. By sending this letter, I have put you in mortal danger. I realize how ridiculous I sound, but I assure you that the danger is very real, and very close. I require your assistance in a somewhat troubling matter which I will entrust to no one but the son of my friend. Unfortunately, due to the nature of this affair, I will also shortly be dead. Terribly inconvenient, but there you have it. That is why you must step into your father's Shoes. Discover my abode. Inside I have hidden more detailed instructions about how you can help me. If you have any sense at all, you will doubt the sincerity of my intentions, which is why I have enclosed something your father gave me a long time ago. I realize it is ill mannered to ask favors during an introduction, but time is short. Find my murderer, or you and your friends will be in grievous peril.

An Imminently Posthumous Friend

Sickly raised an eyebrow.

He sat back in the chair and reread the note, thinking carefully. Then he upended the pouch and something shiny and circular fell out. A signet ring. Sickly picked it up and turned it over and over. It had indeed once belonged to Henry Dodger. The Dodger family crest was imprinted upon it, and engraved on the inside were two initials, H. D.

This indicated that the sender had known his father, though it proved nothing about their friendship. Possibly it had been sent by Henry Dodger's killer, who had stolen the ring and was for some reason looking to finish off what they had started.

Or it could be genuine, and Sickly was being asked to help an almost total stranger. He mulled the possibilities over while reading the short paragraph again. It was vague to the point of frustration, with almost no hint as to how he might find its author. He felt the paper, looked at the ink, the strokes of the pen, and the wording of the prose.

Putting all this together, he could safely assume that whoever had sent this had been born to wealth and education. That meant they were probably part of the aristocracy, especially if it was true that they had known his father. It was easy to infer this because assassins did what they did for *money*, and only the most affluent personages would have had the kind of funds to hire someone with Henry Dodger's skills.

So, he was looking for a soon to be murdered (or assassinated) member of the nobility or merchant class. Someone old enough to have known his father. But it was also clear that the sender had powerful enemies who might have noticed this letter and its recipient.

Sickly reread the bit about being in danger and felt his eyebrow raise. It was so . . . melodramatic. And the little apology for said dramatics lacked style. Still, if the mysterious author was in earnest, then Sickly was at risk. And apparently so were his friends.

Yet if it was assassination, why would his friends be targets as well?

He hadn't wanted to be involved. He hadn't wanted to be an assassin. He only wanted to walk dogs.

Sickly sighed. His curiosity and sense of self-preservation were piqued. He fingered the ring. He had once felt it regularly pressed into his back as his father hugged him on his way to school. It had seemed so large then. With a pang he realized he was able to slip it comfortably onto his pointer finger.

Maybe Henry Dodger would have wanted him to help this mysterious person after all. Sickly crossed to his shoes where he stored the day's newspaper. It was time to check the obituaries.

The snaps on the physician's bag clicked with all the finality of a coffin lid snapping into place. The man rose, pushing his glasses up the bridge of his nose in a practiced motion. Two children with worried expressions perched on the side of the crude bunk where their father lay, his eyes half closed in the manner of the near dead or very drugged. In this case it was both.

Jamie leaned against the shabby wall of the tenement as her mother, Jodie Webb, and the doctor approached, speaking in low voices. Jamie's hand played with a strand of dark braid as her mum's voice rose in a pleading note.

The doctor from the Charity Barnsforth Loving Hospital cut her off sharply. "If you had come to me sooner, perhaps. The Alchemists' Guild has a new serum. But it works only when the disease is in its infancy." As if they could have afforded one of the new serums.

"We've been trying to book an appointment for weeks," Jamie spat.

He jumped and wouldn't meet her gaze, instead fumbling for his glasses as if to give them a clean. "Ah, well, you see. There are a great many people who need treatment. It's not me, see. The hospital administration decides which cases are the most, well, pressing."

He was lying, Jamie knew. Or rather, he was speaking a different language. One in which the words 'pressing case' were synonymous with 'privileged client.'

"We— we thought it was just a bloody bad cold." Her mum, so proud and strong and firm, looked ready to shatter.

"The fact remains, ma'am, that it's River Lung, and only Genulum's providence could save him now."

Jamie's hand continued to work her braid on its own, as if her body was one of the mechanical weaving devices down at the factories. "Happily, there is a remedy, Beaupierre's Curative, which treats the symptoms. All you need do is feed him a spoonful of that tonic twice daily, and he should remain stable for some time. A year or more, if the gods will it. He may even improve. The body has amazing powers, after all." Jodie nodded, her eyes half-lidded and sunken. "I have a bottle with me, if you wish to try it."

River Lung. It came to most dockworkers eventually; those who were smart and lucky enough not die in one of the hundred other easy ways that kept Hambridge ever in need of new bodies working the river. It started as a mild cough that eventually began to produce black sputum and shook the patient's body with wracking heaves. As the disease progressed the victim began to waste away, barely able to cough the fluid from their lungs. At last the sufferer asphyxiated on whatever lived in their own airways.

Everyone had heard of Beaupierre's Curative, for all the good it did. The price of the palliative was enough that it bled the coppers from the unlucky family just as surely as the River Lung bled the life from its victim. Knowing this didn't make their options any different. It just made the choice more painful.

The doctor pulled on his hat with a pale hand and turned. His stoic visage slipped for the first time, not at the tear tracks silently falling down Jodie's face, but at the blank expressions of the two children still by the bed. "I'm sorry for his condition, but there's nothing more I can do."

It would be easy to hate him, Jamie thought, as he stood there with an air of awkward impatience and veneer of sympathy. His posture said that he was only doing his job. It wasn't his fault people got sick. Genulum, god of plagues and alchemy, decided that sort of thing. And at the end of the day he could just walk away and keep living his comfortable life.

Jamie counted out his fee from the purse at her belt, each coin laden with the life she had taken to earn them. She also spent the bitter price for the first bottle of Beaupierre's. The physician nodded and left them to their grief.

As she poured a measure of the amber liquid down his throat his eyes held her gaze. He was too weak to speak, but as the minutes stretched past his breathing eased. The lines of his brow and the creases in the corners of his eyes softened. She could almost fool herself into believing he could recover. That he would be one of the lucky few that pulled through the illness. Idiot.

"What's that face for, my sparrow?" James Webb's voice was husky and cracked like a dropped glass, but it hurt so good to hear it.

"Da," Jamie whispered. "I— "

"Nah, nah, hush now." He managed to bring a huge hand frosted with callouses and scars up to her face. There was such a weight on her chest. "You're a grown gel, Jamie. We both know. You got that fancy schooling, yeah? Now you gotta care of them." He ruffled Connall's hair with his other hand.

Jamie clenched her jaw. He was giving up. He was giving her an easy out. He was telling her to look to the future. He was being sensible, Ten Gods damn him. "Shut it, da." He glared back.

But her mind was racing over the possibilities, calculating the sums. Her prediction at the café, that patrons currently had a wage negotiation advantage due to the surge in young assassins, had not been wrong. The few measly contracts she'd landed since graduation had yielded depressingly small payouts. Still, she tallied a quick budget in her head. How much could she earn per job? How many jobs a month? Less the cost of the curative, food for mum and Connall and Leila. And rent. And her loans.

Her lips drew back to reveal her teeth. It was nothing like a smile. "No. We can do this. I can do this." Jamie stood and hugged her mother who was still standing by the door and mechanically rubbing a braid between her long brown fingers.

"I'm going out, mum. I'm going to handle this."

He was called Crowbar. Well, by his owner, anyway. Everyone else was usually running in the opposite direction. This was because Crowbar was not just a big dog, the biggest of Mr. Stashcrumb's pack, but also because he was not entirely dog. Sickly was pretty sure that within that viscous blood were the most feral elements of wolf and bear. This, coupled with the intelligence of a criminal mastermind, made him not only the smartest, but also the meanest, and most disturbingly quiet of the whole pack.

Crowbar did not lead the pack by fear. Or by respect. Or by any other school of leadership known to humankind. Crowbar did not, in fact, lead at all. He just did whatever the hells he wanted while the other five Stashcrumb dogs followed meekly in his wake. If Mr. Stashcrumb could have bottled Crowbar's essence and sold it to kings, he would have made a fortune.

There were still hushed stories told in the backs of taverns across Hambridge and in the Guild of Postal Workers of Stan Rapkin. Stan Rapkin had been a mailman. And then he had gotten in Crowbar's way. And then he had become, in very short order, lunch. For some reason, there had never been a lawsuit over it.

And of course, Sickly had to walk him.

Every weekday Sickly reported to the big door of Mr. Stashcrumb's mansion in Eel Park, and was greeted by a repulsive odor of week old fish, horseradish and pipe tobacco, and then by Mr. Stashcrumb himself. One might wonder how a predator as evil and temperamental as Crowbar put up with being 'owned' by a human. Crowbar had no love for anything in this mortal coil, at least that part of which he could see, smell, touch, hear, eat, or hump. But when it came to Mr. Stashcrumb, there was the sort of grudging respect one complete bastard holds for another.

"Late again?" Mr. Stashcrumb would rasp, a voice of sandpaper on gravel.

"It's nine o'clock exactly, Mr. Stashcrumb."

"No, it isn't, boyo. If you're late again, I'll teach you a lesson in time keeping you won't forget in a hurry. I could tan your hide with one hand tied behind me back." Sickly would raise an eyebrow. Ignoring this insubordination, Mr. Stashcrumb would turn and call into the foul-smelling interior of his home in a voice tinged with the burr of a high Golraic accent. "'Ere, Crowbar! Gnosher! Gouger! Over 'ere, Gangrene! This way, Gout! Come 'ere, Spoon!" And then, with an evil look in his watery eyes, Mr. Stashcrumb would hand Sickly five leashes in one hand, and Crowbar's leash in the other. "I want this lot back by eleven. You hear me, boyo?" But by this point, Crowbar would already be dragging Sickly down the twisting walk, the other five dogs in their wake.

Surprisingly, there were, in fact, good points to this job.

The bad news was, obviously, Crowbar. The good news was, oddly, Crowbar. Five vicious and otherwise uncontrollable canines followed docilely behind Sickly, because it was always best to keep at least one warm body between them and Crowbar. And so, Sickly was able to walk the dogs wherever he wanted to, provided it was wherever Crowbar was already going.

Sickly had survived the first day only by the skin of his teeth and the skills honed during his college years. At first Crowbar had been a little puzzled to find a living creature still alive after bothering to attack it. And then for the next hour and fifty-nine minutes Sickly had fled all over Hambridge, pursued by an increasingly bemused killing machine.

Somehow he had made it back to the door from whence the six dogs had burst like the hounds of hell, handed the leash back, and then gone and had a lie down for the rest of the day. But he was alive, and that was certainly more than anyone could say for Stan Rapkin, or for the last couple of people Mr. Stashcrumb had hired to do the job.

The next day Sickly had decided to go back. After all, Mr. Stashcrumb had conveniently forgotten to pay him in the kerfuffle. If nothing else, he reasoned, running around for two hours would keep him in excellent— well, better health. Sickly was sickly, after all.

However, after the six leashes were back in his hand, a curious thing had happened. Crowbar turned his head, glared for a full twenty seconds at Sickly, and then started down the path. It took Sickly several days to realize that Crowbar's sudden and above all worrying change was due to the dog's realization that: A) Sickly would take too much effort to kill, B) if Crowbar did kill him, it would take the better part of his walkies, a waste of a perfectly good morning, and C) that Sickly was a sort of parole officer who allowed Crowbar freedom of movement, while in fact being totally helpless to prevent Crowbar from doing anything he damn well pleased.

Sickly always scheduled himself a lie-down before his next appointment. When his head had stopped spinning and his heart had slowed to a gallop, he would then hobble a few doors down to see old Mrs. Cronwall. She owned an aged, half blind Chihuahua which thankfully took an hour to get down the street and back.

Now, several weeks after the first harrowing encounter, they had fallen into a routine which Sickly mentally dubbed The

Walk. The Walk took them from the austere mansions of Eel Park, down through Uptown, across Pigherd's Way, through a narrow alley which opened onto The Crowns, down those cobbles for a few blocks before hanging a sharp right and ducking across late morning traffic on Reiker's Avenue to reach Motley Drive. Finally, after a few alleys, they would at last reach their destination, Reiker's Commons.

At first, Sickly had worried about getting mugged and thrown in the river while crossing Motley Drive, but he needn't have bothered. Crowbar's presence was more effective than a dozen armed bodyguards.

It was a painting day.

Terry had to force himself to move slowly, slowly, slowly so he didn't bump anything with his excitement. First, Terry got dressed. Shoes and socks and shirt, just so. Then Terry made his bed. Then he went to the kitchen which was cold from being lonely all night.

Terry coaxed a fire to life in its ashy home. He got the kettle and the water and his mug. All the while he sang the Tea Song. Soon there would be tea, and this was both right and proper.

He didn't sit about to wait for the kettle to boil. It was a nervous boiler, and could not be looked at. Terry went to the paint shelf, skipping just a little. The floor shuddered beneath him. Terry shook his head. It did not do to have too much excitement. But still, it was a painting day.

Terry took down the easel and the jar of brushes and the water cup and the palette and the carved wooden box of paints. Inside, they were lined up like eggs, just so. He also took down a new canvas, crisp as cream with a cat. In spite of the predawn chill everything felt warm under his fingers. This was right and proper.

Terry put the painting things on his table and tidied up the flat. He put away the pans and dishes from the drying rack. He prepared his toast. He ate his toast. He got out the honey jar for the tea. And the cream. He disengaged the poison arrow at the top of the stairs to the roof and unlocked the door. Terry did not go out yet. That would be peeking at a present before a birthday.

The kettle finally felt brave enough to boil. Terry smiled at it, and hummed as he made the tea. The smell of bergamot filled the room. And the honey. Then the cream. It was almost time.

The canvas, paint box, palette, brushes, easel and water cup were stacked together. Terry carried them in one hand, the tea on a saucer in the other. Slowly, slowly, slowly he climbed the stairs and nudged the roof door open.

There was a blush on the horizon, the kind Sickly and Eveline had when they looked at each other too long. Terry nodded and smiled to himself. He set down his tea. He arranged the canvas on the easel. He prepared the water cup and the palette. This sunrise was almost as shy as the kettle. He sat and waited. He sang the Sunrise Song while the wind played with his hair and the gulls.

And when everything was right and proper, Terry painted the dawn. Just so.

"Hullo, luv!" Eveline grinned as Jamie came toward her across Rue Le Jour, the avenue home to many of Hambridge's finest specialty restaurants and the Guild of Plumbers. When a patron was in gastric straits after a Yakistani curry it paid to have the right people on hand. "You look splendid!"

"Thank you, dear," Jamie replied, with a touch of self-conscious pride. She gripped the edges of her yellow evening gown and half-twirled to show off her finery. In the flickering glow of the street lamps, Jamie looked gorgeous. Her long, dark braids were pulled back and tied with a colorful band of red, orange and yellow. It put Eveline in mind of an autumn forest, colors which complemented the warm brown of Jamie's skin.

"That's lovely! Is it new? Such a good color on you!" Eveline had to admit she was a little jealous of how easily her friend pulled off the whole ensemble. Jamie so often wore working assassin's garb or hand-me-downs that you could almost forget how gorgeous she was.

Jamie shrugged. "Thanks, dear. But no, it's some nob's cast-off I lucked into. But look at you, Vel! Still as stunning as ever."

Eveline shrugged and rolled her eyes with pride, "What, this thing, luv? It's the one I wore to the winter ball last year, remember?"

"Wearing the same dress twice?" Jamie gasped in mock horror. "What would Joanna Martinez say?"

Vel smirked at the memory of that night. "I reckon Joanna would *have* to buy a new dress for every event. At the rate she spills wine on herself, I mean."

"You're terrible, dear," Jamie giggled. "Shall we?"

They turned together and passed the doors of Le Hibou Maigre, which boasted Hambridge's best, or at least most expensive, Bricquébecois cuisine. It is a rule that once any city grows to a certain proportion, a restaurant with an unpronounceable menu, inedible garnish, and disapproving waiters will spring into existence. It will serve very small portions of dubiously conceived meat and paper thin slices of vegetables seasoned with the eater's own confidence in the worth of the price tag.

Like a bed of flowers in formalwear, the faces of the restaurant's clientele turned to follow the two suns that strode into the room. Eveline had to fight hard not to dive for the nearest shadow as she felt eyes rake her up and down. A cold trickle of sweat began to run down her back.

Jamie, by contrast, ignored the situation with a surprising nonchalance. Eveline reminded herself that they were here to enjoy a nice meal, not for a job. That was the trouble with being an assassin; work-life balance was nearly impossible. You started to see threats everywhere.

As they were seated by a fawning waiter, the hairs on the back of Eveline's neck prickled. She glanced sideways and met the eyes of a dandy, who winked a little too knowingly at her. Her glare was cold enough to wilt the rose in the buttonhole of his white evening jacket.

"Disgusting," she muttered, as she pulled her seat forward.

"You're all right, dear," Jamie said. "Just ignore them. That's what they hate the most."

"I don't know how you do it, luv," Eveline sighed.

"Younger siblings, dear, remember? I could ignore a full Hagrippan funeral procession playing stockade drums if I had to. That and two semesters of etiquette with Ms. Perjorice, yeah?"

Eveline took a breath. She could do this. Jamie smiled at her across the acre of table dressing, centerpieces and glassware. "This place sure puts on airs, dunnit?" Jamie murmured, peering around at the décor. Eveline glanced at it too. The dusky atmosphere and the play of candle flames made normal shapes jump and dance in the reflections of knives and spoons.

To distract herself from the images this conjured up, Eveline replied, "Of course it does, why else do you think all these nobs come here, luv?"

"Still," Jamie mused, "give me a pint of cheap ale and a good bar fight any day."

"Well, we can always go down to the Bottle and Four later. Just to watch." As a rule, assassins did not participate in bar fights. It was considered lowbrow. And it was rude to win.

Their waiter returned with a wine and expertly poured the ruby liquid into a pair of crystal glasses. "A '48 Beaumont LaFevre, mademoiselles," he drawled while turning a blind eye as both mademoiselles immediately checked it for poison. They ordered their food with minimal fuss and lounged in their chairs, speaking of idle things.

First the appetizer, then the main course, arrived and they set to. "Oh, damn. Olives," Eveline muttered, as she picked at the little dull-green fruit.

"What's wrong?"

"I hate olives, don't you remember? They give me terrible gas." Jamie snorted indelicately and Eveline couldn't help but grin. The outburst helped her relax. She found she was happy to do so.

The candles at their table burned lower as they talked long into the evening.

In a lull, Eveline regarded her friend. It was good to see Jamie again and doubly good to see her smiling. Yet the little knot of worry that hung thundercloud-like between her brows was, if anything, even worse. Her cheeks looked even hollower than they had back in college.

"How have you been doing, luv? I mean really doing."

Jamie smiled unconvincingly and shrugged. "M'all right, yeah?" Eveline's heart sank, knowing how much those words could hide. "Thanks for the lookout, dear. You've always stood by me."

"Of course, luv! Us scholarship girls have to stick together."

"We really should have done this sooner, you know. But you never respond to my letters."

"I know, I know. I'm sorry, Jamie. I'm terrible at keeping up with people. I haven't seen anyone since graduation."

"Well, you might have if you replied to your post . . ." Jamie sing-songed under her breath. It did not escape Eveline how skillfully Jamie had deflected the conversation to safer ground. Eveline couldn't blame her. Disguising hurt with a brave mask was a defense she had learned long before she took up an assassin's knife. And the deepest hurts often came down to family. Maybe Mrs. Webb hadn't been able to take enough jobs to fill in the cracks or maybe Mr. Webb's health had finally taken a turn for the worse. But Eveline didn't want to press, not if Jamie didn't want to bring it up.

Instead, she responded, "You're right, of course. I'll be better, promise. Maybe I'll send Sickly a letter tomorrow."

"Good. Do it." Jamie paused, looking as though she didn't know quite how to bring something up. "Look, Vel, remember when we were in college and said maybe one day we'd do jobs together . . ." Eveline felt something creep into the conversation, some subtle gristle, lurking far below the cheery surface of the evening. "I recently hooked a patron. A proper one, yeah? But some of the jobs might need a second pair of hands. I thought of you."

"That was kind of you," Eveline said, automatically. She sipped her wine to give herself time to think.

"Her name's Lady Fullfrigate. The coin's been pretty good. Y'know, some help on the side," Jamie went on, staring into Vel's eyes. Vel couldn't hold her gaze. A little voice inside her wondered why, if Jamie was getting extra help, did she look so gaunt? Something about this was wrong. Patronage was excellent, The Ten knew Jamie deserved it, but this had complication written all over it. Complication led to entanglement. Entanglement was . . . dangerous.

"Jamie, luv. Work's been really busy, lately. Lady Margarine Salsa's death has thrown the whole family into turmoil, and Lord Salsa needs me almost all the time to protect his assets." This was mostly the truth. Besides, Eveline wanted to make a good impression with her own patron. By hiring a scholarship student like Eveline, he had invested in her worth as the assassin who took third in the graduation ritual, looking past her social class. She wanted to live up to that investment by prioritizing his interests.

The knot had deepened on Jamie's brow, and Eveline inwardly cursed. The evening had been going so well.

"Look, it's not what you think, Vel. This is different. This is big. These contracts are important. I want you to be part of it, too, all right?"

Eveline sighed. It wasn't that she didn't want to work with Jamie, but that voice was blaring inside her head. It was the voice that had always alerted her to danger back when she couldn't afford new dresses, or even secondhand ones. Back when she couldn't even afford trust. It was screaming that this sudden opportunity was bad news.

Eveline had never heard of this Lady Fullfrigate, though with the ingrown family trees of Hambridge's various noble families that was hardly surprising. Whoever she was, Eveline doubted her intentions were as altruistic as they appeared. It was not unheard of for nobility to headhunt struggling assassins from common stock just to ensure the loyalty of their instruments. Such assassins were considered particularly expendable by their wealthy patrons, and Eveline had vetted her own Lord Salsa thoroughly before agreeing to contract with him for this very reason. But she didn't have the heart to remind Jamie of this, not when she had looked so happy and earnest.

"Thank you, Jamie. But really, I'm doing fine with Lord Salsa. I'm sure you'll do great, too." Jamie mustered the kind of smile that plastered over the cracks of an unmet expectation. Drasilla's docket, Eveline cursed inwardly. She did not have so many friends that she could afford to alienate even one, especially not Jamie.

Dessert arrived, and though conversation resumed, the evening had the same sour notes as the Beaumont LaFevre and the same oversweet finish.

CHAPTER 6

Sickly's thoughts wandered as he took the dogs on The Walk. This was not a good idea if you were within fifty feet of Crowbar and trying to make it to your next birthday. But his mind kept bouncing back to the letter he had received two weeks ago. Since then, he had waited patiently for the murder to actually be committed. The strangeness of the whole thing was not lost on Sickly, who had decided to just keep waiting.

Yet, the letter itself intrigued him. There was something odd about it, and not simply because it was an anonymous letter from someone who thought they were going to be killed. He had read it over a dozen times now, trying to squeeze out additional meaning.

Crowbar gave an unexpectedly hard tug, and Sickly's migratory attention was snapped back to the present. The dog dragged them over to a square foot of paving stones splashed with something vaguely red, nosing it all over. Anywhere else it might have been wine or tomato sauce, but because this was Motley Drive . . . it wasn't.

Like Crowbar sniffing the stain from all angles, Sickly tried approaching the problem differently. Possibly a trap set for him by his father's killer, or possibly a prank. If not, then it was probably a genuine plea for help. Why him? Because he was the son of the sender's longtime friend. Step into my father's shoes. He twisted his father's signet ring on his finger absently. Did that mean he was supposed to think like an assassin to discover who the mysterious letter-writer was?

"AAAAARGH!!"

Sickly looked up to see an unlucky hot dog salesman who had been wheeling his cart down the street wondering where everyone was, and who was now wishing he had never been born. This was because Crowbar had already ripped free of Sickly's limp hand and padded on huge but silent feet up to the poor vendor. The yell petered out into a sort of strangled gurgle as Crowbar gave him a long look.

Sickly was already moving to intercept, to knock the man aside if Crowbar attacked. However, on Crowbar's priority of things he wanted to do, eating a whole tray of cooling sausages ranked slightly higher than disemboweling another defenseless human. It came to the same result, but there was marginally less screaming, and Crowbar was not a dog who liked noise.

"Don't worry, he's very . . ." Sickly trailed off not knowing what adjective to finish that sentence with, though it would probably have been along the lines of, dangerous, angry, or completely psychotic. "Look, sir, just keep very, very, quiet and stay out of his line of sight. I'll pay for the sausages."

"That'll be fifty dollars, guv," whispered the salesman, out of reflex. Sickly raised his eyebrows at this exorbitant price, and opened his mouth.

"Crowbar, come –"

"I'm sorry! I'm sorry, ok? Don't know what came over me, guv! Please take them all! Caestos, just let me live!"

"No, no, I'm going to pay for them. At the correct price." The shaking man took the five dollars Sickly gave him in one clammy hand.

Amazing, Sickly thought. You spent four years learning to poison, maim and kill people in a hundred ways and barely anyone gave you the time of day. But walk down the street with Crowbar in hand and you'd never need to pay for a hot dog ever again.

And since the other five dogs had behaved so far, Sickly gave each of them a sausage too. Gout ate his and, before Sickly could react, snapped at Gnosher's. Gnosher growled in retaliation, causing Spoon and Gangrene to start growling as well.

Crowbar looked up from devouring his twelfth sausage, and glared at the suddenly cowering group of massive dogs. There was instant silence. Crowbar had just enough restraint or indifference that he would give Sickly and the other dogs one warning, not even a growl, before tearing their faces off. Sickly put his wallet away, nodded to the hot dog salesman, picked up Crowbar's leash, and went off down the dingy street.

A cigarette's smoke wafted up to the ceiling in grey, whirling tendrils that pooled in the gaudy ceiling inlay. It was late afternoon and the huge, delicately worked window was white with glare, nothing more than a glowing, opaque square with bars of black wood silhouetted against it. The office was the deep, velvet green of old money accented in mahogany paneling. Anywhere else it would have been a cheap knockoff, something you could buy off the street by the square yard with a grinning gnome key ring thrown into the bargain. Here it was real. The carpet was thick enough to smother mice. It, too, was green.

The figure in the winged armchair sat silhouetted by the light, a stark profile against that backdrop of stoic whiteness. The rest was swathed in shadow richer than the drapes. "It is done, I take it?" The voice had an odd quality, as if shifting through tones and moods.

"Ah, yes," said the second person who stood across the desk.

"But?"

There was an awkward silence, as of a person deciding how much to tell the boss.

"There was . . . one loose end. He sent a package. I tracked it to, ah, Sickly Dodger. Naturally, I checked it, but the item wasn't included. Only a signet ring and a letter. I made you a copy before I sent it on." There was a second pause. It was the pause of digesting unwelcome news.

"Sickly Dodger. Yes, he is an anomaly. Henry Dodger was an extraordinary man, and the boy performed well in the Graduation Ritual." The second figure shifted from foot to foot uneasily. "A man like that would be a man to watch. But instead he has taken up . . . dog walking?" The last two words were spoken in the way an alchemist in a welding mask might use tongs to handle a smoking vial.

"That's right. I doubt he's much of a threat."

"Assassins in our government we can handle, in fact they are a necessity. The plan hinges upon it. Our very society hinges upon it. But assassins who walk toy poodles are unpredictable. Unpredictable is dangerous. Why would he send a letter to Sickly Dodger, I wonder?"

Dead silence from the other person.

"Observe him for now. Find out if he can be useful. But if it becomes necessary, can you kill him?"

The figure hesitated. "I did once before."

"He was blind and wounded."

"Yes. So was I."

Eveline sat and sipped her coffee at the same table that she, Sickly, and the others had shared that rainy day after commencement. She liked coming to Sledge Hammer Coffee, partly for the name, but also because it had a good view of the street through a pair of broad plate glass windows.

The street bustled, and had she been here on business, it would have been a perfect place to watch a target discreetly. And the particular table she was sitting at had its back to a wall, allowing her to survey the café and the street without someone sneaking up on her. In fact, she, Sickly, and the others had chosen it exactly for this reason. They wouldn't be assassins if they didn't fear assassination.

A slight frown crossed Eveline's brow as she watched the cozy atmosphere of the café. He was late. She picked up the newspaper and pretended to look it over, while her eyes glanced back and forth in case of ambush. Even here, in this familiar place, she could never feel entirely safe. She sighed as she scrutinized the passersby outside, none of whom were Sickly.

The dinner with Jamie might not have gone as well as either of them had hoped, but she had at least kept her word and sent a letter to Sickly. She had invited him here at precisely eleven bells, but she ought to have guessed he'd be a half hour late or more.

She read more of the paper. A new building was being dedicated on Reiker's Avenue. There was a sale on vegetables at Aftboro Market, and something about the Headmaster of the Dalton College for Men in Black resigning. She remembered that awful voice and the toothy grin. She allowed herself a small smile. Resigning certainly meant he had been assassinated. Something else caught her eye, a black and white portrait, and a caption including the word 'Murder.'

"Vel!" Eveline's eyes shot upward, as did her hand to a concealed knife. It relaxed when she saw the pale, blank expression of Sickly Dodger framed by shaggy, tangled black hair. She felt herself smile for the first time in what seemed like days.

"Hullo, Sickly!" she replied and waited for him to be seated in the chair opposite her. Barely moving her lips she whispered, "You realize you just sat with your back to the door."

"I know," he said evenly, but his dark eyebrows gave a kind of twitch that she had come to know as his own way of smiling. "But I figured you could watch for me." At this she smiled more broadly.

"Old assassins never change is the expression, innit?" she said, lightly.

"Ever meet any who could prove it?"

"Always the cynic, Sickly."

"As defined by a synonym for realist, I believe."

Vel rolled her eyes. "Cor, didn't realize I was having coffee with a grumpy old man." Somehow, without moving, Sickly's expression darkened. "Oh, come off it, I was just taking the mickey. Here, have a look at this." Vel turned the paper over and pointed to the picture on the front page.

"Huh," he said, which was about all he ever said, even to the most shocking events. Perhaps it was his lack of facial expressions, but Sickly Dodger somehow failed to put emotion into anything, save for the faintest hue of anger or sarcasm in his tones. Vel found it annoying at times, but knew he would be embarrassed if she mentioned it. Well, what passed for embarrassment from Sickly. "Huh," he said again. "You do it?"

"Of course not, Sickly. I don't think *any* of us did it. It said he was murdered, not assassinated."

"Why would anyone murder Bradley Wells, the foreign minister?"

"Politics, innit?" Eveline suggested dubiously. She never got involved in politics if she could avoid it. All right, that was not strictly true. Her job involved her quite often in the daily machinations of statesmen and soon enough their estate planning. But outside of work, she preferred to stay unbiased, and saw the whole political arena as something less pleasant than drinking hemlock.

It was easier this way, many assassins told themselves. It kept things . . . professional.

"If it was politics, he would have been assassinated, don't you think? And it says here that only a few items of his personal jewelry were stolen. Possibly Thieves' Guild, if they had access to his accounts or something. Remember my friend, Booter Squill, at the Thieves' Guild? I could ask him if— oh! Wait a moment . . ."

"Sickly, lay off it," Eveline chided, and Sickly closed his mouth. She surveyed his face, narrow, and with a nearly bluish tint as if suffering a particularly bad cold. Which, she reminded herself, might in fact be true. There was a brief pause until Eveline cast out, "How are you? I haven't seen you in ages."

"Oh. I'm all right."

"That's it? You're 'all right'? It's been two months and that's all you can say? Are you still trying to walk dogs for a living?"

His eyebrows lowered a fraction. "That's right."

"How's that going, then?"

"It's all right." It was her turn to frown. Sickly dropped his eyes, making Eveline feel even more annoyed. "I like the walks, and the dogs. The pay's all right. I'm actually able to rent a flat in Cod Liver Oil Alley."

"Cod Liver Oil Alley?"

"It's a few blocks west of the Dalton College. Apparently famous for its chicken pie. And they call it 'Klowa' for short. As in," and he adopted a Tallow Bells accent, "Oi'm livin' down Klowa way now."

Eveline giggled, half at the street name, half at Sickly's laughable attempt at dialect. His eyebrow twitched.

A waiter came up and took Sickly's order.

"So, how's your work?" he asked distractedly when the man had scurried out of hearing. He kept glancing down at the paper, at the little story Eveline had pointed out.

"Guess." Sickly sighed. It was a well-practiced sigh. "I kill people, and that's what you would be doing if you didn't have this mad idea about dogs."

"It's not mad. It's what I want to do."

"Is it really? Then why did you go to the Dalton College at all?"

"It was my dad's will. It put me through college as long as I went to assassin's school."

"Look at you with your big inheritance."

"Actually, the lawyers are holding it back on account of me not taking contracts. Even if I did technically pass the red test and get certified with the Occisor Cadre."

Vel cut off her instant retort and then paused. She looked at

Sickly a second time. He looked leaner than when she'd last seen him. "I'm sorry." He shrugged, as if he truly did not care. Her temper flared. "Then why in Hagrippa's multifarious hells aren't you taking jobs? I mean real contracts?" He could be so gods-damned stubborn!

"Look, Vel, I don't regret going. It's just . . . Even though I could go around all stab-happy, and yes, I'm embarrassingly good at climbing buildings, and sure, the pay is better but . . ." Vel gave him a look that managed to ride the line of patronizing and frustrated like a skilled jockey on a disapproving horse. "But see, that isn't me! Just because I've got the skills doesn't mean I've got what it takes to be an –" he broke off at a glance from Eveline. "Blacksmiff, 'sis," he finished, dropping back into the Tallow Bells Street slang. "I want ta break out, y'know, do my own fing."

His ear was half on the conversation, and half on what Vel's eyes were telling him. They said quite clearly, "Some intimidating person or persons unknown has come into the shop and is looking around in a casual but very suspicious way." That was quite good for a pair of eyeballs to manage, conversation-wise, but Vel and Sickly had practiced this kind of communication a lot during their college days.

"Look, Al, it ain't the kind of fing mum would of ever wanted you ta do," she argued back, keeping their ruse going. "You know you promised 'er you'd follow dad's craft."

"Yeah, but, like, can't I 'ave just a few years to try being an oyster monger? If it dun't work out, then--"

"An oyster monger, Sickly?" Vel hissed.

"I was debating between that and fish de-boner."

Vel stifled a snort, looked up, and managed, "They're gone."

"What was all tha' about, d'you s'pose?" Sickly said, with an eyebrow-twitch smile.

"Okay, enough. Your pronunciation is terrible." His eyebrow flickered a fraction downward.

"You'd know, would you?" he asked.

"Some of us didn't attend the Dalton College on our family's money, Sickly. We're not all lucky enough to have rich fathers." She had meant it solely to steer the conversation away from her personal life, but Sickly looked, if anything, more downcast.

"Sorry, Vel. I didn't mean . . . sorry."

"It doesn't matter, don't apologize if you don't need to."

"Sorry," he mumbled, sounding utterly defeated.

"What did I just say?" she snapped. "How many times do I have to tell you not to--" she stopped as she noticed him raise his eyebrows sarcastically. "Was that supposed to be funny?" They twitched again. She let out a growl halfway between frustrated and amused. "Anyway. Those men were probably looking for me, either to offer a job, or, well, to complete one of their own."

"What have you been up to that's made you so popular?"

"Mostly work for Lord Salsa. You wouldn't believe how many cousins and in-laws crawled out of the woodwork when Lady Margarine died."

Sickly's tea arrived, a welcome break from the conversation. This was because he had to check for poison, and he made quite show of adding sugar, while really slipping a few grains of a cata-lyst into the drink. When no poison was revealed, Sickly shrugged and sipped at the tea. Eveline sipped at her coffee, mirroring him.

The silence stretched.

CHAPTER 7

"Soooo . . . how's life?" Booter Squill asked as he and Sickly picked their way amiably about Hambridge. It was midmorning, and the sun glinted off Booter's halo of untidy blond hair and slightly nervous expression. Booter moved like a wounded gazelle on the extreme end of the anxiety disorder spectrum.

There is a fundamental law of the universe that says a thief should be called Fingers, with a suitably dashing surname like Slyshadow, or Quickknife. Booter was not this thief. In fact, he was probably the worst thief in the whole world, which was why he was known as "Thumbs." This was a shame, because he was a nice guy and Sickly's oldest friend.

"It's all right, I guess. I get up, go to work, get paid, go home. Nothing special." Sickly jumped lightly out of the way of a passing cart, laden with boxes. The old wound in his back twinged, but he was getting used to it. He skirted a small crowd gathered around a vendor selling honey-coated rats roasted on skewers. "What about you?"

"They still refuse to give me my probationary certificate," Booter mumbled while fidgeting with the small pendant on his necklace. "They keep saying that I give thieving a bad name."

When Sickly and Booter got together to talk, they didn't like to stay in one place. Both of them loved walking the Hambridge streets, seeing the sights and the people, stopping at street shows or dodging prowling gangs. It was just something they did, since as far back as Sickly could remember.

As of last year, however, their outings had become more seldom than Sickly would have liked. Booter often said he was busy – even at odd hours of the evening. Sickly was proud of his friend putting more effort into his studies, but he missed their casual walks through the humanity-choked avenues of Hambridge.

Some might point out the flaw in judgment here: an assassin walking about in broad daylight with no protection and no way of knowing who was watching with a crossbow from the rooftops. But Sickly also knew something that other people didn't. He knew how assassins thought. It *was* monstrously idiotic to walk around so unprotected, ergo, no one would do it. And because no one would do it, it was as if Sickly wasn't there. He evaded potential enemies without doing any work at all. You just had to get past thinking like an assassin, and start thinking like a person.

"But seriously? Nothing interesting?" Booter asked incredulously. Sickly shrugged. "Come off it, Sickly. No midnight assassination attempts? No hiding for your life? No secret assignments?"

"No." Sickly responded flatly. "Look, Booter, I'm a lousy assassin. I hate the idea of killing people. I mean, what reason do I have? You know I didn't go to school to learn how. Honestly, Booter, you'd probably make a better assassin than me."

"What? No, I wouldn't! I can't hurt anyone! Don't say that."

"Sorry, sorry. I just meant that . . ." he trailed off, and then started again. "I'll tell you a secret." Sickly recounted the events of that fateful night when Vel had appeared and assassinated his first target.

As he did, their feet led them up the street, heading towards

Uptown. They could already hear the shouts of street vendors haranguing unlucky passersby with offers of fresh Crab Bread, imported Kaldrian silks, and authentic, edible Reiker's Bridge souvenirs. Sickly fingered the signet ring on his finger as he spoke. It still felt odd and new on his hand.

"I just don't know why she did it," he finished. "Is that what friends are for? Stick up for each other and stick knives in each other's targets?"

"How are you two, by the way?" Booter asked, "You tell her you like her yet?"

"What?" Sickly yelped, "No! I mean, no. She asked me out for coffee yesterday, though."

"Are you a moron? She *asked* you? And you went? And you didn't tell her? Are you a moron?"

Sickly's pale cheeks took on a slightly pink hue. A nearby busker in a colorful shawl played a Yakistani folk tune, the coins sewn into her cloth cap jingling in time with her music. A man shouted about unsanctioned theft of a three-legged goat. All about them was the bustle and noise of the city, but Sickly felt trapped in silence. "Look I— I didn't know how. I think about what I'm going to say to her but then . . . I just lose all the words."

"Sickly," Booter groaned, "She asked you on a date, don't you get it?"

"That's not how it was," Sickly argued. "Even if it was, I mucked it up, right? That was my one chance, right? She probably just wants to be friends. Whatever that means."

"I don't know exactly what being friends means, Sickly," Booter said in exasperation. "But I do know that one of our jobs is to get the other friend pie in time of need. Look, we're nearly at Aftboro Market anyway."

They stepped lightly across the street, causing a passing carter to shout a couple of choice words about their heritage. Then they entered the labyrinth of market stalls that crowded beneath an open topped warehouse, partly roofed in tarpaulins and fishing nets. Booter glanced about with a furtive eye and muttered, "Wait there." He sidled over to a passing gentleman and stuck his hand surreptitiously into the man's waistcoat pocket.

But instead of the smooth steal advertised by the Thieves' Guild recruiting posters, he bumped the gentleman's arm. The man gave a startled cry and turned to see Booter backing away with an apologetic smile.

"I say, were you trying to pick my pocket, young man?" he growled. Booter nodded, smiling and fidgeting with his necklace.

"Sorry sir, Student Thief, sir, got my student license here, sir." He fumbled in a pocket for a grubby card with the tasteful words:

Booter Squill
Student Thief, Thieves' Guild, Hambridge
How's my thieving?
Send post to 468 Unduly Drive

The man strode off, muttering about thieves in his day and how they had the courtesy not to be noticeable when going about their business. "Sorry," Booter said when he got back. "They don't give us any spending money. I think they think we're supposed to steal it."

"Look, it's all right, I've got the money here. You really didn't need to steal it."

"Didn't need to? I'm a thief, even if you're not an assassin. It's in the job description," Booter wailed, looking utterly downtrodden. "And anyway, I was buying."

"Booter, I'm telling you this, as a friend. You're a terrible thief. You're a good person, and a good friend and that's why I'm telling you this. You're a lousy thief." Booter looked at the ground.

"Yeah, I know. Now I need pie, too."

"My treat," Sickly said; raising a consoling eyebrow at his friend's dejected expression. Sickly went to the nearest food stall, selected two small meat pies, paid for them, and brought them over to the disconsolate Booter. "There you go, then." His friend looked marginally happier.

"Thanks, Sickly." They left Aftboro market and meandered through the crowd, heading up the Ham-ward side of Tumult Hill. They found a bench overlooking the river and ate their pies. "You know," Booter said, in the air of a man coming to a conclusion about 'Life'. "You know . . . Even though I'm a lousy thief, and you're rubbish at being an assassin, and though you can't talk to Eveline, and I can't hardly talk to any girls . . . well. At least we have each other." Sickly licked his fingers and looked up at the sky.

"That's kind of sad."

"Yeah, I know." Booter began to chuckle, and Sickly felt sure he would have smiled, if he had been able.

A few happy moments passed as they gazed downward at the grey rooftops. Late afternoon sun, the color of a ripe peach, split the clouds. It glittered off the jade green paint of a Khi Sianese junk bobbing in the sluggish river, offloading a cargo of tea and silks. Pigeons flocked over the Bakers' Guild, dive-bombing the men and women in their little white hats. A stiff breeze blew the smells of pollution and human waste, and the cries of irate bakers over Sickly and Booter.

"I feel sick."

"The pie?" Booter asked. "Need a bucket?"

"I'll be fine, just a little queasy."

"Remind me, Sickly, what *can* you eat or drink that doesn't make you ill?"

Sickly pondered for a moment. He looked, to Booter, like a man wrestling with a complex metaphysical quandary. "There's .. . water. And bread. And peas. Vegetables, you know. There's fruit, of course. And tea without milk or anything, and plain chicken. Oh, and sometimes pork."

"How are you even alive right now?"

"It's better than you'd think. It makes cooking a lot easier for sure." They started off up the street again, dodging a pair of

Civican priests nagging tourists to dispose of trash in city-sanctioned waste receptacles. "You wanted to know if anything interesting happened. Booter, have you heard about the foreign minister?"

"The who?"

"I'll take that as a no. Well, he was murdered recently," said Sickly, staring thoughtfully at his friend.

"See? That's what I'm talking about! Tell me more!" Booter said, avidly. Sickly told him about the letter he had gotten, two and a half weeks ago. "So you think the person who sent that letter was actually the foreign minister?"

"Well, yes. So you haven't heard anything about it through the Thieves' Guild?"

"Nope, sorry. But you've got to admit, it matches the facts."

"Maybe I'll have a look around, then. I'll have to be careful though, the letter said it was dangerous. Bradley Wells thought some powerful people were after him. And he thought . . ." Sickly trailed off, not wanting to frighten Booter with the last part of the letter. The bit that hinted Sickly's friends might be in danger as well.

"I don't envy being an assassin, mate. Worrying about poison and traps and dying all the time? That's no way for a bloke to live."

"That's why I stopped being one. But you've got to admit," Sickly's eyebrows twitched, "I do get cooler post."

Booter grinned ruefully. "Yeah, that's true. All I get are letters about how bad my thieving is."

The art of spying was all about subtlety. A spy had to be quick and fast and clever enough not to get caught by anyone, foe or friend, because every friend eventually turned out to be a foe anyway. There were clandestine meetings in sewers or on rooftops at every time of day and night. Spies slunk through secret passages and listened at keyholes, or peeked in windows.

They attended galas in carnival masques and liaised with the uppermost echelons of society, collecting words that could topple nations. They were not assassins, for while they did poison people's food and drink and put the occasional knife in an unsuspecting back, they did it for politics, rather than a real ideal. Like money.

At least, that was what they wanted people to think, because it made their actual jobs so much easier. Subtlety was what spying was all about, it was true, but contrary to widely propagated popular belief, sneaking down a corridor in some wealthy embassy was not subtle. It drew even more attention than simply *walking* down that same corridor. As a rule, spies did not like being forced to answer questions asked by big guards with truncheons and swords.

And that was why the Spy was doing paperwork. While people searched for her down dark alleys or in secret rendezvous spots, she sat indoors with a cup of strong tea and did research.

The men Lonsk and Calloway who had replaced their unlucky predecessors on the Merchant's Council had both graduated from The Dalton College for Men in Black. Not surprising, really. Of course, not every attendee of the school became an assassin. Many of the non-graduates joined the ranks of the lawyers, the merchants, and other natural Hambridge predators. For instance, there was Simon Digby, another member of the Occisor Cadre who's academic record showed he had focused most of his studies on business. Yet, he had recently been appointed Head of the Guild of Alchemists. It didn't make sense. Unless . . .

The shape of something was forming in the tangled networks of discarded receipts, secret ledgers, and hushed confessions. She could almost see it now but only by watching the way all of the other pieces interacted with one other. And what she saw was not good. It was so far out the other side of insanity that it made a kind of twisted sense. Especially if you were the kind of person that had big plans for the city and didn't care who got hurt along the way.

The Spy rubbed her eyes, took another sip of her tea and continued to read. It was going to be a long night. A long day on the other side of it promised to be just as tiring.

She sighed. This was probably why everyone was so ready to believe in the other stuff. Who would believe that proper spying was more research than sneaking around?

CHAPTER 8

It would forever after be known as the 'That Day on Ardsley Avenue' by various people who thought they had a clue about what had really happened.

In fact, no one did. This was because the crowd was not so much stupid, as deathly, pants-soilingly scared. People panicked blindly, so blindly in fact, that they didn't see what happened. For years afterward they would tell their friends and relatives in hushed tones that they had survived 'That Day on Ardsley Avenue.' Decades later they would sit their plump and happy grandchildren down in a circle and tell them how, bravely, they had fought off the Hound of Hell.

But really, they had no idea.

Only Sickly Dodger, who had been the one person to actually do anything to stop a disturbance from turning into a full-blown, front-page, black and white photograph disaster, would remain quiet about his role in the whole thing. Some might find this a little unfair, and perhaps it was, downplaying the role of a modest hero. However, given what was coming soon, a little unfairness was the least of Sickly's concerns.

It was the day after Sickly's talk with Booter, and he was walking Gout, Gangrene, Gnosher, Gouger, and Spoon back from Reiker's Commons. All six of them cowered in the wake of Crowbar. They ambled down Wobbly Street where the bustle of late morning shoppers, vendors and bystanders was beginning to thin as everyone went indoors to eat. Sickly was already tired from the first half of The Walk, but he had just enough wherewithal to wonder why Crowbar was suddenly being very docile.

Later, when he had time to assess the situation, and when he had grown more accustomed to Crowbar's little tics, he would have been able to spot the problem. And that problem was this: Crowbar was smiling to himself.

Some might argue that dogs can't smile. They are wrong.

All Sickly could do at the time, however, was hope that he got the dogs back to Mr. Stashcrumb before Crowbar committed whatever he was planning on committing. They walked down Wobbly Street without incident. Sickly breathed a small sigh of relief. They turned left and headed up the brick lined road. It was empty of carts, and Sickly was able to maneuver Crowbar so that he was going up the middle. This way, no one would accidentally bother Crowbar.

Sickly had begun to relax a little by the time the pack started up Ardsley Avenue. It was crowded at this time of day because Ardsley Avenue was the main arterial which directly connected the market district and the craftsman district. He began to let his mind wander to the question of the Foreign Minister's death. What he needed was more information about the murder. Maybe his friends could help him?

Sickly and Crowbar had made it halfway when the dog made his move. The wrong neuron fired in the wrong part of Crowbar's brain (i.e., all of it). One really, really violent impulse crossed a sinister synaptic gap, initiating a lightning fast chain reaction. The signal changed Crowbar from passive to homicidal maniac so fast that it could not be measured on the most accurate stopwatch.

First, Crowbar's leg muscles bunched, tensed, and released, sending hundreds of pounds of killing machine flying through the air, ripping the leash out of Sickly's grasp. The chain slid through his fingers, bruising and lacerating, and Sickly stumbled forward.

Crowbar headed for a tight knot of people who barely had time to shriek before he was upon them. Screams of pain erupted immediately as Crowbar's teeth tore into unprotected legs, arms, hands, and backsides. And because this was Hambridge, everyone else wandered over to find out why.

Crowbar was in heaven, or possibly someone else's version of hell. Everywhere he looked there were more targets for him to bite; more squishy, defenseless bodies for him to sink his teeth into, bowl over, and maul. Never before had he been so free to pursue his goal of ridding the world of all these stupid, pretentious primates who thought they owned everything. Well he had news for them, and that was: Die, humans! Die!!!

Sickly's reflexes were very sharp, but even he stood for a few seconds in shocked disbelief before remembering he ought to do something. He tied the leashes of the other five dogs together. "Go find Mr. Stashcrumb! Go on then!" They fled in the direction of Eel Park. Then Sickly ran towards Crowbar, fighting his way through a crowd which was now, as one frightened monkey, running away from a beast whose ancestors had eaten their ancestors and still had ample room for dessert.

In the minute it took Sickly to close with Crowbar, the dog had already left a trail of groaning and bleeding bodies. Sickly's only stroke of luck was that Crowbar was like a child in a candy store. If he killed and ate one human, it meant he was not killing and eating all the others, and this was simply not acceptable. The only solution was to hamstring as many as possible before the bulk of them got away, and then go back later to finish off the wounded.

To Sickly's trained eye, it didn't look like anything the hospitals couldn't fix. Still, it would be best to prevent any further injuries if possible. Crowbar was charging another fleeing group, and Sickly ran as fast as he could to intercept. There was no time to think, just time enough to slam the woman out of the way before she needed a lot of stitches. She yelped, fell over, and was spared for the moment.

Sickly was not as lucky. Rows of teeth sank into his stomach. Sickly was not very heavy, and Crowbar picked him up and began shaking the young man violently. Sickly gasped in pain, felt horribly nauseated, and blacked out.

He awoke a few seconds later, knew that he was alive but bleeding and needed medical attention. Crowbar was about to head off after more people, but he was not gone yet. More importantly, there was no one in the immediate vicinity. Sickly drew in a painful breath and shouted the only command Mr. Stashcrumb had ever taught him. "Crowbar! Go home!"

The dog stopped short, then padded silently over to Sickly. He gave Sickly a long glare that said 'this is not over' and loped off after the other dogs.

Sickly sighed and looked down at his stomach. His clothing might now be suitable for dusters, but wouldn't be acceptable business attire ever again. Only a little bit of blood had stained it, however, much less than should have been there. He sighed, relieved, and lay back. After all, it could have been worse. Crowbar's teeth might also have shredded his body armor.

Sickly and the other victims of 'That Day on Ardsley Avenue' were picked up by the Charity Barnsforth Loving Hospital's wagon, transported safely to the emergency ward, and given immediate treatment. Afterward, members of the Hambridge City Watch approached each of the patients to take down their stories. Sickly for his part, listened to what others said, and copied them. He informed the officer that he had been attacked by a dog but didn't know who owned it or where it had gone. Sickly's loyalty was to his customer. While he appreciated the good work of the Watch, he didn't exactly have to tell them the truth, especially since no one had been hurt . . .

Killed. No one had been killed.

. . .

Mid-morning sun charged desperately through the atmosphere, crashed against the barricades of pollution and made a last stand against the leaves of the majestic elms of Tokeby Court. The few photons that made it through were haggard and hard-bitten when they finally bounced off the three heads clustered around the door of a large mansion.

"Jamie, why are we doing this again?"

"Oh for gods' sakes, Billys! Sickly's in the hospital, the poor dear!"

"So?"

"So he asked you, me, and Terry to investigate while the doctors are sewing him up!"

"So you want me to stop needling you about it?"

Jamie groaned. "And you can take your unimaginative word-play and stuff it."

"Stuff it where, exactly? Maybe you'd like to show me?"

"Billys, you are, without doubt, the most revolting toad I can imagine."

"But you do imagine me?"

"And now *I* wish Sickly hadn't asked you to come."

"At least I'm more interesting than Terry."

"Just shut up, Billys."

"Yep, I'm here." This was from Terry, whose brain lagged a few seconds behind the conversation, rather like an improperly hitched wagon to a fast horse. Billys glanced again at the street to ensure their continued privacy. Tokeby Court was home to the private residences of many political officials. Of course, this did not take into account the myriad number of tunnel systems leading out of the private residences to various wells, abandoned basements or sewers for quick and discrete getaways. After all, if there's one thing a powerful figure fears, it is the absence of an exit strategy, especially when the in-laws are due any minute.

This building had been the dwelling of the late Foreign Minister, the erstwhile Bradley Wells. Currently, Jamie was picking the lock on the door, though not fast enough for Billys' taste. "Look, why aren't we just going down to the Watch and asking them what happened?" Billys grumbled, staring nervously at the empty street.

"Terry and I already did before we met up with you."

"And?"

"They told us to 'stick it where the sun don't shine.'"

"Is that where your lock-picking skills are?"

Jamie took a deep breath and counted to five before letting it out. "This is a Peeble and Cranny X-38 Deadbolt. Top level security. It'll be a minute, even for me, now shut it."

Billys snickered. "Attitude like that, it's no wonder no one'll hire you . . ."

"Listen, you little snot-nosed foul-mouthed piece of . . ." Jamie would have continued, but something at the edge of the door distracted her. "Shite," she finished, staring intently at the edge of the door. "Someone forced this door, with a crowbar, judging by the way the doorframe has been warped. See here?"

"So? The Watch does that to get into houses."

"But there isn't as much splintering as I'd expect," Jamie continued, ignoring this. "It was jimmied from the inside."

"Boring," Billys yawned.

"So it wasn't the Watch, obviously. Drasilla's docket, how can you be this dense?"

"Stop with the sodding lectures and get on with it." Jamie glowered and bent to the lock again. After another minute, Billys added, "Not that I don't love watching you work, but you're never going to get it that way. Just make Terry do it."

"No hard feelings, Terry, dear, but I'm better at locks."

"Maybe, but he's very good at opening doors." Jamie clenched her hands into fists but then sighed and turned to their large friend.

"Terry, dear, open the door please." Terry looked down at the immobile handle, grasped it in one enormous hand, and tugged. The knob was strong, as was the lock, but the hinges of the door finally gave up their battle with age, weather, and Terry. The rusty metal disintegrated, allowing the huge assassin to pick the whole door up and prop it against the wall of the house.

"Dat's not going ta be a problem, is it?" he asked slowly, as if only now realizing that breaking and entering a private home might be considered, as it were, illegal.

"As long as no one was watching, it's perfectly legal," Billys assured him.

"Oh. Dat's all right den."

"Come on you two, let's check this out," said Jamie.

Booter crouched atop a shingle roof, overlooking the empty and almost pitch-black street. From his lofty vantage point he could see out across the city, the river Ham that bisected it, and beyond to the unlit blackness of the Allam Lowlands. Only a few lights shone through scrunched windows. This was not surprising. It was well past 2 a.m. and any sensible person would be at home, in bed, snoring peacefully. Even other thieves were asleep by now. You'd have to be mad to do any kind of crime at this hour, or, Booter reflected, a politician.

Logically, that meant that he was mad. Unfortunately, by the transitive property of insanity, the beautiful, intelligent, and above all very, very dangerous woman crouching next to him was mad, too. And Booter would die before he told her that, or at least, shortly thereafter.

"Hold the rope, Thumbs. Don't drop me." Booter sighed, he really hated that nickname. But he silently grabbed the rope, tied it to the chimney, and gripped it firmly in both hands. Eveline jumped backwards off the roof and disappeared from view. The rope tensed beneath his fingers as it caught her weight, and there was the tiniest of sounds as two booted feet hit the wall.

That was unfair. But that was the thing. Assassins were unfair. They were suave, fashionable, intelligent killing machines for hire. You couldn't fight them and you couldn't get back at them. You couldn't even take the mickey out of them. Because if you tried any of these things, they would find someone to pay them to kill you.

Why did all of Sickly's friends have to be cooler than him? Eveline was, of course, as beautiful and deadly as a Venati tigress. Jamie looked like a fashion model for a catalogue which sold exquisite knives. Terry was strangely charismatic and matchless in strength. Even Billys was uncannily good at gymnastics and fighting techniques. But Booter was just . . . Booter. No skills. No tricks. No weapons. No tactics. He was short, ugly and awkward. He couldn't even thieve properly, and --

The rope gave an unexpected tug and before he knew what was happening, it had slipped through his limp fingers. But the chimney-secured cordage did not snap taut against the weight of a falling body, as it should have. Booter crept to the edge of the roof and peered down. Two very angry eyes glared back. Eveline was hanging, suspended by her hands, from the window ledge.

"Idiot!" she hissed.

"I'm sorry! Can I . . ." his voice trailed off as she performed an effortless muscle up which brought her to a crouching position on the ledge in a fluid motion. Booter could only dream of performing such a maneuver himself.

"Get down here," she ordered. He tentatively grabbed the rope and, one leg at a time, lowered himself from the roof. "Hurry up."

"Look, I'm not very good at this."

"What are you good at?" Booter let this comment slide like the bad rope burn he was currently getting as he descended. Finally, muscles screaming in protest, he got one foot and then the other onto the small platform. Eveline had already used a small pry bar on the window and levered it open. In a flash she was through the opening and into the room. Booter followed her, scraping noisily against the frame as he lowered himself into an office.

The room was dark, limned in pale gray by the moonlight, giving it an otherworldly quality. He could just make out the lines of a bookcase, a heavy desk in the corner stacked with paperwork, a fireplace and a pitted dartboard. There was a single door. Eveline crept forward on hushed feet. Booter followed, wincing every time he put his foot down and heard a painfully loud creak. In the aggrieved silence he could imagine every criticism, as if the back of her head was transparent.

She opened the door without a sound. Through the thin slit a beam of lamplight came into view, as did two watchmen. Eveline stood stock still, rather than darting back and drawing their attention. The footsteps drew closer, and Booter felt his heart thudding horribly against his chest. The feet paused. Oh, Drasilla, Booter prayed, please don't let them check this room.

Assassins, Thieves, and Spies were not, on the whole, a terribly religious lot. In spite of this, they frequently spread religion in the course of their work. For instance, a heartfelt prayer of "Oh god, oh god, please not my other leg," was often found on the lips of anyone who had been late in paying protection money to the Thieves' Guild. However, on rare occasions such as crossing a rain-slick roof while below the Watch were out in full force searching for an individual of your description, a quick supplication to Drasilla, Lady of the Convenient Shadow, was hissed through clenched teeth. Oddly, a constable below the scene offering a prayer to find the bastard quickly and get out of the bloody rain would likely address the self-same goddess. Drasilla, or Thumbscale as she was also referred to, was the goddess of Justice and neither blind nor even believed to be particularly impartial. Hambridgers, in fact, preferred knowing she had a thumb on the scales. They liked even better knowing her thumb was on their side.

"Give us a light, then, constable." The voice sounded tired and held a hint of complaint.

"Sarge, are you allowed to smoke on duty?" said a second and much younger voice.

"I am allowed to have a smoke if it's three in the bleeding morning, and I'm still awake on bleeding patrol duty," said the first, managing to suggest by his tone that if he had his way, things would be very different.

"Only asking, sarge."

"I know, lad. Give us that light then." A match flared, and the aroma of cheap cigar filled Booter's nose. "What a night, then, eh? I can't be up and around at this time of night at my age."

"It'll all be over soon, though, right, sarge? New commander's just putting us through our paces to show she ain't a softie, right?"

"Between you and me, lad, this new commander is no Mr. Burgis. Surprise inspections, extra duty, the reports have to have punctuation, and I don't know what else. Where will it end, I ask you?"

"When she gets in a cart accident too?"

"Right, but supposing--" By the flickering light of their lamp, Booter saw Eveline roll her eyes. In a single motion she drew out a short pipe, fitted a dart into it, and pointed the other end into the hall. She fired, reloaded, and fired again before Booter could get halfway toward her. She opened the door. The two watchmen lay in the corridor, identical darts in their necks.

"Why would you do that!" Booter hissed vehemently. "They were just watchmen! You didn't need to kill them!" Eveline gave him the sort of look that shut him up instantly. It said "Do you want to be next?"

"I didn't kill them. They're knocked out. Now, help me get them in here."

"But why?" Booter demanded as he tugged ineffectually at the smaller of the two.

It must be said that there are two kinds of thieves. There are the pocket pickers, cat burglars and night thieves, and then there are the thugs, muggers and hired muscle. You can tell them apart by putting them into a gym class and then standing back to watch who pounds the tar out of who, even as the victims pick their abusers' pockets. Booter was definitely of the first variety, though only because he couldn't go two rounds with a goldfish.

"Because they were taking up our time."

"But – but," Booter spluttered as he tried in vain to make her understand that this was not how things should be done.

"You want to argue?" Booter closed his mouth. His partner in crime picked up the dropped lantern and stubbed out the still smoldering cigar in an ashtray. Unconsciously, Booter lifted the little copper pendant hanging round his neck and dandled it through his fingers in a calming pattern. They moved down the hall, to a large and ornate door with a plaque on it, which read: Commander of the Hambridge City Watch. Below it was a newer sign that proclaimed: Office of Hannabelle Merc. Eveline tried the handle, which opened. She smirked at their arrogance, and stepped inside.

By the light of the lamp, they could see that it was much tidier and devoid of occupants. The bookshelves were larger, the fireplace more elaborate, and the desk more important. A presumptuous winged armchair sat behind the desk, and several filing cabinets stood to attention against the back wall. Eveline, trailed by a nervous Booter, approached the desk. On it was a small intray, an inkstand, several pens, and a stack of completed papers. In delicate, black gloved hands, Eveline sifted through these documents.

Booter went over to the filing cabinets and examined their neatly penned identification cards. There was a box for thefts, one for fires, one for assassinations, one for murders, and two for complaints. He pulled the 'murders' drawer open. Folders met his prying eyes, and to his relief, he found one marked: Bradley Wells. "Look at this." Booter whispered. He carried the folder over to the desk and opened it. Eveline leaned in and read:

The Honorable Bradley Wells, age 56, was found dead in his residence in Tokeby Court on the forty-eighth of autumn in the year of the Belligerent Cobble. Mr. Wells had been the Foreign Minister of the City of Hambridge for twenty-two years. He was found by his housekeeper, Mrs. Lorris, in the early morning, who ran to the nearest watch station to report the murder and to demand a reward for said discovery.

The door had been forced, and watchmen dispatched to the scene concluded that Mr. Wells had been killed at some point in the night, as he was leaving his office. The murder weapon was not accounted for, though a posthumous examination concluded his skull had been crushed by a heavy, blunt object. Two rings, a gold watch, and Mr. Wells' wallet were also missing. The office showed signs of having been ransacked, possibly for more valuables. A small knife was found next to the body, and identified as belonging to Mr. Wells.

The conclusion of the Watch is that Mr. Wells interrupted a burglary in process and was killed while trying to defend himself. The murderer then robbed his victim and left through the front door. No witnesses have come forward, nor are there any leads to be followed. It is unlikely that the perpetrator will be caught.

The page was signed by Commander Merc.

Booter frowned. "Why don't they think they'll find the murderer?" he asked aloud.

"I don't know. It's very odd. As if they decided to abandon the case. They didn't even mention 'exploring all possibilities' which is what coppers say when they haven't a clue, innit. Let's take this back to Sickly."

"What, steal it?" Booter asked incredulously. "You can't steal from the Watch!"

"You are the worst thief ever, Thumbs," Eveline said, tiredly. Booter went quiet.

They retraced their steps, left through the office window, locking it behind them as they did so. Then they clambered up the rope and untied it from the chimney. Booter dug in a pocket and slipped a small coin under a shingle in thanks to Drasilla for distracting the two guards and for preventing Eveline from killing them.

"Can I ask you, something, Thumbs?"

Booter stiffened, his hands clenching unconsciously. "Yeah?"

"Why are you doing this? You're terrible at it, and I could easily have done this myself."

"Why did you do it?" Booter shot back.

"Sickly asked me to."

"Exactly. Sickly's your friend. But you've got other friends, haven't you, Eveline? But me, I've only got Sickly. He's the only one that stands up for me."

"Then go out and make some friends," she returned, as if it were that simple.

Before he could stop himself, Booter found his mouth spilling the words he had been holding back all night. All week. All his life, really. "I can't. And you know why? Because I'm so bad at thieving even the blind and deaf catch me at it. Because people look at me and see a scrawny, pathetic weakling and think that's all I am. Because they all call me Thumbs. Sickly is the only person who doesn't. He's the only one that sees anything else in me. He's different than them. So why are you friends with him, then?" He took a step back, afraid she might gut him on the spot. Instead, Her masklike expression softened to something almost vulnerable.

"Maybe I haven't got a lot of friends either, Thumbs." Booter blinked in surprise. "You're right, he is different. At college, all the other students just wanted to learn how to kill people, but Sickly looked like he was there by accident. Like all the reading and training was academic to him. Like it was a game or something. He wasn't bad, either, but he's not an assassin. That makes him safe to talk to for the rest of us." She suddenly glared at Booter. "Let's just give him the damn papers." She turned and crept away over the rooftops. Booter followed at some distance.

There was no need for her to ask for his silence. An assassin could trust you because of the horrible things she could do to you if you broke that trust.

CHAPTER 9

$\mathcal{S}$ickly reposed in a hospital bed in the Charity Barnsforth Loving Hospital, feeling rather guilty about the fact.

The CBLH had a reputation as being one of the most mercenary sanatoriums in Hambridge. It did indeed care greatly for each patient, right up until they were safely inside the hospital's gray walls. At this point its executives became rather more interested in caring for the patient's wallet. They funded a number of emergency wagons that rattled to sites of nasty industrial accidents, lethal bar fights, gang wars, and the monthly meeting of the Home and Garden Club to pick up anyone too stunned, hurt, or dead to get away. It was said that if you couldn't get out of the way of one of their gray wagons, then you were already too far gone to be cured by anyone.

In fact, most patients received only the barest of care necessary to keep them breathing until it could be proven that someone could foot the bill or no more pressing cases were available. Sickly had been planning to wait his turn along with everyone else, except that one of the nurses had asked his name. Unfortunately, she had recognized him as the last heir to the Dodger house, after which no amount of refusal or naysaying could prevent them from putting him in a private room. Sickly was sure a number of other potential patients had required more immediate care than he, but none of the doctors or nurses had cared to listen.

The one thing you could say about the Charity Barnsforth surgeons was that they knew their trade. Hambridge being the city that it was, its doctors were accustomed to stitching punctures and lacerations. This month there was even a two for one deal on bleeding wounds. Though it was just a day after his run in with Crowbar, he was already feeling mostly himself.

Now he was reading the report that Vel and Booter had dropped off earlier. That and trying not to dwell too much on the memory of Vel coming in through the hospital door. She had smelled appealingly of the autumn rain.

Right. He was contemplating the oddness that surrounded the death of Bradley Wells. That was what he was doing. The only problem was that he didn't know where to begin. He hoped that Jamie, Billys, and Terry's expedition to Wells' house would give some additional clues, and with both pieces of evidence he might have a place to start investigating. He tried to remember the penny-dreadful crime novels he had read throughout his second year at the Dalton College. He felt a vague urge to find a wide brimmed hat and a tumbler of whiskey. There was always motive. So, who then would have a motive to kill Bradley Wells?

Just then, the door opened. Sickly looked up, expecting a nurse, or one of his friends with some news. It was neither.

Standing in the doorway, shoulders brushing each side of the frame, was Ulrich Munz. The man who had killed him. Ulrich was very tall and broad, but not as mountainous as Terry. Ulrich put you in mind of a circus strong man crossed with a gymnast. He wore his black hair with the casual, messy arrogance of the rich and powerful that was in direct contrast to his beard and moustache. His facial hair was close-cropped, framed his mouth, chin and jaw, and was so ferociously maintained that it could have snapped off a military salute.

Ulrich grinned when he saw Sickly lying there in the bed, possibly because he was glad to see another member of the Occisor Cadre, but probably because Sickly was incapacitated and defenseless. His teeth seemed blindingly white in contrast to his dark hair.

"Hello, Dodger." His voice was low but not gravelly, more like the sound of dark chocolate melting on a black iron stove. He sat down at the foot of the bed, causing it to half-capsize towards the gigantic assassin. "How are you?"

"Just fine, thanks." He couldn't figure out why Ulrich would be here, unless on a job that Sickly played a part in. Specifically the part of victim stabbed brutally to death while lying in a hospital bed. "To what do I owe the pleasure?"

"I merely wanted to visit an old Dalton College friend. I was in the area, heard you were ill, and thought to myself: Ulrich, you should stop by a fellow in need."

"That's very charitable, coming from the man who killed me."

"I say, killed is a bit harsh. You're still here, aren't you?" Ulrich grinned again. It was not a friendly smile. It was the smile of a jackal, prowling the edge of a dying campfire. "More a . . . temporary wounding."

"Not here to finish the job, are you?" Sickly asked lightly.

"That hurts my feelings, Dodger, it really does. Would I kill you, a handicapped opponent and an old friend?" Sickly considered this for a quarter of a millisecond. "Yes."

Ulrich sighed. "So cynical, Dodger. It really is distressing to see a young pessimist."

"Possibly, but not as distressing as seeing an optimistic assassin."

Smiling broadly and ignoring Sickly's comment, Ulrich changed topic. "What have you been up to recently? I hear from very puzzled sources that you are walking dogs?"

"Yes, that's about right."

"Why?"

Sickly was really beginning to get tired of that question. "Because I don't kill people, Munz." Ulrich raised an eyebrow.

"Everyone kills, Dodger. It's human nature. We kill to survive, for revenge, for pleasure. All one has to do is find out what a man will kill for, and then you know the man." His teeth were white as sun bleached bones. Sickly looked back into Ulrich's midnight blue eyes, considering this.

Before the silence was broken, the door opened again. Almost before it had hit the wall, Jamie, Billys, and Terry entered. Billys was already speaking, even before he had crossed the threshold. "Sickly, we checked out that minister's house and found . . . Sickly, why is Ulrich Munz here?" The three newcomers stopped in the doorway, looking as if their train of thought had not so much been derailed, as vaporized.

"And here I thought you were just walking dogs, Dodger," Ulrich said, innocently.

"Something like that."

"Well, as I see you have new visitors, I'll take my leave." He got up from the bed, and gave Jamie a deep bow, to which she returned a look of disdain so cool the room dropped a few degrees. Ignoring this easily, Ulrich swaggered to the door, and turned. "Get well soon, Dodger." His tone was so earnest it was almost a threat. He left through the doorway, pushing past Terry who was staring blankly at the departing man.

"Dat was Ulrik Munts," Terry finally said, breaking the silence that had rushed in to fill the gap Ulrich had left.

"Yeah, Sickly, what did he want? Not here on a job, I hope," Jamie asked quietly.

Sickly finally let go of the small knife he had been clutching in his right hand, hidden beneath the sheets.

"I don't think so. I wonder . . ." It was just possible that the people who had ordered Bradley Wells killed had also hired Ulrich. If so, he was probably sent here to see how deeply Sickly was involved. Bradley Wells had said there would be danger.

"Nothing we can do about it right now," Sickly said, "What did you find?"

"The door was definitely forced," Jamie began, "But from the inside. And when I checked the rest of the house I found a window which had also been forced open. Two entrances, Sickly. Out of character, for a thief, innit. They tend to find an entrance and stick to it, for simplicity."

Sickly glanced down quickly at the Watch report and leafed through the pages. "Ah, it only mentions the door, here. They overlooked the window."

"I think they were supposed to," Jamie said. "It was meant to look like a thief broke in, killed Wells, took what was easy, and left."

"If that's what it was meant to look like," Sickly said slowly, "I want to know what they were trying to cover up. So, what else was there?"

"Nothing that the Watch hadn't already been through," Billys grumbled. "Bunch of old furniture, paintings, lamps, whatever. Someone had even started packing up."

"What Billys is failing to say is that we went into his office," Jamie added, frowning at the short man.

"And?"

"Sorry, Sickly dear, nothing much. A load of old documents on foreign countries, ambassadors, envoys, peace treaties, wars. Lots of *Daily Piccolo* clippings, a picture of a kitten hanging off a branch with the words 'Dinner's Served.' There was . . ." But Sickly was no longer listening, something had triggered his memory, he wanted to look at the letter again.

"Thank you, Jamie. I think I have two ideas. If the Watch overlooked the forced window, they might have missed something else. Let's examine the body. Now, would you mind helping me escape before the official checkout?" They grinned at the thought, or at least, Jamie and Billys did. Terry was smiling because he was thinking about kittens.

A half hour later, when Nurse Maisie came in to check up on

her patient, she found the room empty, a leather money purse with exact payment, and an open window. She tutted, tidied the bedclothes, put the untouched hospital jelly on a tray for the next patient, and looked for the clipboard with the case history on it. The clipboard was there, but the records on this patient were gone, as if he had never been here. Maisie peered about for any lurking hospital admin and then pocketed the purse. Several of her patients were about to be bumped up the treatment schedule thanks to an anonymous donation.

Getting into the morgue was not a problem as Jamie, Terry, and Billys were already known to Mr. Gizzard, the coroner. Most assassins rapidly became good friends with the doddering old man, who was no stranger to men and women wearing all black coming in at odd hours to 'examine' corpses. So long as there was enough of the body left to bury at the end of the night, Mr. Gizzard tipped his shapeless wool cap, smiled a toothless smile, and turned a cataract-blind eye.

Mr. Wells was lying on a slab in a cold room, covered by a sheet that had bid farewell to better days. He was an older man with well-trimmed grey hair, a salt and pepper beard, and wrinkle-lines around his mouth and eyes. That was the picture Sickly formed of him before his murder, because now the side of his head was defaced by a blood-caked crater. Sickly tried hard not to look too closely; he already felt nauseated at the smell of formaldehyde.

Jamie was unaffected, and pulled the sheet back farther, exposing an expanse of dead, pale flesh. Death was not kind to beauty, but Mr. Gizzard had performed his duty honorably with respect to embalming and preservation. The body had been cleaned, drained, and, not to put too fine a point on it, emptied of anything that might have begun to stink. Even with no obvious bloating or seepage, Sickly's gorge rose.

Jamie peered at the corpse with the critical eye of a professional. "No struggle wounds, no bruising on the hands or arms. No superficial lacerations or abrasions, nothing but the impact on his skull, nothing but . . ." she trailed off and peered at a spot beneath the ear on the side with the wound. "Look at this, Sickly."

Sickly, against his better judgment, looked where Jamie was pointing. Beneath the ear was another wound, and a fairly sizable one at that. "What am I looking at, Jamie?"

"Sharp force trauma, innit? Give me a moment." Jamie prepared her hands by clawing a slab of grey soap, leaving a residue built up under her nails. Next she gathered a set of instruments and bottles from a nearby table and proceeded to clean and examine the area around the injury.

Sickly tried hard not to look at the corpse and even harder not to vomit. Terry stood still as a statue, a faint smile on his face. Billys inserted a pinky into his ear, twisted vigorously, then examined his findings.

"Sickly, look here," Jamie said at last. "There are two bruises around the opening, and the hole itself might show a diamond pattern," she finished.

"Might?" Sickly asked. Jamie gave him a pitying look.

"Sickly, dear, wounds are rarely as clean and straightforward as the pictures in the Forensics 101 textbook. Life and death are messy things. The skull can get chipped or shattered. The body may twist while the knife is still inside. Blood clots and dries over everything."

"Exsanguination," Terry supplied. Sickly and Jamie turned, but Terry didn't seem to have anything else to add.

"Sorry," Sickly said at last.

"Haven't I told you not to apologize unnecessarily?" Jamie replied, archly.

"You and Vel both," he muttered. Jamie's lips pursed for the briefest moment at the mention of Vel's name. Sickly found this odd.

"I don't think Wells was killed by the gash in his head," Jamie continued, as if nothing had happened. "It appears to have been inflicted postmortem. I think he was killed by a dagger. A Hambridge baselard, to be exact."

"What does this mean?" Sickly asked.

"Well, a baselard usually has an inward, crescent-shaped cross guard and pommel, but the Hambridge variety cross guard bends outward. That would have made the bruises near the hole. In either case the blade has got a diamond cross-section. That adds strength, especially for piercing attacks, to punch through armor. It's a killer's knife, Sickly. Whoever did this knew what they were doing. A single wound that pierced his brain. Killed him without a fight. It's a move that would take speed and skill that a common burglar or even someone trained at the Thieves' College would find difficult. The postmortem damage was meant to cover the killing blow, make it look like a murder."

"So, he *was* assassinated," Sickly finished, feeling a sense of excitement and progress at last. "Good work, Jamie."

But how had the Watch failed to find this? Sickly wondered. The report had mentioned nothing about a knife wound. The hole in their story matched the one in Wells' head. Coppers might not be clever, but they weren't stupid. The report had either been tampered with, or purposely left out details.

Sickly returned his attention to the matter at hand. "That leaves the question of whose baselard killed Bradley Wells?"

"That's a bit harder," Jamie said, and Sickly sighed. "Or it would be, if I hadn't taken The Art of Backstabbing: Historical to Modern Approaches. It covered a lot of material, including popular assassination trends through the ages. The Hambridge baselard, as a weapon for assassins, wasn't popular until a few years ago. Most of the older assassins still view it as little better than a fashion accessory."

"Oh yeah, that sounded like an interesting class," Sickly said, remembering the fall syllabus. "Why didn't I take that?"

"It was cross-listed with Political Science, innit," Jamie reminded him, "and you had already got that requirement out of the way with Mockiavelli."

"Oh, right. So we're looking for a younger assassin, maybe someone from our Occisor Cadre," Sickly finished. "Who uses baselards from that group?"

"Me, actually," Jamie said, gesturing to a crescent-hilted blade at her hip. "And Billys."

"What are you saying?" Billys snapped. "I didn't do it!"

Jamie gave him a scathing look. "Obviously. I'm just listing everyone I know who uses this kind of dagger. Let's see. Vel, sometimes, though she tends to go in for misericorde daggers. More fashionable for coup-de-graces. Ulrich uses them, Sable Levania, Joanna Martinez, and I think I saw Doyle Gaspard use one, a few times." Jamie finished ticking the names off on her fingers, and gave Sickly an apologetic look. "And that's just the people from our year, innit. No telling how many from other years, like Gertrude Hanklebaum, Rupert Plunkett, the Caduceus brothers, and Yasmin Rinkali, to name a few."

"That's a lot of names. Hold on though," Sickly said, as Jamie began scrubbing her hands in a basin. "How big was the window that was forced at Wells' house?" Billys held up his arms about a foot and a half apart. "That's not terribly big," Sickly mused. "If that's where they got in, they couldn't have been Terry's size. Thinking just about our class, Ulrich and Doyle are too big. That leaves Joanna and . . . Sable." Billys, Jamie and Sickly shivered, and not just because they were in a cold-room. "It could have been Sable Levania." Sickly said. "That's a dead end if ever I saw one."

"Cheer up, dear," Jamie said softly, putting an arm around his shoulder. "What was that other lead you mentioned at the hospital? Don't give up," she gave him an encouraging smile.

Sickly shook himself. "All right, then. Let's go buy a newspaper."

"I still say we should've snuck in here when it was dark," Billys grumbled. Everyone else rolled their eyes.

"If we did that it would make us look like thieves," Jamie explained tiredly.

"But that's what we are!"

"No, we're assassins. Ten Gods, Billys, start thinking like one," Jamie groaned.

"All I'm saying is, why does it have to be me?"

"Because you're the one who's had the most experience with the Hambridge Watch!" snarled Jamie.

It was true. For some reason, Billys seemed to have an almost magnetic attraction for the City's Finest, who always appeared at the wrong moment and demanded to know why, as if they had the right, a man dressed all in black was climbing out of a nobleman's bedroom window at, say, 1 a.m. There was little the Watch could do to arrest an assassin for doing their job, but there were endless ways to detain them by asking pertinent but difficult questions such as, "Why?"

Billys had first been detained in the second year of college when he had been given a practice assignment, and though no harm had been done, he still had to spend a night in the lockup. From there, it had only gotten worse.

"Come on, you lot." Sickly and his three friends had gone straight to News Street from the morgue. News Street was home to three major newspaper companies who all had the same motto: "The people will know!" blazoned across the fronts of their buildings. It was the city's best place to gather information, though all three companies were unfailingly misinformed. Sickly led the way, still wearing his tattered, muddy, and blood-stained clothes from Crowbar's rampage. Behind him came Billys, small and dressed in black, Jamie, slim and dressed in black, and Terry, huge and dressed in black. They crossed the street, starting from a rundown café, and headed not for *The Hambridge Times*, but for the second largest newspaper, *The Daily Piccolo*. The street was busy, and the group of four oddly dressed strangers caused a bit of stir, but at least this allowed Sickly to forge ahead in the gap created by confused passersby.

As they neared the presumptuous white columns of *The Daily Piccolo*, an old man approached them. He wore several patched and faded coats, a rotting scarf and a face harrowed by the years. He jingled a rusting tin cup at them. "Please, m'lords. Spare a coin for an old soldier?"

"Go find a soup kitchen," Billys muttered, barging past. Terry touched his forelock and passed by wordlessly. Sickly dithered, never knowing how to deal with this kind of situation.

Before he could move, Jamie went up to the man and pressed a fiver into his hand. "There you go, sir. Keep warm, keep safe."

"Civica bless you, m'lady," he murmured, tipping his hat. Jamie smiled and grabbed Sickly's arm, hurrying him to catch up with Billys and Terry as they entered their target building.

The inside was not what Sickly had been expecting, after the huge columns outside. Much of the interior was devoted to a large, open room where perhaps fifty journalists, writers, and editors were working at individual desks, or bumping into each other as they ran back and forth between these islands of relative peace. Here and there people sat in huddles around a single desk, their heads bent, speaking loudly because of the noise. The room was alive with curses, cigarette smoke, and flying pages, some of which were not poorly folded paper gliders. A mechanical clacking and thudding could be felt through the floor from the printing presses.

Undaunted, Sickly threaded his way through the melee that was *The Daily Piccolo*'s life blood, to the back where it was easy to find the obituary editor's desk. It was the one that featured, by way of decoration, silver-framed certificates of death. Also by way of decoration, there was a chipped mug with the hopeless little message: "You don't have to be sane to work here. Help."

Mr. Harold Nosey, as introduced by a placard in the center of his desk, was seated and drafting something on a typewriter. He glanced between it and a long list of scrawled notes.

"Excuse me," Sickly said quietly, which got no response. "Excuse me!" he tried again, with the same lack of response.

Sickly tapped his shoulder, at which the man spun around and stared up at Sickly with an air of barely contained intensity.

"What?" He yelled, loud enough to be heard over the din.

"Did you write the obituary for Bradley Wells?" Sickly yelled back.

"Yes!" The little man motioned emphatically, and continued in a thick Golraic accent. "Follow me! I hate this bloody room! Can't hear the dead people, you know. They tell me how they want their obituaries written." Sickly raised an eyebrow.

Mr. Nosey finally appeared to notice the three people in assassins' clothing behind him. To his credit, he paused for barely a second before saying, "Your, ah, friends can come too."

That was the thing about assassins in this city. They were a fact of life. They weren't common, but it was understood that they were around, doing quiet little jobs for huge sums of money, and because they were assassins, they advertised. No assassin in their right mind would walk down the street in plain garb when they could swagger down it, dressed in the latest fashion, turning heads all the way. It was a matter of style, and because of this, people found out. And since regular people probably weren't important enough to assassinate, assassins were tolerated as long as they were polite and didn't go knifing anyone in public.

Mr. Nosey stood, though the difference in his sitting and standing height was negligible. He was quite spry, despite his portly appearance, and marched quickly towards a door at the back. Sickly motioned to his friends and trailed behind the bobbing head covered in short, curly red hair. When they were all through the door, Mr. Nosey shut it behind them.

"That's better," he mumbled, polishing his thick spectacles. "Now, what is it you wanted, mister . . . ?"

"Thomas. Gordon Thomas." Sickly shook the proffered hand gingerly, trying not to think about the words, 'Can't hear the dead people, you know,' and failing. "I wondered if you knew something about the position of Foreign Minister, about Bradley Wells, his murder, and who replaced him."

"Know something about it? Why, young man, I know everything about it. Everything!" Sickly resisted taking a step back from the editor who was practically vibrating with as yet uncommunicated knowledge. "Bradley Wells, a very interesting case. Of course, I follow all the major political figures quite closely, and when one is murdered, well, sir!" He beamed, as though murder was the most wonderful thing that had happened all morning. "I do take an interest."

"Wait, major political figures? I thought the Foreign Minister wasn't a big job," Billys said confusedly.

"That was a bad joke, right? You can't be that bloody ignorant," Jamie scoffed.

"Enough, both of you," Sickly said. "I'm sorry, Mr. Nosey, you were saying?"

"What, laddie? Ah, yes, Bradley Wells. Foreign Minister. Not very well known but incredibly important. Conducts all the, erm, foreign affairs of the city. Naturally, that includes the ambassadors and embassies but, and not many people know this, also the Guild of Spies. Not ground-shaking inside the city, perhaps, but vitally important for any negotiations with the other Autarchic Cities and the kingdoms beyond. Parliament is still bickering over who is to replace old Wells. We shall have to see if the fresh blood is as adept as the old fox, eh?"

Sickly nodded, but internally he felt his excitement growing. Leadership of the Guild of Spies. Now there was something worth killing over. Between this information and what Jamie had unearthed at the mortuary, he finally felt he was getting somewhere.

"I'm sorry, laddie, has something upset you?"

Sickly raised his eyebrows in genuine surprise at the small man. "Oh no, I'm quite thrilled."

The man was frowning at his face, and Sickly thought he knew what was coming. "Ah, right, then. You just, ah. You looked, ah. Nothing, nothing, never mind. Is there anything else you wanted to know?"

"Er, no, thank you, Mr. Nosey, you've been very helpful. Now could you just point me towards the personal boxes?"

As they left, Sickly could imagine Mr. Nosey's eyes on the back of his head. He could almost hear the man mutter to himself "Did you see that, eh? No expression at all." It was like Joanna had said. He was a freak.

"Billys, are you ready? You're up next."

"Great." Billys mumbled faintly.

"Come on, Billys. Get on with it," Jamie said, snidely.

The corridor opened out into a small room which was nearly filled by a large desk and an even larger man wearing an official *Daily Piccolo* uniform of gray tweed. The man's expression and posture suggested that his eyebrows had been permanently glued together, and he was not happy about it. There was a door behind the desk, though it was conspicuously locked. The guard had been reading an old issue of *Unsporting Sport Hunting*, but looked up when he saw the four assassins approach.

"May I help you . . ." he paused and his eyes passed over Sickly's tattered shirt, Billys mess of greasy hair, Jamie's shabby clothing, and Terry's blank expression, "people?" His voice was gruff and confrontational. Billys stepped forward, his usually slouched shoulders snapping to attention. His normally flippant tone was replaced by military firmness.

"Yes, you can. The Watch is currently investigating the murder of one Bradley Wells, who, we are informed, had a personal box here. Due to the nature of our search we need all information, however trivial, to be brought back to the station. The Watch would appreciate your help in locating the box in question."

The man at the desk, whose nametag announced him as HiMyNameIsBrutus, leaned forward with the air of a person who is about to gleefully make someone else's life hell. "Sorry sir, can't do that sir, you understand sir, I'm sure. It's just that, sir, you don't look like Watch officers, sirs and lady, and it just wouldn't do to let anyone in, sirs and lady. If you could just show me some identification, sir."

Billys didn't flinch, but instead answered in the time honored way of the watchman, "I think you are wasting Watch time. Do you know what we do to people who waste Watch time?"

Unfortunately, this did not work. Brutus' grin grew even wider, and he pulled from behind the desk a large and unmistakably loaded crossbow.

"I think that you are some of the sodding worst bunch of street thugs I have ever seen. Do you know what *I* do with street thugs who come onto Piccolo property? I get to shoot 'em. And since I'm the guard, that makes it legal. If you was proper watchmen, you'd know that. So get out of here. Go on." Brutus aimed the crossbow at Billys' chest.

Had Brutus been as smart as he thought he was, he would have noticed that Billys didn't flinch at all when the gleaming tip of the arrow was leveled at his heart. But this was only his first big mistake.

Billys turned questioningly to Sickly, who shrugged and motioned for them to leave. It wasn't worth starting a fight over something when they could just come back later and deal with a more reasonable guard. They turned to go. And that was when Brutus made his second big mistake. "Yeah, walk away. Cowards." All four of them stopped in their tracks.

"Now?" Billys asked in a carefully neutral voice. Sickly demurred for a second, then nodded.

"You cheeky little prick, you don't have the stones to -- Oh." Faster than blinking, the knife's point pressed into the man's large nose. Billys' face grinned down at the suddenly very, very worried security guard.

"Achoo, Brutus?" Billys asked, as the man's piggy eyes began to water.

"You're, uh, that kind of watchman, then?"

Billys grinned. "That's right. The kind that doesn't have to ask nicely, see?"

"I'll, uh, just have that door open in half a tick then, shall I, sir?"

"Yes, I think you will." Brutus lead them cautiously through the door into a room filled with neat cubbyholes, each labeled with a name.

"Nice going, Billys," Sickly whispered appreciatively. "But was the handstand onto the desk as you drew your dagger really necessary?"

Billys shrugged and failed to suppress a smirk. "I've been trying to learn ripjigging from some of the dockworkers' kids on my street. It's bloody tough."

Sickly kept his eyes on Brutus as their newly servile guide searched for the box. "Isn't that the dance where you spin around wildly, do backflips, and hold poses? Haven't people been hospitalized for it?"

Billys grin grew wider. "I know, right! It's great!"

Brutus bowed deferentially. "Here, sirs and lady, and will sirs and lady be wanting anything else, sirs and lady?" His voice oozed helpfulness.

"No, that will be all, *sir*," Billys said, and the relieved Brutus left as quickly as he could.

"What's this about then, Sickly?" Jamie asked as Sickly opened the cubby door.

"Mr. Wells sent me a letter, about three weeks ago, and explained that he was going to be murdered. He said that he would leave me a more detailed explanation at his house. But you three checked through it and only found information about the murderer, not the man himself. The only clue was that he left a bunch of old newspapers, *Daily Piccolos*, lying around. See, I've got this habit of leaving the paper in my shoes until I need to use them. I picked it up from my dad. And the only grammatical error in Wells' first letter to me was about my father's shoes. Putting two and two together, and knowing that the *Piccolo* has these newspaper boxes, there was a good chance he might have hidden something here."

"That's bloody esoteric, innit? You figured that all out your-self?" Jamie asked, and patted him on the back. Sickly felt rather proud, and his eyebrows twitched a little bit.

"Thanks, Jamie."

"So, what's in da box, Sickly?" Terry probed.

"Let's find out." Sickly reached his hand into the dark interior, explored a little and found . . . nothing.

Sickly couldn't believe it. He had been so sure. All the clues pointed to this. "It's empty," he breathed. "Someone give me a light."

Billys produced a grubby match, scraped it against the floor and held it up to the box. Sickly peered inside and almost sighed with relief. In the back wall of the box there was a small engraving of what looked like the Dodger family crest, mirrored. Sickly removed his father's ring from his finger and pressed it against the little imprint. There was a soft click.

"Brilliant," they all whispered, in unison. Sickly pulled the ring back, and as he did so the back panel opened forward. Sickly took the match and squinted into the dark cavity. He could make out the form of a small book and a bundle of papers. The match died. Sickly scooped up the contents of the box, closed the back panel, and slid the ring back onto his finger. He slipped the book and papers into his coat pocket.

"Thanks for your help, everyone, let's go before Brutus gets smart again. After all, we wouldn't want anyone to get hurt."

CHAPTER 10

"It isn't necessarily Sable," Jamie argued as they neared the front door of Sickly's apartment building, "Joanna also uses baselards. And I've heard she's been doing some high level work lately."

"Yeah, for ole Annette Martinez herself," Billys whispered. "What do you bet Lady Ironside wants to be foreign minister? She's already got influence outside of Hambridge, I hear. But if being the foreign minister is as powerful as that cracked journalist said, and she got Wells' job, well . . ." he gave them a knowing look.

"That's not a bad thought, Billys," Sickly said, impressed. "Want to go talk to Joanna about what her mother's been up to?"

"Why's it always me?" Billys asked, indignantly.

Sickly raised an eyebrow. "Weren't the two of you seeing each other back in our second year?" Billys shrugged but stood taller, making him almost five and a half feet tall.

"Yeah, until she dumped you for that wanker, Traplek," Jamie muttered. Billys deflated.

"Now den, no fighting," Terry said placidly.

Sickly gave him a grateful look, and the man returned a serene smile. "Give it some thought, Billys?"

"Maybe, all right? But you'd owe me one. I've got a lot on my plate already." Jamie rolled her eyes.

"I fink I ought ta go get ready for da night shift at da Merchant's Consul. Bye, Sickly,"

"Bye, big guy," Sickly said. Terry strode after Billys, and the two figures rapidly disappeared down the twisting streets of Cod Liver Oil Alley. Sickly looked at Jamie, and a thought occurred. She was the smartest person he knew.

"Want to come in? Maybe you can help me sort this out."

Jamie toyed absently with a braid. "Well, I don't have a job until later tonight. And I am a bit curious." Sickly raised an eyebrow gladly and led the way to his ground floor flat.

"Tea?" he asked as they took off their coats. "I've got some sugar, even."

"I couldn't put you to any trouble, dear," she protested.

"I'm putting the kettle on." As it warmed, Sickly continued, "How have you been?"

"Can't complain," she replied airily. Sickly nodded and busied himself about the tea. "I managed to snag a patron – Lady Full-frigate – at last."

"Jamie, that's wonderful," Sickly said, excitedly.

"It is, isn't it? It's been good to have work."

"I know what you mean. I feel like I get a bit cooped up on days off. What kind of contracts?"

"This and that, yeah? Client confidentiality and all. But yeah, it's been good." Something about her tone made him turn around. She stood by his table, twisting a braid of hair between her fingers. She looked up and smiled, or at least her mouth went up at the corners and her teeth appeared. Sickly raised an eyebrow questioningly. "Can I tell you something?"

"Sure, anything." He waited, expectantly, but she remained silent. He knew it was hard for her to bring up issues affecting her personal life. After a moment, he prompted, "How's your dad?"

Jamie stiffened, a look of anxiety flashing across her normally controlled features. "He's fine." Her hand twisted over and over. "He's been a bit ill, is all."

"Gods, I'm sorry."

"He's all right for now, I guess." Sickly floundered like a three-legged camel in a snow drift. Not knowing what else to do, he came forward and put his arms around her. She returned the gesture a bit stiffly, but said, "Thanks, dear."

"Anything I can do?"

"No, no, it's fine. I'm fine."

And really, what was there to do? Sickly wasn't the type to pray to Genulum, and it sounded like Jamie had things under control. "Jamie, you're one of the strongest people I know. You'll get it sorted, I know you will."

She nodded. "Yeah. Thanks, dear."

They turned their attention to the matter at hand with steaming mugs of tea and a small fire to warm them against the Hambridge chill. Sickly pulled the notebook and the bundle of papers from his coat pocket and laid them out on the table. The top one was a letter, which he opened first.

To the Son of Henry Dodger,

Congratulations on finding this. I'm sure your father would have been proud. As I'm sure you've worked out, my name is Bradley Wells, Foreign Minister of Hambridge. I am also one of the few people alive who knows what danger threatens this city. Now I must pass this burden on to you, and you alone.

Half a year ago a prominent member of the Merchant Consortium, Mr. Otto Blotter was slain in a tragic fire. Two months ago the head of the Hambridge Watch, Commander Burgis, died in a cart accident. A month ago, Wendy Stimpson, Head Chemist of the Alchemists' Guild, was assassinated. Three weeks ago Mr. Hopkins, Master Thief of the Thieves' Guild died in a bar fight. Last week several more members of the merchant's council resigned their posts for mysterious reasons. By the time you find this letter there will be others.

These are not random happenings. They are murders. Murders committed by assassins paid not in gold, but in power. These killings have been orchestrated by the man who will have me murdered. I do not know who he is, but it is clear that he is trying to seize Hambridge. The successors to the newly vacant positions are all assassins trained at The Dalton College for Men in Black.

Someone is using the assassins to wage a silent war on our city. For being in contact with me, you will surely become a target. Your friends are in danger of becoming pawns in this game, and if they refuse, they will be terminated.

Your only hope of survival is to find whoever is staging this coup, and kill them before they kill you. He will not be one of the new heads of the guilds, those positions are too vulnerable. It will be someone in the dark, standing in the shadow behind the throne. The Traveler will come for me soon, I can feel it. My position is highly valuable as I run the ambassadors, embassies, and most importantly the Guild of Spies. The ambassadors must bow to the ruler of the city, but the spies will still answer to me. However, if they get their hands on my notebook, they will be in control of the spies as well.

That is why I have entrusted it to you. It contains a list of all my agents, their whereabouts, assignments, and covers. I need you to keep it safe, foil this plot, and pass it on to a successor chosen by Lord Reiker and the parliament. The information held within its pages is too important to lose. Without this book in the hands of a competent and trustworthy Spymaster, Hambridge will be vulnerable to infiltration by outside forces. Nor of course, can you allow it to fall into the hands of the murderer.

Get in contact with one of these people; they are my eyes in the city. They will help you. If you doubt their identity, which you should, they will tell you this phrase: The white crow listens in the well of silence. Tell no one of this. Anyone might be part of the plot.

Sickly sat back and whistled softly. So Bradley Wells believed there was some kind of plot going on, a plot to take over the city. Sickly wondered if the man was crazy. Of course he was. Anyone who rose to be the leader of Hambridge's Guild of Spies would be have to be paranoid. That did not, however, mean he was wrong.

Tell no one of this. Anyone might be part of the plot.

Sickly passed the note to Jamie. She scanned it quickly, her brows climbing higher as her eyes sped down the lines. She reached the end of the document and grunted. "I heard about Commander Burgis, but still, this is a bit much, innit?"

Sickly shrugged. "They are watching you," he murmured. Jamie looked uneasy. Sickly rose and drew the curtain to mute the mid-afternoon sunshine leaving them in candlelight. Together they pored over the next piece of paper which had three names on it: Kerry Adams, Earl Watkins, and Quentin Verk. There was also a list of instructions about how to contact each one of them, and a list of aliases that they might go by.

Beneath it all was a small, red notebook. Sickly opened it and found page after page detailing information about all the spies currently operating in foreign countries and cities. There were names, pseudonyms, reports, and whereabouts. Much of it also seemed to be written in a code of Wells' own devising, suggesting that some secrets were too valuable to leave for just anyone. If knowledge was power, then whoever had this notebook would be very powerful indeed.

"What do you reckon?" Sickly asked as he passed Jamie the notebook.

Her eyes on the pages, she responded slowly. "Well, there's certainly a lot here. I dunno know, though. A grand plot to seize Hambridge seems pretty mental to me."

"But all of it together. All these freak accidents and mysterious deaths, one after another. It could be worth looking into."

Jamie looked up, her face pulled into an expression of logical abstraction. It reminded Sickly of their introductory alchemistry classes when Jamie would work a problem through in her head before pulling the stopper off any bottles. "Well, dear, if there was a plot, would it be so bad if assassins ruled the city?"

Sickly raised an eyebrow. "Let's see. Assassins are mostly a danger to each other and the upper class. They're not supposed to attack everyday people. There would probably be a lot less political infighting."

"Which might mean things get done around here quicker," Jamie mused.

"Yeah, but what things? They're not acting like assassins. They're not killing for money. This is more like a . . . a coup. Whoever controls them would get more control over the city than anyone's had since the Reikers first settled here. And all we know so far is that they're dangerous. By the sound of it, they've already killed a load of people for their own ends."

"Being dangerous doesn't make someone evil, dear. I'm dangerous. Vel is dangerous. You're dangerous, Sickly," Jamie reminded him.

"Come off it. You know I'm not like you or her. But I take your point. Still, if Wells is right, then I'm not the only one in danger. Vel, Terry, and Billys might get targeted. *You* might get targeted now that I've shared this with you. Who knows? They might even go after Booter. I can't take that chance." As he said it, he realized he meant it. He wouldn't let a cabal of murderers threaten his friends.

Jamie frowned, as if she saw gaps in Sickly's argument, but eventually said, "Well, dear, what are you going to do about it?"

At the very least, Sickly had a duty to warn his friends. But who first? Booter wasn't an assassin, so he was probably safe for the moment. Eveline? Much as he wanted to go to her first, for reasons not entirely related to the conspiracy, he shouldn't. She was shielded by Lord Salsa's reputation and more than capable of defending herself. Who else? Terry worked for one of the guilds, he couldn't remember which. Jamie was here with him.

"Billys," he said, and Jamie quirked her dark brows at him. "I might be able to convince him to look into Joanna's family. Then maybe I'll try to contact one of these spies. See if they know anything."

Jamie twirled a braid in her fingers. "If you're going to get mixed up in something dangerous, you might as well take out some insurance." Jamie picked up a few of the papers they had been perusing. Sickly raised his eyebrows at them. One was a recipe for Mincefish Streussel, another was a piece of sheet music from the score of *The Marriage of Pigaro*. "I'd bet these are keys to the codes in Wells' notebook, dear. And if you don't want that information falling into the wrong hands you need to separate the lock from the key."

"Brilliant, Jamie." Sickly knew he had made the right choice in getting her opinion on the matter. "I want to keep the notebook on me at all times, but you're right. We should hide the rest of these documents. Would you be able to do that for me?"

"You're sure?" Jamie asked, in surprise.

"Well, if they get me, I don't want to make it easy for them to crack the codes. Be easier if I didn't know where they were hidden, right?" He grabbed the page of notes detailing how to contact the late Foreign Minister's agents in Hambridge and proffered the rest to Jamie.

"Well, all right then, dear. I've got a job tonight and I can hide them on the way." Jamie took them and Sickly felt a weight lift from his chest. They finished their tea quickly and rose to go. As Jamie drew on her coat, Sickly crossed to the chest at the foot of his bed. He opened it and folded his arms, ringed finger tapping against left bicep in a contemplative motion. It had been almost three months since he had last used any of his equipment.

For the first time, Sickly wished that he had bothered to keep up his training.

"Arrêtez. Arrêtez! That means halt, mademoiselle Lucrezia." There were scattered snorts from the assembled watchers.

Eveline curtailed her lunge and flicked a glance towards the Dalton College fencing professor, Maitre Brossard. His cold blue eyes regarded her from their perch above a nose that could have been registered as a valid tournament weapon. "Your foot has, yet again, found its way off the piste. That is to say, the strip of play."

She risked taking eyes off her opponent a second time and saw that, indeed, her left boot had edged over the inlaid wood of darker grain which indicated the edges of the legal area. "Monsieur Gaspard, I award you the penalty."

Behind the glittering mesh mask, Eveline could see Doyle's blocky face contort with a smile. Grinding her teeth, she backed up the required distance and assumed her stance again.

"En garde. Prêts? Allez!" Maitre Brossard's voice snapped lazily through the still air of the Dalton College fencing gymnasium. The Bricquébécois art of fencing was renowned for its emphasis on speed, precision and grace. Eveline had registered for the class because she had hoped it would be an easy A as she tried to find her feet in this new world of higher education. After all, on the streets of Hambridge you were either fast or dead.

What no one had told her was that the art of fencing also emphasized rules. Endless, finnicky rules that made no sense and would get you killed in a real fight. She surged forward like a spring loaded alley cat towards Doyle who stood in the traditional fencer's crouch, sword forward and back hand raised comically over his head.

Eveline lunged, the long, whippy, and above all ridiculous sword diving for the man's chest. He managed a quarte parry, brushing the tip of her blade away from his heart. Before he could riposte she leaned outward, wary of the edge of the strip, and struck again for his side. She felt her blow connect, but a second later there was a tug on her own thick fencing jacket. Doyle had managed to strike her shoulder.

"Arretez! The touche is yours Monsieur Gaspard." Eveline turned in disbelief and rage to their instructor.

"But I hit him first!" she managed, incensed.

"Perhaps, but riposte has priority over remise. And priority, mademoiselle, is everything in this world."

The set finished quickly. Doyle was not fast, but as he boasted to anyone within earshot, he had been trained in the art since he was four on his family's estates. Eveline's grasp of the esoteric swordplay etiquette became more tenuous as her anger grew. As the class wore on, Maitre Brossard continued to narrate the finer points of each fencing phrase, addressing her by name each time someone committed an infraction of which she too had been guilty.

Eveline forced herself to endure. A skill she had honed since childhood. Even as they pulled off the thicket vests and pads afterwards, she was not safe. Her skin crawled as air cooled the sweat-soaked training clothes they all wore beneath the protective gear and memories threatened to flood her mind.

Doyle, on his way out of the room, paused beside her. With a smirk he said, "Perhaps you'd care for some extra practice? I could teach you one-on-one. Even let you score a few points." Her whole body was already taught as a crossbow at full draw. She kept her eyes fixed on the coarse fabric of the fencing jacket. One hand crept to the knife at her side. "Of course, you'd have to let me get in a few touches of my own, if you follow me."

Her face was as steely and expressionless as the mask she had worn all afternoon. Only her eyes betrayed the hatred and disgust boiling inside her as she considered killing him. Drop low. Elbow to groin. Dodge clumsy counterattack. Use momentum to sweep left leg. Pin arm with knee. Draw knife and sever jugular.

Then run for the escape route she had plotted on her first day here. She had dared to hope it wouldn't be necessary. But there were predators here as well, just as there had been where she'd grown up. The only difference was that at Dalton they were called students.

Remise, she thought. Not counterattack.

Doyle chortled and walked on.

"You're Eveline, right?"

She jumped and whirled, drawing the knife, and falling into a defensive crouch. A boy was watching her, expression oddly blank for someone with a knife pointed toward them.

"Come on then, have a go at me, why don't you," she spat, eyes darting back and forth in case he had friends.

He raised his eyebrows. "I'm sorry, I didn't mean to upset you."

Eveline frowned. "This is a trick, innit?"

The boy's dark brows flickered in uncertainty. "No? I've upset you. I'll go." He turned and began to amble away, never minding the fact that he was leaving his back open to someone wielding a knife.

"Who are you?" she called after him, despite herself.

"I'm Sickly. Sickly Dodger," he repeated, when she looked confused. Now she remembered seeing him around, always in the background, always below the notice of their professors and peers.

"What do you want, then?"

He shrugged. "I don't know. I guess I was just curious how you learned to fight like that. You're really good."

Her instant reaction to such an insult was to go for his throat, to show him just how good she really was. But something about his tone gave her pause. It was almost as if he meant what he was saying.

"You – you reckon?"

"Yeah, I mean, in a real fight you would've killed Doyle easily. It's a bit silly, isn't it? All this emphasis on fighting by the rules when the whole point is to train us for something where there are no rules. That's just what I think, anyway."

"Yeah, it is a bit dodgy," she muttered, still staring at him with wary disbelief.

"I'm headed to get some lunch with another first year. Terry Andrews. Want to come?"

Uncertain, but oddly fascinated, she followed him out of the room.

Standing by a worktable in her attic, Eveline smiled to herself. She finished sharpening the long dueling saber and hung it on a wall rack. Even after she had learned the rules of play, learned to control her temper, and taken first in the Maitre Brossard's class over Doyle Gaspard, she had never liked fencing. Still, at least one good thing had come from that first semester at Dalton.

Billys' flat was like the man himself: short, unkempt, and obtrusive. It lurked in the bad part of Hambridge, which was to say everything within a few blocks of the river Ham's docks. Officially, the district was known as Murktown, and unofficially as "Murder Town" because more knifings, barfights, and casual killing took place here in one night than in the rest of the city in a whole year. It was said that if you wanted a body disposed of, you simply had to leave it at the edge of Murktown, and within the hour someone would have eaten it.

But Billys was safe because he was an assassin. Even the belligerently drunk and the very stupid would think twice about breaking into the residence of an assassin. Sickly walked up the cracked steps and knocked on the door. No answer. Sickly sighed and turned around.

"Got'cha!" There was Billys, pointing a crossbow at Sickly's nose.

"Hi, Billys," Sickly said resignedly. Billys lowered the bow, and Sickly relaxed a little.

"Fifteen to zed," Billys crowed, walking around Sickly and opening the front door.

"What?" Sickly asked blankly.

"I've gotten you fifteen times, and you haven't gotten me any. I win."

"Gotten me?" Sickly repeated.

"Yeah, you know – got you." Billys looked slightly put out. "You know the problem with you, Sickly?" Sickly raised an eyebrow. "You're no fun, and you can't take a joke. Is it because your face is so messed up?"

Oh yes. There it was: that pent up feeling you got whenever you were near Billys for any length of time. It was the kind of feeling that, when it built for too long, caused quiet, considerate people to pick up the nearest pair of sharpened office scissors and make the front page of the evening news.

Sickly followed him inside, silent. It was difficult to stomach Billys for any great length of time, say fifteen seconds. "Would you mind putting the kettle on?" Billys asked as he took a seat.

Sickly mustered further reserves of patience and crossed to the small fireplace, where he set about making a fire. "What are you doing here?" asked Billys as he put down the crossbow and propped his booted feet on the table.

"You remember why I sent you to Bradley Wells' house?" Sickly asked as a tiny flame roared to life beneath his fingers.

"Who? Oh, him. Something about a burglary, right?" Sickly went to the water basin and filled the pot, and then hung it over the fire.

"As it turns out, it was actually a murder, disguised as an assassination disguised as a burglary."

"Yeah?" Billys said, sounding bored.

Sickly explained quickly about Bradley Wells, the ongoing murders and the plot to replace powerful Hambridge figures with assassins. "And now that I know about it they might come after me and my friends," Sickly finished. It was Billys' wrinkled his brow in disbelief. "So I thought I'd warn you."

"You don't think he was completely mental?" Sickly made a noncommittal grunt. "Listen, Sickly, it sounds like he was just old and paranoid, and someone paid one of us to bump him off. But he got scared and didn't want to lose his job, so he called on you because he knew you aren't an assassin."

Sickly looked into the fire which was now tickling the pot's underbelly. That had certainly been Jamie's opinion at first. Just because she had agreed to hide the papers didn't mean she agreed with his conclusions about a grand machination. "Maybe. But I'd rather guard against something that isn't real than get killed by something I ignored."

"Sounds like a 'you' problem, Sickly."

"I came to warn you."

"Against the ravings of a barmy politician? Is that tea ready yet?"

'Look,' came the insistent voice in Sickly's head, 'it's all right to kill him if he's being really, really annoying.' Sickly shook his head to quell these thoughts. Billys' reaction, while not unexpected, had shaken Sickly's conviction in Mr. Wells' letter and the conspiracy theory. Perhaps there wasn't one. Perhaps Sickly was overthinking it.

After this, he would go home and sleep, and in the morning he would walk dogs. Jamie would hide the papers, just in case. He could finish warning his friends and then let the rest of this plot, real or imagined, pass him by. It was probably the safest option.

"Have a look at this. I've been assembling it all day!" Billys raised his crossbow. Sickly took a closer look. It was a heavy thing with a black stock and polished steel fittings. "The latest Burlington model, the 'Pandemonium X-treeem'! It's got a custom T-eight-six dot oh-three oak stock, and the limbs are horn and sinew with the built in gyro-cycling from the P-oh-eight model. The riser is omega grade temp steel manu'ed by Guillotine Smelters, and 'AD' at forty is barely point-nine! I got it preordered and, as part of the deal they threw in a hand bow version and sixty crossbow arrows."

Sickly was far out of his depth, but managed to pick out the last few words. "Don't you mean bolts?" He asked weakly.

"No, the arrows are much higher accuracy, due to..." Sickly's mind wandered, adrift on a sea of acronyms, abbreviations, numbers, and model types. Every so often he caught a few words before they were rushed away, screaming, by the tide of gibberish. Thankfully, the tea began to boil, which gave him something to do other than sit and feign interest.

When it was ready, Sickly brought two steaming mugs over and placed them on the table. Billys paused briefly, and looked up from describing some feature on the bow. "Oh, thanks." Sickly nodded, feeling the pressure of built-up anger abate. He sat back and sipped his tea as he listened amiably to the stream of chatter.

"So what do you think?" Billys finally asked, jerking Sickly from his reverie.

"It's a very nice piece of equipment," he supplied, dutifully.

"No, about Anemia Cassidy!" Sickly's mind raced over the past couple of seconds, but came up with nothing more than a dull, pleasant buzz.

"Who?"

"Anemia Cassidy? The girl at the City Watch station on Raft Street. Do you think she'd like it?" Sickly looked at the crossbow, and then at Billys. A dim memory was called from the back of Sickly's mind. It came, pulling on a bathrobe in haste.

"Hang on, is she that girl?" Billys nodded. "That girl you got arrested by three months ago? And last year?" He nodded again. Something finally clicked. It wasn't surprising that it had taken this long. The thought was so alien it hardly dared to be thunked. "You're not . . . sweet on her, are you?" To Sickly's amazement, Billys blushed.

"Well, she always makes sure I've got a cuppa when I'm down at the station, even if she wasn't the one to arrest me," he said, rather proudly.

"I thought you always liked . . . well, y'know. Jamie." Billys flushed.

"Well, yeah, but. But anyway, Anemia. You think she'll like it?"

"You think she'd like the Burlington?"

"Just for show, you know."

"You think a girl would like that."

"Well, yes," Billys said, suddenly sounding a little uncertain.

"A real, live, actual girl?"

"All right, all right, I've got the point."

"A real girl," Sickly repeated, quite enjoying himself.

"Thank you, so much," Billys growled.

"Got'cha, I believe."

Billys glowered, then his face broke into a boyish grin. "See, Sickly? You're not hopeless! One to fifteen!" His face darkened. "But you don't think it'll actually work?"

"I'm not the best person to talk to about relationships, starting them or otherwise," Sickly said defensively. "I mean, there was Helga Blitzkrieg back in second year, but . . ."

Billys nodded. "Yeah. Sorry about that one, mate."

Sickly shrugged. "Anyway, what I mean is, I don't have much experience with any of that."

"Me neither," Billys agreed emphatically. "Only Joanna, but we barely even snogged." He considered this for a moment. "Fine, Sickly, you win. I'll go and talk to Joanna about her mum and Wells and all that. But you've got to help me with Anemia!"

Looking at the hopeful expression on the man's face, Sickly had to supply something. "How about this: next time you get arrested, and she's bringing you the tea, ask her when she has time off. Take her to Sledge Hammer Coffee and ask if you can buy her something. Only pay if she says yes. Ask what she likes, and if she likes bows, then bring the bow next time."

Billys squared his round shoulders, an event Sickly would have paid money to see. "Right. That's what I'll do." He paused. "You're a good friend, Sickly." Sickly's eyebrows rose.

"Thanks. And thanks for checking into the Martinez family for me."

"I bet me and the Burlington'll really impress Anemia. I bet she's never had such a cool beau."

CHAPTER 11

Night inundated the city of Hambridge, extinguishing the day's activities. But where one life ended, another began. The nocturnal comings and goings of the city's thieves, assassins and merchants was in full swing by the time a lone figure ascended to a dark rooftop.

Sable Levania straightened and examined his gloves for any trace of grime. Reassured of their purity, he glanced about to ensure his solitude and find a place to wait. A line of soot stained chimneys rose from the peak of the roof. They would not do. The neighboring building was slightly higher, its roof overshadowing one side of the shingles. Sable nodded.

The black garments he wore blended in perfectly with his chosen shadow. He was invisible. No, he was more than invisible. Being invisible made you overconfident, and anyway, you could still be detected by sound and scent. Sable stirred with every breeze, sighed with every breath of wind, shifted with every rattle of a distant door. He had altered his odor with a range of designer assassin camouflage scents. For all intents and purposes, he did not blend in with the background. He *was* the background.

He readied the crossbow, a slim, beautifully utilitarian thing which stored enough power in its stubby limbs to send an arrow through a brick and kill a target on the other side.

He waited for the cart, knowing, with utmost assurance that he would be successful.

A coach came down the street. It bore the livery of the Hambridge Palace and was pulled by a team of four horses. Though it was richly appointed and large enough to hold six men, streaks of mud spattered its sides and caked the wheels. The driver wore the garb of the Ponsingham Palace Guard. He sat between two soldiers wearing chainmail and swords. The cart was flanked by four cavalrymen, wearing palace tabards over full plate armor.

Sable sighted down the bow and dispatched the driver with barely a second's pause to adjust the shot for a draft. The driver lurched forward and the guards on either side of him, despite their training, let out small yelps of surprise. The horsemen lifted their own crossbows as one and fired them toward the assassin's hiding place. Four bolts thudded heavily into the roof.

Sable was already moving, gliding through the air without leaving any trace of his passing. The horsemen guided their steeds into the shadows of the buildings, spreading out but keeping up with the coach. One of the guards on the seat grabbed the slackened reins, while the other informed the coach's occupants of the attack.

To Sable, from above, they were as powerless as infants. He withdrew from the folds of his cloak a blowpipe and fitted into it a poisoned dart. Sable had no qualms about using poison, it made things . . . simpler.

The two horsemen on the opposite side of the street were the first to fall. Like Eveline, Sable could put a dart into a neck with pinpoint accuracy. Unlike Eveline, the only sleep induced by Sable's poisons was the final respite of Hagrippa's cold realm.

By this time the coach had begun to pick up speed. Sable replaced the blowpipe on his belt and withdrew a specially weighted throwing knife. Knife was not the correct term, but 'machete' did not do the fine lines of this weapon justice. He pulled his arm back and hurled.

The coach shuddered as something struck the rear wheel and shattered it. Its five passengers pitched forward in their seats as the rear axle struck the ground and began to drag. An awful crunching noise came from the paving stones. The other wheel shuddered. There was a long moment as the cabin tipped sideways, threatening to hurl its occupants into the wall. Finally, the guards outside managed to bring the frightened horses to a stop, and the coach ground to a halt.

Inside the coach sat four guards and one terrified man wearing a fancy hat. His name was Cole Nebble, and among other jobs he was Lord Timothy Reiker's Steward. Oh yes, the guards were on edge because they were under attack, but Nebble was the only one who knew exactly how much trouble they were in. He clutched a briefcase to his brocaded vest. It was perhaps the only thing that could save the city.

There was a scream from outside, an awful, pained cry that latched onto the amygdala and sent fear crackling through the body. There was a second scream and then a silence more ominous than the shrieks of dying men. "Stay down, Cole," ordered the captain of the guard.

"Matthews," Cole began, his voice choked. The captain's bearded face turned to him. "You can't win this one. They're not . . ."

"We'll do what we can, sir. As soon as we get out there, you run. I'll send Higgins and Chu with you. Get back up the road, get as far as you can. Can't have the godfather of my kids dying in the street."

The steward shook his head. "They're on to *me*. This isn't a back alley koshing. It's the assassins." The guard's face tightened. They both knew what that meant. "Just get your squad out, when they chase me."

Matthews slammed a mailed fist onto the bench. "Gods damn

it, Cole! I took an oath. To the crown. And I don't mean to break it." They stared each other down.

Cole grinned. "You daft crownie." Matthews grinned too, but his eyes were over-bright. The captain signaled to his men. "Right then, Higgins and Chu, you're with us after all. Let's show this bastard what being in the Reiker Guard means!" His squad let out a ragged cheer. They threw the doors open and charged out into the street.

Cole waited for all attention to focus on the guards before he crept out the front end of the carriage. As he ghosted down the street, he turned back for a last look at his old friend. The guards spread out to surround a solitary figure in the center of the street.

Thumbscale, you old bitch, if you're up there look kindly on them. For me.

Then he fled, carrying his briefcase and the knowledge of a terrible plot with him. He ran until his lungs ached, cursing his own laziness and the neglect of his physical abilities over the past few years. After only a minute his legs burned like fire and unaccustomed sweat poured down his brow.

The shouts of dying men spurred him forward.

When he could take no more, he dodged sideways into an alley. Up ahead the alley opened onto a main thoroughfare. He could hear voices. Figures in armor carrying lamps — the Hambridge Watch!

He tried to call out, but managed only a whisper. No matter. He clutched the leather folder, thought of Matthews and managed a step forward. He *would* warn Lord Reiker.

The knife plunged through his back, passing straight through his heart. Sable's face was beside Cole Nebble's as the man's last breath slipped from his lips. The Steward died instantly, slumping backward into Sable's cold embrace. Sable withdrew the fatal knife, let the Steward slide gently down, and cleaned the dagger with a black cloth.

Then he inspected his gloves. Stained with soot and grime

despite his best efforts. That was the trouble with this city. It was so polluted you could hardly perform a job without getting its taint on you. He would need a new pair. No matter.

A good night's work, all considered. The carriage guards had delayed him slightly but at least they had died well. The Traveler, god of death and messengers, might need a new set of boots after tonight's journeys to the underworld for each soul. Drasilla, please look upon their passage into the cold realm favorably.

Assassins did not usually dispose of the guards of their targets because they were not common killers. Assassins only targeted, well, their targets because collateral damage lacked style. You could measure quality work by the precision of the instrument, and assassins were the most precise instruments gold could buy. You can tell how civilized a city is by the means it uses to kill its own people. Hambridge was a very civilized city indeed.

Their deaths had not been in vain. This was all for the greater good.

Sable took up the briefcase from the dead man's hand and stowed it in his bag. Best, all in all, that neither Cole Nebble nor these documents reached Lord Reiker. The Steward had come dangerously close to revealing the game early. Dangerous for the Steward, that was.

Sable was gone in the blink of an eye, melting into the shadows.

"Oh, sure I'll help you, Sickly. No problem, Sickly. Don't worry about me, Sickly, I'll just sit here in the cold and the dark in this stupid bush for hours on end without a drink or time to take a piss. Oh no, I'm sure it'll be fine. What could go wrong? I bloody well like sitting in this gods-damned bush. But you knew that, obviously, didn't you, Sickly? With your crazy pretend plots and your sodding face that never moves. Sure you'll help me with Anemia. Everything will be peaches and gravy and piss all."

Billys paused in his whispered tirade to shift position so that he could fart more quietly. A branch that he had carefully maneuvered in front of his eyes suddenly whipped backwards and stung him across the cheek. "Bloody bloody bloody sodding—" a rain drop landed on the cloak of his hood. The foliage around him suddenly came alive with the sound of droplets impacting leaves and ground.

"Scuvirion's sodding sack," Billys cursed. Scuvirion, god of agriculture and fertility, was often depicted in harvest scenes involving two large sacks of grain which was undoubtedly the origin of this popular Hambridge oath.

Billys stood and stretched his cramped muscles. It was time for a pint at the corner pub and an early night.

Before he knew what was happening, his body reacted to the sound of a crossbow unleashing an arrow. It pierced his erstwhile resting place even as he dived across the slick grass. The Burlington flew into his hand, and he came up from the roll on one knee, pointing his weapon into the dark. A figure swathed in black clothing stood in the middle of the path which ran up to the manor house Billys had been spying on. It was paused in the act of reloading a bow.

"Don't move," Billys hissed across the intervening space.

"Who are you? Assassin?"

Billys tipped his head fractionally so his hood slipped back, revealing his face.

"Ugh, Williams Kid?" said a woman's voice, now thick with disgust. He grinned.

"Joanna? Is that you?" She nodded, tight-lipped.

"Don't tell me you're here to fulfill a contract on my mother."

"No."

"What? On me then!"

"No! I'm not here on a job."

"As if I'd believe a toad like you. Tell the truth. I have a right to know your client."

His temper flared. "I'm not lying!" He grimaced and lowered his crossbow. Joanna's posture relaxed momentarily, but became defensive again as Billys started forward. "I'm here because of Sickly, all right?" Now that they were closer, Billys saw Joanna's face flicker to shock for the briefest of seconds before settling on suspicion. "Look, Joanna, what's Annette up to now?"

"Business. None of it yours," Joanna shot back.

"What do you know about the Foreign Minister?" Billys pressed.

"What, that cracked old politico, Bradley Wells? Sounds like he finally kicked it."

"And where were you on the night of the murder?"

"I don't have to explain myself to you, Billys. I thought I made that perfectly clear when I dumped you."

Billys flinched, and Joanna smiled nastily. The rain came down, filling the silence between them with a symphony of plunks, drips and splashes. "How are you two, then?"

The smile played around Joanna's mouth. "Oh, Hamilton and I are fine, thank you ever so much. And how have you been?"

"I've been brilliant, thanks for asking. You hear about Cuthbert Rawley? Yeah, that was me."

Joanna looked surprised in spite of herself. "I heard he was guarded by a pair of Umundi jackal warriors."

Billys smirked, "Actually it was four jackal warriors. What jobs have you done then?"

The brief look of amazement was replaced by her usual square-jawed contempt. "Oh, no, you're not getting anything out of me that easily. You can tell that freak Sickly Dodger not to go poking his nose into other people's business."

"Hey, don't talk that way about Sickly!"

She glared at him. "You said yourself he's a freak."

"Yeah? Well I take it back. He's not a freak, and I'll fight anyone who says different. So maybe you better shut up about my friend."

The front doors of the mansion opened, spilling yellow lamplight across the assassins' faces. A butler came down the steps and called across the lawn. "Young miss? The Lady Martinez requests your presence posthaste. It is a matter regarding her parliamentary agenda, I believe." The blood drained from Joanna's face.

"Scared of your old mum, are you?" Billys mocked.

"You would be too, if you knew what was good for you," Joanna spat. "You and Sickly better watch your backs if you keep prying into affairs that don't concern you." She turned and hurried up the drive, leaving Billys alone in the rain.

CHAPTER 12

Sickly awoke and looked at the window. There was something suspicious about the very bright light filtering through the cracks in the curtains. It was Friday. Late morning. Friday. That meant . . . something.

He was late for work!

He shot bolt upright, and then clutched at his head. It felt like someone had put an axe through his skull. To make matters worse the scar on his back throbbed dully. Cursing his poor constitution, he got up, dressed clumsily, made a cup of tea, and ate a hardboiled egg.

Where was he supposed to be? Oh yes, Mr. Stashcrumb's. Cramming a piece of bread into his mouth, he got his coat on, and as a precaution, took his set of throwing knives and several long daggers which he hid strategically about his person. He patted the pocket of his coat and felt the reassuring edges of Wells' notebook.

Then he dashed out the door, wincing a little at the light which assaulted his eyes, exacerbating the headache. The journey through Hambridge was quick for someone who knew the city as well as Sickly. Fifteen minutes later he was standing in front of the Stashcrumb mansion in Eel Park. He knocked loudly, and a moment later, Mr. Stashcrumb aggressively opened the door.

"I've had it with your lateness, boyo! One more time and you've had it! You're sacked, understand? Proper timekeeping is essential! Oi! Gnosher, Gouger, Gangrene, Gout, Spoon!" The dogs arrived at the door and stood to attention as their tyrant approached. It was clear that Crowbar had not forgiven Sickly. The calculating look the dog gave him said that there would be blood today, and that it was going to be human. "And where've you been, eh? Three days I've had to walk these pups meself. Gone soft, 'ave you?"

"I suppose so, Mr. Stashcrumb. There was a bit of an incident on Ardsley Avenue, and Crowbar attacked some people, including me. Regrettably, I was in the hospital."

"Hospitals." He spat onto the porch. To Sickly's surprise, his gravelly Golraic tones softened for a moment. "Doctors. Nutters. Can't trust 'em, boyo. And being injured's no excuse! Why, in my day, we used to walk dogs uphill, both ways! And we were always cut up and scraped from something, so don't tell me being in hospital is an excuse to skive off!"

"Yes, Mr. Stashcrumb."

"Don't be fresh."

"Yes, Mr. Stashcrumb."

"And don't be late!" Sickly took the leashes and was hauled down the drive by Crowbar.

Sickly was ready for an immediate attack, but it seemed that Crowbar was biding his time, waiting for Sickly to lower his guard. But Crowbar would not have been Crowbar if he didn't emphasize his displeasure by pulling more forcefully, dragging Sickly around right angles at high speeds, and stomping through every kind of muck he possibly could.

But they made it to The Crowns and then through Motley Drive, and finally to the park. Sickly let the other dogs free, knowing that they would behave as long as Crowbar was around.

Crowbar glowered at the other dogs, and then turned to face

Sickly. He did not have to look up very far. Sickly was terribly aware of how large Crowbar was, especially when his hackles were up. Crowbar's lips drew back, revealing two-inch incisors and a formidable amount of black gum. Those huge, onyx eyes narrowed to slits, trained on Sickly. The dog looked like death on four paws. Crowbar dropped into a crouch, the better to launch himself at the human that had ruined his version of the Winterwatch holidays.

Sickly got ready to drop the leash and dive under the inevitable leap.

"Good day, Mr. Dodger." Sickly and Crowbar looked around in astonishment. There, standing atop a park bench, was Ulrich Munz. Neither Sickly nor Crowbar had heard him approach. Ulrich wore a loose tunic and hose that unquestionably concealed body armor. His sable doe-skin boots were buckled with non-reflective metal, and his hands were clad in black gloves. He held the twin of Billys' new Burlington, cocked and loaded with a steel-tipped bolt.

"Good day, Mr. Munz." Sickly replied automatically. "Here on business, I assume?"

"I'm afraid so," Ulrich said jovially, smiling his wide smile. He ran one gloved hand over his elaborately groomed black beard and moustache, still pointing the weapon at Sickly. "Out for a little walk, are we?"

"Actually I'm on business as well." Sickly gestured at Crowbar who was giving Ulrich a calculating stare. Ulrich's grin broadened, if it were possible, and he let out a booming laugh.

"Oh that is rich, Mr. Dodger, it really is." Sickly glanced left and right, looking for an exit. Unfortunately, Ulrich was not alone. Sickly recognized the man holding a long sword on his left as Hamilton Traplek. On Sickly's other side Joanna Martinez held paired daggers, her face split in a predatory grin. A backward glance told him a fourth man, unknown to Sickly, was closing in with a crossbow. "I see you have noticed my associates."

"Ms. Martinez," Sickly said, inclining his head a fraction of an inch towards the woman. "Mr. Traplek." His tone was as neutral as always. One didn't show fear to an assassin. It was the same mentality as staring down an irate Crowbar. "A lovely day for a date in the park, isn't it?"

They laughed without a hint of mirth. "You call this indigent mud-pit a park? Fraternizing with that Webb girl must have really lowered your standards, Dodger," Traplek snorted.

Sickly's eyebrows lowered a fraction, but he returned his attention to Ulrich. "Who hired you and your . . . associates?" Below his calm façade fear blossomed from his gut, and above it, his mind raced like a rat in a maze. It wasn't unheard of for someone to hire two assassins for a really tricky job, but four? And just for Sickly? When Ulrich was perfectly capable of killing him on his own?

"Well there's the trouble of it all, really. I haven't been hired exactly. We were simply asked by the right person," Ulrich went on.

"And who is the right person?" Sickly asked quickly. Ulrich continued to smile, drinking in Sickly's helplessness, reveling in it.

"Where's the notebook, Mr. Dodger?"

"What notebook?"

"Please don't play silly blintzes with me. I know that you figured out Bradley Wells' clues, and that you took something from his personal box at the *Daily Piccolo*." Sickly raised an eyebrow, he had been right! He would at least die knowing that he had gotten it right. There was some kind of conspiracy!

That still left the problem that he was going to die.

"Why not just kill me in my sleep?" Sickly asked, his heart thudding.

"Call it . . . professional courtesy."

"You walk dogs too?" Sickly retorted. Ulrich laughed again, Joanna and Hamilton joined in.

"I always liked you, Dodger, I really did. Now where is the notebook?" Ulrich's tone became more businesslike.

"You're just going to kill me, even if I gave it to you."

"Yes."

"That's not much incentive to tell you, is it?"

"You can hand it over now and I can kill you quickly, or you can try to be smart with me, and we'll take you alive. The person I work for doesn't mind how I ask questions, as long as I get the notebook, you follow me?"

"Please fight, Dodger," Joanna cut in, twirling a dagger suggestively. "I'd love to see how much it takes before even you make an expression."

"Stooping to the old cliché," Ulrich added, "easy way, or hard, Mr. Dodger?"

"Fair enough." Sickly pulled the notebook out of his coat's inner pocket and displayed it. Joanna made a tiny noise of disappointment.

Ulrich nodded to Sickly. "You are a man of honor, and I respect that. Now, I can see it would be dreadfully rude of me to take up anymore of your time."

"I can't remember offering to kill someone quickly ever appearing in *Miss Demeanor's Compendium of Agonizing Social Nuance*. Was it in the appendix? I always skip the appendix," Sickly said apologetically.

He turned to Crowbar. The hound had been motionless throughout the conversation but was now glancing from Sickly to the assassins. A growl vibrated at the bottom edge of Sickly's hearing. Crowbar was not a dog to share the bloody delight of retribution with a pack of undeserving humans who also had it out for Sickly.

"Just like old times, isn't it, Mr. Dodger?" Ulrich said, smiling happily.

"Not quite. Crowbar? Sic 'em."

Whatever the assassins had expected, it was not 200 pounds of pent up testosterone and vengeance flying towards them. The assassin Sickly didn't know, the one holding the crossbow, was bowled over by the force of Crowbar's leap. Ulrich and his two friends watched, dumbfounded as Crowbar's massive jaws sank into the man's neck.

Sickly didn't wait for them to come to their senses. He pulled a throwing knife from his belt and hurled it at Joanna's arm. He hadn't practiced in months, and the knife caught her in the leg instead. As she doubled over, Sickly would have winced in sympathy if his face could have managed it. Then he sprinted for the nearest tree.

Ulrich recovered first. Sickly dove behind the tree just as Ulrich fired. He heard the twang of the bow and the sound of the air being ripped in half. The bolt buried itself in the wood. Sickly's eyes swiveled to see the steel tip protruding from the bark, an inch from his face.

"Hamilton! Get the dog! Joanna, you're with me. We take Dodger!" Ulrich bellowed. Sickly did not waste any more time. He flung himself away from the tree and dived through more foliage. A knife flashed past him and he kept running, dodging this way and that, jinking and weaving, trying to remember every scrap of his training.

Always keep something between yourself and the enemy; that was the thing to remember. Sickly ran for the nearest clump of trees and slipped between them, forcing Ulrich to go around and slow down. Sickly risked a look over his shoulder, and to his very small relief saw that Joanna was far behind, slowed by her wound. But Ulrich was beginning to gain on him. Sickly returned his attention to the path before him. It led to a small, walled garden. Perfect.

Sickly drew another one of his throwing knives and clamped it in his teeth. Just as he reached the wall he leaped, caught the top of it with both hands and slammed against it from the speed of his run. Grunting with pain he pulled himself up, over the top, just as a second bolt from Ulrich's crossbow flew past his shoulder, barely missing. Sickly tried to ignore the burning pain in his muscles, his headache, and the breathless ache of his lungs. He dropped to the ground and took the throwing knife from his teeth. Then he threw it with all his might towards a thick bush so that it shook as the knife passed through it.

To Ulrich, coming over the wall, it looked as if Sickly had just dashed through to the other side of the bushes, and he charged after him. Sickly knew the man wouldn't be fooled for long, and he heaved himself back over the wall. The other trick was to know how an assassin thought. An assassin chasing a mark would expect the target to dodge and weave, to pull maneuvers like Sickly had just done. An assassin would not expect the mark to head back to the place of the initial attack if the assassin had accomplices. It wasn't simply a matter of bad strategy. It was idiotic.

Sickly ran towards where they had first attacked. That still left the problem of Joanna. Sickly burst through a bush and nearly ran into her. It was almost worth it to see her stunned expression. Even so, she did not stay stunned for long, and Sickly drew one of his combat knives from its place on his belt. "Sorry about the leg, Joanna. How was your summer?" Sickly said as he jumped away from her first swipe.

"Get out of it," she growled, voice taut with pain, "Don't pretend like you didn't send that little creep Billys to spy on me. You're nothing but a soft, underachieving, scrawny weakling." She pivoted on her good leg and blocked Sickly's halfhearted attack, her other dagger flashing forward.

"Sorry to hear the job market is so slow," Sickly said, while jumping back again and trying to work out how he could use her injury to his advantage. "Since you're reduced to fulfilling contracts on scrawny weaklings. You could always walk dogs."

"Shut up and die," she hissed, face twisted in rage and pain, "you emotionless freak."

"I really don't hold it against you," he said, mildly, "all those time you called me that."

Sickly grasped his knife in both hands and waited for her to advance. As she started forward he swung downward, and she caught his weapon with both of hers, crossed over her head like an 'X'. As soon as her daggers had stopped his blow she would be able to free one of them, allowing his knife to slide harmlessly off while she gutted him with the free stiletto.

Before she could do this however, Sickly kicked her wounded leg. "Well, maybe a little."

Joanna crumpled to the ground, choking back a scream of pain. Sickly looked down at her. He had won, hadn't he? He could kill her; it was what she would do in a second, had their positions been reversed. It was what Henry Dodger would have done. Or Eveline, now that he thought about it. One swift blow to the back of her neck, and she would never call him a freak again. She would never hurt another soul. Or laugh or cry. It was sickening. It was exhilarating. There was a headiness to it, the lethal knife clutched in his hand.

He shook his head. "I'm not a killer, or an assassin." He kicked her weapons from her hands. "And I'm not a freak." He kicked her hard in the leg again and then fled, leaving Joanna moaning behind him.

Hamilton Traplek had graduated from The Dalton College for Men in Black eighth in the class. He was good at what he did. He had already undertaken three successful contracts, one against a prominent noble. He had no qualms about killing men, women, or, if necessary, animals. He did not know why Jameson had allowed himself to be killed by this dog. Perhaps it had just gotten lucky. He advanced on the large mongrel of indeterminate variety, holding his sword on guard. Honestly, Dodger didn't even bother to walk canines with real breeding.

If he had not been as confident in his abilities, he would have paused to wonder why the massive creature, blood dripping from its jaws, was not acting like a normal dog when approached by a stranger. Its hackles were not up, it was not growling, it wasn't cowering or running or barking. If anything it was grinning, showing a lot of red teeth.

Hamilton gave it his trademark smirk and raised his designer sword to dispatch it.

And then Crowbar leaped.

Sickly arrived back at the clearing a moment later. It was a grizzly sight.

Crowbar sat by the corpse of the first assassin, licking his lips and smiling in a self-satisfied way. There was a gash in his side, oozing blood down his black fur, but he didn't seem to mind. He turned to Sickly and regarded him critically with the eye of a county fair-winning pie-eater sizing up one last raspberry tart. Sickly waited, but after a second Crowbar turned his head away. Vengeance could wait a few more days.

Sickly turned to follow his gaze and saw the distant figure of Hamilton Traplek fleeing at a dead limp. He had even dropped his sword. Sickly demurred for a second, then bent the expensive blade on an iron bench and hurled it into a nearby pond.

He wondered how much time he had before Ulrich caught on, found Joanna, and then found Sickly. He ran forward and dug in the pockets of the dead man, trying to ignore the blood, viscera and dog drool. He didn't find a contract of any kind, nor any kind of identification as to who it was that had contracted them. No, not contracted, Ulrich had said. *Asked*.

"Bugger," he muttered and stood up. "Crowbar, if you were to round up the other dogs and go home, it might be a really good idea." It was *not* a good idea to order Crowbar to do anything. Sickly was just lucky that the dog had decided Ulrich and his cronies were enough of a threat to respond to Sickly's first command. "And next time we walk I might find some more sausages for you."

Crowbar gave him a look that said, 'you are so transparent,' but rose to his feet and gave a single bark. Instantly Gout,

Gangrene, Gnosher, Gouger, and Spoon came running and sat at attention, staring at their tyrant like a group of expectant pups. Spoon turned to Sickly, tongue lolling and wagged his tail hopefully. Crowbar snorted and wandered off, the other dogs in tow, but Sickly was already gone.

The adrenaline was starting to wear off, and Sickly became aware of a burning pain. He glanced down and saw a long gash in his left arm, oozing blood. How had he gotten that? Maybe Ulrich hadn't missed with his second shot after all. Sickly wasn't dead yet, so if there was poison, it wasn't of the instant variety. His head began to swim at the sight of his own blood. For the umpteenth time he wondered why he had been born with the intestinal fortitude of an elderly lapdog.

Poison didn't seem like Ulrich's style. He liked to confront his prey head on, reveling in the challenge of it. And to an assassin, style was everything. Style was why they wouldn't kill a fellow assassin in his sleep. Style was why Joanna hadn't yelled for help. Style was why Ulrich wouldn't resort to poison.

But now that their head-on assault had failed, they would surely target his house. It would not be safe to return to Cod Liver Oil Alley. It was lucky that he and Jamie had split up the notebook and papers after all.

Where would he be safe from an unknown but probably large number of assassins? The answer was far away, under a rock, of course. Somehow that didn't seem like a very feasible option. Anyway, he wasn't going to leave his friends to their fates, whatever was in store for them.

He paused at the edge of Reiker's Commons, ripped the bottom half of his black shirt off and wrapped it around his arm, tying it off with his teeth. He noted with some chagrin that once again he looked like a vagrant that had been living on the streets for several days. His thin coat was torn from thorns, crossbow bolts and Joanna's knives. His shoes and trousers were muddied from his acrobatics. The bandage on his arm and the torn shirt completed the picture.

He sighed and walked into the late morning stream of traffic, matching their pace so as to be less conspicuous. With luck, Ulrich would assume Sickly would go to ground in the first place possible, not walk about the city with no protection. But that was a lot of assumptions for one day, and Ulrich wasn't stupid. Sickly needed to find a sanctuary fast.

The girl lay in the dark of the closet and sweated. On the top shelf she nestled in tattered blankets and the remains of a straw pillow, trying not to breathe. Her chest rose and fell in staccato, dancing to the rhythm of her frantic heart. Air whispered in and out of her lungs in the stifling, warm dark. And she sweated through the rough-spun nightshirt that covered her fragile figure. It was the sweat of the heat of the closet. It was the sweat of the warm summer night. It was the sweat of pure terror.

She couldn't move from her suffocating prison. She knew it to her bones that the only thing to do was to wait for it to be over. This certainty did nothing to calm the panic and fear infesting every thought in her head, every inch of her body.

She lay. She breathed. She sweated.

And then the screaming started.

It pierced the walls of her prison and set her teeth on edge. It was the wail of an animal, trapped and dying. It shrilled through the air and bit into her eardrums with the ragged edges of a howling throat. She screwed up her eyes against it, every muscle tensing but still it went on and on, breaking in waves against the girl's hunched form.

As it peaked, a terrible crash shook the closet. The door eased open a crack, and light poured in, even as the scream was cut off.

The girl looked past her blindness and into the face of the outside world. It was awash in red stains and flickering yellow lamplight. Silhouetted against the alien light, monstrous figures shifted and wavered. They turned in a slow, eerie dance, turned and moved forward.

She could no more blink than she could have moved. Her throat stuck in a scream that would never reach the air. She lay, sweating, trapped, and dying.

Eveline was jerked from sleep by a loud knock at the door. Silently she twisted in the mass of sweaty sheets and blankets. Her stomach roiled with nausea, and her heart thudded savagely within the confines of her chest. One hand snatched the knife from beneath her pillow.

But it was just a dream, she thought. Just that dream. The same dream she'd been having for fifteen years.

She shook herself and listened as the knock came again.

The Dalton College for Men in Black trained its students to recognize all manner of secret knocks, from coded messages about targets to death threats. There was a secret knock for establishing a meeting at almost any location in the city, there was a secret knock for delivering payments, there was a secret knock for asking for the listener's immediate help, and there was even a secret knock for the traveling pie seller.

This was a very strange secret knock. The strangeness of it was that it seemed to be a perfectly ordinary knock at the door. She frowned, trying to pick up some subtle undertone or scratch or rattle at the handle, any of which would signal something.

But no. Whoever was at the door was completely untrained at giving secret knocks. They weren't even knocking the same way twice. It was an icepick under the fingernails of her soul. Eveline got up from her bed and put on a bathrobe reinforced with a very fine, stainless steel chainmail. It hadn't been cheap, but nor was hiring an assassin of her caliber.

The knocking came again, a totally random set of taps against the door. She winced and crossed soundlessly to the hall, where a clever system of mirrors was arrayed. From a certain point, she could see the front door, the back door, the dining room, the first floor hallway and the roof. In the corner of a mirror she thought she caught a glimpse of flickering light and spattered red and wavering figures — No. Not here. She was safe. She was.

She glanced at each mirror, focusing on the here and now. It appeared that there was only one person, standing on the front porch. Concealing her knife in the left sleeve of her robe for easy draw, she walked quickly down the stairs. The figure outside had stopped knocking and was standing very still. Readying an attack? Some kind of signal? Or, perish the thought, it might not even be a trap.

She pulled the door open a hair and waited for some kind of blade or gas weapon to be shoved through the slit. Nothing.

"Well?" she asked, in a business-like tone.

"Hi, Vel, it's me." Eveline, throwing caution to the wind, pulled the door open.

"Sickly?" He stood there meekly, his hands in the air. She glanced past him at the street, and at the low rooftops across from her house. Everything was deserted. But this was a secondary concern. Eveline was suddenly uncomfortably aware that she had just awoken, drenched in sweat and hadn't brushed her hair at all. To make matters worse she was wearing nothing more than a nightgown and bathrobe combination. It was no way to present herself, no matter that either garment could stop an arrow at a hundred paces.

Sickly didn't look very presentable, either. Twigs and leaves ornamented his black hair, his shirt was ripped, his clothing was muddy and torn and a bandage covered in fresh blood was tied round his left arm.

"May I come in?"

Eveline blinked, then nodded and stood aside. She shut the door quickly.

"You can put your hands down, by the way." Sickly lowered them. "You didn't think I'd shoot you, did you?"

"To be honest, I find it safest to be cautious around assassins."

"Get threatened by crossbows a lot on your dog walks?"

"More than you'd think, actually."

He wore his usual flat expression, but there was something

new in his eyes. It was a mix of fear and something else. Excitement? From Sickly?

"Someone's been trying to kill you, haven't they?" she asked. She could read it in his stance, a little crouched as if he was about to fight or flee. The bandage on his arm looked hasty, so he must have been on the run. There was less blood than she'd initially guessed, so the wound was likely a graze.

"Um, yes."

"I'm not sure if that's surprising or inevitable."

"I was pretty surprised," he said mildly.

"Sickly, I keep telling you. You don't stop being an assassin. You went to The College, so you're one of us, whether you like it or not."

"Can we not, right now? This is serious." As if she needed to be told. Whoever had done this had better pray for Drasilla's protection, because nothing short of divine intervention would save them from her.

"Come into the kitchen and we'll take care of your arm," she said aloud. "And leave your boots by the door so you don't track mud on the carpet."

"Oh, of course, sorry." He sounded sheepish and awkward, as if he didn't quite know what to say. That was all right by her. She didn't know what to say, either.

Eveline led him through the first floor hallway to the kitchen. She lit the lamp at the center of the table with the flick of a match. "Sit," she commanded, and Sickly pulled out a chair, using his good arm.

Eveline went to the special indoor privy which she had paid an extra 2,000 Hambridge dollars to have installed. She opened the medicine cabinet which held an extensive array of bandages, gauze, tape, medical scissors, needles, fine thread, oxidized water, and a number of other vials containing a range of cures for common poisons.

"Are you poisoned?" she called to the kitchen.

"I don't think so."

He'd better be damn sure. She brought the kit back to the kitchen.

"Cut your bandage off, and I'll get some water and a cloth." He grabbed the scissors and set to work. By the time Vel got back, he was clumsily unscrewing the cap of the bottle. "Wait, I'll do it." Her eyes swept the wound, and saw it was sticky with blood. She did not see bloodstains coating the walls. She did not, because they were not there.

Vel took the bottle and expertly began sterilizing the wound.

A hiss of air escaped Sickly's lips, but that was all the response he showed to what must have been a painful process. As she worked she couldn't help noting that his arm, while wiry with muscle, was not, on the whole, impressive. She examined the wound for signs of abnormal necrosis, rubbed some of the fresher blood between her fingers and peered intently at his lips.

"What are you doing?" Sickly asked, sounding mildly concerned for her mental stability.

"Checking for toxins, obviously."

"I told you I don't feel poisoned. Don't you trust me?"

She couldn't help coloring a bit. "It's not that. I just wanted to be sure."

"Thanks, then." His lips did not look overly blue, so blood was probably flowing as normal. She bent over her work to avoid looking further up his face.

"So why are they trying to kill you? And, while you're at it, who's they? And why did you ask me and Thumbs to break into the main office of the Hambridge Watch?"

He quickly recounted the events of the last couple of days, from Bradley Wells' first letter to the attack in the park led by Ulrich. "Once I got clear of them I ran here. Don't you see? They sent four assassins after me! I was right! There is a plot!"

There it was again, that alien look of . . . yes, excitement, in his usually listless green eyes. Above his flat expression his brows knit into a look of worry. "You do believe me, don't you? I know I sound mental."

Yes, he did. Eveline had been listening for the past few minutes in a state of disbelief. Assassins weren't murderers or thugs. They didn't assassinate political leaders without the promise of healthy amounts of gold. They wouldn't just go attacking someone on a non-client's orders. It contradicted everything an assassin was. But Sickly had been targeted by no less than four assassins, and he was almost insignificant in assassin hierarchy.

The only explanation was that he knew something he shouldn't.

"I believe you."

His eyebrows rose up in one of his odd 'smiles.' "Thank you." For once, there seemed to be real emotion flooding through his voice.

"What do we do first?" Eveline asked, feeling a little of Sickly's excitement course through her.

"We've got to reach the others. Terry and Jamie and Billys. We need to stay together, for protection."

"We're assassins. We don't need protecting. People need protection from us."

"I keep telling you, I'm not an assassin."

"Yes, Sickly, you are! You went to the school. You took the bloody graduation test, you're an assassin." Why was it so hard for him to get that through his head? Oh, gods, he was actually glaring at her. His eyebrows formed a V over his eyes, even while his mouth stayed resolutely flat. Was this about the night of his red test?

"Pretend for a moment that I'm not." Eveline had never seen him this angry before. Why was he looking at her like that?

"Vel, I'm not strong like you or Jamie or Billys or Terry. I can't kill people. You know that better than anyone. Remember a certain night before the graduation test? A certain noble you killed?" She wanted to look down, but his eyes held her. She knew she shouldn't have interfered. She'd done it anyway. "Vel," he pleaded, "I need your help. I need your protection. I need all my friends. I trust you."

Oh gods, he trusted her. The silly, sweet boy. The first thing they taught you at the Dalton College was to never, ever put your faith in another. Especially not an assassin. It was a lesson she had already learned by heart in a different life, long ago.

"All right," she said at last, unable to break his gaze, let alone that blind trust.

Sickly found that his fists were clenched with the effort to convince her, causing the band of his father's signet ring bite into his pointer finger. A deep, insistent ache had begun in his arm, spreading up to his shoulder. The nausea had returned, so he took a few deep breaths. His nose was filled overpoweringly with her smell. Like sweat and some kind of dried flowers. His heart thudded at the thought of being so close to her. He blinked and Vel looked away.

"I can't go back to my flat, obviously. I only have a few combat knives. Oh, and this." He retrieved the notebook from the tatters of his coat. "If Sable Levania is behind all these murders, then maybe one of the spies knows who he's working for."

He glanced down at the single piece of loose parchment he'd saved. "Once we've got everyone together, we'll get in contact with Kerry Adams, or one of these others. Maybe one of them will know who Sable's reporting to. See, I've got this theory that it's Annette Martinez."

It was Vel's turn to raise an eyebrow. "Old Ironside you mean?"

Sickly nodded. "We'll collect Terry first, then Jamie, then Billys. That way he won't have had time to annoy us too much before we get everyone else."

He glanced up to see Vel giving him an odd look. Was it pity? "What?"

"It's a decent plan, there's just one thing." He raised his eyebrows. "You're not coming with me."

"Wait a minute, I –"

"You'd just slow me down. Besides, they're not looking for me, yet. They're looking for you. You stay here where it's safe. Rest, heal, and retrain yourself. You're no good to anyone until you're back in practice." She began to stand up, as if this settled things. Sickly's breath hissed between his teeth in frustration.

"I came here because you're safe, not this house. Without you here to protect me, I'm a dead man. They could figure out that I came here. When they do, do you honestly think I can survive four assassins again?" It was Vel's turn to growl in frustration.

"Damn it, Sickly, you make everything so complicated."

"You know I'm right." She pursed her lips as she weighed the two evils in her mind, leaving Sickly here, vulnerable and alone, or taking him, wounded and out of practice, with her.

"Fine."

"Thanks. Um, could I get some weapons, first?"

Eveline crossed to a wall panel and pressed a hidden button. The panel slid aside to reveal an alcove filled with weapons. "Take any you need, I'm going to change."

Sickly turned, confused, and for the first time it registered that she was wearing a bathrobe. He looked away, then back, then away again. Her hair hung lank as if she had just run a mile, and there were bags beneath her eyes. "Oh, of course." She scoffed and exited the kitchen.

Right, just the essentials.

Sickly restocked his supply of throwing knives with a pair of Number Eights, three Number Sixes, and a Number Two. The knives were forged of Inrove steel, a special alloy produced solely in Hambridge which could hold an edge sharp enough to split a leaf dropped on the upturned blade. The metal was smoky grey so that it wouldn't reflect light and alert a target. He also belted on a slim short sword with a vial of poison in the grip. He pocketed a pair of brass knuckles and several attachments which could be screwed in to add weight, spikes, or venom. He took a blowpipe which could be unscrewed into several pieces and stashed it in his boots, as well as a miniature bandolier of darts, their shafts encoded with raised grooves for easy selection in the dark. In a pants pocket he stashed a roll of lockpicks, and round his belt he wound a thirty foot length of fine cord guaranteed to hold up to 50 stones of weight. In another pocket went a grappling hook which folded down for easy storage.

He felt a bit awkward about taking Vel's equipment, but she *had* offered. It was true that assassins didn't really need all the devices and fiddly little specialty weapons. All you needed was a knife, your wits, and a body honed by years of training. Even the knife was optional, if you were really keen.

But for most assassins, carrying the extra accessories was a matter of pride, of honor, of style. It meant that you knew how to use all the weapons you carried. It meant that you would be ready for any situation, no matter how dire or dangerous. It meant that some of the younger and overeager assassins needed help getting up if they tripped.

It was called Shling.

Vel came back into the kitchen. Sickly was about to apologize for taking so much, when the words died on his tongue. She was wearing custom black leather armor that hugged her figure, protecting her completely from neck to toe, yet somehow managing to accent her physique. The black clothing accentuated her delicate features, heart shaped face, and shoulder length wavy red hair.

Her feet were wrapped in knee-high black leather boots with knives ringed around them. At her hip was a butterfly sword and swinging from her belt a quiver of crossbow bolts. Over her shoulder was the crossbow, and on her fingers were an assortment of rings which, while complementing the beauty of her hand, were also poisoned, spiked, and able to turn into an assortment of lock picks. Assassins never wore jewelry unless it was functional *and* beautiful.

She looked stunning, which was probably the least violent thing she was capable of at the moment. Drop-dead gorgeous was a much more accurate description.

"Um, wow, Vel." She smiled. "You ready?"

"We were trained to be ready for anything," she retorted, still smiling at his look.

Ready for anything? Then why was it so hard for him to come up with anything to say? "Let's go, then," he finally managed.

"Oh no, not like that, you're not."

"Like what?" She pointed at his ripped shirt, muddy trousers, and bird's-nest-style hair.

"Oh."

She strode forward and reached up to his hair. Sickly felt himself go red, and ducked his head, partly to help Vel, who was shorter than he was by a few inches, but also in the faint hope she wouldn't see his blush. He sensed a peculiar tingling in his finger-tips, like they were full of hot, red pins and needles. It was the most exhilarating thing he had ever felt, standing next to her.

"There, that's a bit better, innit."

Sickly began to breathe again. "Uh, yeah. Can we go collect everyone now?"

"Not wearing that, you can't."

"Is now really the time?"

"If we walk out the door, it will be too late." Sickly was glad of this argument, it gave him something to focus on other than the fact that she stood barely a foot away from him.

"Fine, what do you propose?" She stepped back, admiring him critically.

"Well, I don't have anything in your size, so there's not much I can do for your pants or shoes."

"Oh, so I should stay here and be killed by assassins to avoid a fashion disaster?"

"Don't be ridiculous. You're more of a fashion peccadillo."

"What do you even care?" Sickly asked. She looked a little hurt.

"Well, what do you think I do in my free time, shoot targets? Work out?" He quirked an eyebrow. "Ok, fine. But I do other things!" she said, offended. "I have hobbies. Killing people isn't my life. Jamie and I used to go out Volpi-dancing every Thursday night, don't you remember?"

Sickly did. He had not so much toyed but no-holds-barred-wrestled with the idea of accompanying them, so that maybe, just maybe, Vel would ask him to dance.

"But we're wasting time, follow me." Sickly obeyed, and she led him back into the hall. She opened the coat closet and withdrew a leather duster. "Try this on."

"It's a bit . . . well . . ." he said uncertainly, not knowing how to put it, "assassin-y?" She gave him a look that said, 'Brilliant observation, no *really*.' He hung up his tattered jacket and tried on the duster.

It was an excellent coat, well-tailored, made of good material, and as elegant as its owner. Yet somehow it felt wrong on Sickly, and not just because he was shaped differently than Vel. Sickly knew anyone looking at the pair of them together would believe they were assassins. This was fine, in Vel's case, but he, Sickly, didn't kill people. Still, it was a nice coat...

"Lucky you're so thin, or your shoulders wouldn't fit at all," Vel remarked, breaking him out of his reverie. Sickly mentally translated this to: you've got the body of a twelve-year-old.

"Come off it," he mumbled, "do I have to?"

"I am not walking with you in public unless you wear something over that shirt."

He was about to protest, but realized the futility. Instead, he shoved the notebook into his new garment.

"Now, let's go before it gets any later," she said impatiently.

As if he had been the one wasting time.

CHAPTER 13

Walking in public was not how Sickly would have described their journey across Hambridge to the Merchants' Guild. They used the rooftops at Vel's insistence. Sickly would have been inclined to argue, except that this put them on a level with anyone trying to attack them, rather than down in the streets, easily picked off by crossbow fire.

In any other city, two black-clad figures bearing weapons moving across the rooftops might have provoked the suspicions of the townsfolk or at the very least the City Watch. In Hambridge, with its Guild of Thieves, Guild of Spies, and Guild of Assassins, the maze of rooftops, clotheslines, catwalks, and chimneys was just a breezier type of sidewalk.

The river Ham bisected Hambridge from north to south. The merchants, tradesmen, and bankers lived, for the most part, on the West Side, while the nobles and city offices were predominantly located on the East Side. On the other axis, poorer districts sprawled to the south and richer ones clustered further north, as if afraid to be seen in such company. Ponsingham Palace, Lord Reiker's residence and home to the two houses of parliament, sat in pride of place on Tumult Hill in the northeast of Hambridge.

As it was, they kept to Murktown as much as they could. Though there would be more muggers and thieves about, the dirty, soot covered rooftops would discourage most assassins from staying too long and looking too closely. No assassin in their right mind would willingly sully their boots on such common shingles unless there was a serious bonus promised.

There was some traffic over the clay roofs by gangs of large, hairy men and women, each of whom had more weapons than the group's combined number of teeth. But Sickly and Vel were not accosted. If you didn't learn to recognize an assassin by sight, you couldn't learn at all, and you didn't survive up here. As they passed, Sickly felt their eyes rake the duster and he cringed. He knew that their fear of him was better armor than a piece of chainmail, but it was still off-putting to know his entire person had been reduced to a threat signal by a piece of clothing.

Sickly's bandaged arm burned with the effort of hauling himself up and down. Soon his other arm and both legs added their own complaints as he struggled to keep up with Vel. She made it look easy, jumping from rooftop to rooftop, ascending walls like a fashionable spider. Though it was a cold autumn day, he soon felt sweat trickling down his back as his heart pounded and his breath puffed.

Sickly kept half an ear on the chatter of the city. Over there was the Street of Mostly Reputable Goods, one of the many places around Hambridge where thieves fenced stolen property, and nobles rebought it. And there was Tin Can Alley, where, it was said, you couldn't walk five feet without being mugged, pick-pocketed, and thrown in the river. Below them was Heart Street, home to the main house of the Courtesans' Guild and their private army. Then they passed over the muddy streets closer to the River Ham, where men drank, smoked, swore, gambled, fought, killed, and, when times were really tough, did an honest day's work.

The smells wafting up from below were a mixture of raw sewage, stagnant water, garbage, blood, booze, and eye-wateringly powerful fish. With a slight breeze from the right direction, the nose also detected the aroma of industrial waste from the river. Sickly motioned to Vel to pause in their journey across rooftops. "What?" she called, frowning.

Sickly shook his head for a moment, then bent over the rooftop and vomited all over the dingy thoroughfare below. Passersby in the street didn't even look up. No wonder assassins avoided these areas like the plague.

"Better?" Vel asked kindly. Sickly shook his head. "Let's keep moving then, before the smell sets into our clothes." Sickly thought it was a little too late for that.

The streets directly adjacent to the river were slightly cleaner and more often patrolled by the Hambridge Watch. It was all well and good for thieves and muggers to kill each other over money that was already in the city. It was thieves interfering with the flow of money into the city by threatening shipping that they had a problem with. Out here, where the chimneys thinned out to make room for the docks and jetties, the smell of industrial pollution was worse, but at least there was more wind.

They crossed the river by jumping from roofs to gantries, gantries to masts, masts to gantries and finally back to the roofs on the opposite side.

When Sickly and Vel reached the warren of shops and businesses that was the Merchants' Guild they climbed down from the roofs and stood warily at street level. They walked swiftly towards the center of the district, indicated by the increasing opulence of the buildings they passed. Finally, they came to Velver Square. "What now?" Vel asked.

"We go and ask the front desk." He pointed to a large kiosk at the center of the plaza.

"Must we?" she said, looking uncomfortable.

"I don't have an exact address."

"It's just that . . . well. I don't like talking to people, all right?"

"I know, Vel. But we've got to find Terry as quickly as possible."

Eveline unconsciously squeezed the knife under her coat, before finally nodding.

They walked forward, drawing a few nervous glances from passing merchants, their guards glaring suspiciously at the two assassins. Vel glanced about, her hands twitching toward her weapons.

The Merchants' Guild was a huge network of offices from different trading companies, each with a design to expand into the markets of their neighbors. Here was the beating pulse of Hambridge's economy, where giant company mergers or schisms occurred, where partners shook hands and smiled as they silently aimed crossbows under the table, and where, more than once, there had been all out war between private merchant armies.

The most important companies had their finest offices here, in a loose ring around Velver Square. More than a dozen couriers were running to and fro, their leather satchels full of the papery lifeblood of trade agreements. Several merchants and their guards stood and gossiped in the square, forging pie-crust promises. Wealthy nobles and traders came and went, conducting their business, buying and selling unimaginable volumes of product.

The plaza itself also served as an offering site to Caestos, god of war and commerce, second only to his great temple on Ten Street. Like assassins and thieves, many merchants tended toward cynical atheism, though they still made offerings of coin and good vellum to the Lord of Pen and Sword at the little dog-headed altars guarded by heavily armed war clerics. Doing so was viewed as purchasing insurance against the off chance there really was anything to expect after death. Priests of other temples might have flown into a rage at such cavalier disregard for higher powers, but the clergy of Caestos just smiled. They knew the law of diminishing marginal returns extended to all things, even faith. Disingenuous devotion was acceptable so long as it was *optimized*.

Sickly felt overwhelmed and was glad that he had already lost his breakfast. Now that he thought about it, he hadn't eaten anything but an egg and a cup of cold tea all day. Maybe there would be time to grab a bag of fish and chips after getting Terry. As long as the fish was plain, and there was no vinegar on the chips, he amended.

Sickly led the way up to a free clerk at the kiosk. The man eyed their clothes warily and spoke in a melodic, nasal whine characteristic of natives to the Duchy of Lelywijk. "I'm afraid I can't help you if you're here today on business. By guild ordinance one-six-oh-nine dash oh-seven-three B, paragraph two, I am strictly prohibited from aiding or abetting non-guild-sanctioned criminal activities."

"We're just looking for Terry Andrews, an assassin currently employed here," Sickly said.

"As I was saying, I am expressly forbidden to assist anyone trying to harm guild –"

"We're not here to kill him!" Vel said in exasperation. The clerk raised his eyebrows at her. "By my oath to the Occisor Cadre and Drasilla's sagging scales, we are not here on business."

"Really!" Sickly added, unconvincingly. The clerk, out of a sense of duty or stupidity, hesitated.

"Do not force me to find someone who will pay for you to die," Vel said, in tones sharper than Inrove steel. The man sighed.

"Very well, very well." He swiveled his chair and looked through a filing cabinet for a moment or two, grumbling to himself. "Here he is. Terry Andrews, resident assassin, currently in the employ of the Merchant's Council, at the moment tasked with guild compound security. Apartments in a suite on the top floor of the Woffler Building, just over that way." He pointed southward.

"Thank you very much," Sickly said as warmly as he could manage. The man frowned, scrutinizing his face, which was at odds with his tone. As so often happened, Sickly could imagine the man come to the conclusion that Sickly was 'not quite right.'

"Have a nice day." The clerk's tone suggested that by saying this, he was giving up some portion of the niceness of his own day.

They climbed the alley side of the Woffler Building. It was a five story affair, the design of which suggested that the architect had been trying out all the pillars he had ever studied in school and had been offered a special deal on carvings of bunches of grapes. The climb wasn't out of any desire to avoid the front entrance. To an assassin, the window *was* the front entrance. You climbed it because it was there.

Inside, they found a long corridor, lit by mid-afternoon sunlight and paneled in oak. A well-kept green and gold rug ran the length of the hall, and several doors stood closed on either side. "Hello?" Sickly called, a little doubtfully. Vel glared at him for this breach of secrecy, and he felt a pang of guilt, not from giving away their presence, but for disappointing her.

In answer, a mechanical hum came from the walls. Two spinning metal circular saws erupted from concealed panels on either side, each at a different height. Sickly tensed, but they did not close in, yet.

An enormous man in Merchants' Guild livery emerged from one of the doors and pointed a hand crossbow at them. In his other hand was a cord, ready to release the trap on Sickly and Vel. "Who's dat?" came a low voice.

"We're friends. Uh, is that you, Terry?"

"Dat's right," said the man. Sickly looked again. There was no mistaking the huge frame which almost blocked the entire corridor. "Now who're you?"

"Terry, it's me, Sickly Dodger. And this is Vel-- Eveline." Terry squinted at the two backlit silhouettes in the window.

"Oh. Dat's all right den." He banged on the wall with a massive fist and the two saws folded back. He lowered the crossbow. They came forward, cautiously, out of the glare cast by the sun. "Sickly!" Terry said happily. "Dat really is you! I'm glad ta see you. Very glad. Come in, I'll make tea. Hullo, Evline."

He led them through the door into a little parlor with furniture that seemed much too small for its owner. Everything was decorated in blues and whites, with several pictures of the sea and river hanging from the walls, signed by Terry himself. The morning's *Hambridge Times* was open on a coffee table to the crossword. The dishes were cleaned and left to dry on a draining board. Everything was clean and well cared for.

Sickly was impressed. Billys' flat had lived down to his expectations, and Vel, as one of the best up-and-coming assassins, had a magnificent house. But somehow Sickly had expected their large friend to live in a much shabbier place. Sickly was uncomfortably reminded of his own austere living conditions.

"I'm afraid we don't have time for tea, big guy," Sickly said, as gently as he could. Terry was easily upset.

He turned to them, his huge face falling. "Why not?"

"The thing is . . . someone's trying to kill me. Something bad is going on in the city."

"Yes."

Sickly paused, Terry was not usually this . . . informed. "Yes?"

"Yes. Bad things happ'ning. Lots of big men resign from da Merchant's Consul. Not coming back. Some people saying I don't do good enough job protecting dem. Saying I should get replaced." Sickly's eyebrows knit.

"I'm sorry, big guy."

"S'okay."

"Well, whoever is assassinating the big men from the Merchant's, er, Council is also killing off heads of the other guilds. There's this, uh, plan to take over the city. And I know about it, so they're trying to kill me. I know you have your own problems, but --"

"I will help." Terry said simply. "You're my friend. I will protect you." Sickly was taken aback. He hadn't expected it to be this easy, not after Jamie had doubted him, Billys had disregarded him, and Vel had been so hard to convince.

"Thanks, big guy." Terry turned to Vel.

"You helping Sickly, too?" She nodded, and he gave a wide,

childlike smile. "You always my friend too. Now we help Sickly together." Sickly's eyebrows rose, and he turned to Vel. She was wearing an odd expression, but then mustered a smile.

"Actually, could I get a little something for the road? I'm starving."

"You want some bread?" Sickly nodded. "One ting dough." They waited, expectantly. "Sickly, is dat a new coat?"

The injured arm grumbled as she fought the weathered window with both hands, trying to close it behind her. Jamie let out a groan to match that of the ancient timber as the window jerked inward. It would be another struggle to open it again, but that was a problem for later. That done, she slumped down against the wall.

She was so tired that for a moment all she could do was stare blankly at the rotting boards peeking from behind holes in the plaster. Somewhere, a leak dripped. At least she had gotten Sickly's papers hidden on her way to Eel Park. It had made her late though, and she'd had to improvise on the entry plan she'd spent a week calculating. When Jamie closed her eyes her target's look of surprise and fear flashed across her mind. She had died without a fight. With barely a sound. A clean death, Jamie hoped.

Her head pounded with the beginnings of a migraine. She knew she ought to rise and tend to her arm. Get a candle lit. Eat the last of the bread. She would have to buy more tomorrow. Right after she collected the coin for tonight's work from Delia Wiggins, her employer's snivelling clerk.

Then she could think about paying this month's rent. Or she could risk putting it off again and go to the Charity Barnsforth Loving Hospital to get another bottle of Beaupierre's Curative for Da. It had kept him stable, at least for the time being. Even with the extra coin from her patron, the expenses and bills continued to mount, especially since the curative had tripled in price a month ago.

That reminded her of the monthly payment on the loans she'd taken out to pay for the Dalton College. The scholarship had made her attendance possible, but she had still ended up with more debt than she could feasibly manage, even without considering support to her family.

Connall and Leila would be home with Da, acting as nursemaids. They shouldn't have to worry about all this. They deserved a little more childhood yet. She ought to buy them something. Perhaps candied fruit or the roasted nuts from the street carts on Tully's Bridge. She ought to get the candle lit. She ought . . .

Her head was full of hot cotton wool, scratching the backs of her eyes, but tears wouldn't come. Some assassins killed the nerves in their hands and arms by repeatedly striking unpadded training dummies to deaden their pain reflexes. Right now her emotions felt just as detached, senseless. All she craved was to sit here in the dark until sleep overtook her.

After a long moment, she shook herself. Sitting on your arse wouldn't get the cows milked. It was a saying of her father's, though she was never sure why. He had been born in Hambridge and never seen a pasture. It just seemed like a saying that everyone's da' said.

Gritting her teeth, she rose and fumbled for the candle. Suddenly, she missed seeing his lined face crack into a grin and the gleam of pleasure in her mum's brown eyes. It had been too long since she'd visited the tenement on Maven Street. Of course, there was no way she could return to live with her family. Not as long as she was an assassin.

Not for their protection, but for hers. The Webb apartment would be the first place a potential enemy would look for information about her, and it was safest if innocents like them were never told where she lived. Every assassin knew that obscurity protected better than leather or steel. And yet, at times, she wanted nothing more than to curl up with her head in Da's lap while he stroked her hair and sang shanties in his gusting bass.

She walked to the front hall, examining the damaged armor plate covering her shoulder. The pain was secondary. Bodies healed, armor didn't. Cost of repair would further eat into her earnings. Maybe she could do a patch job herself and spin the wheel of fate again, gambling her luck against Merafey's Rule of Consequences.

First some rest. Then maybe a wash at one of the cheap public baths that had been instituted by old Lord Saucer Reiker's wife, without whom Hambridgers would be even more odorous than they were now. As no good deed goes unpunished, the grateful citizenry had instantly dubbed her the Wife of Baths.

Jamie stooped to remove her boots, and saw that a black envelope had been shoved beneath her door.

Cautiously, she picked up the letter. Her stomach knotted itself as she spotted the seal. Imprinted in the blood red wax was a flowering rose.

Jamie Webb knew what it meant.

CHAPTER 14

As they climbed down the Woffler Building to the alley below Vel stopped, looking over her shoulder at the crowded streets and shops. "While we're here, should we do some shopping?"

"Shopping?" Sickly asked, turning his head to her.

"For supplies. I'd like to pick up a few more weapons, some poisons, and a few traps."

"Do you really need all that?"

"Said the man who's wearing half my arsenal? Besides, you can use the time to figure out how to contact one of those spies."

"Shopping!" Terry cried happily, a few seconds behind the conversation once again.

They climbed the rest of the way down and Vel led them to a street lined with shops for the stylish assassin. "This is my favorite store," she said, pointing to a large black sign with gold lettering. Sickly read Bernt and Daughters, Purveyors of Specialty Instruments for the Discerning Assassin. In the shop window was a large display of knives, bows, quivers, garrotes, and tiny vials, all immaculately arranged on an acre of blue satin in concert with bouquets of flowers in red, pink, and white.

"I can see why," Sickly said, drily. Vel gave him a look. They entered the shop, a room filled with elaborately worked weapons that were graceful but deadly, and smelling of the finest perfumes. His eyes picked out a stiletto dagger in a beautifully tooled black leather sheath, as if the buyer might be tempted to assassinate a target while on her way to the opera.

One or two patrons browsed idly while a man tended the counter. Towards the back a young woman was wrestling a large sign depicting Grandma Winterwatch out of a backroom.

Winterwatch was a traditional Hambridge holiday dating back centuries as a means to control children through judicious use of carrot and knitting needle. The legend went that on Winterwatch Eve a little old woman in coal black skirts would scuttle from door to door, picking the lock with her knitting needles and entering illegally. Children judged to have been 'good' were given ancient sweets that tasted of talc, fourth-hand handkerchiefs, and scratchy wool clothing in patterns and colors that, at best, constituted a hate crime. Bad Children were flogged with size 20 knitting needles and roundly upbraided. Very few Hambridge children reoffended.

"Bloody typical," Vel muttered, "they bring out the decorations earlier every year. Would it kill them to wait the extra week?"

In this overpriced, chic store Sickly felt how Terry looked: out of place. There was a bench on the other side of the window display, and Sickly strayed towards it.

Vel saved him by saying, "I'll get the supplies. You and Terry stay here, watch the street, and get to work on those spies." Gratefully, they sat down. Terry's huge presence made Sickly feel like a child waiting with his father while his mother did the shopping.

To dispel this disturbing notion, he pulled out the contact instructions and began to peruse the page. Terry made a little noise in his throat.

"What's that?" Sickly asked, after a moment.

"Pretty. I like dat one." Terry pointed, not to a weapon, but to a silver necklace in a display case. It was hung with tiny geometric bangles.

"You could get it, if you like," Sickly reminded him. "I like the one next to it." It was also a silver necklace, but this one had only a single pendant shaped like a rose with shards of garnets clasped by the metal petals. "The stones are nearly the same red as Vel's hair," Sickly said, without knowing why. Then he, too, went red.

"It is also pretty." Terry conceded, scratching his curly dark hair. "Maybe I will get dem."

"Come off it," Sickly said, embarrassed. "Just get yours."

"Oh. Ok. I understand." Terry got up and went over to the counter. Sickly returned his attention to the paper. Kerry Adams could be reached by leaving a coded message with the bartender of the Bilgewater Tavern. Earl Watkins, alias Cole Nebble, would seek you out if you left him a note in Thief Sign on a specific wall of Ponsingham Palace. Quentin Verk would contact you if you waited in an abandoned warehouse next to pier 27 on the Hambridge docks at sunset. Sickly mulled the possibilities over.

He certainly didn't like the idea of leaving his own description on a wall where someone besides Earl Watkins could read it. Kerry Adams would have been a good option, except that the Bilgewater Tavern was back on the East Side of Hambridge, and it would take them far out of their way to get there. But Quentin Verk, and the warehouse next to Pier 27, was within running distance over the rooftops of the houses in Billys' part of town.

Sickly looked up to see Terry coming over, putting his purchase into a pouch. Behind him Vel was cramming something large into a paper bag, and Sickly got a glimpse of a long spike before it disappeared from view. She came over, smiling a little to herself, and handed Terry the shopping.

"After we get Jamie and Billys we'll try and find this spy, Quentin Verk," Sickly said.

"Oh, no," Vel interrupted, "First, we're buying you some new body armor."

"Vel, I don't have that kind of money on hand. I walk dogs for a living! And I doubt they'll just let me borrow against the Dodger family name," Sickly protested.

"You can pay me back when it saves your life," she said firmly, and led them to a second store.

The sign above it proclaimed: Amos Quality Armor and Formal Wear, Stop an Arrow in Style. After speaking to the proprietor, a tall, lean man with onyx skin wearing a beautifully tailored blue suit, Vel motioned Sickly over. "We need to fit my friend here with the works, Amos." The proprietor nodded and ushered Sickly to the back of the store.

Sickly felt distinctly awkward about his appearance next to Amos in his blue suit and air of authority. Even more so when he was asked to strip down to his underclothes. Sickly's dampened emotions didn't stop him blushing as Amos deftly measured him with a little gold-edged tape. "Let me see what I can get you, sir," Amos said with a flash of white smile and the trace crispness of an Umundi accent. He disappeared into the recesses of his shop with the air of a librarian who knew exactly what book a visitor needed.

The man returned moments later with a bundle of straps, fittings, and carefully crafted armor pieces. He expertly helped Sickly adjust and size every greave, cuisse, brace, vambrace, and fauld. Once they were done, Sickly admired himself in the mirror. He looked older, somehow, wearing all this utilitarian finery. "Is it to your liking, sir?" Amos asked, discretely.

Sickly started. "Oh, yes, it looks wonderful, Mr. . . .?"

"Amos, please," the man said, giving Sickly another smile. His teeth were as white as Ulrich's, but warm like the sand on a tropical beach, rather than icy and cold. The man was looking at him, as if expecting some facial expression in response. But for once, the smile did not falter when met by Sickly's stony features. Amos' eyes twinkled kindly, and he went on, "May I help you find anything else today, sir? Perhaps an evening jacket to impress the Lady Lucrezia?" If Sickly had been blushing before, it was nothing to the inferno that roared across his cheeks now.

"Erm," he mumbled, "It's not like that."

Amos raised an eyebrow, "Oh? My mistake, sir," he said diplomatically, and made to help Sickly with the straps on his new armor.

After mentally and physically squirming for a few moments while he and Amos worked to take off the armor, Sickly opened his mouth. "Actually, I recently lost access to my, er, wardrobe. Would you mind helping me pick out a few outfits? Maybe with an eye to impress . . . certain people."

Amos smiled. "I was hoping you'd ask me that, sir. It would have been such a shame."

"What would have?" Sickly asked, bewildered.

"The interest of a woman like Mademoiselle Lucrezia is difficult to pique, and not to be discarded lightly. And, if I am not being too bold, sir, you have her interest." Sickly hadn't thought his cheeks could burn any hotter than they already were. He had been wrong.

Amos helped Sickly find an array of tunics, pants, shirts and underclothes in a surprisingly short amount of time. And because this was an assassin's shop, they were all exquisitely well cut, tasteful in color and style, artfully sewn with handy pockets, and jaw-droppingly expensive.

"Actually, er," Sickly began again. "This coat belongs to Vel, er, Miss Lucrezia, and I, well, wanted to give it back."

"I believe I understand, sir," Amos added with a diplomat's grace. "Perhaps we could find something a bit more understated for you?" He disappeared again, returning with a grey coat of thick wool that no one would mistake for belonging to an assassin. Sickly's eyebrows twitched.

At the end of forty-five minutes' jumping in and out of all styles of clothing, Sickly stood by Vel at Amos' counter. Two large brown bags filled with Sickly's new clothes and armor lounged on the polished oak. Amos presented them with the bill, and Sickly winced at the size of Vel's eyes as she spotted the total.

"I didn't bring you here to buy half the shop," she hissed under her breath, taking Sickly aside.

Sickly hung his head in shame. The things Amos had said to him about Vel had probably just been a sales pitch to get Sickly to buy more clothes. "Oh, gods, of course. Sorry, Vel, I'll put them back," Sickly mumbled.

Vel exhaled through her nose. "Don't you dare, Sickly Dodger. You looked right fit in those outfits."

He raised his face gratefully, then realized. "You peeked!" Sickly whispered back, half horrified, half wondering if his face could actually be permanently dyed scarlet from embarrassment.

Vel gave a roguish smile. "Thought I wouldn't appraise what I'm paying for? And you, a smart university boy," she teased. "Just promise to dip into that inheritance and pay me back, yeah?"

"Of course!" The heat on his cheeks could have melted glaciers. "But you . . . only when I – erm, well, uh, had the clothes on, right?"

Vel had already turned back to negotiate the price with Amos. Amos clasped each of their hands in turn, and bowed them out of the shop. As Sickly turned to leave, he thought he saw the proprietor give him the smallest of knowing winks. And perhaps it was simply Sickly's imagination, but Terry was smiling faintly, too.

Lady Fullfrigate, Jamie's employer, hadn't been nearly so generous as the Merchants' Guild when it came to providing lodging for her retained assassins. Instead, she had been forced to rent a flat at the edge of Murktown. Sickly's heart lurched as he saw how desperately small and dingy it was. Even Billys' place was better than this. Guilt wrapped itself around his throat as he thought of the pile of gold that had put him through college and the expensive new armor he had just acquired.

The three of them walked to the actual front door to allow Jamie to open it and see them. This way they would avoid the scare they had had with Terry's traps. Sickly went up to the brass knocker and rapped a few times. Both Vel and Terry winced in unison.

"Oh, come on, Sickly. Give a proper knock," Vel urged him.

Sickly sighed and tried to remember the secret knock for being in trouble and needing the listener's help. First, he gave five panicked taps, followed by a short pause, then four louder, more insistent knocks, another pause, and then as many rapid taps as he wanted, to correspond to the level of emergency currently experienced.

They waited.

"She's probably just out, right?" Sickly asked. As one assassin, Vel and Terry turned and surveyed opposite ends of the street, the rooftops, and the buildings around them. "I mean, they'll be after me first, won't they?" Vel unlimbered the crossbow, loading it and cocking it with a practiced motion. Terry crouched, dropping the bags and pulling on a pair of massive gauntlets studded with spikes and armor plates.

"Get the door, Terry," Vel ordered.

"Is that really necessary? It doesn't mean that she's . . ." Terry didn't hesitate; he brought one massive fist around and shattered the door, sending splinters and boards spiraling through the air.

"Inside, quickly," Vel barked. "You first, Terry. Watch for traps." Once again, Terry obliged, stepping in smartly and raising his fists, ready to block a potential attack. None came. Vel pushed Sickly through the doorway, and they ventured a little further into the hall.

"See? She's just out," Sickly said. "We smashed her door down for nothing."

"I will pay her back," Terry said earnestly.

As soon as they reached the tiny kitchen, they could tell something was wrong. It was too cold. A draft tugged at a few papers scattered across the floor, and it wasn't from the door they'd smashed down. "Over dere. Broked window, watch your step," Terry rumbled. They inched forward on silent feet. The window was broken, and on the shards were drops of what was unmistakably blood. A handmade trap lay in pieces, strewn over the glass.

"Jamie . . ." Sickly breathed. His throat constricted automatically. It felt like his insides were filling with hot smoke, stinging his eyes. "I dragged her into this. This is all my fault."

"We should keep searching, there might be a clue as to who killed her," Vel said, her voice dangerously flat.

"She might not be dead," Sickly argued, though it sounded hollow. "You didn't see a body, right?"

"Um, friends? Look," Terry said, pointing to a second broken window. But this time the broken glass had landed in the mud outside the house.

"She might have made it!" Sickly said excitedly. Please let her have made it.

"Maybe," Vel allowed, relief palpable in her voice. "Whatever else, we need to get out of here. We'll get Billys, and then we're finding that spy. We need to know who's after us."

This time when they arrived at Billys' flat he was not there to brandish the Burlington. Sickly kept hoping his pinched, grinning face would pop out at them, ready to laugh at their surprise. But there was no sudden, jeering laugh. Sickly knocked, this time using the secret 'help me' knock immediately. Once again there was no answer.

"Gods damn it!" He kicked at the ground in frustration. How many more of his friends was he going to lose? Vel put her hand in his, sending a tingle through his body. The weight of Terry's hand descended on his other shoulder.

"We are still here, Sickly," Terry said reassuringly. Sickly looked down, fighting the urge to scream. It had seemed like a joke till now. Or, if not a joke, a game. A puzzle. Since this morning's attack, however, it had all become real. Two of his only friends might be dead. His arm hurt. He was tired and hungry. If he hadn't been so selfish and asked Billys and Jamie to help him, they might still be . . .

He blinked back tears, focusing on the doormat to keep from

crying. A strip of white caught his eye. He bent down and picked up a piece of paper.

By Order of the Hambridge City Watch,
The occupant of this dwelling has been taken in for questioning about the death of Sir Cuthbert Rawley. Please forward all mail to the Hambridge City Watch House on Raft Street.

"He wasn't killed! He was arrested!" Sickly said with a strange, hysterical laugh. His hand was actually shaking with relief; he had been terrified of losing anyone, even Billys. At least he was safe, in the watch house, even if they didn't know where Jamie was.

"Should we go bail him out?" asked Vel.

"No, he'll be surrounded by watchmen, in a cell. He'll be safe. Anyway, it's almost sunset."

CHAPTER 15

*P*ier 27 was closer to Murktown than Sickly would have liked. The warehouse itself was a long, low building covered in gang graffiti and peeling paint. It was unequivocally abandoned, the perfect place for a clandestine rendezvous, or a trap. "Spread out, but keep in sight. Don't get ambushed. Stay low," Eveline advised, though she hoped that Sickly and Terry didn't need the warning. "And, Sickly, don't call out." He nodded.

They entered the grey building and paused at the entrance, surveying the scene. It would have been an open space had it not been filled with huge, wooden cargo boxes decaying with age and moisture damage. It was a maze of blind corners, dead ends and possible traps. Chains hung from the rafters, and the floor was a mixture of mud and stone. In the last rays of the setting sun, the gloomy interior of the warehouse was decidedly creepy.

"Spies." Eveline spat the word. Only a spy would think a place like this was a suitable meeting point. "Stay in sight. I'll take point. Terry, guard the rear. Sickly, watch the sides, got it?" she whispered, her voice getting lost in the huge space. They nodded, grimly.

She set off, not giving herself a chance to get nervous. They turned one corner, and then another. The tiny sounds of their boots sucking at the mud were immediately swallowed by the consuming darkness above and around them. All else was silence, eerie and unknowable in the grey twilight of crates and dangling chains.

As they moved farther in, the greyscale shapes began to swim before her straining eyes. Her heart rate increased, in spite of all her training. Eveline kept her mind off her growing panic by listening for any sound, staring around for any possible ambush. She tightened her grip on the crossbow to stop her hands from shaking.

The thing was that assassins got scared like anyone else, under the right circumstances. They were strong, but not all powerful. They were trained to kill, not be killed. But they were not invincible. It was an illusion they cultivated for their own benefit, but in the end they died, just like anyone else. Though they invoked the Traveler with each kill, they did not walk with him. Assassins dealt in death. They did not understand it.

Eveline rounded another corner. She looked up, toward the silent chains overhead, the ends of which were lost to the dark. She pressed on, down the passage formed by crates and boxes, smelling of mold and damp. They turned right at the end, waiting for a voice, for a sign that they had come to the right place.

The silence battered her ears with the force of a gale, a deafening stillness. What was that over there? Eyes flicked to dancing spots of color welling and pooling in the suffocating dark. Eveline felt her heart break into a frantic run against her chest, a frightened animal dashing itself against a cage it could not comprehend. It was nothing, she told herself, just shapes her eyes invented in desperation to see something. Her hand bumbled against a crate, she recoiled, then plunged on into the inky void.

The moist darkness pressed in, like the walls of the closet. Drasilla cast your shadow on me, Eveline prayed silently. Sweat beaded on her forehead in spite of the evening's chill. She was trapped, boxes and clothes all around her. Somewhere outside the screaming would begin any second now.

It was wrong. This was all wrong. Instincts from a time when her ancestors had lived in great forests and hidden from huge cats were telling her to turn and run. Assassin or not, she was going to turn around and sprint toward the exit, ignoring all caution and the reason they had come. Somewhere in the echoes of her own mind, the first shrieks caught up to her.

She halted, hands shaking. Sweat trickled down her back.

Something touched her hand.

She flinched and was about to bolt when she realized it had come from beside her. Sickly had slipped his hand into hers.

Sickly needed her help. Eveline mastered the overpowering urge to run. She squeezed, his hand and managed to go a step farther. She took another step, and suddenly it became easier. Her training came back to her, and she was able to lead them down to the end of the passage. This was not the closet.

The corridor opened onto a cavernous pitch black maw at the center of the warehouse. Eveline could feel the emptiness yawning in front of them, even if she couldn't see. Her night vision was good, but even assassins had their limits. Behind her, Sickly and Terry had both stopped, waiting for her.

She closed her eyes, the better to focus on aural and nasal information. She opened her mouth, the better to hear and smell. There was no sound other than her own breathing, and the breathing of Sickly and Terry. She concentrated. A drop of liquid, quite close by, fell through the darkness to splash on the floor. She inhaled, scenting the air, letting the smells fill her up. She could smell mud and water and the heavy earthiness of rotting wood. She breathed in again, her chest expanding with the effort of gathering every aroma.

Yes, the mud and moisture were fitting, but there was something else. Something past them. A darker, metallic scent. A scent she knew well. There was blood here, a lot of blood. The bards sometimes sang of 'the smell of death' and people thought that it was just a clever phrase. But Eveline knew it was a real scent, something visceral and ugly, a blackness which oozed into her nose, crawling into her brain.

Someone had died here.

"Get a light," she whispered. "Get. A. Bloody. Light." A match flared behind her. Its tiny glow seemed pathetic in comparison to the consuming darkness all around them. She fumbled behind her and felt the heat as Sickly placed it between her fingers. She lifted the little flame over her head and walked forward.

A shape loomed out of the blackness, so quickly that she hesitated. It was large and long and dangled grotesquely from a chain, it was --

The match died.

This time Eveline fished in her own pouch for a matchbox, and struck the match herself. It illuminated a body, hung by its neck from one of the chains on the ceiling. Its hands were tied behind it by a cord, and blood had dripped down to the floor, staining the mud below. A rough sack was thrown over the head of the corpse.

Behind her, Sickly threw up. Eveline was not scared of dead people, but even she had to struggle not to retch at the sight and the smell. But that was secondary, a reaction of her body against the awful sight. Her mind spun silently, detached from the scene. She lifted a hand to the bag and ripped it off.

Long matted hair fell over a face that was so bruised and shredded that it was barely recognizable as human. The most she could tell was that it had probably been male, and that whoever had done this had done so with the utmost precision. The man had died in surgical agony.

Eveline let the match fall where it hissed into silence in the mud.

. . .

Night had fallen by the time they exited the warehouse. Sickly was still shaking, his hands jerky as he wiped vomit from his mouth. It was growing colder. He hoped that wherever they went next, it would be inside. He took a few gulps of the night air, trying to calm himself. He had never seen anything like that. The image of that face, puffy and swollen, blue with bruising and air loss and laced with gashes oozing red, had branded itself across his mind. Every time he shut his eyes he saw it again. He could imagine the man's feet twitching and writhing as he slowly suffocated, alone in the silent dark.

"Bad," Terry stated. Vel nodded.

"That must have been Quentin Verk," she said. Her tone was business-like, as if she encountered this every day. It frightened Sickly. He wondered if she could commit such an act against anyone. "Someone was sending a message with that body. That's what'll happen to anyone who digs too deep into this conspiracy."

"Yes," Terry agreed, "bad."

"We -- we need t-to," Sickly stuttered, "we need to find one of the others. Watkins or Adams." Vel looked at him with what might have been concern. He shook his head.

"Adams, then. It'd be suicide to wander the Merchant District, waiting for Watkins to come to us. Where is she again?"

"B-Bilgewater Tavern," Sickly managed. His hands shook, fingers stiff and cold in the night air. He had to clench them to prevent his father's ring slipping off his index finger.

"Right, follow me," Vel commanded, then paused. "Sickly, do you want Terry to carry you?" She said it kindly, but it stung like a blow.

"No!" he barked. She looked a little taken aback. "No, I can make it."

As they descended to street level on Shadhopper's Lane, Sickly almost dropped from exhaustion and hunger. The city's clocks had struck ten maybe fifteen minutes ago. Terry put a hand on

Sickly's right arm, steadying him. He managed to raise his eyebrows, and Terry nodded solemnly. Vel was already heading across the street toward the lit windows of the tavern.

The Bilgewater was the kind of tavern which was rowdy in the front and quiet in the back. Once you ducked past the flying chairs, booze, and mugs of the evening's bar fight, there was a little ring of quiet near the bar. Here were the people intent on getting down to some serious drinking without interruption. Folks ready to not only drown their sorrows, but water-torture them under the taps of the house special. But it was a good kind of quiet, not the oppressive silence of the warehouse.

Sickly, Vel, and Terry approached the bar, and, as if by magic, the seats nearest the bartender emptied. There were many perks to being an assassin, and one was that you never needed to wait to be served at a bar. Sickly pulled out the note and examined the instructions about how to contact Kerry Adams.

"What'll it be?" asked the barkeep, a man hardened by years of experience running a tavern near Murder Town.

"I'll have a Thief's Purse, on the rocks. And make it exactly right." Sickly tried to sound confident, as if he did this every day. In truth, he had only ever been in a bar once, with Vel, Jamie, Terry, and Billys on the night they celebrated the end of the first year at College. That was how he had discovered his body's inability to tolerate alcohol. Alcohol poisoning happened to him after just a single drink.

At his words, the bartender turned his back and asked, calmly, "Would you like a lemon with that, sir?" Sickly consulted the piece of paper for the response to this code phrase.

"Just an umbrella. A blue one." The bartender nodded and disappeared through a door behind the bar.

"Not bad, Sickly," Vel said encouragingly.

"What do you mean?" Sickly asked. He wanted to lay his head down on the bar.

"You look like you do this all the time."

"What are you on about?" he protested, heat rising to his cheeks.

"No, she is right. It's your face. You were very con-vin-sing," Terry added. Sickly shook his head. They were just trying to make him feel better. Treating him like a child. He put his head in his hands. He missed his warm bed in Cod Liver Oil Alley. Or his bunk in the Dalton College dorms. Or, even more wistfully, his bed at the Dodger House with the ticking of the grandfather clock in the hall while his father snored in the master bedroom. He was tired down to his marrow.

The bartender returned, carrying a stack of coasters. He poured the drink and slid it over to Sickly, on top of one of the coasters. The man glanced expectantly at Vel and Terry, but they shook their heads. He sidled off to serve another customer.

"That's it?" Sickly frowned. He had expected the bartender to tell him how to get in contact with Kerry Adams, or possibly for the spy herself to appear. Instead, he had just received a cocktail he couldn't drink. He looked down at the piece of paper. Hadn't he done everything properly?

"There must be more to it," Vel insisted, she looked over the bar, and peered around the room. Terry picked up the Thief's Purse.

"You mind?" he asked.

"Go ahead." After quickly checking for poison, Terry drank it in two massive gulps, setting the glass carefully down on the bar. "Totally normal?" Sickly asked in desperation.

"Wheat vodka, triple de-stilled. A earthy, cherry liqueur. Notes of lemon and a undertone of bitter ash from da soap used ta clean da glass." They stared at Terry. "Not bad. Totally reg'lar dough."

They had reached dead ends everywhere. What else could they do? Sickly stared at the coaster, which had the Bilgewater Tavern's logo stamped atop it in blue ink-- a sinking ship in a muddy river.

"This place is a dive." Vel grumbled. Sickly paused. The

bartender had gone to get a stack of coasters, hadn't he? Sickly turned it over, and on the back was a scribbled message:

I have what you're looking for. Alley next to burned house, 920 Olney Street, East Hambridge. Midnight tomorrow, on the hour.
Kerry Adams

Sickly's eyebrows rose. At last. He passed the note to Vel and then Terry.

"Midnight exactly, I ask you," Vel muttered when she had read it. "Spies."

He felt overwhelming relief. At least this gave them some time to rest. But as tired as his body was, his mind still raced. Billys was safe at the Raft Street Watch House. There didn't seem to be any way of finding Jamie, dead or alive. Vel and Terry were both here, with him. Who did that leave out?

A knife of dread pierced Sickly's brain, leaving fear and adrenaline sizzling in its wake. "We have to get to the Thieves' Guild, quickly," he snapped, all tiredness suddenly gone.

"Sickly, what –" Vel started, but Sickly ignored her, his mind racing.

Whoever was behind this had not limited themselves to targeting just assassins. Quentin Verk's fate proved that. And the mysterious murderer was exceedingly well-informed of Sickly's movements, since Ulrich had known about the notebook, which he, Sickly had only gotten . . . yesterday?

It felt like ages ago that he, Jamie, Billys, and Terry had extracted the little red notebook from the *Daily Piccolo*. But this meant that whoever was watching him knew about his friends. They would know about Booter Squill, the lowest member of the Thieves' College.

"So dis note is from da spy lady?" Terry asked slowly, holding up the coaster. Sickly had to remind himself that Terry took a long time to read anything.

"Yes, and before we meet her, we have to get Booter."

Terry nodded, pocketed the coaster, and plunked a few coins down on the bar next to the empty glass.

CHAPTER 16

The Hambridge Thieves' Guild, and by extension the Thieves' College, was located on the West Side of the Ham in proximity to the Merchants' Guild. This was so the extortionists didn't have to walk as far to hire extra muscle for their enterprises. To get there, Sickly, Vel, and Terry decided to use Reiker's Bridge, rather than exhaust themselves with further acrobatics across masts and loading gantries. Besides, Reiker's Avenue was well patrolled by the Watch even at this time of night, and the Thieves' Guild was just one street removed.

This compound was much more compact than the Merchants' Guild, and had a large iron fence around it, though the reason why was anyone's guess. No one would willingly enter a den of thieves, despite the strict code that all its members adhered to. Both the Assassins' Guild and the Thieves' Guild had very rigid creeds about the actions their members were allowed to take. There was crime and assassination, but it was *organized* crime and assassination. And it was government-sanctioned crime and assassination, meaning it was all legal anyway.

Sickly strode purposefully toward the front gate. Four guards leaned to attention, picking their teeth or paring their fingernails with knives in a very nearly non-threatening way. They wore brown bowler hats and brown coats over tweed vests and starched white shirts. Scars crisscrossed the backs of their hands and their faces. When they smiled, or rather leered, gold, brass, and even lead glinted dully in the lamplight. As Sickly, Vel, and Terry approached, their eyes flicked upward, and their leader limbered himself off the wall.

"Don't bother searching us for weapons. We're assassins, we have weapons, and no we're not giving them up." Vel glared defiantly at the man who wore a smirk that said: what do you take me for?

"Scaffer Dunkirk, at yer service. And what might yer business be, this fine night, milords?" His tenor voice lilted with the characteristic Scoffborough brogue of the northern lowlands.

"We're looking for a thief here named Booter, Booter Squill," Sickly said flatly. The man cocked his head, like he was giving this some serious thought.

"Booter? Can't say as I've heard of him, serrah."

Sickly sighed, and, with a pang of guilt, said, "You'd know him as Thumbs." The thief's face broke into a smile full of yellow teeth, only a few of which were gold.

"Yer looking for ole Thumbsie, eh? He's in tonight, gov'ner. You're like to find him in Mess Hall." Sickly was suddenly aware that the man was standing too close. They both glanced downward, to where Scaffer's hand was halfway into Sickly's coat pocket. The hand retracted, slowly, palm up to show it held nothing. Sickly eyed the man's grin. "Just doing me job, milord, yer free to pass, so long as you's don't go knifing no one you weren't paid to."

"Keep your hand on your wallet at all times. Make sure no one gets closer than two feet, and don't attract attention," Vel advised as they entered through the front doors. Sickly nodded and Terry just smiled, looking up at the stonework, humming to himself. "Terry, mind the shopping." She stopped a young thief passing in the other direction. "Mess Hall?" she demanded.

"What'll you give me for it, lady?" he asked, unwisely.

"I won't give you this knife, in your throat," she said, just loud enough for him to hear her.

"Pull the other one! You're not allowed to kill me 'less some-one's paying you."

Vel's body tensed and Sickly wondered just how on edge she really was. Sickly got ready to intervene.

Terry chose this moment to give the boy a dollar. His eyes went wide. "Over that way, two doors down, on the left," the boy said, and stuck his tongue out at Vel. Sickly put a hand on her shoulder and steered her toward the Mess Hall, Terry following.

There was a reason that this room was not named the cafeteria, the refectory, the canteen, or the lunchroom. Mess Hall summed it up to a fault. It was crowded and dirty and smelly, bits of food littering the floor, with dogs scrapping under the tables. Here and there fights were going on, egged on by supporters eagerly betting on the outcome. At the tables themselves, the thieves, muggers, and enforcers ate, drank, and swore, all the while sneaking their hands into the pockets of their neighbors.

If money was made to move, economically speaking, here was where it came to put on its sneakers and sprint. Money changed hands and pockets so quickly that it wasn't a matter of owning it, it was a matter of keeping score. Those who could thieve the most spent and gambled the most, and it all went round and round, like a game of Find the Lady except with pockets instead of shells, and everyone was a con artist.

Even though it was around midnight, the guild was in full swing, thieving being best done by night, as was assassination. Terry and Vel seemed to be wide awake, despite the hour, even while Sickly wanted to crawl into a corner and sleep. But he had to find Booter, and make sure that his friend was all right.

Sickly and the others skirted the main part of the room, moving around clockwise to the less occupied tables. But between the mess, the crowd, and the exhaustion, Booter was nowhere to be found. Just as he was going to ask someone, a snatch of conversation caught Sickly's ear, and, as if by magic, he homed in on it.

"Lay off, all right?"

"You're free to go, Thumbs."

"Yeah, right. Free to go through Two-Pence Doppler and Cudgel Capone, you mean." There was a burst of nasty laughter. Sickly knew what this was about all too well.

Being small, unpopular, and too nice for his own good had gotten Booter far in life, but mostly in the downward direction.

It was how Sickly and Booter had first met, backed into the same corner by a gang of eight-year-old Lady Rangers, led by Henrietta "Half-Brick" Lovelace. They were ostensibly selling chocolate biscuits to the neighborhood, but had taken it upon themselves to put a dent in the overhead by extorting pocket money from other kids. In later years, Sickly had learned self-defense for the both of them, insofar as kicking someone in the shin and then running like the blazes, Booter in tow, constituted a martial art.

Sickly peered through the small crowd that was gathering for that evening's entertainment of thoughtless cruelty and violence inflicted upon the weak.

Booter crouched at the center of a ring of thieves, blue eyes darting nervously from grinning face to grinning face. His cheeks were flushed with embarrassment and fear, and his hands were half-raised, ready to shield his face from a blow. He looked ready to cry, and Sickly's heart went out to the poor man. How often did this happen to him? Sickly got the sense that it wasn't an uncommon event. He should have noticed. He should have been a better friend.

"Tell you what, Thumbsie," said the leader, a woman of medium height, light bronze skin, and black hair. Her dark green eyes were beautiful, as was her smile. Yet the cruelty beneath her expression and her treatment of Booter did nothing to endear her to Sickly. "We'll let you go if you give us . . . five dollars? Call it . . . guild dues." She glanced around at her cronies, who, on cue, gave thuggish laughs.

"You know I haven't got five dollars," Booter growled.

"Not got five dollars? And you, a thief, trained for five years at the Thieves College?" the woman said, in a tone of mock amazement.

"Five and a half," someone added, and there was a burst of laughter.

"That's right!" she crowed, smiling dazzlingly. "You didn't graduate this summer, did you, Thumbsie?" Booter's jaw clenched in frustration, his cheeks burning. "How many times is it that you've failed the graduation exam? Six? Seven?"

"Nine!" jeered the wag in the crowd.

"That must take some real skill, Thumbs, failing nine times in a row. You'd think, after spending five-and-a-half years of your life in training, that you'd have something to show for it. I guess it was just wasted effort. Now, since you can't pay up, I'm going to have to take something else from you. How about that necklace you're always fingering, the one dear old mum gave you?"

"Get away from me!" Booter's voice was high pitched and full of fear.

"Two-Pence, get it from him," the woman ordered. Two-Pence Doppler lunged, but Booter must have learned something, because he ducked out of the way, sidestepping his large attacker. Cudgel Capone blocked his escape, but Booter kicked him in the fork of his legs, and he went down, cursing. Then the woman moved in a flash, and all Sickly knew was that one moment Booter's necklace was around his neck, and the next, she was holding it in one hand, ruby lips framing a triumphant smile.

Sickly, Vel and Terry finally managed to elbow to the front of a crowd past a rat-like man in a blue waistcoat and a curvy young woman nearly covered in tattoos. "Leave him alone," Sickly called, and there was silence. Booter's primary tormentor turned to look at the three newcomers, still smiling.

"And who exactly are you?" she purred, looking Sickly up and down. She had a thick Murktown accent from somewhere near Motley Drive with the barest hint of a rolled 'R' that Sickly couldn't quite place.

"I'm . . ." He trailed off. It was not a good idea to announce his identity to a crowd of unknown people, any of whom could have been hostile. More hostile than your average thief, anyway.

"Sickly!" Booter exclaimed. Sickly gritted his teeth. He had been hoping to avoid this.

"Sickly?" The woman raised an eyebrow, and then comprehension spread across her face. "You're that Sickly Dodger Thumbs is always talking about, aren't you?" She gave him a second look, and a demure smile. "My name's Madeline, but you can call me Lady." She extended the hand not holding the necklace. Sickly, hesitated, then shook. She had a monstrously strong handshake, but Sickly used it as a distraction, lunging forward with his free hand.

Madeline was no fool, and dodged his swipe. There was nervous laughter from the crowd. "Why Mister Dodger, you barely even know me!" she trilled. "That was hardly the act of a gentleman." From somewhere, Vel made a small noise of disgust. Sickly realized how close he was standing to Lady, and that her eye lashes were very long. He stepped back and finally allowed her hand to slip out of his. He wasn't stupid. If you got near a thief, you'd better be damn sure where both her hands were.

"Give him back his necklace, Lady," Sickly said flatly.

"I'm afraid that guild business is no concern of yours, Mr. Dodger. I'm going to keep this until your friend Thumbs can steal it back from me. It might be a while though." A snicker broke out among the assembled watchers.

"Give it back to him," Vel ordered, and drew a knife. Instantly, the crowd bristled with knives, cutlasses, stilettos, blackjacks, saps, and even a chicken leg, all pointed threateningly toward Sickly, Vel, and Terry.

"You're in no position to make me do anything," Madeline said sweetly. Vel reluctantly sheathed her knife, and, slowly, the thieves lowered their weapons, and in one case, took a large bite. Madeline walked over to Booter and bent slightly to look him in the eye, still smiling.

"I didn't know you needed others to fight your battles, Thumbsie," she whispered. "I guess I'll remember that the next time you have anything I want."

Booter let out a roar and charged forward, shoving the surprised Madeline backward, his fingers clawing desperately at the hand which held his necklace. Despite her shock, she managed to keep it out of Booter's reach, even as she fell backward, right into Sickly. Sickly caught her in one arm and used the other to pluck the necklace from her grasp.

She looked up, startled, at Sickly's impassive face. "Why you!" she hissed, the smile finally gone, replaced by a snarl. Sickly handed Booter the necklace, which he clutched in one hand, his chest heaving with rage and humiliation.

Madeline looked down at his arm around her, and her smile returned. "Oh, my, Mister Dodger, I didn't know you felt this way about me." She eased herself backward, pressing into Sickly, who was suddenly made acutely aware of the curves beneath her clothing.

Sickly shoved her away hurriedly. Suddenly nervous, he patted his pockets and felt the reassuring edges of the notebook. "We'll be leaving now," he managed.

She smiled. "A *pleasure* to meet you, Mr. Dodger. Drasilla shade you."

"Don't threaten Booter ever again." Madeline's smile wavered for a fraction of a second.

"He's lucky in his friends. That's for certain," she finally said.

As they exited the Mess Hall, Booter continued to shake with anger or fear, Sickly couldn't tell. "I hate that woman." Uncharacteristic venom filled his voice. They passed Scaffer and his cronies as they exited the Thieves' Guild gate.

"Madeline?" Sickly inquired, his voice light. He hadn't eaten in hours, and his muscles felt like molten lead.

"I can't believe you stood up to her like that."

"Why not, Thumbs?" Vel snapped. Sickly's brows inclined slightly, and he shook his head at her, over the top of Booter's unkempt hair. "I— I mean, why not . . . Booter?"

"Because she was the best thief in my year. Maybe the whole guild. You know why they call her Lady? Because the other part of that nickname is Fingers. She can steal the shirt from your back without you noticing." He sounded a little awed. Sickly had to remind himself that Booter wasn't an assassin and was a little more credulous of people's abilities. Training to be an assassin had taught Sickly a great many things, especially about where reality stopped and myth began.

Even so, he felt the red notebook in his pocket one more time, to be completely sure.

"She's Lady Fingers, and I'm Thumbs. She's the best, and I'm the worst."

"Come on, Booter, that's not true. I saw you dodge away from Two-Pence," Sickly tried.

"You said it yourself, Sickly, I'm a lousy thief. Nine times." Now more than ever did he sound like he was going to cry. "I hate her," he repeated and refastened the necklace about his neck. "But she was right."

"About what?" Sickly asked sharply, he hated to see his friend in such a state.

"That I need other people to fight my battles."

"Five on one odds is hardly a battle," Sickly pointed out.

"That's not what she meant. Even if she was alone, she could take anything she wanted. I'm such a failure."

"You're not a failure, Booter! You're just not a thief," Sickly protested, knowing it wouldn't convince his friend.

"Yes, I am! I am a thief! I spent five-and-a-half years training to be one, how can I not be?" he asked, desperately.

"I spent four years training to be an assassin, and I'm not one." Behind him, Vel tutted. "And look, Booter, about not fighting your own battles? Even though I had four years of training, here's me with two whole assassins for protection."

Booter looked marginally happier. "Come to think of it, why are you here?"

They returned to Vel's house well after one o'clock in the morning. Vel directed Terry to haul some cushions into the living room and then set up three makeshift beds. Sickly and Booter would sleep on sofas, and Terry, due to his size, would sleep on the cushions on the floor. He didn't seem to mind. Vel, of course, would sleep in her own room, but, everyone decided, they needed to keep a round-the-clock watch. Vel volunteered to stay up first.

Terry passed out almost as soon as his head touched the pillow, and Booter's breathing slowed after a few minutes, but Sickly's mind raced. His body ached from the day's exertions, and he should have been able to fall asleep instantly. Instead, he worried after Jamie. Was there really any hope that she could have survived? He had involved her because he'd thought knowledge would be better protection than ignorance. Had he been wrong? He turned over, trying to shelve his doubt and worry since there was nothing he could do to change it in this moment.

That was when the image of Quentin Verk's mutilated face began tracing across his eyelids. A vision of that sickening body, dangling from the chain, alone in the dark.

He tried thinking about something else. How had Ulrich known about the notebook but not the papers? They must have known about the notebook from before. Wells must not have kept it as secret as he thought. So they already knew they were looking for a notebook, but they didn't know they were looking for reports from spies.

They must have been watching him go into the *Daily Piccolo*. And they knew to watch him because . . . because they had intercepted the mail. That was the only tie between him and Wells.

They must have been watching the old Spymaster's every move. They had used Sickly to find the notebook, but they hadn't expected him to escape Ulrich.

From another room there was a clatter and Sickly tensed before remembering that Vel had gone down to set up some of the traps she had bought at Bernt and Daughters.

Sickly got up. He was still wearing everything but his boots, gloves and the new coat he had bought at Amos' Quality Armors. After all the attention he had received over Vel's duster, he had hung it up in the hall closet with satisfaction. Quietly, so as not to disturb Terry and Booter, he snuck out of the room.

A flicker of motion caught his eye as Vel disappeared up a flight of stairs. He needed to talk to someone about Quentin Verk and about what was happening. He followed her heels up the stairs, which creaked loudly with every footfall. Sickly reached the top of the stairs and stopped. Vel was staring directly at him, her hands behind her, holding something that Sickly couldn't see. She was also glaring.

Sickly cast about for something to say. "Erm, what's with your stairs?"

"They're specially made to creak unless you know exactly where to step. Why are you following me?"

"I couldn't sleep."

"So you decided to sneak up on me?" she said testily.

"No, I just wanted to talk. And what are you holding behind your back?"

"It's nothing," she said too quickly, and Sickly's suspicions were aroused.

"What?" he asked, raising an eyebrow. He came toward her, and she backed up, still hiding whatever it was behind her back. Now really curious, he feinted left, then jumped right as she tried to hide it behind her.

The mysterious object was a unicorn.

Vel glared at him, patches of pink rising in her cheeks. "Sickly," she hissed, "you had no right . . ." Now that he had seen, she let the clay unicorn fall to her side. Sickly had to look again, just to be sure. A unicorn. And yes, now that he could fully see it, there was no other word to describe its . . . pinkness. And then Sickly remembered their shopping excursion and Vel stuffing something with a long spike into her shopping bag.

"You bought that at Bernt and Daughter's, didn't you?" he accused, feeling his eyebrows rise.

"Shut up," she hissed, looking absolutely mortified. "If you breathe so much as a word to the others, Sickly Dodger, so help me I will ram this horn up your --"

"Don't worry! I won't tell! I promise! I was just . . . curious. A unicorn." His eyebrows rose still further. She glared. "But, erm, can we talk?" Vel glanced ruefully at the toy and then shrugged. She led him through a door, into what had to be her bedroom.

"Whoa . . ." Sickly said, his voice trailing off. The room was painted white with pink trim, and everywhere were toy unicorns and horses, in all different colors, but mostly pink.

"You promised," she said warningly.

"Right, not a word," he agreed. "It's just . . . I never thought . . ."

"Oh please, it's not like I decorated the whole house like this. And you can sit down, by the way." He sat gingerly on the white bedspread. Vel went over to a shelf already half full of clay, porcelain, and wooden ponies and placed the unicorn beside them.

Sickly took in more of the room and noticed that, while it was extremely cutesy, it also featured training weights, hand tools, and a weapons chest decorated with painted flowers. Sickly inferred this from the nine-ring broadsword and katana poking out from one corner of the box. And while the horses and unicorns were distinctly saccharine, they were also better armed than any other toys Sickly had ever seen, concealing knives, spikes, caltrops, and a wide variety of toxins, which just proved that assassins were assassins to the core of their unicorn-lined hearts.

"I know it's stupid," Vel admitted, sounding half awkward, half defensive. "But . . ."

"But if it's what you like, then what's the problem?" Sickly asked. The light of the lamp cast a warm glow over her face as she smiled. Hurriedly, she turned and began to fuss with the shelf's equine arrangement.

Sickly watched her putter for a moment, but his mind descended back into the dark current running below the surface. He couldn't bring himself to conjecture aloud about Jamie's fate. He felt, somehow, the longer he could avoid voicing it then the longer she remained safely bound in uncertainty. Instead, he said, "I keep . . . keep seeing Verk's face, over and over."

She stiffened for a second, her hand over an ornate knife. "It *was* horrible."

"But you stayed calm. You got us out of there."

"I did what I had to." Her fingers wrapped around the dagger, and she began to spin it habitually in her hand. Wavy red hair hid her expression.

Sickly took a deep breath. "Could you do that to someone, Vel?" He half expected, and was hoping, for an indignant response. Her silence frightened him. The knife kept twirling.

"We were trained to make quick, clean kills. Precision. Accuracy. Efficiency. That's what it's all about, innit. That's what we're paid for."

"I know, but . . . but if the client paid you to do . . . *that.* Would you?" Her hesitation was all the answer he needed.

"It's an ugly world, Sickly. Some people deserve it."

"Oh, really?" he snapped, suddenly angry. "They deserve to be tortured and hanged? To be alone in the dark? Suffocating?" His voice broke.

Vel hung the knife on a small hook, pointing down over a toy pony with a mane so pink it looked sticky. Her response was dangerously flat, next to his emotion, "What if they did that to other people first? We don't get paid to kill innocents."

"You sound like Ulrich," Sickly said, disgustedly, "He said

'everyone kills. You just have to find what will motivate them.' Normal people don't think like that. Assassins are messed up."

She grabbed a misericorde from where it had lain in a pile of dirty clothes. "You reckon? Remember Lord Kistrel Reiker? Remember the bodies hung from the palace walls? Remember what he used to do to 'traitors' caught stealing bread? The Pits of Repentance? You know, Sickly, when two assassins dropped him in his own pit, no one even tried to stop it. Some would call that justice." The little blade spun round and round in her hands.

"Evil breeds evil," Sickly said hollowly. This side of Vel scared him. Suddenly, he wished he hadn't followed her up here. She was facing him now, her eyes downcast toward the blade, and her expression indrawn.

"Perhaps it does, but we're not the ones who decide what evil is done. We just carry it out. We're not," she cast around, "not auditors of death. Just the instruments."

"And you're happy to be an instrument?"

"If it means I don't have to beg or scrounge or . . . or sell myself. You don't know the real world, Sickly. The scholarship that those idiot nobs at the College sneered about? It's everything to people like me and Jamie. It wasn't a choice for us. Billys and Terry, they're pampered second sons. You chose it because of your father. He was a full graduate, right?"

"I never chose to be an assassin, I just didn't want to . . . lose the money," he realized.

"Exactly, Sickly. You can afford not to kill people." Her knuckles had gone white around the handle.

Vel's words hit him like a metal fist to the gut. He felt ashamed of himself. She was right. He could afford not to use his college training to make a living. He didn't have debts like Vel or Jamie. "I'm . . . sorry."

"Forgiven," she said, amiably. Suddenly, she set the dagger down and sat lightly beside him. "Sometimes it is about the money, and that's okay. Everyone's got to eat, right?" Sickly said nothing. He felt more tired than ever, body and soul. "Cheer up, you still haven't killed anyone." Her voice was almost bitter.

"Oh yeah, great comfort." He laughed, trying lighten the conversation. "Thanks, though." There was a pause. "What do you think about all this?"

"This plot, you mean? Sounds like someone's got grand plans, innit. Assassins in power? I guess we aren't just instruments after all."

He thought about the day's events, getting ambushed, going to Vel, getting Terry, and then going to the Thieves' Guild. "I'm glad we got Booter out of there. That necklace means a lot to him, if Madeline had --" Vel huffed and Sickly paused. "I notice you haven't mentioned her."

"I'm glad you noticed," she replied, and then paused for a long moment. "I noticed you shoved her away."

"Yes well . . . thanks for noticing." Suddenly the silence had become very complicated. Sickly wasn't sure how to interpret what had just been said. He wished . . . he wished more than anything to unburden his heart to her. But as much as he admired her cold certainty, he was also afraid of it.

"Feeling better?" she asked. He wasn't sure, but at least he had said some of the things that had been most bothering him, even if he didn't know what to do with Vel's answers. "If you want, you can use my bed, I know that couch isn't very comfortable." At his look of panic, she added, "I won't be in it, cleverdick. But I'll keep watch, on you and them." She rose and gestured downstairs. "Your choice, innit."

Uncertainly, Sickly stretched out on the mattress. His head was unbearably heavy. The sheets were very soft. They smelled like her.

CHAPTER 17

The scent of frying eggs and bacon woke him. He looked around muzzily, and let out an involuntary gasp of surprise. A double barreled weapon of some kind was being pointed at his face, and Sickly raised his hands, in a gesture of capitulation to *force majeure*.

After a while, he realized that he was staring down the nostrils of a toy horse positioned over the bed.

Feeling rather foolish, he rose and stared around him until he remembered where he was and what was happening. He looked down and froze. Not an inch from where he was standing, Vel slept in a tangle of cushions, sheets, limbs, and red hair.

As quietly as possible, he left the room and creaked his way down the stairs.

Terry was asleep in the middle of the living room floor, but Booter's couch was empty. Sickly padded silently into the kitchen, where Booter was making breakfast. "Muh-mooorning," Sickly yawned. Booter jumped, whipped around, and aimed a spatula at him.

"Don't do that!" he muttered, embarrassedly. "Make some noise, or something. Bloody assassins."

"You on watch?" Sickly asked as he helped himself to a piece of toast.

"Yeah. Terry woke me up half an hour ago and went back to bed. He said Vel said you were sleeping in her room." He gave Sickly a significant look. "In her room," he repeated.

"No, Booter. Eveline and I are not . . . walking out together."

"It's not the walking part that I'm thinking about." He grinned, and Sickly gave him a dirty look.

"Don't even go there."

"I'm just saying, a dazzlingly beautiful woman, and a . . . bloke, forced to take refuge together, well, certain things might –" Sickly threw his toast at him.

They ate their eggs, bacon and toast in amiable silence, in that early-morning-not-really-ready-for-higher-brain-function kind of way that so often marks the early hours.

It was a little after noon.

"So what now?" Booter asked.

"The next step is to meet Kerry Adams and find out what she knows about all this. That's at midnight. For now, we let them sleep, and then I expect we'll do some practicing. It's been ages since I really trained."

"Yeah, you're looking a bit frail, now I come to think about it."

"Get stuffed," Sickly said, only half joking. There was a moment of silence.

"I never thanked you properly for coming to my, er, rescue, last night. Thanks."

"You're welcome."

"You didn't save me any?" Sickly and Booter both jumped. Vel was standing in the doorway of the kitchen, wearing a loose, white dress. Soft sunlight from the windows caught in her hair, giving her a rosy aura. Sickly found himself remembering pieces of last night's conversation, pieces that suddenly had his heart pounding. His eyebrow twitched.

"Did you both sleep all right?" Vel asked.

"Like a rock. On a bed of rocks," Booter grumbled as he set about making more food for Vel.

"I slept fine, but woke up to your --" Sickly stopped, he had promised not to reveal Vel's little equine secret. "Trap," he finished, lamely. "Right over the bed. It was quite surprising."

"Trap over the bed?" Vel sounded confused, "But the only thing above -- oh. Yes. I can see how the *trap* would have that effect."

"You guys sleep with traps over your beds?" Booter asked incredulously. "That's insane." Sickly gave Vel a knowing look. She tried to scowl back, but couldn't quite hide a smile.

As Sickly was washing up the dishes, a knock came at the door. Five raps, a pause, then four steady knocks, and finally a frantic tapping. The secret knock asking for help. Or a trick.

Vel jumped to her feet, yanking a length of chain from around her neck, at the end of which was a steel weight. She gripped it in both hands and began whipping the business end up to speed. Sickly set the plate down and drew a combat knife and a Number Six throwing knife. Booter was still staring towards the front door, a look of fear on his face.

"Stay here, Booter," Sickly and Vel ordered in unison.

"I'll check the mirrors," Vel said and hastened off toward the hall. Sickly crept into the living room and nudged Terry, who came instantly awake. Sickly gestured toward the door, and Terry nodded, pulling on his gauntlets. Vel entered the room and whispered, "All clear, just one, out front, as far as I can tell."

They set up in the hallway with Terry in the middle, Vel and Sickly at the sides. On the count of three, Sickly pulled the door open, and Terry and Vel charged out.

Jamie Webb stood on the front step, or, more accurately, slumped. Her dark braids were tangled and matted with blood and sweat. Her clothes stuck to her in patches where blood had caked over wounds. A barbed metal chain had tangled around her right leg, which oozed blood.

But she was alive. Sickly felt lightheaded from relief.

Vel's face drained of color at the sight of Jamie. "What did those pig-shaggers do to you?" she demanded.

Jamie smiled weakly as Vel and Terry helped get her inside. "Don't worry, dear, I lost them when I went over the river the second time." Booter came hesitantly into the hall then gasped at the sight of Jamie.

"What happened?" Sickly asked, trying to sound soothing.

"Yesterday, I got a . . . a Rose Notice." Vel's eyes widened and Booter gaped. A Rose Notice was a gentlemanly letter from one assassin to another, usually warning of an impending attack by the sender. It wasn't mandatory, and had often resulted in the reversal of killer and victim, but some old timers still held that it was the only honorable way to fight a colleague.

"Couple of assassins broke in. Helga Blitzkrieg and an older one I didn't recognize. Asked – ouch! Asked if I knew what Sickly took from *The Daily Piccolo*. Told them I didn't —ah! I didn't know what they were talking about. They attacked . . . I escaped out the other window. Ran all over Hambridge. H-had to find you, Sickly . . . Spent all night and day searching . . . had to find you. Warn you. I heard . . . on the street they say . . . dead. Sickly, dear . . . he's dead."

Jamie slumped sideways, still mumbling, incomprehensible with pain and fatigue.

Terry helped lift her to the bed in the living room. "Terry, can you and Booter treat her wounds?" Sickly asked.

"Yes. We need ta help Jamie," Terry stated. Booter was already kneeling, his sleeves rolled up. Quicker than Sickly had ever seen him move, Booter began stripping away the metal chain on Jamie's leg, easing out each barb with measured precision.

"Terry, get me some bandages," Booter ordered, and Terry hastened off.

Seeing that Jamie was in good hands, Sickly said, "Vel, you and I are going out."

"What? Where?" Vel demanded, still clutching Jamie's hand in her own.

"To get information. Something happened last night. They killed someone, and Jamie risked her life to tell us."

"You're right, Sickly." She bent to Jamie, and whispered, "You're going to be fine, luv."

"Sickly, be careful," Booter warned, still not looking up from his work.

No need to tell him twice. Or even once.

The rain didn't keep the Hambridgers from their daily business, but it did hurry them. And there was something else that Sickly, as a denizen of this city, sensed. People did not simply hurry. They *slunk* through the streets. They glanced nervously about. It wasn't just the weather that soaked into Sickly's clothes and made him glad of the exercise as they traversed the roofs. Something had happened, and it was making Hambridge uneasy.

Sickly breathed a sigh of relief when they finally got to the south end of News Street. They climbed down a drainpipe into a nearby alley and emerged onto the main thoroughfare.

Assassins normally got a wide berth when they went out in public, but today Sickly and Vel seemed to actually repulse people by their physical presence on the street. Even a group of Kaldrian tourists, wearing floral-printed shirts over sandal-length *thaubs* and *abayas*, glanced up and then hurried away at their approach. "That can't be good," Sickly said and Vel nodded. As they moved through the crowd, a bubble of space and silence surrounded them.

Sickly pointed and led them over to a hot dog salesman, a sure source of street gossip.

The young man stood shivering in the rain and holding a newspaper over his cloud of curly black hair. He bore the stoic stare of a hot dog man on a hard day. That was, right up until he noticed Sickly and Vel walking towards him, at which point he got the kind of hunted expression people wear when they are approached by tax collectors and there is nowhere to run.

"What's happened? What's going on?" Vel demanded, as they neared.

"Um, what do you mean, guv? There's lots of things been happening. It's the third straight week of the cabbage shortage, an' Lord Salsa's dog went missing yesterday, an' Lady Ironside is making a new law in the House of Uncommons, an' someone's mum knitted the biggest sock on record, an' there was a fire in the Alchemists' Guild, *again*, an' —"

Sickly cut him off. "She meant why's everyone acting like this?"

He stared hard at Sickly, and then his eyes went wide. "Wait, you're the one with that —that dog!" Sickly raised an eyebrow at him. He quailed. "Well, cos of, er, well . . ." His eyes darted left and right in a desperate search for help, which came up lacking, "Cos they say Lord Reiker's been assassinated, guv." He squeezed his eyes shut at the mere mention of this.

"You don't think we wanted to hear that first?" Vel asked, voice dangerously low.

He opened one eye. "Begging your pardon, miss, but I thought you already knew, what with you being an assa— er, you know," he trailed off, looking guilty. "Want to buy a sausage? Special discount on account of the tragedy and you not bringing that dog ever again?"

To the man's great relief, Vel and Sickly left, to have a hurried discussion under an awning which was suddenly empty of passersby.

"Lord Reiker? Assassinated?" Sickly said.

"It makes sense. If they've got assassins in position everywhere else, then they'd surely go for the Hambridge throne." Vel pointed out. "This has all been about gaining power over the city, right?"

"But only another Reiker can succeed the last."

"Don't be naïve, Sickly. Whoever succeeds Lord Timothy Reiker will be a puppet. It's all been about controlling the throne."

"That doesn't make sense. If it was just about the Hambridge throne, why did they bother to have assassins take over everywhere? And why are they so interested in Bradley Wells' notebook? I think they're planning something bigger. I just hope Jamie was able to hide the keys to the codes."

Vel bit her lip, thinking. "This is bad, innit, Sickly? If they've staged a successful coup, they've won, haven't they?"

"Not if we're still around. We know the truth, and we have the notebook. And Kerry Adams is still alive, since she passed us the note at the Bilgewater Tavern."

"That could have been a trap, to lure us to that alley where they'll shoot us all. Don't forget they found Quentin Verk, even without that book. Maybe they found Adams, too."

"It's a risk we'll have to take. We don't have many other choices."

"We could run." Her voice was so soft, Sickly could barely hear it.

"Oi! Boyo!" Sickly and Vel turned, their hands flying to concealed weapons. Mr. Stashcrumb was ambling up the street, wearing a truly horrific knitted cap with a bobble on the end, and an expression like a mule's arse. He was being dragged along behind Crowbar, and leading the other dogs. "Late? Again? You're fired, you hear me!" Vel gave Sickly a look of absolute confusion, and Sickly couldn't stop his eyebrows from rising.

"Mr. Stashcrumb, the dogs, yes. I'm sorry," he said, adopting the neutral tone of an employee ready to weather the storm of the boss' anger.

"Sorry doesn't begin to cover it! You're sacked! You're through!" A bony finger was jabbed into Sickly's chest. Crowbar took a step toward Sickly. "Chsh," Stashcrumb chided. "He's mine." The dog snorted, gave Vel a cursory glance, and then began nosing his way toward the hot dog man, who appeared to be wetting himself.

"Mr. Stashcrumb, I'm afraid I'm going to be putting my dog walking business on hold for a while. I'm having . . . financial troubles," Sickly invented. The old man looked him over appraisingly, and his expression, for once, softened.

"Don't be too hard on yourself, boyo. You did good work – once you finally showed up, that is. If you ever start up for business again I'll consider rehiring you. I'm letting you off easy, this time. One time deal. And . . . if you's ever need a little help, you can come by me house in Eel Park." Sickly's eyebrows shot up in utmost surprise. "But don't think that entitles you to come by whenever you want!" he clarified. "We are not friends!"

"Yes, Mr. Stashcrumb."

"And don't be fresh!"

"Yes, Mr. Stashcrumb." But the old man was already wrenching Crowbar away from the cowering vendor and hobbling off, up the street.

"What the hells was all that about?" Vel asked.

"That is an excellent question."

"Glad you are back," Terry stated, lowering his spiked gauntlets.

"Any problems? How's Jamie?" Sickly asked worriedly as he and Vel crossed the threshold of her house.

"No problems. Jamie is hurt, but doing ok. We took care of her. Come see."

Jamie still lay on Terry's bed in the middle of the living room floor, but her wounds had been cleaned and bandaged neatly. All things considered, she looked a lot better. Her head was propped up on a pillow, but she was still asleep. Booter knelt beside her, a wet cloth in one hand, his sleeves rolled up.

"What are you doing, Booter?" Sickly asked, bewildered. Booter colored.

"You know," he mumbled, "when someone's hurt someone else always seems to be dabbing their forehead with a wet cloth. I thought I might as well do it." Sickly raised his eyebrows. "She still hasn't come round for more than a couple of seconds, and each time she was delirious," the young thief added.

"Thanks for looking after her, and thanks to you too, big guy," Sickly said. "Lord Timothy Reiker is dead. Assassination, they say." Everyone was quiet for a moment.

"Then what are we doing?" Booter's voice was small as its owner.

"We're still going to meet Adams. I'm still trying to solve this murder."

"What, the murder of Bradley Wells?" Booter scoffed. "I'm sorry, but it's a bit pointless now, don't you think?" He swished the cloth in a bowl of water and reapplied it.

"I think it's more important now than ever. Whoever this murderer is, they've just gained power. We've seen their methods. They kill people who get in their way. What do you think that'll be like when that person runs the city? I haven't the slightest clue, and that scares me even more. That's why we need to find them. We can, and we will." He tried to sound confident, aware that they were all looking at him.

"Sickly, you're such a romantic fool." Vel sounded resigned, and Sickly's heart dropped. "But they hurt Jamie. I'm in." His eyebrows rose.

"I will help too," Terry agreed.

"You're all mad, but . . . but I'll follow you," Booter said, looking a little green. His hand fled to the copper pendant at his neck.

"Now that that's decided, if you're going to be of any use in combat, you'll need some practice," Vel announced, in a business-like tone. "Sickly, follow me." She led him down the hall, past the kitchen and bathroom and through a far door.

The room looked like a training hall transplanted straight from the Dalton College, replete with weapon and armor racks, target dummies, padded floors, and even a small climbing wall inset with spikes and traps to make it more interesting. As Sickly gazed about, impressed, Vel crossed to a hand-carved weapon rack and pulled down a set of blades.

"Since you favor throwing knives, we'll start with those. Though if I were you, I'd just take a crossbow."

"I like knives better. With a crossbow, I might hurt someone." His eyebrow twitched sarcastically.

Vel set her jaw. "Right This is going to be harder than I thought. For both of us, apparently." Sickly took hold of a knife, turned toward a target, and tried to remember his training. He pulled his arm back, and let the knife fly, soaring end over end, in a beautiful trajectory.

It bounced off the wall a good three feet from the target. "Again," Vel ordered. He tried again, and this time it hit the target pommel-first and bounced off. "Again." Sickly glared at her, but she glared right back, her arms folded in determination. Sickly gritted his teeth and threw again. It hit the wall several feet from the target and stuck. "Again."

Five minutes later, he had collected the scattered knives twice, only a few of which had landed in the target. He was improving, it was true, but not nearly quickly enough, by Vel's standards. He tensed his arm, ready to throw, when she said, tiredly, "Stop. This isn't working. Your arm is too high, and you need to breathe out when you throw." Sickly nodded and tried this. The knife hit the target handle first. "Better, but you're still not getting the spin right." She came over and grasped his throwing hand.

A thrill coursed through his body at her touch, like static electricity, but a thousand times better. He had to fight hard to concentrate on what she was saying as she shifted the angle of the knife, and how he was holding it. ". . . and you want to think about how far away the target is. You remember this, don't you?" He nodded, focusing solely on the knife, and definitely not on how close she was to him. She pulled his arm back in slow motion, guiding his wrist movement. "There. That's where you want your hand to be. Now try again."

As the afternoon progressed, Sickly became more confident in his knife-throwing skills. He was hitting the target nine times out of ten, and getting the knife to stick, blade first more often than not. It wasn't perfect, but it was better than nothing. Eventually, Vel had him switch to practicing his close combat skills, with both knife and short sword. "I don't want to tire you before tonight, so we'll go easy, got it?" she said, as she readied her own swords.

By the time they took a break for dinner, Vel had beat the living hells out of him. She had spent a full hour raining blows on his defenses, bruising every inch of him with their padded training weapons. Sickly staggered out into the hallway and collapsed, drenched in sweat, his limbs shaking. Vel called after him in a voice of perky maliciousness, "One more round? I'm sure you'll do better *this* time!"

Booter poked his head out of the kitchen. "Oi! Would you keep it down, we're – Sickly, what are you doing?"

Sickly grasped at Booter's legs from where he had fallen. "Take me away from all this," he pleaded.

Booter's normally worried face broke into a rare smile, and he laughed out loud, "Okay, but you'll owe me, Sickly. Dinner's ready!"

Booter and Terry had made a hearty stew from provisions in Vel's larder. As they sat down to eat, Booter asked, "What's the plan for tonight?"

"Vel and I will bail out Billys, and the three of us will go to meet Kerry."

"I want ta come," Terry sounded a little hurt that he had been left out again. Sickly looked at him, feeling guilty.

"I know, big guy, but Jamie isn't going anywhere fast, and you're the best one to protect her. You and Booter need to look after her, so that we'll all be at full strength." Terry still looked upset, as if they were back in college, and he and Sickly were the last to be chosen for teams; Sickly because he didn't put much effort into the games, and Terry because everyone thought he was big, and slow, and stupid. Which he was, a little, but in a nice way. He didn't deserve this, but Sickly needed Vel by his side. She was the strongest of all of them.

"So, I'll be here?" Booter said. It looked like he didn't know whether to sound happy or disappointed about this fact.

"Yeah, help Jamie."

"You already have, dear," came a voice from the doorway. Jamie was standing there, a little shakily, but a bit more color had returned to her russet cheeks.

"How do you feel, luv?" Vel jumped to her feet but paused. A look passed between her and Jamie. Then they both grinned. Vel leapt forward and nearly tackled Jamie with a hug.

"Easy, you! I feel like shite, and I lost my job, but —"

"But at least I'm not a gods-damned nob," Vel said, joining in the end of the old rhyme. They grinned at each other. Jamie turned to the others, her laugh quickly stifled. "I'm better. Much better. Thanks, Terry. And thanks, Thumbs." Sickly was the only one to notice Booter wince.

"What happened?" Sickly asked.

"Two highly trained killers came after me. What did you think happened?" Her face twisted in consternation. "Sickly, dear, Lord Reiker's been assassinated!"

"We know," Vel said, sounding tired.

"You know? You mean I ran all over the city, chased by assassins, to get you vital information, and it was all for nothing?" For some reason, she sounded put out. She came and sat down in Sickly's vacated chair, and Sickly placed a bowl of steaming broth before her.

"No! We wouldn't have found out without you. And more importantly, you survived." She huffed, but looked happier. "Here, drink this."

"Thank you, dear." Jamie took a spoonful of stew, and smiled. "This is good, innit! Vel didn't make it." She winked at Vel, who scowled. "So who . . . ?"

"Me," Booter said, almost inaudibly.

"Really? Well thanks, Thumbs." He shifted uncomfortably, and Sickly gave him an apologetic shrug.

"I got those codes hidden, dear. That's what all this is about, innit?" Sickly nodded and felt a weight lift from him. "Guess you were right about that plot after all." He twitched his eyebrows, and she gave him a rueful smile. They quickly filled her in on all the events she had missed in the last day. "Have you been able to narrow down the list of suspects? Either for the murder of that nob or whoever's behind all this?"

"Well . . ." Sickly hadn't had time to consider the suspects since yesterday morning. "No. I mean, Sable Levania might have murdered Bradley Wells . . . but he's a Dalton *graduate*, he's got money, titles, and land already. What more does he need?"

"Hang on a minute," Jamie interjected, "you said Wells thought this person wants to be the power behind the throne. Joanna took some big contracts over the last month, and rumor has it her mother, Lady Ironside, is making a move to take over the whole Merchants' Guild."

"You're right," Sickly said. "I asked Billys to check into it for me, but he got arrested."

Jamie gave him a patronizing look. "Sickly, dear, you sent Billys. What did you expect?"

"But he knows Joanna!"

"That's what I meant, dear."

"I guess we'd better go and bail him out then," Vel grumbled.

CHAPTER 18

Raft Street was in the middle on a scale of Tumult Hill to so-close-to-Murktown-you-could-smell-the-corpses. Therefore the Raft Street Watch House was not staffed by the shiny, going-to-the-top officers of the Main Watch House, nor was it crewed by the meanest, ugliest and most cutthroat guards, many of whom were separated from murderers only by the width of a silver badge. Symbolically silver, in most cases, so that it wasn't pawned for cheap beer. Instead, the watchpersons of Raft Street were simple coppers, through and through, patrolling their beats and keeping the Reiker's peace because it was their duty.

As a rule, assassins didn't sully their social class by interacting with guards. The Watch didn't investigate assassination, and the assassins only killed the people they were paid to kill. That did not mean, however, that the Watch and the assassins got along. The assassins viewed them as little more than an impediment to their jobs, and the watchmen saw the assassins as nothing but glorified murderers with a loophole in the law.

But, put one toe out of line, mess with an officer, and that loophole became a noose because they came down hard on assassins in revenge for all the upturned noses they had stared up over the years.

Sickly and Vel knew this, and therefore approached the Raft Street Watch House cautiously, at street level, and with their hands obviously visible. Watchmen who stayed alive as watchmen had to be devious enough to deal with the Thieves' Guild, smart enough not to tangle with the assassins, and steel enough to track down real killers.

A big man wearing a dented but well-maintained breastplate stood at the door, eyeing their approach. He had a good face for being a copper. It was large and blank, and betrayed nothing of what he was thinking. It was a little like Sickly's face, except that Sickly couldn't turn it on and off. "Evening," the guard said carefully, when they got near enough that he was sure they weren't just passing by.

"Good evening," Sickly replied. "We're here to see a friend."

"Official business is it?" His tone was as flat as Sickly's.

"No, he really is a friend. He's been arrested."

"We've only got one person in the cells tonight, and I know you aren't looking for him."

"Why's that?"

"Because no one would ever be friends with him."

"That's Billys. Can we at least get in to see him?" The man seemed to give this some thought.

"You are free to enter a watch station. It is, after all, a public building." Sickly and Vel started forward. "However, we will be running . . . scheduled maintenance in a quarter of an hour, so you'll have to clear out by then." Sickly nodded.

"All right then." The man made no move to allow them past.

"Unfortunately you are not allowed to carry weapons inside the premises; you will have to leave them with me." They both let out exasperated sighs.

"It'll take all night to hand you all of them! Let alone fifteen minutes," Vel complained.

"Just give me your visible weaponry and don't even think

about getting smart with the rest of it, because I can tell you that that would be very . . . dumb."

Sickly shrugged and handed over a few knives and his short sword. Grumbling, Vel gave the man her crossbow, her butterfly swords, and a few other objects obviously recognizable as weapons. The guard nodded at them, and they walked inside. Sickly noted a weathered carving of Drasilla's scales in the woodwork of the doorframe as he passed the threshold.

If it was true that crime did not pay, apparently neither did being a watchman. The interior of the watch house was shabby, all peeling paint and worn, creaky floorboards. They walked into a large room which served as both a lobby and an office. Half a dozen coppers sat at rickety tables, bent over paperwork, trying to work out where to put the punctuation. Apart from them, a sergeant sat on a stool behind a desk with a duty roster, a couple of constables sipped tea in a corner, and a bunch of off-duty men and women were coming out of a back room, looking as if they'd had a long, gritty, and above all, tiring, day.

At the arrival of two assassins however, all work in the room ceased, and every head turned toward them. It was more than a little unnerving. "We're looking for Billys, that is, Williams Kid," Sickly said, his voice small in the silence. All of the watchmen were glaring at them.

"Are the two of you assassins?" asked a constable, making it perfectly clear that the only answer which could defuse the situation was 'no.'

"Yes," Vel said, before Sickly could come up with a lie. Mentally, he groaned. The glares from around the room intensified. If anger was heat, their rain-wet clothes would have been steaming.

"Look, we're just here to bail out Mr. Kid, we're not on official business," Sickly tried.

Luckily, the sergeant chose that moment to bark, "Get on with it, you lot." The watchmen, with some muttering, went back to their activities, but kept glancing up at Vel and Sickly. The sergeant eyed a wall clock. "Bail for the prisoner Williams Kid has been posted at five hundred dollars." Sickly and Vel glanced at each other.

"Is he really worth five *hundred* dollars?" Vel asked dubiously.

Sickly lowered his voice. "We need to know if he found anything on the Martinez family. And we'll need him tonight to meet this spy. Is it worth it to leave our backs unprotected?"

Vel quirked an eyebrow. "We're talking about Williams Kid, Sickly."

"He's a git, I'll grant you, but come on, Vel. I swear I'll pay you back for this and the armor once it's safe to go back to my flat." Vel narrowed her eyes but eventually opened her bag and gave the Sergeant a receipt to her bank. Sickly didn't want to think about confronting the barristers at Kharnassi and Rolls, but he wanted to be a burden to Vel even less. Maybe he could write it off as a business expense, now that he was technically doing work related to assassination.

The sergeant made a show of looking the note over, but nodded stiffly. "That seems to be in order. However, since this man was arrested in connection to a possible murder case, there is a certain amount of paperwork which needs to be filled out before I transfer custody." He produced a sheaf of papers.

"Would you just tell us what it boils down to?" Sickly pleaded. The man smiled coolly.

"In a nutshell, if he goes around killing, stealing or participating in other illegal activities, it's your head on the line. She won't get her money back until the bailee shows up on the court date and all proceedings are dealt with." Sickly shrugged and put his name, address and signature on various pages of the document as quickly as possible. "Very well. Constable Ramirez, Constable Dean, escort these . . . citizens," a word which sounded, in the mouth of the Sergeant, remarkably like the words bottom feeding murderers, "to cell number one." He dismissed his men with a salute, and Sickly and Vel followed in the wake of the two officers.

They left the lobby through a door in the back left wall, proceeded down a corridor and entered a small anteroom. Constable Ramirez spoke briefly with the warden, who rose from a chair behind a desk, took out a ring of keys, and moved smartly to a heavy oaken door. The warden unlocked this door, which allowed Vel and Sickly to step through into a stone cell block. Billys slouched in the first cell to their right.

He already had a visitor.

A young woman wearing a breastplate, chainmail, and badge leaned against the bars outside Billys' cell, and the two were conversing animatedly. She had short black hair and a pretty face, and was about as tall as Billys. At Sickly and Vel's approach, however, the unlikely pair looked up. "Finally came to bail me out, have you?" Billys said, by way of greeting.

"Yes," Sickly said flatly.

"Well, good."

"Care to introduce me to your friends, Mr. Kid?" the young woman said politely.

"This is Sickly and Eveline," Billys said offhandedly. "Sickly, Eveline, meet Anemia Cassidy." Sickly bowed a little awkwardly, and Vel nodded. The watchwoman returned Sickly's bow, equally awkward. The Warden unlocked the padlock on Billys' cell door, and the assassin stepped out.

"You're welcome," Sickly said, in response to gratitude that seemed unlikely to come. "Now, we need to get going, Billys."

"No," Billys said, and Sickly frowned. "I'm staying here."

"Why would you want to stay here?" Vel sneered, finally speaking.

"Because Ms. Cassidy and I are going to the dance together." Billys' cheeks flushed, but he also looked very proud. Silence met this announcement.

"What?" Sickly asked, after an awkward moment.

Anemia smiled shyly, and said, "It's been bad recently with one thing and another, so me and some of the constables organized a bit of a fundraiser for the Watch Widows and

Orphans Fund. Our captain's been very stressed, and it's his birthday today, so we decided to turn it into a sort of party to raise morale. Since Mr. Kid is our only prisoner, I thought it would only be fair to invite him to join." Sickly and Vel took a moment to digest this. Sickly thought back to his conversation with Billys. It still seemed impossible that any woman, let alone one as pretty as Anemia, would be interested in Billys.

Sickly took Billys' shoulder and steered him down the corridor, leaving Vel and Anemia to stand around awkwardly. "Listen," Sickly began, "that plot I told you about is real. Yesterday, I was almost assassinated in the park, and since then I've been trying to survive and find out who's behind all this. Sometime last night, Lord Reiker was assassinated, and the murderer, whoever it is, has taken over. We need your help." Billys looked, for once, a little stunned, but then rallied.

"No, Sickly. You said if I talked to Joanna about Wells' death you'd help me with Anemia. And now you're ruining my chances with your stupid paranoia!"

"Hold up a minute, you talked to Joanna? What did she say?"

Billys shrugged offhandedly. "Not much. But Lady Ironside is definitely up to something big in parliament. Joanna said to stay out of it or we'd be sorry."

"No kidding. She was one of the assassins who tried to kill me!" Billys looked shocked.

"Joanna? Really? Well now I'm glad I stuck up for you. You're welcome, by the way." Sickly lifted his eyebrows in surprise. "But I'm going to this dance whether you like it or not." Sickly opened his mouth to protest. "Don't you raise your sodding eyebrow at me!"

Sickly knew they needed Billys. Terry and Booter were dedicated to protecting Jamie and the house. Even Vel wasn't a match for an ambush set by a large group of assassins. "How long is this dance?" he asked quickly.

"I don't know, a couple of hours," Billys said, taken aback.

"Billys, if we go to this dance thing for a few hours first, will you come with us?" Billys eyed him thoughtfully.

"Okay," he said at last. "But don't you dare mess things up for me with Anemia!" Sickly raised his eyebrows in a gesture meant to convey that Billys didn't need Sickly's help for that. They walked back to Vel and Anemia.

"Vel, we're staying for the dance." Vel opened her mouth, but Sickly forestalled her argument by saying, "We'll be warm, dry, and safe for a few hours, and then we'll be on our way before midnight. That is, if it's all right with the Watch." Anemia bit her lip, looking unsure.

"Well, you are friends of Billys. I can talk to the captain, if you like."

"That'd be great, thank you."

Anemia led the way back through the cell block door, nodded to the warden who closed it behind them, and then through a passage which opened onto an indoor drill yard, currently cleared of equipment so that it was now just a large, open space. Watchmen were milling around at the edges of the room, clearly waiting for the party to begin.

The low buzz of talk which had permeated the room ceased when Anemia and the three assassins entered. The watchmen were glaring at Sickly and Vel. One even spat on the ground.

Anemia marched straight up to the watchmen who had spat, and, in steely tones, barked, "Constable Grant!" The man looked shocked at her sudden rage. "If I see you do that again I will report you for willfully defiling Watch property!"

"But they're assassins, corporal," Constable Grant managed.

"What about it, constable?"

Grant's surprise hardened into sullen anger. "Didn't you organize this charity thing? You know about Captain Matthews of the palace guard! Whole patrol wiped out by assassins. I used to go drinking with some of them! Chu was a friend, corp! And we get stood down over it? You can't tell me that's right. And it was their kind that done it!" His finger scythed towards Sickly, Vel, and Billys.

"So what? Do you know it was those three in particular? No, you don't. We're the Watch, not the army! That means we need evidence before anything else."

"Come off it, corp! They're wearing assassin's clothing," the luckless Grant mumbled.

"I don't care. I'm wearing my official Watch uniform, but I am not on duty. Are you on duty, constable?"

"No, corporal."

"Well then, constable, as you are not on duty, and as they are not, as it were, on duty, I don't see the problem. Now clean that up." She gestured at the saliva on the floor.

Sickly's eyebrows rose. He had taken her to be a rather shy young woman, but clearly there was more to her than met the eye.

Talk was beginning again, and the accusatory glares had fallen away in the face of Anemia's outburst. She turned back to them. "Sorry about that. Sometimes being in the Watch is no picnic."

"It's not a laugh being an assassin neither," Billys said importantly and Anemia laughed.

"I'm sure," she said smiling. Sickly shook his head. He didn't know what tiny sliver of charisma she saw in Billys, but it probably indicated that she had microscopically good vision.

They stood around in that time-honored awkward way that is unavoidable at the beginning of large social events, making small talk about Anemia's work, and slyly dodging questions about their own. It was dangerous to give away casual information to a copper, even one off duty.

Eventually, a large man in a worn grey suit appeared. He had black hair shot with grey and a large, waxed mustache. His face was weathered but handsome, with a cast to his eyes that told Sickly he had seen it all, and it had not been family friendly. He frowned as he walked over to them, never a good sign in a policeman. He was probably compiling a mental list of all the offenses he could charge them with.

"Father," Anemia began, to Sickly and Vel's shock and horror, "would it be all right to invite Mr. Kid and his two friends to the dance?" Anemia's father, the captain of the Raft Street Watch House, turned his gaze to Billys and looked him up and down, but mostly down. He frowned, then looked into Vel's eyes, and the frown lines deepened. Finally, he turned to Sickly.

The iron grey eyes drew Sickly in for a startlingly long time. In spite of his blank expression, the captain appeared to be reading him like a billboard.

Sickly managed to drop his eyes, and saw, to his astonishment, that the man was holding out a hand. Sickly grasped it, to his immediate regret. Mr. Cassidy could have crushed a fistful of mixed nuts into granola with ease. Sickly was glad he couldn't wince. "Captain George Cassidy, Hambridge City Watch, Raft Street Branch," he said formally.

"Sickly Dodger, part-time dog-walker." At this the captain raised his eyebrows, but turned to Vel.

"A pleasure to meet you, madam. George Cassidy."

"Eveline Lucrezia." Sickly noted he didn't crush her hand as he had Sickly's. Instead, he bowed politely and kissed her extended fingers.

"Father," Anemia muttered, embarrassed. The captain turned to Billys, and his eyes narrowed. The temperature in the room dropped palpably.

"And I already know you, Kid."

"Yeah, see if I care, Cassidy." George Cassidy turned stiffly and clapped his hands once, bringing the assembled members of Hambridge's finest to organized, if poorly washed, attention.

"All right lads, you're just as tired as I am, so I'll keep it short. I know it's been bad, these past couple of weeks. Commander Merc," he paused as if displeased by the name, "is leading investigations into Lord Reiker's death. That leaves the rest of us stretched thin on the streets keeping the peace for his nephew,

Lord Scoke Reiker. The best thing we can do right now is our jobs. That means keeping the peace, upholding the law, making sure people are protected from themselves.

"You've all got an old mum out there, or maybe a sister or a grandfather, and they need protecting." He paused and fidgeted with the hem of his suit. "But see, it's like this. People are scared, people are hurt, people are angry. And all those people out there, the ones who'd sooner shove a brick through your skull as look at you, well, they've all got an old mum too. That could just as easily be you out there on the street, furious and with good reason. So you'd best think twice about how you treat 'em, or you'll be out on your ear faster than you can blink. We're coppers, not soldiers, understand?"

The assembled watchpersons stood absolutely quiet.

"I won't lie to you, we've got our work cut out for us. We've got no room for error. Too much work and too few good coppers to do it. Let us remember those who dedicated their lives in service to Hambridge." He listed off the names of Captain Matthews' entire squad, and led them in in a moment of silence. Sickly, Vel, and Billys shared awkward glances. The captain went on, "And let us remember those they left behind." He withdrew a crisp note from his wallet and placed it in a collection tin labelled 'Watch Widows and Orphans Fund.' There was a murmur of assent from the crowd and a queue formed at the tin. Sickly and Vel stood well back, though surprisingly Billys joined Anemia in the line.

"But tonight is also a chance to relax a little, before it gets real bad. And, of course, to celebrate my fifty-fourth birthday. Thank you to everyone who sent me a card detailing just how young I look for my age, you bunch of bootlickers." There were titters from the crowd, little hisses of steam from a pot ready to boil over with stress. "And since you're all coppers, every one of you to the core, there'll be lots of free beer!"

The tense crowd exploded into relieved cheers and applause. Music struck up from a three piece band with an accordionist, a fiddler, and a dog that howled along to the rhythm. The men and women of the Watch swarmed the large kegs of social lubricant and the buffet table which displayed many of Hambridge's signature dishes: Last Week's Fish Stew, Crab Bread, Allpork Sandwiches, Probably Salad, and without fail, yesterday's lunch.

After the initial five minutes of loud talk and alcohol consumption, a few people began to edge toward the dance floor with hopeful looks at potential partners. Sickly threw a sidelong glance at Vel, and saw that she was watching the whole display with distaste.

"Pardon me." Sickly turned and met the iron gaze of Captain Cassidy.

"Yes, captain?"

The man smiled thinly. "Mr. Cassidy will do."

"Yes, sir," Sickly said, carefully. "Can I be of assistance?"

"No need for all that. I just wanted to get to know one of my guests a little better."

"You let us stay because of me. Please don't try to deny it. I saw the way you looked at Eveline and Billys." The captain smiled to himself.

"You're quite perceptive, aren't you?"

"Why me? Did I look vulnerable?"

"Ten Gods, no. I know you young assassins carry all that Shling about you, and that you can use it, too. No, it wasn't that."

"Then what--"

"I look at Mr. Kid and see a petulant, bratty little child who'd like to think he stands atop the world. He wouldn't last a minute against some of the men in Murktown. But you assassins have everyone scared so much they don't bother you at all. But I can see right through him. And your friend, Ms. Lucrezia. She's got the eyes of a killer. A ruthless one, at that. I know the eyes of a killer, Mr. Dodger. Anyone who walks the beat long enough learns to tell. But I looked in your eyes, and saw a good man."

Sickly took a while to digest this. "So you don't believe a good person can be a killer?"

"I see it like this. Some of the ones we catch would gut you as soon as shake your hand. We've had a few real nutters, over the years. Who maybe should have died for what they did to little kids or young women. But we arrest them properly, if we can help it. My coppers don't kill. That's not their job, that's not their justice.

"But some folk who kill, well, maybe it's because they just couldn't see a different way out. They got too scared or desperate or lost and figured the problem would look smaller dead. But on the other side of things, the guilt makes it all the worse. This one woman who killed her husband. He'd been beating her, bad. One day she'd just had enough, I suppose. I sympathize, but it was still murder. I reckon throwing that kind of person in prison don't help much, except make it easier for folk like Lord Reiker and Lady Ironside to forget about 'em.

"And sure, she'd killed a man. But gods, we should have put a stop to him before it got that bad. I arrested her because I had to, by the law. But I don't think she was bad. There's been a thousand cases like that, where Drasilla's justice is greyer than a cloudy day, as they say. And here's me, a captain of the Watch."

"Are you a good man?"

The captain gave a bark of laughter. "You're sharp, Mr. Dodger. I can't say as I am a good man, but my daughter loves me, and my wife too, and I keep the streets safe. Well, safer, at any rate."

"I think that soon we may all have to make a choice of which to uphold more strongly. The law, or the good in people," Sickly said as diplomatically as he could manage. He knew he was in dangerous territory. Captain Cassidy seemed honest, but then, when was anyone what they seemed?

"So sharp you'll cut yourself." Sickly regarded the party, and the captain followed his gaze to Vel. "You may want to watch out for . . . sharp things, in the near future." Sickly turned his face directly to the captain.

"She's my friend. I trust her with my life."

"I believe you do at that. But you might want to ask her why you wouldn't trust her with someone else's. People don't kill without a reason." Sickly considered this.

"That's why I'm not an assassin. Like you said, I'm not a killer. But I'll do what's right."

"If I was you, I'd hold on to that belief very, very tightly."

"Captain!" someone called, causing Mr. Cassidy to look round.

"Excuse me, Mr. Dodger," he said.

"A pleasure, Mr. Cassidy." They shook hands, Sickly tried not to pay attention to the sensation of grinding finger bones. After the captain had gone, Sickly looked around for Vel, or Billys, or even Anemia. The latter were talking next to a small group of coppers, but Vel . . . ?

"Looking for me?" Sickly fought back the impulse to jump, and turned around slowly. There was Vel, smiling oddly at him.

It is said that it is easier to be brave when you must be so in front of a woman. Sickly now knew that this was not true, at least, not if you were trying to pluck up the courage to ask said woman to dance. He cleared his throat in an attempt to flare off some of the wild panic building inside of him.

It didn't work. His stomach heaved at the prospect of asking. What if she said no? What if she just wanted to be friends? What if it made things worse? And, oh gods not this, what if she said yes? And then his mouth took over while his brain watched in stupefied horror. "Would you, erm, you know, like to, uh, to pass the time, well, as it were, if you want to . . . um . . . dance?"

She gave him a pitying look. "Yes, Sickly." This solved one problem, rather unexpectedly to be sure, but presented him with a whole range of other metaphysical quandaries such as, *why* did she say yes? Was she taking pity on him? Did she just want to dance? Or was it about passing the time? Did he actually have a chance with her? Was he overthinking this? Was he under-thinking this? Could he actually dance? He couldn't remember. Where the hells was the exit?

Vel seemed to notice that he was getting nowhere fast, so she took him gently by the hand and led him to the dance floor, while his brain spun in ever more confused circles. For a few moments, Vel took the lead, eliciting much beery laughter from the surrounding crowd, but Sickly didn't even notice, because he and Vel were embracing. His whole body filled with a deep, rich joy he couldn't remember ever experiencing. His mind went blank which at least allowed him to take the lead during the next dance.

The Dalton College had taught them more than subtle slaughter. Palace-style dancing had been a popular class during their third year, and Sickly began to remember the steps as he and Vel spun and turned to the music. After his initial panic, he began to relax and enjoy himself. He raised his eyebrows at Vel, who smiled back at him.

They danced for what seemed like no time at all, and yet, as is the way of things, for an eternity as well. Every once in a while, Sickly caught sight of Anemia and Billys wobbling across the dance floor. Billys waltzed like a neurotic ferret clutching a greased time bomb.

Finally, Sickly and Vel slipped off the dance floor, their faces flushed from the exertion. They went to the drinks table, where Sickly poured himself a glass of water, and Vel got a stein of beer. Sickly raised an eyebrow, but she just smiled and downed it easily. He drank the water, watching the undulating rhythm of the dance. When he turned around, it was to find that Vel had disappeared, and he was alone.

Not sure what to make of this, Sickly made his way around the room, trying not to bump into the other people, listening to snippets of conversation. He found and ate a couple of lost-looking celery stalks at the buffet table, which had otherwise been picked cleaner than the bones of tourists to the Taffatiti Desert. By the clock on the wall, it was only a quarter after ten.

Sickly slipped past two women holding each other tenderly, around a group laughing at someone who'd taken a drunken spill, and over to Billys and Anemia. They were still talking, and, surprisingly, Anemia was still smiling. But Mr. Cassidy arrived first, his expression somewhere well south of friendly.

"Mr. Kid, I want a word with you about my daughter."

"Father!" Anemia exclaimed.

"I just want to have a little chat, man to," he sneered, "man."

"Oi!" Billys said, but Anemia cut him off.

"Since when do you decide anything for me, father? I've been washing my own clothes since I was eight!"

The captain looked nonplussed, but tried to rally, "Anemia, I'm not sure how that --"

"And do you know what else? I've been washing *your* dirty socks since I was *ten* because Mum had too many chores and you never help! Do you have any idea how much scrubbing it takes per sock?"

Mr. Cassidy opened and closed his mouth, looking as though he had been clubbed over the head by a haddock. "I, um, I've really no –"

"Exactly! So where do you get off telling *me* who I can and can't go out with?"

The captain tried to regain a little ground by sounding indignant. This was a mistake. "As your father, I have a certain responsibility –"

"Oh, you want to talk about responsibilities? How about washing the dishes after you come home? How about sweeping the fireplace? How about cleaning the house? Or going to market? Or darning your filthy socks? You want those responsibilities on top of being in the Watch? Because I've got them!"

"Nemi, calm down."

"No!" There were tears in Anemia's eyes, "Why do you hate him so much?"

Sickly looked around. The room had gone absolutely quiet. Every watchperson appeared to be engrossed in what they had been doing, and was therefore eavesdropping intently. "Anemia," The captain's voice was suddenly hard as when they had first met him, "we are not having this conversation here, understand?"

"Leave her alone!" This was from Billys. He shoved his way between Anemia and her father, and glared up at the captain. Billys was little more than half the captain's height and the man glowered down at him. "You got a bone to pick with me? I'm right here. Come on, if you think you're hard enough." Sickly internally winced.

The captain let out a laugh as warm and pleasant as a privy seat on a winter morning. "Can you really be that idiotic? To attack a watchman, on Watch property, in front of thirty officers who are itching to inflict some of the Reiker's Peace on you pompous, self-absorbed assassins?"

There was an angry stirring from the assembled watchpersons. They had been unwilling to pick sides in a matchup between Anemia and George Cassidy, but an assassin was an enemy they could unite behind. Constable Grant stood with his arms folded, wearing an expression of vindictive pleasure. Luckily, Billys remembered where he was, and who surrounded him. He still wore his sneer like a badge of honor, but he assumed a less combative stance.

"You're both being ridiculous!" Anemia said, in the tone of a mother who has just come upon two children fighting in the mud and is about to put her foot down.

"Face it, Kid, you're just an assassin. And in this room, in this place, that leaves you with nothing. Less than nothing. All you do is make people hate and fear you."

"Right, because no one hates and fears the Watch."

"Do I need to put you both in time out?" Anemia said, rolling her eyes, though she was largely drowned out by the testosterone roaring in their ears.

"Anemia deserves better than a man who only knows how to kill."

Billys bit his lip; it looked like the captain had won. "Nemi, come away from him," Captain Cassidy urged.

"Wait." Billys stuck his chin out, the old fire back in his eyes. "Play some music."

The band hurriedly set to their instruments, the dog crooning away in the background. The waltz plucked at the crowd's feet, urging them to move. The bow danced over the fiddle strings spinning notes and twirling them into the air. The accordionist stamped his feet in time with the beat of the song. The assembled watchpersons were just off-balance enough that they allowed Billys to pass. The short man with greasy, brown hair walked to the center of the room and . . .

Sickly blinked, and missed part of it.

Billys was dancing, but not in any manner taught at the Dalton College for Men in Black. Billys had begun to do back-flips, spins, rolls, and handstands to the rhythm of the music. The crowd watched, dumbfounded, as he turned a backflip, then a second, and landed with a flourish. Without giving himself a second to breathe, he dove to the floor, rolled, leapt and pushed off from the ground on one hand, spinning head over heels to land on his feet.

Billys stared at the captain defiantly. "Flashy, I'll grant you," Captain Cassidy grumbled, still glaring at Billys. The crowd looked expectantly at the pair of them, unsure now who to support. "Of course, a real ripper dances in jig time."

"Set to it then," Billys commanded. The band redoubled their efforts, striking up a capricious, lively tune. The notes capered through the air, the fiddler's bow flashing across the strings like a living thing.

Billys became a blur of rhythm as if possessed by the music itself. He spun like a leaf in a hurricane. He bent his body in shapes that made Sickly queasy. At one point he remained balanced on just his hands, legs thrust defiantly skyward, for fifteen seconds while his whole body undulated to the beat.

For almost a full two minutes Billys ripjigged through the room, his face red with concentration, hurling himself into the heart of the music. He became its physical incarnation. It wasn't long before even the most hardened and cynical watchman began to clap. As Billys turned his last flip, the applause built and built until everyone was stamping to the beat of the music. Billys stood there, his chest heaving, staring defiantly into the iron eyes of the captain.

George Cassidy looked around at the crowd of coppers smiling and cheering for the young man who had defied every expectation they had of an assassin. He shook his head and said, drily, "Nothing to see here, then. Move along." The assembled Watch let out a great roar of beery, relieved laughter. Some of the younger guards formed a circle and began to showcase their own ripping styles.

"What in the name of Thumbscale was that?" Vel asked, once again appearing beside Sickly.

"Don't look at me, he failed Intro to Palace Dance. Twice, remember?"

Billys bounded up to them. He was drenched in sweat, but smiled arrogantly at the turbid expression on the captain's face. "Anemia, would you like to dance?"

"Yes," she said. Without looking at her father, she followed Billys onto the dance floor.

"He's really not as bad as all that," Sickly said, feeling the need to add something.

"Loyalty is a fine trait, lad. Blind acceptance is not. I meant what I said, earlier. Merafey's devils could learn a few lessons in egotism and crassness from him."

"And you were right. Billys' foot has taken up permanent residence in his mouth, but he has his good moments. That was one of them."

"If you see another one coming, please alert me so that I might leave the room."

Sickly sighed, and tried a different tack. "It's clear you love your daughter."

"Of course."

"And you trust her?"

"She's already a better copper than I was at corporal. She's got twice the brains and a better grasp of the law than many a grey bearded officer, let alone our new commander. Of course I trust her. I'd trust her with my life."

"Then why don't you trust her to make her own decisions about who she likes?" The captain turned to face him, and once again Sickly tried not to shy away the intensity of his gaze.

"You've got me there, Mr. Dodger. I just don't like Kid."

"You don't have to. Let Anemia handle that part."

"Perhaps you're right." He turned back to the crowd of dancing coppers, and a wry smile spread across his face. "Look at them. Haven't seen them so happy in . . . well." He let out a bark of laughter, and Mr. Cassidy said, "That is some dance, Kid."

CHAPTER 19

It was a quarter to eleven when at last they convinced Billys that it was time to go. Vel had reappeared and helped Sickly win Billys over. He wanted to stay and keep dancing with Anemia, but Sickly and Vel were adamant, and eventually he allowed himself to be steered outside. He kept up a constant stream of dark imprecations as they retrieved their weapons and climbed to roof level. Vel led the way towards Olney Street. Sickly tried to ignore his growing anxiety over the meeting by looking out for enemies, and listening to Billys' threats.

"Billys, tell us again about Joanna and Annette Martinez?" Sickly asked to shut him up.

". . . and stuff it in the wrong end of a pig. What? Joanna? Oh. Look, she was pretty cagey about it. I asked her if she knew about the Foreign Minister, and she told me to stick it. Bloody rude, I thought. But she already knew about his murder, and I thought that was weird."

"Joanna wouldn't pick up a newspaper if her life depended on it. Too busy reading that trashy fashion mag Glarmour," Vel added.

"She's definitely got her nose to the ground. Maybe Lady

Ironside is making a power grab in parliament, like Jamie thought," Sickly mused. "Hopefully Adams has something on her."

They reached Olney Street with two minutes to go, found the burned building, and slunk across to the alley. They entered, after Vel scouted for attack, and peered into the darkness between houses. No one and nothing was visible in the gloom. They waited, alert for ambush. The more Sickly thought about it, the more likely it seemed that this was a set up. They had no way of knowing who had sent them the note. He tried to calm down, but the nervousness kept creeping up out of the pit of his stomach, infecting his mind with panic.

He jumped when the clock tower on Tumult Hill began to toll. "Mr. Dodger, I presume?" Sickly turned round so fast his cloak fanned out. Vel and Billys aimed crossbows into the darkness. "Please put those down, I mean you no harm."

"Out here, where we can see you, then," Vel ordered.

"But of course." A woman appeared from the shadows of the alley. She wore a loose, dark green tunic and hose that somehow managed to break up the edges of her form, so that she was difficult to distinguish from the gloom behind her. Everything she wore, from her boots to her gloves, was the same mottled dark green, not quite black.

Assassins wore black because it was traditional and stylish, not because it offered perfect camouflage. Undiluted black made you stand out against other shadows unless it was a moonless, cloudy night. This meant that Vel, Sickly and Billys, wearing head to toe midnight, could be seen by a trained observer. This woman in dark green was only visible because she allowed it.

Her hair was dark and pulled into a knot at the back of her head. Her face was covered by a half mask, something out of a masquerade ball, elegant and curved, fitting snugly around her eyes and forehead. The lower portion of her face was covered by a scarf the same color as the rest of her attire, though she removed this as she stepped forward. She had fine features and a small pointed chin. Her mouth was delicate and precise, and curled into a half smile.

"Are you Kerry Adams?"

"Among other names, yes. And please, lower those bows."

"We only have your word."

"Such a cynical world we live in." She sighed. "Very well. The white crow listens to the well of silence." Billys and Vel stared at her blankly, but Sickly remembered the note Bradley Wells had left for him at *The Daily Piccolo*. That was the correct phrase, and unless they wanted to be really picky, they would have to trust her.

"All right, that's Adams," Sickly said, and gestured for Vel and Billys to lower their weapons. "What do you have to tell us?"

"So direct, how refreshing," she said, with a small laugh. "I don't often get to the point this quickly in my line of work."

"Hurry up," Vel snapped. "We're wasting darkness." Adams' mouth turned downwards.

"Ask her about Lady Ironside," Billys whined.

"Tut tut. Today's youth and all that. Oh, very well. There is a plot against the city orchestrated by Hank Winderstint."

Vel and Billys' mouths dropped open. Sickly's stayed flat, but he raised an eyebrow.

"That pathetic excuse for a headmaster is trying to do us all in?" Billys exclaimed, loudly.

"Shut up, Billys," Vel hissed, then turned back to Adams. "Let me get this straight, Hank Winderstint, the old, *dead* headmaster of Dalton College, is the murderer?"

"Wherever did you get the idea that he was dead?" Adams scoffed.

"The paper said he resigned," Vel retorted.

"Yes, and?"

"The headmaster of the Dalton College only ever resigns posthumously!"

"I'm afraid that he, as they say, 'put one over on you.'"

Sickly interjected. "We thought it was Annette Martinez! Her daughter, Joanna—"

"Is working for Winderstint," Adams finished. "The elder Martinez may be turning a blind eye to her daughter's activities, I do not know. But she is not behind *this* plot."

"All right, so if Hank Winderstint is the man who's behind everything," Sickly allowed, "What's his plan? Why take over Hambridge with assassins?"

"He doesn't just want to rule it, but control it, every piece of it. He offered the younger assassins power they hadn't dreamed of. Positions as the heads of guilds or city offices they would have had to toil and scheme for years to achieve. Simon Digby was accelerated to Head Alchemist despite his ineptitude with reagents. Hannabelle Merc was offered command of the entire Hambridge Watch though she's never patrolled a city street. Winderstint is offering them a chance to make the rules, not just enforce them."

"Enforce the rules? You make it sound like the assassins are some kind of . . . of police force," Sickly said, thinking of the watch station they had just visited.

"They most certainly are, Mr. Dodger. They do not control the public, the workers, the masses. They control the authorities. They watch the watchers, and, when necessary, kill the watchers. They check the balances. They keep the politicians in place through reputation and merciless action. It's no accident that our matron, Drasilla, is the goddess of justice. Justice in all forms, not just that practiced by the courts.

"Hank Winderstint threatens to upset this balance, and use the assassins to gain control. But he doesn't just want power over Hambridge, or he wouldn't be after Wells' notebook. With the knowledge it contains, he could find all the Hambridge spies in every city on the continent and replace them with his assassins."

"So what? You spies aren't anywhere near as good as us, but everyone knows you'll kill when you need to," Billys sneered. Adams gave him a distasteful look.

"Spies are old hat. People expect us, even if they can't find us. But Winderstint wants to use the assassins' reputation, the fear they inspire in people, as a weapon against other nations. Imagine what he could do with a silent, invisible army that strikes terror into the hearts of everyone in every city."

"The other cities have assassins of their own, they won't go down without a fight," Vel objected.

"They already have. You assassins are good, but no one is a match for three or four others at once."

"Assassins don't work together like that," Billys argued.

"Nor are they supposed to assassinate people for power, rather than money. Yet here we are."

"And the other cities still follow rules like 'assassins work alone.' That makes them easy prey," Sickly guessed. Adams gave him a small smile.

"Very good. It happened here in Hambridge. Winderstint eliminated the older assassins here, the ones who would have objected to his plot. As cunning, as quick, as intelligent and deadly as they were, they were no match for a coordinated group."

"How do you know all this?" Sickly asked.

"Thumbscale, save me from stupid questions. What do you think I'm wearing all this for? A costume party?"

"Right, sorry."

"I've been watching, and listening, and investigating the bodies left behind, and bribing the low-level officials, those who see things but aren't important enough to kill. Wells had figured out some of it, and I've put as many extra pieces together as I can. My associate, Earl Watkins, was supposed to go to Lord Timothy Reiker with everything we'd compiled on Winderstint, however . . ." Adams sighed, "I haven't heard from him, and Lord Timothy was obviously killed."

"So what do we do? How do we stop him?" Sickly demanded, painfully aware of how exposed he felt. The night seemed to close in on them, shadows everywhere.

"This whole plot revolves around Winderstint. He is the spider at the center of the twisted web. You must kill him, at any cost."

"I'm sorry, but it's just not that easy," Sickly said, "First, I don't kill people."

"We do," Vel and Billys piped up.

"Secondly," Sickly continued, "the Hambridge Watch should handle this, if Winderstint murdered Lord Reiker."

"They assassinated him," Adams countered.

"No, they didn't. They didn't do it for money, and while I admit assassins kill people for power all the time, it's for someone else's power. Hank Winderstint did it for his own power, and that makes it murder."

"The Hambridge officers are bound by the law, a law which is written by the Reiker family and the politicians. Who do you think controls both?" Sickly groaned in frustration. "They can't touch Winderstint," Adams said. The shadows seemed to grow even longer, but Sickly tried to focus on Adams.

"Thirdly, how are we, a handful of people, supposed to take on Winderstint and this silent, invisible army you told us killed even the smartest assassins?"

"But you and your friends are not bound by the code of assassins either. You can be just as unpredictable as Hank Winderstint."

"I'm sorry, but that's not worth a lot," Sickly said.

"You have something they don't."

"What?" Sickly asked, skeptically. Adams opened her mouth, but did not speak. Sickly, Vel, and Billys waited on tenterhooks for her next counterargument, but it did not come.

A strange little moan escaped her lips, and she relaxed backwards.

Sable Levania removed the knife from the Spy's back, and allowed the corpse to fall to the ground. Adams' body was nothing more than chaff from which her life had been removed by Sable's scything knife.

"Thank you for drawing that spy into the open. She was by far the cleverest of the ones I've been briefly acquainted with." Sable spoke conversationally as he fastidiously cleaned his blade with a dark cloth. Billys and Vel took half steps backward, their expression shaken. Nevertheless, they pointed their crossbows at Sable. "Do you really think you could hit me?" He tossed the dirtied cloth nonchalantly aside.

Sickly couldn't even move. His mind reeled from the shock of how quickly Adams had died. Just like that. No more than a gasp.

"I'll take my chances," Vel replied coldly and took aim.

"You're here to kill us?" Sickly asked, dumbly. Just a gasp.

"Goodness me, no. I've been searching for this one." He gestured to Adams's corpse. "But since Munz failed to kill you, you've been marked as a target of opportunity to anyone who can find and assassinate you. Would you like to go one at a time or all at once?"

Sable did not smile. He simply stared at them with his head cocked to one side, curly black hair falling over his eyes. He almost looked innocent, with his pale, handsome face and a detached but interested cast to his eyes. "Eveline, would you like a rematch? A second chance, as it were?"

At these words, Sickly's reeling mind was snapped back into focus. Not Vel. Anyone but Vel. "And then what, Sable?" he asked, louder than he'd intended. "You kill us and then Winderstint makes you what? A duke? Sable Levania, Duke of Hambridge and professional murderer?"

"Mr. Dodger, if you had paid attention in history class, you would know that the House of Levania has held the title for centuries. Killing you is but a step on the long road ahead of us."

"A long road ending where? Ruling every city through fear and assassination?"

"Yes. But it isn't as bad as the spy made it sound." He cocked his head to the other side. "Have you been down on the streets of Murktown, Mr. Dodger?"

This was so far from what Sickly had expected, he answered without thinking. "No?"

"I have. I've walked its alleys, docks and abandoned jetties. It would be a place of magnificent industry if it weren't for the pestilence, the famine, and the death. Every day scores of people die, beaten and bloody, drowning in pools of their own filth, passing into the dark.

"And the politicians do nothing but talk. Countless human beings are wasted while those pasty old men sit and smoke their fat cigars and pat themselves on the backs for improving the world. You want to throw around the word murder? There are your true murderers. When we rule, there will be no arguing the cost-benefit analysis of saving a life. We will not talk figures. We will not negotiate net incomes. We will simply make the difference."

Sickly was stunned. He had never really thought about why Sable would kill, but there it was. "That's a noble ideal, to be sure," he said carefully, "but at what cost?"

"Any cost. I'm a bit of a historian, you see. And history helps put things in perspective. There are always rich people, and therefore, always poor people. The rich care only to remain rich, and the rest of the world is ground beneath their heels. But what would happen if one privileged man were to awaken and use his power to create, not destroy? To feed the hungry, to clothe the ragged, to heal the sick? If we must have a system of lords and peasants, let them be benevolent lords. Sadly, to challenge the momentum of our existing cycle, extreme measures must be taken. Surely you can see this? To that end I will assassinate men, women, and children. Does this satisfy you, Mr. Dodger?"

"Not quite," Sickly said, his voice flat. "You see, while I've been distracting you, two of my friends have snuck up to the rooftops and taken aim at you with Burlington crossbows. You might be able to kill all three of us," he gestured to himself, Vel, and Billys, "But even you, Sable, can't take on five of us all at once."

"You're bluffing," Sable stated with absolute confidence.

"Am I?" Sickly asked, face expressionless, voice flat, eyes unreadable.

"Yes. Because my associates will have found your two friends and killed them."

"And now you're bluffing," Sickly retorted. "You didn't come here with backup, Sable. It's not your style. You're the perfect assassin, and the perfect assassin works alone."

"I'm flattered. But if so, why are you hiding behind these two?"

"I'm not an assassin," Sickly replied. "I let myself have friends, and friends protect one another." And now, because Sickly was watching Sable very closely, he saw the briefest flash of doubt in those dark eyes. "Your move, Levania."

"If you really had the numbers to take me, you would have ordered them to kill me." Finally, Sable smiled. It was an unnerving, childlike grin.

"No. I don't kill people, not even self-justifying murderers like you. If you think you have to kill people to get what you want, then you're just as sick as those politicians. But I won't be the arbiter of your justice. Leave now." Sickly and Sable stared at each other for a long, silent moment, but Sickly had a poker face that would have left even the Thieves' Guild's best gambler cursing him for a stone.

"A most entertaining evening, Mr. Dodger. I do look forward to our next encounter," Sable breathed, eyes never leaving Sickly. With that he gave a shallow bow and ghosted back into the shadows of the alley.

"Sickly, what –" Billys began, but was cut off.

"Not now. Not while he could be watching. Get back to the house first. Billys, take rear guard. Vel, take point. Take the most convoluted route you possibly can." They retreated in silence, following Vel's path up walls, across rooftops, back down to alleys and side streets, and once even through a section of sewer. It was well after 3 o'clock in the morning when they finally slunk to the back door of Vel's house.

Terry met them at the door. "Hullo Sickly. Hullo Vel. Hullo Billys. How was your trip?" Vel and Billys turned to Sickly.

"Excuse me?" Vel asked, icily.

"What?" Sickly felt exhausted, he had never been so scared.

"Terry and Jamie weren't up there protecting us?!"

"Well, no," Sickly admitted, "But Sable didn't know that."

"Are you out of your bloody mind?" she shrieked, grabbing him by the shoulders. "You bet our lives that you could convince Sable Levania, the most dangerous assassin out there, that he was facing five-on-one odds?"

"Er, yes?" Sickly squeaked. Vel seemed to sag, as if all the air had been let out of her, and she released him.

"You're suicidal. Bloody suicidal," she breathed.

"Wait, you lied?" Billys asked, sounding half impressed, half angry. "Shite, Sickly, you lied to Sable Levania and got away with it?"

"I guess so."

Billys let out a huge laugh. "That's brilliant!"

At that point, the adrenaline wore off, and Sickly's legs became as limp as overcooked pasta. He slumped to the ground and lay there, trembling with fear and exhaustion. He had done it. He had saved all their lives, protected them against Sable Levania, without even drawing a knife.

"I don't feel so good," he mumbled.

"Terry, please get this fool to the beds in the living room," Vel said, sounding as if the night's events had accelerated her to the next age category. Terry picked Sickly up and carried him gently to the sofa bed. He helped Sickly take off his boots, the jacket, all his weapons and his socks, and then Sickly got into bed.

"Well done, Sickly," Terry whispered, and tucked Sickly in, like a huge, immensely strong mother. Then Terry blew out the lamp and left.

Consciousness plagued Sickly, his mind still running around in frantic circles, a mouse caught in a maze of possibilities. How had Sable found them? What were they to do apart from keep the notebook safe? How could they defeat Winderstint? What if Sable had called his bluff? What if they had all died because of him?

Dimly, he was aware that the others, Vel, Terry, Billys, Jamie, and Booter were discussing something in the kitchen, but he could only make out bits of it. ". . . never do that again . . . should we do? . . . what a laugh . . . come off it . . . better safe than sorry . . . *never* safe . . . that's why . . . look at the clock . . . with no . . . face it, it's impossible . . . we should . . . stupid! . . . shut up, Billys!"

Eventually, Sickly succumbed to sleep and dreams. He was in the Thieves' Guild, watching Booter dance with Lady Fingers, who kept stealing Booter's watch. Then Billys arrived, wearing a belled jester's cap. He and Sickly began to waltz around the dance floor, and suddenly, Billys had turned into Vel, and they were smiling at each other. Vel asked him something, but he had no reply.

But then Jamie and Terry came and the scene shifted to the graduation test at the Dalton College. Sickly was surrounded by his friends, who were all staring at him. They drew knives and began to fight each other. Sickly tried to stop them, but found he couldn't move or speak. Pain pierced his back and he awoke.

CHAPTER 20

Sickly was sore the next day. It was light out, and judging by the glare on the windows, a little after noon. He reflected on the poor hours kept by assassins and spies, and wished he was just walking dogs. It had all been so simple, getting up, going to work, walking the city. No fear of assassination, no pain other than that inflicted by Crowbar, no complicated silences around Vel when they were alone. He rubbed his eyes gingerly. His head pounded, and he felt weak, a headache coming on for sure. That and the old injury from graduation was twinging worse than it had in a month.

"Sickly!" some cruel and unthinking person shouted loudly into his ear, and was therefore Billys. Sickly groaned in response. "Rise and shine, sleepyhead! You've been out for hours."

"Not bloody long enough."

"I've decided I'm never playing poker with you, Sickly. Unless you really suck at it, but I don't think you would, because you bluffed Sable Levania." Billys prattled on, and Sickly cast a bleary-eyed glance around for his clothes. "I did laundry. Can you believe it? Eveline made me do laundry! Terry's socks are disgusting! And yours were no basket of lemons either. One day, I swear I'll get her back for this. Caestos help me, I'll – oh, yeah,

Eveline also said that you need to take a bath today because you're starting to stink. Between you and me, she's right. You smell like week-old fish left in the sun, covered in sewage, and doused with aniseed. You –"

Sickly grabbed Billys by the collar and pulled him down to eye level. "Shut up, Billys."

"Ok, sor-ry, you sure are grumpy in the mornings, aren't you?" Sickly narrowed his eyes and Billys lapsed into silence.

They spent that day training and recovering from their previous exertions. While Sickly would have liked to have Vel to himself again, Billys and Terry joined them. Booter and Jamie remained on the sidelines. Booter fussed about aimlessly, while Jamie buried herself in a book on poison-craft that Vel had been meaning to lend her.

Dinner that night was loud and happy with the six of them seated around the dining room table. Terry ate vast helpings of meat, salad, bread, and anything that was within reach. Billys flicked peas at everyone with his spoon until Eveline threatened to shove it up his left nostril. Booter laughed awkwardly and made forced attempts at conversation which everyone but Sickly ignored. Jamie and Vel gossiped about other assassins' romantic interests. Sickly tried hard to both ignore and eavesdrop on this conversation.

After dinner they cleaned up and then retired to the living room. Sickly sensed that this was the time when plans would be made, so he began. "I heard you lot talking last night. Any ideas?" Vel and Jamie shared a glance.

"Look Sickly, we know you want to save the city from Sable and Winderstint, but there's five of us, six if you count Thumbs, and he can't fight to save his life, or ours, so he doesn't count. Five assassins against Sable, Ulrich, Winderstint, and all the others. They have control of everything in the city. They're unbeatable." Jamie's tone was firm, but her face betrayed an apology.

"Not the spies," Sickly argued.

"Yeah, but if you hadn't noticed, there are fewer and fewer of them around, and they're no match for assassins," Billys pointed out. "Why don't we just burn the notebook and be done with it?"

"Bradley Wells was clear about that. If we burn it, then the next Spymaster of Hambridge won't have anything to go on. We'd be putting Hambridge in danger from other powers. Besides, I doubt they'd stop chasing us even if we did. Look, Adams said we have something they don't."

"What? What magical weapon do we have that can beat them?" Vel demanded.

"Well," Sickly demurred. "She didn't exactly say. Sable kind of killed her."

"And that's exactly what's going to happen to us if we don't run." Vel flushed as if the word itself was something embarrassing or dangerous. Billys and Booter nodded vigorously in the background. Sickly stared stonily at Vel, who looked ashamed yet defiant.

"Vel's right, dear," Jamie said. "The numbers don't work out."

"So you don't think we can do this."

Vel exploded. "This? *This* is madness, innit? This is the charge of the light platoon and Davide Cloquette at the À La Mode all wrapped into one! Think it through logically. You're good at that, right? You must be really logical because you show as much emotion as a statue. Hells, Sickly, if you didn't have such a blank face, we'd all be dead right now, because Sable would have killed us." Vel stopped, looking horrified. "Oh, Sickly, I'm so sorry, I didn't mean that."

"Yes, you did." Her words drove like shards of ice into his mind, freezing it solid. Vel thought he didn't have emotion, thought he was a freak. And who could ever love a freak? "You want logic? Well, here it is. We can't run. You heard Adams same as me. They will control every government in every city. No matter how far we go, they will be there. It's true, we could hide out in slums, change our identities, or live in the countryside, but is that the way you want to live?"

"Hey, I just want to live," Billys snapped.

"I wasn't finished. Thanks to Sable they'll know that we know their plan. We endanger their power simply by existing. Even if we ran and hid in a cave, they would track us down because of the threat we pose to their authority. How long do you think we'd last, hunted by groups of assassins that never give up?"

Vel shook her head. "If we attack Winderstint, we'll die for sure."

"Die now or later, that's the choice we have to make," Sickly retorted.

"I choose later," Billys said instantly.

Sickly softened his tone. "But we can make a difference if we stay. Listen to me. I know that none of us wants to die. Neither did the people Sable killed. Every one of them had a future, a family, a life which he took away because he thinks he's making things better. And if we run, he and Winderstint will keep taking lives to fuel their dream."

"But Sickly, dear, didn't Sable say he was trying to fix things for normal people? I hate to say it, but he's not totally wrong." Jamie had spoken quietly, but everyone paused.

Sickly took a moment before responding. "If I thought that he could do it, I'd agree with you. But if they're trying to make Hambridge better, what do they care about taking over the rest of the world? Since they've started all this, they've done nothing but grab for more and more power. Things are as bad as ever, worse even. You should have heard them at the watch house last night. Hambridge is about to boil over. Maybe Sable really does want to help people. But he said himself that he's willing to kill children! There must be a way to help people, but this is not it. At this moment, we're the only ones who know what's happening. It's our responsibility to stop them.

"Adams said that we have something they don't. I figured out what it is. We have each other." Jamie, Billys, and Eveline rolled their eyes as one. Sickly frowned, but continued.

"What I mean is . . . every one of you is here because you're my friend, and I trust you with my life. I asked you once before to help me, and you did. I'm alive because of it. And I'm about to ask for your help again. I can't do this alone, if we're going to succeed, we all need to be in on this. If you want to run," he paused, "I won't stop you. If every one of you decided to walk out that door right now, I'd let you. But I'd still try and stop Winderstint. You're all worth it to me. You're all I've got."

He looked around at them. Terry was nodding slowly, Booter looked uncertain, Jamie was massaging her temples, looking unhappy. Vel bowed her head, so he couldn't see her expression.

After a long moment, Billys broke the silence. "What's that phrase? Oh, yeah. Never doubt that a small group of thoughtful, committed assassins can change the world. What the hells, let's do it."

"I want ta help," Terry added.

"I don't see how I matter either way, but I'll support you, Sickly," said Booter.

Jamie's features were calculating, as if weighing all possibilities on tailored steel scales. "Sickly, dear, if I thought I could convince you otherwise, I would. But I can't, can I? And, given that we don't have the numbers or resources for a protracted engagement, I believe your strategic assessment is sound." She paused, mustering a smile. "Let's give the bastards hell." Booter let out a small cheer.

They all turned to Vel, who shifted uncomfortably. "I think we should run," she began, and Sickly's heart sank, "but I'm not going to let you throw your life away because I did the smart thing and you didn't." She addressed Sickly directly. "It's mental that you see this as the only option. But I'm not going to let your stupidity get you killed, at least not while I'm still alive."

Sickly could have fainted with relief. "Then we need a plan."

"How about kill them before they kill us?" Booter said after a moment of silence.

"Good start," Sickly said encouragingly, "but maybe something a bit more --"

"That's my favorite kind of plan!" Billys said, gleefully. "It's the same as what assassins always do! Only now we get to call it strategy!"

"Hang on, I thought your favorite was the Toboggan Gambit," Sickly interjected. "That thing you pulled second year?" Billys paused, and a malevolent grin spread across his face.

"Oh, yeah. But come off it, Sickly, we'll never collect enough pickled herring in time."

Jamie and Vel groaned in unison.

"I got ta see a fire wagon," Terry reminisced happily.

They argued long into the evening, discussing strategy, diversions and contingencies. Vel suggested that Booter could take the notebook and hide it, as Jamie had done with the cipher codes. Sickly was against it, but relented when Booter himself volunteered for the plan, worried face composed into an expression verging on determined. Billys and Vel got into a heated discussion about poisoning and the merits of Fadelock, Black #6, Burning Serum, and haggis. As the candles burned lower, the plans became more and more elaborate and ridiculous. Finally, Sickly called a halt so they could get some rest.

Since Jamie no longer needed constant tending, Vel put her up on a cot in the training room so that she would be within earshot of the others, but have a little privacy. Vel then retired to her room, and Billys rolled onto a couch. Booter and Terry went to the dining room, to sit the first watch. Sickly wasn't tired. He was still too full of ideas about how they could break in to Ponsingham Palace. He followed Terry and Booter, and they sat around the dining room table. "We should probably go to the hall to watch the mirrors," Booter sighed.

"Yeah," Sickly agreed, but no one made a move to get up.

"Not going to bed?" Booter asked softly.

"I'm exhausted, but not tired, you know?" Booter nodded, looking worried. "How are you holding up, Booter?" The small man shifted uncomfortably under this hail of cross-examination, his hand clutching his necklace.

"I guess it's better than the Thieves' Guild. I'm not bullied every day, no one except Billys has tried nicking my stuff, and even though I'm last in line for meals, it's a much shorter line. On the other hand there's, you know, problems. Like these are all your friends, Sickly, and while they're fine people, except Billys, we don't really have much in common. Then there's the constant worry of being on alert for a bunch of assassins to burst in and kill us all. I'm still game to hide the notebook, but it is stressful. And finally, I'm really, really bored."

"What can I do to help?"

"Get me some knitting needles and a ball of yarn?"

"I meant about the friends thing."

"Oh. Well, I don't think there's anything anyone can do about that." There was an awkward silence. "Everyone I know calls me Thumbs, except you. So, thank you, Sickly." He took a deep breath, like a diver about to go for a record in shark infested territory. "But in the last couple of years, you've been really busy, and I understand that, I just miss . . ." He gulped for air, "I miss hearing my name. My name is Booter, not Thumbs. And when you're not around to call me Booter, everyone makes me into Thumbs, the worst thief ever. It's a person I don't want to be, and without you, I'm forced into it." He paused, abashed. "Sorry."

"No," Sickly said softly, "I'm the one that should be sorry, Booter. I know I haven't been there for you, and I promise, when all this is over, I'll make it up to you."

"Look, I know I could've reached out more, too. I've also been . . . busy. Sorry."

Sickly raised an eyebrow at the brief hesitancy in Booter's voice, but said, "You're all right, Booter."

"I will be your friend," Terry stated, surprising both of them. It was very easy to forget that Terry was present since he was quiet, and didn't move much.

"Wh-what?" Booter asked.

"I will be your friend, Booter, and will not call you Thumbs." Sickly sat back and watched Booter's puzzlement. "What is your favorite color?"

"Blue?" Booter answered, bewildered.

"Now ask me mine."

"What's your favorite color?"

"Black. What's your favorite animal?"

"I don't know, um, cats, I guess."

"I like cats, too. And doggies." Sickly got up quietly and left the room as Terry was asking Booter when his birthday was. Booter looked nonplussed, but his face held the faintest glimmer of a smile.

In the hall, he ran into Jamie, who was wearing a set of Vel's pajamas that clinked when she walked. Sickly suspected that they were capable of producing any number of weapons from hidden pockets. They were also patterned with adorable bears.

"Are you feeling better?" Sickly began.

"Yes, thank you, dear. Something you needed?"

"Well, not exactly. I just haven't been able to talk to you since you were attacked. I'm sorry that you're in this mess on my account."

She laughed bitterly. "Don't be sorry, dear. I would have been in this situation either way. They came after me, remember? This way, at least I'm among friends, yeah?"

"I'm glad you survived."

"Me, too. Sickly?" He nodded for her to continue. "I hate to bring this up, but how much do you trust us all? I know at dinner you said you'd trust us with your life, but how can you be sure that, well, one of us isn't a traitor? Working for Winderstint, I mean."

"Because you're all my friends."

"Sickly, dear, this is why you failed to graduate. You're like me. We're both too loyal to friends and family. Don't raise your eyebrows at me, I'm serious! What do you really know about us? Terry wouldn't hurt a fly that he wasn't paid to. He's a big softie, but the others? Vel's my best friend, but we don't share everything. Billys is a lewd little shite who'd do anything for bit of attention or money. What makes you sure he isn't a traitor? Or me, for that matter?"

Sickly stared into her tawny eyes and thought back to a scene from three years ago. Upon learning that he and Vel were both orphans, she had invited them to visit the Webb household for dinner.

He remembered Jodie hugging him warmly by way of introduction and the peculiar sense of heartache the gesture had evoked. James Webb pretending to be stern and critical of Sickly before breaking into wheezing chuckles halfway through dinner. The gap-toothed grin of Jamie's little sister as she whispered in her brother's ear. All the Webbs, Jamie blushing furiously as she joined in, gathered around their hearth, singing a round of sea shanties for their guests. Awkward though it had been at first, Sickly had found himself genuinely moved by the experience.

"Because I know you all. We all got through Dalton together. Terry and I were shy and awkward, and we didn't know how to reach out to other people, so we sort of crashed into each other. And Billys can be really sweet, when the fancy takes him. You haven't seen him when he's around Anemia Cassidy, but he's practically a different person. And all those posh kids that looked down on you and Vel for your scholarships? Well, who bloody cares? Jamie, you're a really great person. Remember dinner with your parents? You brought me into your family, of course I can trust you."

"I remember! My da was so sure we were walking out together, I thought I was going to die of embarrassment." She smiled fondly. "You're wonderful, Sickly, dear, you really are. It'll get you into trouble one day, but only because the rest of us can't all be as good as you." She smiled and shook her head. "Well, if you're sure we can even trust Billys, then that's good."

Sickly shifted uncomfortably. He had one question he really

wanted to ask her, but couldn't quite find the words. "Something else, dear?" Jamie asked, kindly.

"In here," he said, and led her into the living room where Billys was snoring loudly. "No way we'll be overheard over all that." Jamie nodded encouragingly, and Sickly took a deep, shaky breath. "Would you – I mean, could you tell me, ah, no. What I mean is, about — about Vel. What does — no, I mean. Gah. This is all coming out wrong." He took another breath and tried again, looking anywhere but at Jamie's face. "Should I . . . Jamie, is it even possible that Vel might . . ." Finally, he let his gaze snap to Jamie's golden brown eyes.

She was trying hard not to smile, giving him a half pitying, half laughing look that Sickly found mortifying. When she had her face under control she patted him on the arm a few times. "Sickly, dear. I love you dearly, and I would do a lot of things for a friend like you. But in this case, all I can say is: you should ask her." Sickly let out a hysterical cough of laughter.

"But Jamie, I don't want things to be . . . I don't know. Weird. Between her and me. I couldn't live with that."

"Sickly, you can't live like this either. You've got to ask her, whatever the consequence. She's a strong woman. But between you and me, Vel is terrible at this sort of thing. If you wait for her to come round, you might be waiting a long time, see? That's all I'm saying." Sickly sighed. It was the answer he had expected, but it didn't make him feel any more reassured. "I know it's hard, dear, but you can do it. Now, I suggest we get some rest before –"

She was interrupted by the living room window shattering.

"The hells?" Sickly asked in the sudden silence.

"Down!" Jamie shouted, grabbing Sickly's collar and yanking him to the floor after her. Billys startled awake and reflexively rolled off the sofa. In answer to this outburst, two crossbow bolts thudded into the house. One stuck in a beam, but the other passed through the space where Jamie's head had been seconds before. For a moment, nothing more happened, and Jamie put a finger to her lips. In the quiet, Sickly could hear a fitful hissing noise reminiscent of an alley cat accidentally confronting Crowbar. "Poison gas," Jamie whispered, looking as though she was doing some quick calculations. "We need masks."

"Training room," Sickly whispered back.

"What in the name of Hagrippa's hairy nethers is going on?" Billys groaned. "And what's that smell?" Sickly grabbed Billys' arm and heaved him back. Jamie leapt forward and helped Sickly drag him toward the hall. Before they could reach it, however, a figure dropped through the shattered window and landed with a soft crunch of broken glass. It spotted the three of them and raised a hand crossbow. Jamie hurled a knife at the attacker, striking them in the chest. There was a grunt of pain, but the assassin fired anyway.

Thanks to Jamie's knife, the bolt flew awry, piercing a painting of a village girl balancing an apple on her head. Billys had begun to cough, and Sickly clamped a hand over Billys' mouth to stop him giving away their position. But it was only a matter of time before he and Jamie succumbed to the gas as well. Jamie was hurling more knives at the intruder, who had taken cover behind the couch. Sickly tugged at her arm, and nodded toward the hallway, then dragged Billys along after him as Jamie covered their retreat.

They reached the windowless hall, which was mercifully clear of gas. A faint clicking could be heard from the front door, as of someone trying to open it with lock picks. Billys tapped Sickly's hand twice, and Sickly released him. They ran as quietly as they could to the training room, listening intently. The assassin Jamie had wounded peered around the corner, and Jamie threw another knife, causing the head to duck back. There was a crash from the back door, the snap of a tripwire being broken, and a scream of pain quickly cut short. Sickly inwardly flinched in sympathy, in spite of the circumstances. But what had happened to Terry and Booter?

They reached the training room and closed the door behind them. Quickly, they discovered four gas masks. "Only four?" Jamie whispered incredulously.

"She lives alone, four is more than redundant," Sickly hissed back. "I hope she's all right. Vel will have one in her room, but that still leaves four masks between the rest of us. I won't take a mask."

"Don't be ridiculous, Sickly," Jamie protested, "You're our leader, sort of, so you need a mask. Four masks, five of us. Thumbs is the least effective, so he'll have to go without." Sickly was about to argue when the door crashed open, revealing the assassin from the living room.

Sickly grabbed a short sword from a nearby weapon rack and parried the first attack. Jamie slipped around to the side and shoved a wrist blade into the exposed armpit. The assassin let out a muffled scream of pain, and Jamie kicked out, sending the attacker to the floor. She pinned their opponent with one arm and her knee, but paused before delivering the killing blow.

"You reckon we need a prisoner?" Jamie hissed.

"Good thinking," Sickly whispered back. "But first we have to get to Booter and Terry!" "Right then," Jamie wasted no more time in knocking their victim unconscious.

Sickly stooped and examined the assassin who wore a full facial mask with a filter on it, to protect from poison. "Brilliant, now Thumbs can have a mask too," Jamie said, and ripped it off. "It's us or them, dear, and I choose us." Sickly didn't argue.

Instead, he stood and whispered, "We've got to get to the dining room to find Terry and Booter, and then cure Billys." They each put a mask on, and wrestled one over Billys' greasy hair. Sickly pocketed the other two masks while Jamie grabbed Billys.

"You're so beautiful," the man mumbled through the filter.

"I'll drag this idiot," Jamie said, voice muffled. Sickly took the short sword, several throwing knives and two melee daggers. He crouched low and advanced toward the kitchen, trailed by Jamie and an increasingly unsteady Billys.

There was no way to tell how many enemies they were facing, assassins being silent, after all. The hissing of the poison gas had ceased, leaving in its wake a hollow silence that was somehow worse. Above them, they heard a trap trigger, but there was no answering scream. The silence pressed down on their ears, magnifying the panicked rhythm of Sickly's heart. He felt as though he was playing a game. A game where, if he was found, the older kids wouldn't just laugh at him. They would kill him.

Palms sweaty, lungs already complaining of the stale air filtered by the mask, he crept into the dining room. It was empty, the main window splintered, a gas canister lying on the floor. The candles by which the room had been lit were blown out and lay on their sides.

The silence was disrupted by an earsplitting clash of metal on metal. Sickly stood and ran towards the kitchen, following the source of the sound. Jamie tugged Billys along behind her, muttering "Move it, you limp wick!"

Sickly rounded the corner to see Terry fighting a pair of enemies in the moonlight. Both had the slender build of the archetypal assassin, one taller, the other shorter. Blood spattered the tile of the kitchen floor, and Booter was nowhere to be seen.

Sickly jumped forward, slashing with his sword, aiming for a leg. The tall woman sensed his approach and leapt back, turning to face Sickly. Jamie made to help Terry, while Billys sank soundlessly to the ground, overcome by the poison. Sickly retreated quickly as the masked woman swung a pair of short, deadly sickles at him.

Before Sickly knew what was happening, she had grabbed his weapon in the crook of hers and yanked it from his grasp. The other sickle sliced the air above his hand, barely missing. Sickly backed into a counter. Fear clouded his vision. He tried to draw a pair of combat knives, but it was too late. The blades scythed downward with terrible efficiency.

Sickly closed his eyes, a fatal mistake by any assassin's standards no matter the circumstance. There was a loud clang and the woman toppled into Sickly. Sickly opened his eyes and saw Booter standing there, wearing a wet dishrag tied round his face, and holding a heavy, wrought-iron frying pan. "Booter, how?" Sickly gasped through the mask.

"I always liked frying better than dicing."

Somehow the quip calmed him enough to regain his wits. "Put this on," Sickly ordered, and thrust a gas-mask at Booter who exchanged his dishcloth for it.

Jamie and Terry were fighting the shorter assassin, and a third who had just arrived. "Take this, give it to Terry when I make an opening. I'm going to help Jamie." Sickly shoved the mask into Booter's startled hands and then leapt up to the counter. Half crouching, he ran along it, forcing the enemy assassins to retreat or risk being flanked, giving Terry time to fall back and Jamie room to press them.

Sickly didn't have time to think. His heart pounded wildly in his ears, and time seemed to slow down. The man's arm jabbed toward him, steel shining in the light. Sickly felt his arm moving to block it, while at the same time his other arm riposted. The diminutive assassin blocked Sickly's counterattack with his left hand, retreated a pace, and crouched low to spring at Sickly. Sickly leaped to the side, slashing as the man went past, but his knife parted only open air.

In the moment that the pair was disengaged, Sickly had time to register Jamie fighting the final enemy, and Booter giving Terry first aid.

Then Sickly and the assassin faced each other in the moonlight again. The assassin made a single, cat-like step to the side, and Sickly mirrored him. Fights could be like this, Sickly thought, distractingly, endless moments of balance where both assassins circled, waiting. Waiting for the other person to step an inch out of place, to falter, to show some tiny weakness.

Sickly could feel the attack building in the other assassin as they maneuvered in the confines of the kitchen. The attack was about to come, the assassin could see where Sickly had misplaced his step.

Then Jamie grabbed the man in a choke hold from behind. "Nice work, dear," she said calmly, arms clamped around their enemy's windpipe. Sickly stared as he struggled desperately. Jamie casually dragged him off balance to keep him from kicking her. "Stay behind the walls so we can't get picked off by crossbows." Sickly nodded dumbly as Jamie let her victim drop heavily to the floor, unconscious. Twice already tonight his friends had saved his life.

The adrenaline was beginning to wear off, leaving a feeling like clammy sweat clinging to the inside of his veins. He crouched low on shaky legs and stepped over to Booter and Terry, slumped against a cabinet. A crossbow bolt sliced past Sickly's face, and he felt a stinging pain on his left cheek. He took cover behind the counter. Booter had gotten the mask over Terry's face, and wrapped several layers of bandage around the man's wounds.

"Sickly, dear," Jamie said through the mask, voice muffled, "I'll protect Thumbs and Billys and Terry. You go and find Vel. Bring her back here. Then we can form a strategic defense, got it?"

He nodded and went to retrieve his short sword from where it had landed.

He heard Booter say, "Jamie, antidotes for Billys and Terry are in the bathroom, over there. Look for a bottle labelled Wundergast's Elixir. It ought to work."

Sickly wasted no more time and dove into the hall, avoiding another bolt which ricocheted off a pan with a satisfying clang. Once in the hall, he started up the staircase. His feet followed the pattern Vel had taught them all, making sure her creaky stairs did not give him away. Though every muscle in his body urged him to run as quickly as he could, he had to caution himself not to make any noise. If Vel was hurt –

By the time he reached the landing, the clamor of battle was gone. Sickly looked around him but saw nothing. He padded silently across the hall and into Vel's bedroom. The door was already ajar, and, though he was afraid of what he might see, he peered into the room.

It was a grisly sight. Toy unicorns with maniacal grins and shining glass eyes surveyed two bodies lying at painful angles on a floor awash with red. One assassin's throat had been slashed so that she now wore a necklace of liquid garnets, and the other had been run through on the horn of a white unicorn quickly staining red. Neither body was Vel's. Sickly breathed a soundless sigh of relief and turned back to the hall. In Vel's study, he found a disarmed trap near the window, but no sign of his friend. Fear of what might have happened to her roiled his stomach.

He turned to go back out into the hall, but froze when he saw a shadow making its way across the passage. Outlined by the faint moonlight shining through the shattered windows was Ulrich Munz. The assassin moved stealthily down the corridor, away from Vel's bedroom. As he passed the study, he looked inside, and Sickly's heart stopped.

Sickly would have been found, had he not been below the window line, examining the trap just as Ulrich happened by. The bright moonlight blinded Ulrich just enough that Sickly went unseen. Sickly didn't dare to breathe as he watched his old class-mate go by. Just as Ulrich was almost past the door, he whirled around and stared right at Sickly.

But then his gaze moved on, sweeping the room once more. At some sound, Ulrich tensed, but instead of jumping towards Sickly, he sprang down the corridor, heading for the third floor. Sickly heard his footsteps going up Vel's creaking stairs.

He had a choice. Follow the man who had killed him and risk history repeating itself, or leave Vel to face Ulrich and Ten Gods knew how many others alone.

Sickly didn't even hesitate.

He darted up the stairs after Ulrich, his heart thundering.

The third floor was a large, open storage space crossed with a workshop for Vel to work on traps, poisons, weapons, and toy ponies. Vel stood in the middle of the floor, a knight in shining, armored bathrobe. In one hand she held a crossbow. Steely chainmail glittered beneath the spattered red and white of the robe, marked in blood from her earlier encounter. She faced Ulrich Munz, who held a pair of short, unadorned blades.

"Hello, Ms. Lucrezia," Ulrich said, and his teeth flashed as white as ice. A lock of untidy long hair fell in front of his eyes, but he was too focused to brush it away. His beard and moustache were as strictly regimented as a military redoubt.

"Mr. Munz," she replied.

"Happy to run into you, even if it is such a late hour. I wonder if you remember that little rivalry from our college days?" He wasn't moving, but he was poised to charge in an instant. Sickly, exploiting Ulrich's habit of talking to his victims, moved as cautiously as he could onto the landing and began inching his way forward.

"Yeah, we used to fight until both of us were so battered and bloody we couldn't see straight," Vel said levelly.

"Would you care to go again? Assassin against assassin, *mano a mano*, or, I suppose, *mano a womano*. A clean fight, and a sole survivor."

"All right, if you want a clean fight, tell your mates to come out of the shadows where I can see them." Ulrich's smile was as hard and sharp as two rows of cut diamonds.

"Oh, I couldn't do that." He launched himself toward Vel. Two others broke from cover and ran at her, triangulating on her position. Vel fired her crossbow at Ulrich, but he managed to duck aside. She dived under a table which blocked an incoming blow from one of the other two, and rolled to her feet on the far side. She kicked the table toward her attackers, one of whom dodged, while the other was caught off-guard. Ulrich leapt over the toppled furniture and pursued Vel, who had grabbed a sword from a nearby weapon rack.

Ulrich and the luckier assassin backed Vel into a corner. She raised the blade in her left hand, Ulrich readied his swords and the other enemy leveled a short spear. "No!" Sickly shouted, startling everyone. But everyone in the room was a trained assassin, and Vel and Ulrich didn't take their eyes off each other.

"Ah, Mr. Dodger, so happy to find you here!" Ulrich gloated.

"Sickly, run, get to Jamie or Terry!" Vel screamed, fear in her voice.

"Doyle, please excise Mr. Dodger," Ulrich said, conversationally. Then, without warning, he swiped at Vel with his left sword, followed by a fast jab with his right. At the same moment, the other assassin had lunged with his own weapon. There was a sickening crunch of steel and a spray of blood. Sickly blinked in shock.

Vel had deflected the swipe, ducked the jab, and before anyone else could move, shoved a wrist blade concealed on her right arm up, under the chin of the spear-wielding assassin. The spear dropped to the ground, closely followed by the dead man, and Vel leapt over his corpse, dodging past Ulrich.

Doyle Gaspard, unmoved by his partner's death, closed in on Sickly. Sickly wondered briefly how many fellow members of the Occisor Cadre were going to try to kill him.

"You'll regret what you did to my friend," said the stocky assassin.

"I — what?" Sickly said, nonplussed. Doyle glared.

"You set that half-breed beast on Hamilton," Doyle spat, seething with rage. "It nearly tore half his face off. Your death is for him. I'm going to enjoy every minute of it."

"Hagrippa's hells." Just what he needed. Another assassin with a vendetta.

"Sickly!" Vel shouted. She blocked Ulrich's incoming attack and retreated. Sickly could now see that she had not escaped unscathed. It was clear the spearhead had driven through the armored robe and pierced her torso, not fatally, but enough to handicap her for the coming fight. Not only that, but Ulrich had slashed at her side as she leapt past him. A red stain was spreading on the white of the nightgown beneath Vel's robe. "What are you doing? Get out of here, please!"

"I really wish I could," Sickly said with heartfelt honesty, parrying a thrust from Doyle. "But I've been overcome by a surge of idiotic bravery." Sickly and Doyle circled each other like large, wild felines, waiting to pounce.

"Mr. Dodger, I've been meaning to ask you," Ulrich said, as he caught Vel's blade on his and shoved her reeling back into a table covered in vials. Ulrich raised his voice over the sounds of shattering glassware as the vials tumbled to the floor. "Where did you find that dog? You do realize it killed my colleague Jameson Hoopenmeier?"

"Occupational hazard, I guess," Sickly said, never taking his eyes off Doyle.

"True," Ulrich replied, slashing at Vel, who barely dodged away. "Assassination is a dangerous job."

"I meant dog-walking," Sickly retorted. He blocked Doyle's next two handed strike, the shock sending waves of pain through Sickly's arms. He let the blade slide off his short sword and hacked at Doyle who retreated. A few feet away, Vel hurled a bottle at Ulrich's feet. It burst into a mushroom cloud of red dust, fountaining up around Ulrich.

"Don't you know I've built up a tolerance against most gaseous poisons?" Ulrich scoffed as the dust reached his face. "I barely even need a mask."

"It's not poison. It's blinding powder."

"Oh, blintz." Ulrich hissed in pain as the same dust he had once used against Sickly assaulted his eyes. Sickly felt a small sense of closure at the sight of Ulrich jumping back, clawing at his face.

Doyle lunged at Sickly, who dropped and rolled past him. He changed his sword to his left hand, drew a throwing knife, and hurled it at Doyle, who managed to parry. Sickly pulled another knife, not for Doyle, who reflexively dodged what he thought was an incoming attack, but at Ulrich. Sickly's knife throwing skills were much improved by the last couple of days training sessions, and Ulrich was still blinded. Sickly's knife hit him, pommel first, in the hand that covered his face, causing Ulrich to drop his sword.

Vel pressed their advantage by slicing at Ulrich. Doyle charged again, and Sickly barely blocked. But Doyle, it seemed, had had enough of games, and careened into him, sending them both crashing to the floor. Sickly's shoulder hit a table leg, and Doyle's weight crushed the wind out of him. Sickly struggled vainly to breathe through the suffocating mask, only dimly aware of Doyle, above him, drawing a knife.

"I promised Joanna I'd let her have you, but this is too good. After I kill you, that gutter-born whore Lucrezia is next," the man hissed.

Suddenly, Vel was above them, she grasped Doyle's head and snapped his neck in a fluid motion that was all too practiced.

"I've been waiting to do that for four bleeding years," she said to no one in particular.

The dead man slid off of Sickly, who raised his head to look around at the destroyed workshop. Ulrich had backed up to a window, still half blind and all the madder for it. "This isn't over, Lucrezia! Dodger!" Vel made to follow him as he climbed out the window, but a sniper's crossbow bolt forced her to duck back into the safety of the room.

"Is that it? Are they gone?" Sickly gasped breathlessly, as Vel helped him to his feet.

"I think so. Ulrich and what's left of them will retreat, but Winderstint will send a new wave as soon as he finds out the first attack failed."

"I can't believe they did fail," Sickly said.

"Yes. Did we lose anyone?"

"I don't think so. Jamie and Booter were looking after them all downstairs. We need to move, just gather the essentials and go to a hostel until we figure out a plan to take them down. I'll go check on them downstairs."

"Thanks," she said, quietly.

"No problem," Sickly replied, suddenly feeling awkward, "I'll just --"

"I meant for saving me." She was staring at him with her green eyes. Sickly felt himself begin to panic, not for the first time that night, but in a very different way.

"Oh, well, I . . . I mean, I didn't really. You were the amazing one. You killed two assassins! Four if you count the ones downstairs. You saved me from Doyle."

"Ulrich and the others would have killed me. Even I'm not a match for three at once." She held his gaze. "Thank you, Sickly."

"Um, you're welcome." He coughed, not out of a particular need to clear his throat.

"We should probably find the others," she said. "You go. I'll just grab a few things."

Sickly left very quickly, trying to stop his hopes from soaring into the heavens.

"Thank the Ten you're alive, dear!" came a voice from the dark of the living room.

Sickly whirled round to see Jamie and Booter crouching over Terry and Billys. "We heard fighting," Booter whispered, voice constricted with fear. "We thought --"

"We won, somehow," Sickly began, still dazed and beginning to feel the aches and bruises of the fight. "But they'll be back. We need to get out of here."

"Billys and Terry are hurt bad," Booter warned.

"We don't need to go far, just far enough," Sickly said, though he was mostly convincing himself. "We'll pack medicine, a few traps, basic clothing, and lots and lots of weapons. Jamie?""Don't forget toiletries, dear. Being well armed is one thing, but we'll all be sorry if we forget toothbrushes." Sickly blinked in surprise but nodded. "Hang on a moment," she said, then dashed off toward Vel's training room. She returned a moment later, wearing a grim expression. "Our prisoner's gone. They must have extracted him, along with all the others we knocked out."

"The important thing is we got to Terry and Booter in time," he reminded her.

Sickly first changed into his new body armor and new clothes and then grabbed all his favorite weapons. Booter had found a small suture kit and deftly sewed up the injuries on Vel and Terry. Meanwhile, Sickly and Jamie sorted everything into six bags. Vel dissuaded them from the notion of the food, water, and traps, as they needed to travel light. This restriction did not, of course, extend to weapons.

Jamie was calm and efficient in packing. Terry bore up well despite his injuries, and Billys had returned to hazy consciousness. By the time everyone was ready, Sickly was queasy with anxiety, expecting another barrage of poison gas any second.

They gathered around the front door. "Vel, Jamie, do either of you know a decent inn that isn't too expensive? We need to keep a low profile, and the high class places are where they'll look first, once they miss us here."

"I know a place. It's a bit of a walk, but we'll make it," Vel answered.

"Good, we'll follow you."

Vel went to the coat closet and got out the leather duster. Sickly grimaced at it, and Vel smirked as she put it on. As she did, the notebook and a crumpled paper fell to the floor. Sickly knelt to retrieve them but froze. The little red journal had fallen open to a bookmarked page bearing a hasty cartoon. The sketch depicted two fingers raised in a lewd gesture, with an exaggerated kiss mark atop them.

A sense, very much like that possessed by animals that live on tropical islands and know when a tidal wave is coming, began to stir inside Sickly. Slowly, he reached down and paged through the rest of the book. All the other pages were blank.

"What's the sodding hold up?" complained Billys.

Sickly's heart hammered against his ribcage. His mouth had

gone bone dry, but his hands were suddenly clammy. "She nicked it."

"What?" Billys asked.

"Lady Fingers nicked the journal. She must've swapped it with this copy."

"Are you serious?" Vel shrieked. "Bloody thieves!"

Sickly continued, tonelessly. "She knew the whole time who I was. Someone must have tipped her off, someone working for Winderstint. They've been playing us since the beginning. Winderstint got his hands on the notebook."

Sickly felt as though he had just signed the death warrant of every single person in the Guild of Spies. The realization tightened like a noose around his throat.

Booter gulped. "So that's it then, isn't it? They've won?"

Sickly licked his lips. "They've won," he repeated, feeling as though the words took all the life out of him.

"They don't have the keys to the codes, dear," Jamie reminded him. "That book's as good as rubbish without them." Sickly felt a faint flicker of hope in his chest. "But if we attack head on, we'd be playing right into their hands."

Sickly looked up. "You're right. We can't risk them capturing you. They wouldn't hesitate to torture you or your family for the information." Jamie nodded, her face resolute. "We have to pull back, reassess strategy. Maybe we do need to retreat for now, get out of Hambridge. We'll go to the inn and set out first thing tomorrow morning."

His friends nodded. The words still left a bitter taste in his mouth. He had wanted to make a difference, to use his training to help Hambridge in some small way. Even if Winderstint couldn't crack the codes, he and Sable were still in charge. Sickly had let everyone down.

Booter walked over and hugged Sickly, who did not return the gesture.

"Let's go," Vel said, after a moment. "They're still after us."

The inn that Vel had picked was called the Lord's Feet, either as a sign of deference or political satire, Sickly couldn't decide which. The innkeeper wasn't happy with the appearance of six heavily armed persons on his doorstep, well into the night, most of whom were assassins. But he took their coin without too much fuss; after all, coin was coin, no matter whose blood stained hand it came from, right?

He led them up a flight of stairs to a hallway and four rooms. Terry and Booter would sleep in the same room, Sickly and Billys in another, Jamie in the third, and Vel, as the financier of the voyage, took the fourth. Sickly was too tired to question why Vel didn't share a room with Jamie. Their guide told them to keep the noise down, there was a bath at extra cost, the privy was out of doors, and his wife would be making breakfast tomorrow morning. Terry tipped him, and he retired downstairs.

Terry and Booter went to their room with their share of the luggage, Vel took her bag to her room, and Sickly shepherded Billys into their lodging. Billys looked closer to death than sleep at the moment, so Sickly helped him into bed before making his own preparations.

There was a wash basin in the corner, and Sickly used it to

brush his teeth. He stripped off his outerwear and the body armor but then paused. His shoulder bore a huge, purplish bruise from when Doyle had knocked him over, and his arms were achy. When he touched his face, he felt dried blood from the cut caused by the crossbow bolt slicing past his face. He washed off the worst of it and applied some healing ointment to his wounds. Finally, he checked the dressings on the wound Ulrich had given him two days ago in the Commons.

Billys was already beginning to snore. Sickly made to crawl under the covers of his bed, when there was a very soft knock at the door. His heart leapt like a dog beaten once too often. He grabbed a knife from its sheath on his leg and got ready to ambush the attacker when they came through the door.

"Sickly?" The faintest whisper could be heard through the heavy wood door. Sickly's mind paused in its frantic preparation for battle.

"Vel?" he asked hesitantly.

"Yeah." He unlocked the door and opened it a crack, allowing a glimpse of the corridor and a thin sliver of her face. "Can I talk to you?" Sickly opened it wider. She beckoned him into the hall, and he closed the door behind them. She was wearing a conservative black nightgown that could probably deflect a barrage of arrows, and he felt remarkably exposed, wearing only a pair of woolen pants and a shirt.

"Yeah?" he asked, wondering what she could possibly want to talk about at this hour.

"In here." She led him into her room. He followed, exhausted, and still weak with defeat. They had won the battle but lost the war.

Vel managed to read him, despite his blank face. "Look, Sickly, I know you wanted to make a difference here, but it was a long shot, at best. Right now, the best thing we can do is survive to spread the message about Winderstint and Sable to other cities."

"You know we can't do that. If we go shooting our mouths off, they'll shoot our heads off."

"Maybe, but it's something. We might stop them, you never know." When Sickly continued to look forlorn, she added, "At least we still have each other."

"Oh, yeah, an annoying little shrimp with a name like a pair of goats, a big, shy guy who adores puppies, the worst thief in the city, and . . . well, Jamie's damn clever at least."

"I wasn't talking about them," she said. She was standing very close to him, and Sickly began to get that same, panicky feeling he had had earlier, right after the fight.

He wanted to hold her. He wanted to be close to her. But the memory of Vel snapping Doyle's neck as easily as Crowbar slaying a squirrel intruded upon his fantasies.

"What?" she asked. He steeled himself.

"The night of my assassination test, why . . . why did you kill my target?"

She shrank back, as if his words had repulsed her. She turned and went over to the bed. "Honestly?" she asked, her tone more business-like than it had been. "Because I knew you couldn't." She sat down.

"But if you knew, why did you do it? You knew they'd make me an assassin," he tried not to sound accusatory. "Did you do it so that I would have to become one?" She took her time in answering, and when she did, she was staring at her feet.

"I suppose part of it was because I couldn't stand to watch you fail."

He wanted to believe her. He did. But George Cassidy's words came back to him. People don't kill without a reason. "How? How did you kill him?"

"I slit his throat." The response was flat, unemotional.

"I don't mean . . . how he died, I mean, how is it that you kill a man? You, Ulrich Munz, George Cassidy, you've all told me that no one kills without a reason. Why do you kill, Vel?"

This time, Vel was even longer in answering. Sickly stared at her, craving her answer, but she didn't seem to know what to say. When at last she spoke, her voice was as small as a mouse's whisper. "I don't remember much about growing up. My mum and da' worked as clerks at a small shipping company, I think. We weren't rich, see. We lived outside of Murktown." Sickly wasn't sure where this was going, but the way Eveline was speaking, it had to be important.

"I guess they must have been in on something below the table, though. When I was six, a bunch of men came to our flat. My da' went to the door to see who it was, and they grabbed him. Mum hid me on the top shelf of a closet. It was midsummer. Hotter than anything I'd felt before. Like I was being baked alive." Sickly, without realizing what he was doing, came over and sat by her on the bed. Her voice, usually as unemotional as Sickly's face and as calculating as Jamie's mind, sounded on the verge of breaking.

"I just lay there and sweated. Waiting. All I could do was listen. And then my parents started to scream. It went on and on. And the men laughed. They knew no one was coming to help." She gulped for air. "Then they — they killed them. Left their bodies in the middle of the floor around a gang sign. The Watch did an investigation, but because my parents had broken the law, they didn't look too hard. Why worry about criminals k-killing criminals, right?"

She paused and took a shaky breath. Her hands had begun to unconsciously ball the fabric of her nightgown, twisting the material.

"They put me in an orphanage. I ran away. Joined a gang of kids that used me as a distraction while they did their thieving. They taught me how to survive. How to run. How to fight.

"I figured out which gang it was by their symbol. The Iron Fishers. By the time I was eleven, I had them tracked down. I waited three years for my chance. Scraped up the money for a potion from a back alley alchemist. And I – They –" She paused again. "One night, after stealing a fortune from a merchant they started to drink. They drank and ate and drank more, never realizing I'd poisoned it. They could barely stand. I went in. They didn't recognize me. How could they? A little girl from eight years ago that they'd never even seen. They gathered around me, st-staring at me. Like I was another prize. Like I was a doll. A *thing*. But I smiled, and told them how, when I was a girl, they killed my parents."

Her voice strengthened and the words rushed out.

"Then I killed them. At first they tried to fight, but I was small and fast, and they were sick and drunk. Their leader almost made it to the street before I caught up with him. I took him alive, dragged him back to their hideout. I tied him down and – and I made him watch as I cut open his friends. So he knew what was coming before I got round to him.

"There was so much blood on my hands. Sickly, it – it felt so *good*. For once I wasn't just a thing. I wasn't prey. I was the hunter. It was like . . . like being one of the Ten. A god. I was *their* god. He begged me to let him die. I did. Eventually.

"I stole their haul, used it to survive, to get off the street. To buy anonymity. When it ran out I found another ruthless gang. Again I waited for them steal a huge bounty, drugged them, and killed them. It wasn't revenge. It wasn't to justify killing them. It was economics. The most cutthroat gangs always made the most money. It was a matter of convenience. Of money. It was even easier, the next time.

"I survived like that for about four years. I thought I was being careful, hiding my tracks. But one day, while I was scouting a hideout, I got caught. He came up behind me. I thought he was going to shoot me on the spot. Sometimes, I wish he had. He said his name was Professor Rector, and he wanted to offer me a place at the Dalton College. A full scholarship thanks to my . . . my talent."

Sickly felt queasy. Those were memories which he did not want to have, even if they were not his own. He wished he could forget the images that had flooded his imagination, yet he basked in the trust she had shared with him. This had to be the first time she had ever spoken of this to anyone. Probably not even Jamie knew all of it.

He looked at her, and was surprised to see her face was tear-streaked, fresh drops coursing down her flushed cheeks. "That was the only time I killed for – for y'know, for anger or, or passion, or whatever. That night I avenged my parents. And now look at me. A butcher for hire. I don't know why I think I need so much money. Habit, I guess." She paused and gave him a despairing look. "You were right, Sickly. Assassins, we – *I'm* messed up. Taking the lives of human beings. For money."

"That's not true," Sickly said. Vel's mouth opened in surprise. He wasn't sure if he believed it himself, but he kept rambling on. "When you killed my target you didn't get any money for it. You killed him so I wouldn't fail. You killed him for me. And you didn't kill those assassins tonight for profit. You killed Doyle to protect me, not for any worthless money."

Vel thought about this for a moment. "That's true." She said it softly but there was conviction in her voice. "I'll kill for you, Sickly."

"That's not quite what I meant," Sickly said, half flattered, half disturbed by the thought. "I meant there's more to you than just a killer. I asked Captain Cassidy if he thought a killer could be a good person, and he didn't know. But I do. You are a good person, Eveline Lucrezia, no matter your past. At least to me."

"No one's ever told me that," she said, looking surprisingly small. Her eyes met his, "They tell me I'm good at my job, that I'm a ruthless and efficient assassin, and that I'm beautiful."

"You are all those things," Sickly replied. "Especially that last." He coughed. "But you've heard that before."

"I could stand to hear it again." Her tentative smile brightened the whole room. Sickly seemed to have become a human funnel, filling and draining over and over with waves of sickening adrenaline. The next wave caused the following moment to become hazy and surreal.

She bit her lip, not looking at him directly. "Sickly, trust me."

"I do trust you, Vel."

A shadow passed across her face. "I know," she said, soft and sad. Sickly felt as if he were trapped on shifting gravel above a great precipice. No matter what move he made he was sure to begin sliding. The revelations about her past scared him. He could never relate to that experience. But Jamie's words burned in his mind. He had to tell her how he felt.

"Vel, I – I really . . ." Her eyes flicked up to his, held his gaze. His heart fluttered in his chest, blood coursed through him. "I really like you a lot."

Her face brightened again with a smile, small but genuine. "I know."

"Really? How?"

"Because you're always so tongue-tied." There was a pause, stretching like a great elastic band, ready to snap. Or perhaps like a chasm opening between them. Sickly held his breath as he waited for her to say something, anything. This was not how he'd imagined it. She was supposed to have said something by now, wasn't she?

The silence was fractured by a frantic knocking on the door. Even as Sickly turned to look, a knife appeared in Vel's hand.

"Eveline! Eveline! Sickly's gone!" Booter's voice issued from the door, panicked and shaky. Before either of them could react he threw the door open and took a step inside. "Sickly, Vel, thank gods you're here. I don't know where he's gone, he might have got some fool notion to do something stupid. He was so upset about –" Booter stopped short and stared. "Sickly, what are you doing here?" In the candlelight Booter's face went red to the roots of his blonde hair. "Ooooh."

"Will there be anything else, Thumbs?" Vel asked, her tone light and amused.

"Um, n-no," he stammered and backed out of the room. "Have fun, you two." He gave Sickly an exaggerated wink and departed.

If Sickly really was as icy as his face made him appear, he would have melted into the floor from the heat of his embarrassment. It certainly would have made for an easier escape of the situation.

But then Vel burst out laughing, breaking the tension. "Perfect timing, Booter," Sickly groaned.

"Don't be too mad, Thumbs was just trying to look out for you. He's a good friend."

"Yeah," Sickly grumbled. "Also, please don't call him Thumbs."

It was Vel's turn to flush. "Oh, of course. Speaking of timing, it is late."

"I didn't mean to overstay my welcome, sorry."

Vel smiled and grasped his hand. "You didn't. Sleep well, Sickly."

Sickly was loath to take his hand out of Vel's, but he forced himself to rise and say goodnight. As the door closed, he rubbed his hands over his eyes, mind racing. He had known Vel for years. He knew she had been orphaned young, but the graphic details of her life before Dalton had always been mysterious. Yet she was still Vel, right? His friend? He still cared for her, even if he now had to untangle that care from these new questions. If it hadn't been for Booter's interruption . . . Sickly shook himself. He dared to hope that this would not be the last time that he and Vel would be alone together.

Hank Winderstint scrawled a looping signature on a promissory note with his favorite gold-inlayed fountain pen. He had purchased it specially after earning the title of Dalton College Headmaster, and it reminded him daily that no matter what the world threw at him, he could always turn a bad situation to his advantage. Just as he had done here.

"Pleasure doing business with you, m'lord," drawled the thief in her atrocious street accent. Really, Hank thought to himself, something would have to be done about the disrespect commoners like her showed to civilized people such as himself. "If you ever need any other services from the guild, I'd be ever so ecstatic to assist you." She smiled ingratiatingly, like a dog begging for attention.

"Yes, very good, Miss Fingers," Hank said, shaking hands over the desk between them. He would have to wash it later. And have the desk cleaned.

She smiled again, taking the note he had just signed. She flicked her wrist and suddenly it appeared in her other hand. "It's Lady, actually. And if this don't spend, I'll be back."

Hank gave her a smile as tight as a noose. "Of course." Sable watched them both from one wall of the room. Hank longed to give the command to end her, but unfortunately she was the best. She might be useful later. She had brought him the notebook after all.

Lady Fingers flounced from the room, blowing Sable a kiss on the way by. No peasant should legally be allowed to exhibit that much swagger.

Hank took the notebook in his hands and ran his fingers across its weathered cover, savoring the feeling of victory. These pages contained the power to extend his reach beyond Hambridge. To finally turn his dream into reality. To catapult Hambridge from city-state to empire. Great things were afoot, and the name Winderstint would finally carve its rightful place in the history books.

A cloaked figure appeared from a side door and whispered with Sable. He turned to his master. "Sir, the team we sent to the Lucrezia house has returned. They report heavy casualties and failure to slay Mr. Dodger."

Hank pursed his lips. "Mr. Munz has botched the contract on Dodger several times. His failure is becoming . . . embarrassing. No matter, we have the notebook." His eyes lit greedily upon the pages covered in detailed notes.

"Sir, I wanted to speak with you about the reforms. I believe the late Mr. Wells' estate could be seized and turned into a public trust."

"Ten damnations, Levania, can't you focus on the greater good for one moment? We still have enemies." His hand thumped a briefcase of dark leather. "You read the steward's reports yourself! Wells was on to us. Ironside is plotting something. The reforms she's trying to shove down our throats in parliament are practically proof of it! That is why we agreed to keep Ms. Joanna out of this!" Sable stared at him blankly. Hank shivered.

As a professor he had instructed Sable in several classes. Even in those days the man had unnerved him. It was something about his eyes, the way they looked at you with alien logic and terrible certainty. "I . . . apologize. You raise a good point. We must use our power to ennoble the city. When time permits I will have a word with our young Lord Reiker on the matter." Sable nodded his head slightly, and Hank relaxed.

He returned his attention to the notebook and squinted at the page before him. Much of it was gibberish, a random assortment of letters and numbers almost like . . . a code. Winderstint flipped through the rest of the book, growing increasingly frustrated.

"Sir?" Sable asked.

"The old fox had one more trick up his sleeve, it seems," Hank said, keeping his temper tightly under control. Sable stepped forward and ran his gaze over the encrypted texts. Hank clenched his fists. Caestos curse it, he was so close! He just needed the key to the code. That was all. But where to find it? "Send another team to track Dodger," he ordered coldly.

"Our informant will likely be able to learn the whereabouts of the key to this cipher, if we allow a little more time . . ." Sable suggested. Hank drummed his fingers on the leather briefcase and considered his enemies.

"No, this cannot wait. You will lead the team. You will find it yourself, and then you will kill Dodger and his friends." Sable nodded. "Don't worry, my dear boy, I will be sure to move the public works projects forward tomorrow. In fact, if Dodger knows nothing, we may find something useful at Wells' estate while we, ah, convert it. I'll draft a note to Scoke immediately." Hank reached down. "Where is my pen?"

"I believe Lady Fingers stole it, sir."

Blood coursed through Eveline's veins, filled her chest, rouged her cheeks. It pumped from her head to her toes, rushing faster with each exhilarated breath like a red tide. It enlivened each fingertip, curled around the crossbow stock. It seduced her to action, to reflex. She was a creature of motion, of instinct, of kinetic energy at its most sinuous and feral. A rider in tempestuous Gwyloch's endless hunt. She would be the victor of the graduation ritual.

Blood. That was what it all came down to. Not the way nobles thought about it, in an abstract way that meant nothing but which scion inherited the fortune. Not the way bigots thought about it in black and white, superior or inferior. Not the way that alchemists thought about it, detached, taking notes and trying to bottle wind without first breathing it, but –

Blood, the surge of it in the hunter and the prey, an instinct that drove them both. The lioness and the gazelle. The hound and the stag. Blood united them, transduced them into a single being of scent and motion and –

Blood.

Eveline Lucrezia craved it. The prey was before her, beckoning her in the tilt of its legs, the cant of its back.

She raised the crossbow and fired. Not a kill shot. Too quick, too impersonal for the sacred, profane bond of predator and chosen.

The man fell. Eveline holstered the bow in a reflex action that was a footnote to drawing the knife. The man rolled aside as she stabbed downward. He tried to defend himself, pulled a dagger, slashed at her.

She avoided him with ease, caught him round the neck, and pulled him off balance all the while carving a loving gash on his arm. He dropped the knife, mewling in terror. She smelled his blood. An aphrodisiac, a stimulant, a lust for the kill.

She held his life in her gloved claws, toyed with it for a long moment. The feral ancestor screamed for the kill, to taste the life as it slipped away. She fought it, choked its furred throat, suffered its raging slashes and bites, forced it back into the dark place. After a terrifying moment that took no time at all, she knocked the man out with the pommel of her blade.

She stood and wiped the blood on her knife carefully on a rag from her pocket. A second later she heard a muttered curse and a body drop to the floor. She looked around, ready to become the hunter again, but then saw the pale, blank face of Sickly Dodger. He was awkwardly drawing a knife from a hidden sheath. She could so easily knock him out, spare him the rest of this grueling graduation test.

But no, not easily. Hurting Sickly was never easy.

"Put it away, Sickly," she said, tiredly.

"Vel?" he sounded hesitant, fearful. The poor man – boy, really – was terrified.

"Yeah. It's all right, I'm not going to kill you unless we're the last two, ok? We're friends."

"That's very comforting. But how do you know you'd win?" She resisted the urge to smile. His defeat was written all over his stance. His body clearly said: prey. She decided to be tactful.

"Come on Sickly, I've been in school with you for four years. I know how you fight, and anyway, if you'd wanted to kill me you would have drawn those throwing knives and picked me off while I was finishing Denner over there. And finally, there's that whole thing where you don't kill people."

"Oh."

"Hello, you two." Jamie Webb had just rounded the corner. Eveline raised her knife and dropped into a crouch. She really didn't want to think about fighting Jamie. Not her best friend. "How are you dears doing?" Jamie asked politely, melting the tension between them.

"Surviving," they said together. Vel turned and smiled at

Sickly, he returned it with an impassive stare, and she inwardly sighed. She wished he could show any kind of emotion.

"I marked 'Yesterday' Sam and Roderick Gablehaus but only just escaped ambush from Sable. He's teamed up with Ulrich Munz, of course. They're killing anything that moves," Jamie said. Eveline relaxed a bit more.

"I saw Terry go down, but the doctors got to him quick I think. Haven't seen Billys anywhere," Eveline supplied, and sheathed the knife before reloading the crossbow.

"Sable finished him with a punching dagger," Jamie said callously. She detested Billys with a cool fury, not least because he tried to come on to her and Eveline at least twice a week.

"Just us then?" Sickly asked to fill the silence.

"Yep. Do you want to make a go of it together? I bet we'd have a chance of giving Sable some exercise," Jamie said, smiling.

Just then, Eveline's ears picked up light footfalls from the end of the hall, and without thinking dived sideways. Jamie moved a second later, but Vel heard Sickly grunt. She prayed that he wasn't permanently hurt.

She fired her bow down the hall, toward the two men who were almost upon them. Sable and Ulrich. The crossbow arrow missed, punching through the distant wall. She hadn't expected to hit, only to make Ulrich and Sable dart apart, so that Sable would come at her, not Sickly.

Sable obliged. His step was so smooth that the word run was too crass. He glided like a hurled knife straight at Eveline, as she rolled to her feet. They faced each other for a long moment, two predators longing for the kill.

But she couldn't focus, couldn't call up the same lust for the hunt that had allowed her to defeat the luckless Denner. Not with Sickly to worry about. Her eyes flicked to Sickly and Ulrich for just a second, and Sable moved. Something exploded at his feet, the air around the man darkened with smoke, and he was quickly obscured. "Damn," Eveline muttered. "Jamie?"

Jamie nodded at her, and Eveline backed up, sighting down

her crossbow. Jamie grabbed a bag of caltrops from her belt and scattered the contents into the quickly expanding cloud.

But before Jamie could retreat to relative safety, Sable emerged from the haze and fired. Jamie screamed and fell. Eveline whipped her bow round and pulled the hair trigger, felt the cord snap, the steel limbs flex with shock. The arrow sprang from the bow like a living thing, and sheared past Sable, grazing him.

Eveline could spare no time for her friend, and dove for Sable, but he had already faded back into the smoke. Eveline allowed the roiling cloud to engulf her as well.

She sensed the blade coming toward her, pivoted on one foot and blocked the attack with a knife. Steel rang on steel, and Sable was gone again. But his foot kicked one of the tiny barbs that Jamie had strewn across the carpet, sending it tinkling into several others. She followed the sound, slashed blindly, felt her knife drag across armor and possibly flesh.

And that was exactly what Sable had expected. Even as her knife pierced his armor, it gave away her position in the smoke. Eveline felt a blade impact her skull, sending her tumbling to the floor. "I think we're done now," said his calm, silken voice above her.

Eveline woke with a start, sheets tangled around her, clammy and suffocating.

CHAPTER 22

Sickly rose blearily with a knock at his door. The barest hint of a grey dawn poked its fingers through the curtain over the window. "Sickly, come on. We need to go now," Terry rumbled through the door.

"Coming," Sickly groaned. He rousted Billys from his bed and went downstairs, hauling his bag behind him.

In the inn's small but well-appointed common room, Vel, Jamie, Terry, and Booter were seated around a table digging into a meal. Only one or two other patrons of The Lord's Feet were up at this hour, sullenly nursing cups of tea. Jamie and Vel shot them suspicious looks every once in a while, alert for danger.

The innkeeper's wife, Mrs. Gritch, was built along the lines of a sack of potatoes and bustled about Sickly until he was surrounded by a mountain of breakfast including eggs, sausage, bacon, chips, pies, fried tomatoes, and gravy. Sickly crushed his stomach's usual protests under the sheer weight of hearty food and actually managed to enjoy the meal. It was only marred by Booter throwing him knowing looks across the table. Sickly tried to ignore him but couldn't help glancing at Vel every once in a while.

"There are a few things we need to decide. For starters, if we're running away, where are we running to?" asked Jamie. "The other Autarchic Cities are close by, but I'd be worried we'd have to run again once Winderstint starts expanding beyond Hambridge. We practically rule them already just talking economic power alone. We could head north to the Golraith Uplands, maybe get to Koleitos or Matagka by barge or on foot in a few weeks."

"I want to go to a city, not some backwater village that thinks pissing is running water," Billys stated.

"There's always Bricquébec. They've cut off diplomatic relations with Hambridge since the Julienned Squid Scandal two years ago," Vel suggested. "The Hambridge embassy eventually shut down due to all the protests. It might be safe."

"I hear their coppers – sorry, *gendarmes* -- arrest Hambridgers on sight, dear," Jamie pointed out.

"We'd disguise ourselves and learn the language," Vel argued.

"I've always wanted to visit Hai Vong City. Have you seen the clothes the Khi Sianese merchants wear? Plus, it'd definitely be far enough away," Booter said, his eyes wide with sudden excitement.

"Yeah in a sodding jungle," Billys sniped, "I'd rather be shot than eaten by mosquitoes or snakes or whatever else they've got."

"Badagoza?" Sickly tried.

"Nah, they're at war with the Jevites," Vel said dismissively. She began to tick names down on her fingers, "The Duchy of Lilywick would confiscate our weapons since we're technically at war with them, the passes through the Sternmetz are going to be snowed in soon so we can't get to Yakistan or Guhnstadt and I frankly refuse to go to The Soggens."

Terry broke in. "What 'bout Klodge? Y'know, in da Kaldrian Caliphate." They all turned to look at him in horror.

"Terry, dear," Jamie said, "That's uh, not the best idea."

"What's wrong with Klodge?" asked Booter, confused. Every assassin turned an accusatory look on him. "What? What?"

"All the buildings are one storied!" they chorused, in unison.

"The houses are just domes, so there are no good rooftops," Jamie shuddered.

"They have streetlamps everywhere and it never rains or even gets cloudy," Billys sneered. "Not to mention they build with light colored bricks."

"And worst of all, the coppers there think assassination is murder!" Vel finished disgusted.

"Terry, that's – that's brilliant! No, Vel, listen to me. It's perfect," Sickly asserted. "An assassin's nightmare. We'll go to Klodge." A frisson went around the table at the decision to go to such a backward city, but no one argued the point, not even Billys.

Jamie set her jaw. "If we're going to do this, we better do it properly. They might have eyes on the docks in case we try catch a ship out of here. It'll be easier to sneak out one of the gates and take the Robber's Ribbon east to Dunder. We'll find a ship there." They nodded.

While Vel was paying the innkeeper, and the others were using the privy one last time, Billys sidled over to Sickly.

"What about Anemia?" he demanded, glaring up at Sickly.

"What about her?"

"Well, you get to take your girlfriend."

Sickly choked at the last word, and Billys snickered. "Vel's not – I don't know what you're talking about."

"Thumbs said he found you and Vel together last night, if you catch my meaning."

"I'll kill him," Sickly vowed, darkly.

"It's not my fault he woke me up because you were gone. Anyway, did you shag her?"

"Billys!" The man grinned. "We didn't, I mean we just –"

"Just a bit of harmless hanky panky, eh? Can't blame you, she's got great pair of tits."

Sickly felt himself go red from embarrassment and indignation. "Billys, you can't say that. Vel's a human being, not a window display! Anyway, we're just friends." Billys looked rather put out. "And she's coming because she's the best assassin we've got on our side."

"Well, I want to take Anemia," Billys pouted, returning to the attack.

"Look, are you two even going out?"

"Not yet," Billys sighed. A cruel look crept across his face. "Then again, compared to you I'd say I'm moving at record pace."

"Shut up, Billys," Sickly growled. "Anemia's with the Watch. She's safe."

"We're assassins, and we're supposed to be the toughest things around, so why are we running if there's nothing to fear? I just want to make sure," Billys retorted. He had actually made a decent argument, Sickly thought in surprise. The little wanker.

"Fine," Sickly growled through clenched teeth, just as the others arrived. "Change of plans. Billys wants to go to the Raft Street Watch House one last time to visit his fake girlfriend," Sickly announced, not without some asperity. Billys scowled, but declined to comment.

"We don't have time for this, Billys," Vel said instantly.

"Fine, don't come. I'll just go by myself," Billys retorted.

Vel looked ready to let him.

They set off without any more delay, dressed as commoners, concealing their weapons beneath baggy clothes. Despite Sickly's pleading, Vel threw caution to the winds and wore her black duster underneath her cloak. They also decided to take one of the ubiquitous horse carts that trundled about the city. Though it was a bumpy ride – shocks having been considered a design flaw because they would add weight and comfort – it was faster than the rooftops.

Today, sleet hissed down, and they pulled their wool cloaks around themselves and drew the hoods down to keep the worst of the cold and wet out. Vel refused to sit next to Sickly, and though he was mostly ignorant of the complex dynamics of relationships, he managed to work out that this was a bad sign. She and Jamie occupied the other side of the cart and kept their voices low. Sickly huddled next to Terry's bulk to keep warm. The man was a furnace, protecting against the onrushing winter weather.

Sickly felt despondent. It wasn't just because Sable and Winderstint had won. He wasn't quite sure what he had done to offend Vel, whether it was solely because he had decided to help Billys and endangered them all, or if it was more. Perhaps, after last night, she was rethinking how much she liked him. It felt impossible that he had been so happy. Why was everything always so complicated?

"You are sad," Terry stated.

Sickly looked around, startled. "What? No, big guy. I'm all right. Everything's . . . fine."

"I will make you happy," Terry continued, and, before Sickly could respond, reached into his bag. He brought a massive fist out and opened his hand, palm up, to reveal the rose pendant necklace that Sickly had noticed in Bernt and Daughters.

"Oh, Terry," Sickly breathed, "you didn't have to."

"I know. You liked dat one but too manly to buy it yourself. I get it for you." He gestured that Sickly should pick it up. Sickly did so, and marveled at the tiny emerald fragments that made up the petals.

"Thanks, Terry," Sickly said, after a while.

"I think you like Evline a lot. You should not be fighting."

"Well, it's not quite that simple. You're right. I do like her a lot, but I can't just –"

"Go talk to her," Terry commanded.

"But I –" Sickly started.

"Go on." And without any choice, Sickly got up, steadied himself on the cart, and went over to Vel.

. . .

"Jamie, are you sure about this?" Eveline muttered, while peering out at the street. Slithey Alley? No visible enemies, but she would have to recheck it. Rooftops? Difficult to make out through the sleet. Good cover for snipers. Burrow Street? Crowded with people not currently assuming an offensive posture.

"Are you?" her friend shot back.

Eveline sighed. "Look, I've wanted to run for a while now, even if it means abandoning my life here for a bit. But you've got your whole family to look after!"

Jamie's brows furrowed. "Don't think I hadn't considered it, luv. But they're safe, at least for now. In the meantime, we've got to get clear of this place. Once things settle down I'll come up with a new plan."

"If we get clear of this place," Eveline grumbled, "with Billys weighing us down like a set of bloody lead boots."

"Vel, dear, we're not going to be killed. It's a quick detour, innit? Five minutes while that girl rejects his greasy arse and then we're out of here. Two minutes, if he really mucks it up."

"You know perfectly well how dangerous this is, Jamie. Why is Sickly such an idiot?"

"Because he trusts people. It's his greatest weakness, dear. Possible ambush sites include that alley, the street vendor's cart, and that crowd. But if he didn't trust people, would you still like him?"

Eveline exhaled her frustration. His trust was so blind, so innocent it was infuriating. No one had ever used it to stab him in the back. It was precious, in a way, that untarnished faith in other people. "No, I suppose not."

"See? He's lovably stupid, innit? Especially when it comes to you." Her friend smiled.

"I just wish he wouldn't be so stupid when it comes to Billys. That moron is mooning over a girl obviously too good for him."

"Oh, sweet Ten, yes. I saw her that one time, remember? He doesn't deserve a three-legged piglet, let alone a girl like her,"

Jamie agreed. "But tell me about last night." Even Eveline couldn't stop herself from blushing. She looked out at the street to give herself time to reply.

Current street status? Clear of visible caltrops, traps, easily removed sewer gratings. Rooftops still occluded by sleet. Burrow Street? Still no visible enemies. Twigmy Alley? No visible enemies. "Well?" Jamie pressed, "Was he as flat as his expression?"

Eveline's cheeks were burning. "Scuvirion's sack, Jamie!"

"Well, you know how hard it is to get a rise out of him."

"Jamie!" Vel squealed again. "He barely got around to telling me he liked me."

Jamie grinned. "That's our Sickly."

"Anyway, there'll be plenty of time for all that after we get out of here."

Jamie winked. "Oh! Looks like we've got company!" Eveline snapped her head around to check the street for attack before realizing that Jamie had only been referring to Sickly.

He came and sat down next to her, and she grudgingly made room. "I hate these carts," Sickly started. "Booter and I always liked walking better." Why did Sickly always want to talk about his friends? It was always Thumbs or Billys or Terry. "What about you?"

"Walking," she replied shortly.

"Oh, right, you were in a gang when you were younger."

"What's that supposed to mean, 'I was in a gang'? That's not all there is to me, Sickly. I like walking because I like the feel of the ground underneath my feet, not because I was 'in a gang'." Sickly was silent, and Eveline felt a small sense of victory, quickly crushed by overwhelming shame at this feeling.

"Look, I can tell I'm only digging myself in deeper here. I do like you, Vel, and I'm scared that if I mess up, it'll get weird. And I wanted to say sorry for siding with Billys. I reckon he's afraid something would happen to Anemia. And I know it sounds silly, coming from me to you, but I understand how he feels."

Idiot, Eveline thought, fondly.

"Sickly, I'm," scared, but her mouth translated this to, "angry that Billys is endangering us all for his stupid crush. We all know she's safe! We could be too, right now, outside Hambridge, and on our way to Kaldria."

"I know," he whispered, barely audible. "I just want us all to be together. And I know that you and Billys, and Terry and Jamie are all really good assassins. But Booter and I – and Anemia too, I suppose – well . . . we aren't. We need you to keep us safe." Eveline finally looked him in his eyes. "I need you to keep me safe."

Sickly was such a romantic fool. "And I know gifts aren't the way back into your good graces, but I wanted you to have this." He held up a silver necklace. It was a terrible cliché, but the color of those emeralds would accent her eyes beautifully. That was eerily keen, for Sickly. And it would go so well with the black dress . . . but which dagger? And which shoes?

Eveline snapped back to the present, took it, a little hesitantly, still not sure if she had forgiven him. Feeling Jamie's smug presence behind her, she put it on and let the rose rest just below her collarbone. "How do I look?" she asked.

"Wow," he breathed, making Eveline smile. "I have phenomenal taste." Jamie burst out laughing.

"Oi!" Eveline said, half indignantly and swatted at Sickly, whose eyebrow twitched. Then she smiled. "Hah, you certainly do, Sickly Dodger." His eyebrows drew up into what was for him an expression of worry.

"You're not mad?"

"Don't be an idiot, of course not. It was just surprising, coming from you."

"I have hidden depths," Sickly said humbly.

"Yes, you do." Eveline said playfully, "I can't wait to find more of them."

Jamie's face looked like it was going to cave in on itself from the crushing weight of her suppressed giggles. Terry hummed to himself. Across the cart Billys stuck his tongue out and pretended to vomit, but over his head Booter winked at Sickly.

Sickly went scarlet.

CHAPTER 23

When they reached the watch house on Raft Street, the guard outside the door hailed them with a nod. They disembarked from the cart and paid the driver. He shook the reins, eager to find another fare, even in this weather.

They approached the guard who, upon recognizing Billys, grinned from ear to ear, as if enjoying a particularly good joke. "You're Williams Kid, the man who ripjigged in front of the captain," he said. Billys gave a careless shrug that was bursting with pride. "You are, aren't you?"

"Yeah, that was me," Billys allowed, smugly.

"I would very much like to shake you by the hand sir," the guard said. "Constable Jerome at your service." The rest of the party shook their heads in disbelief.

"We need to see Corporal Anemia Cassidy," Billys stated importantly. Jerome suddenly looked sheepish.

"Could be a bit of a problem, there. See, Mr. Cassidy's not too keen on weapons in the station, at the moment. And though you hide it very well, I can still spot a lot of Shling on you, and that means you're assassins." He looked uncomfortable. "It's not me, see, it's the captain's orders. So, if you could just leave your weapons with me, that'll sort it all out."

"What, all of them?" Jamie asked, indignantly.

To forestall an argument, Sickly quickly said, "Billys, how about just you and me? It'll be faster." Billys grumbled but handed over his bulky weaponry, as did Sickly. Then Jerome led them inside, and up to Anemia's desk. Sickly sensed that the constable was mainly interested in the fame by association to the infamous ripper.

This conversation was clearly going to be intimate, and naturally the room wished to give Billys and Anemia ample privacy. It came as no surprise therefore that all the watchpersons put down their pens so as not to disturb them with the sound of their scratching.

"Hello, Billys," Anemia said as they approached. "And . . . Sickly Dodger, isn't it?"

"Hi, Anemia," Billys greeted, his voice suddenly changing from its normal nasal whine to something much more tolerable.

"Is there something I can help you with?" she asked politely.

Billys colored and mumbled, "We're here to make sure you're safe. See, it's been really dangerous lately, and, well, we, uh, *I* just wanted to be sure."

"Oh, well, thank you very much. As you can see, I'm fine."

"Right, yeah, good." Billys gathered his courage. "Anemia, would you come with us to Klodge?"

"What?" Anemia said, nonplussed. Sickly covered his face with his hand. So much for secrecy and a clean getaway from Hambridge.

"Do you want to come with us to Klodge?" Billys repeated.

"Is this some kind of prank, Billys?"

"We're going to Klodge because we'll be safe there. I want you to be safe, too, so you should come with us," Billys said, with the air of one laying out a sound mathematical proof. Anemia gave an uncertain laugh.

"You're really not having a go at me? Billys, I can't just leave, I have —" she stopped midsentence at a shout from outside, "Oh, Drasilla! What's —" Sickly spun on his heel and looked out the window to see Jamie, Terry, Booter, and Vel ducking for cover.

Eveline barely had time to draw her butterfly swords before the first crossbow bolts burned holes through the sleet. "Incoming!" she yelled.

She evaded the first two bolts and ran for the cover of the watch house, but was cut off from retreat by more shots. Eveline looked around for cover from the barrage, and saw Thumbs, huddled and alone in the middle of the street.

Damn it.

Jamie was pressed up against the wall of the station, and Terry had taken cover behind a newsstand. For a second the hail of bolts ceased, and she had the chance to dash for the cover of the building.

But Thumbs – Booter – was still out there, and Sickly would be broken if he died.

"Jamie!" she screamed to draw her attention. Jamie's eyes were wide and fearful.

"What are they doing here?" Jamie asked, her voice panicky.

"Focus!" Eveline hissed, "Take Booter and get into the watch house." Jamie bit her lip but nodded. "Terry, you and I draw them off!" Eveline couldn't see if he had heard, but she had to hope for the best.

Six assassins in combat gear were advancing down the street, reloading crossbows. She backed away, hoping that the assassin's instinct to chase a fleeing quarry would prevail. It worked. They ran at her, and she turned and fled, glancing over her shoulder to be sure. Four followed, but two stayed to take care of Booter and Jamie. Damn Booter. Damn Sickly. They were both too vulnerable. "Terry!" she shouted again, and the huge man nodded. He dashed back to intercept the last two and help Jamie defend the lost lamb of the Thieves' Guild.

Eveline had no more time to spare for her friends and focused every part of her mind down to the task of dodging, weaving, and running. A few more arrows ripped past, but they had no chance of hitting her while firing on the run. She led them to the end of Raft Street, then, instead of running down Cloaker Avenue, jumped into the last gap between two apartments.

The wounds from last night's battle began to burn, but she fought the pain down. She sped down the tight corridor formed by the two tenements, then doubled back to the right, running parallel to Raft Street. At the next opportunity she turned left and came out in an empty cul-de-sac slick with slush. All she needed now was a little luck from the Lady of Convenient Shadows, and she could slip back to Sickly and the others.

Her breath came hard in her lungs, and she turned to look behind her. For the moment, she seemed to have lost her pursuers. Maybe they had gotten lazy and gone back to finish Terry, Booter, and Jamie. Hopefully, the three of them had made it inside the watch station.

Her hands moved without conscious thought, raising her swords to deflect an incoming strike. The knife skated off her blades, and Eveline took an automatic step backward.

She looked past the knife for a second and saw –

Sable Levania.

Eveline retreated, parried, and swung desperately. Terrified.

Her counterattack was so slow that Sable seemed to almost walk around it, positioning himself to strike at her left arm.

The knife sluiced through her armor and bit into her flesh. Pain blossomed, but she kept herself from screaming.

She back stepped again, parrying Sable's attacks with her right sword, her left arm falling uselessly to her side. Sable, assured of the kill, gave her a moment's breather. "Ms. Lucrezia, not at your best, I see."

"Had a spot of bother last night," she panted, trying to center herself. Blood coursed down her left side. "Did Munz enjoy my blinding powder?"

"Mr. Munz is no longer . . . associated with our interests. His low success rate contributed to the decision to let him go this morning."

"By your master, you mean? We know your secret. You're an assassin who doesn't work for pay."

"You are mistaken," Sable said, conversationally, as if Eveline had made the faux pas of thinking he played hearts, rather than bridge. "I fear you may have fallen into the trap."

Eveline had had enough of a breather, and attacked without warning, hoping to prolong the encounter. Hoping for what? That Drasilla might grant her a little more luck. That someone would come. Foolishly, she prayed it would be Sickly.

She whipped her blade around in a shining, flashing arc, but Sable blocked easily. She sidestepped, keeping the motion of her sword going, sleet hissing off her blade. "What trap?" Keep him talking, buying time.

She knew how useless it was.

"You see, the trap that so many of our kind fall into is not of steel or wire, it is a trap of the mind," Sable mused. "Thinking that gold is all-important."

She made two fake slices toward Sable before committing herself to another attack. Sable dodged, still talking blithely. "I sometimes think that the influence of Caestos is more virulent than any malaise concocted by Genulum, if you'll forgive a religious analogy. That arm must really be hurting you. You must know that you're not just paralyzed. You're bleeding out."

"It occurred to me, yes," Eveline managed, through clenched teeth. She struck again, but Sable blocked easily and jabbed the wound on her arm. She screamed as the pommel of the knife impacted her injury, sending blinding pain though her body. Her vision flashed, and she nearly blacked out.

"Has Mr. Dodger shared any papers with you?"

Papers? Then that meant Jamie's trick of hiding the keys had really worked. It also explained why he hadn't just killed her straight out.

"I'd n-never tell you," she managed, hating herself for how her voice shook.

"I suppose not. In that case, are we done here?" Eveline was bent over, feeling tears or meltwater sliding down her face.

"Yes," she said, defeated. Sable gave a little sigh and his knife whined through the sleet.

Before he knew what was happening, Eveline blocked with her right sword and struck with her left.

Sable blinked in astonishment as the sword cut him in the side. It didn't tear through him as she had hoped, but she had wounded him. "My arm is hurt, not paralyzed." Eveline said, through gritted teeth.

It did burn though, and he was right. She would eventually bleed out, even if she could move her arm. Before Sable could recover, Eveline attacked again, pressing him back towards the middle of the cul-de-sac. Sable was no longer dodging as easily, and Eveline managed to give him a second gash on his leg, even though her arms were shaking with exhaustion and pain. Her vision swam from mist and blood loss.

"The gleaming trap, I call it. And the fascinating thing about it is that we willingly walk into its jaws, as if we expect it to be different for us." Sable, in spite of his injuries, resumed conversation as calmly as ever. Gods, Eveline hated self-righteous nobs like him. She searched for an opening, a weakness, anything.

And then Sable shifted his footing just wrong, and Eveline could see the kill shot. Like a game of chess, Eveline used each of her moves to force Sable into the trap.

Sable kept talking, oblivious to the danger. Back and forth they battled, swords and knife flashing away in the sleet. "The jaws of the gleaming trap are made of hope, plated in greed. And when those jaws close, they never let go."

"I hope you know you're insane." Eveline struck with her right sword, forcing him to block, exposing his wounded side to an attack. Her left arm quavered with pain as she struck.

The jaws of the trap closed. Sable's knife caught her in the stomach.

"No." Sable said, sadly. "It is insane to hope."

And Eveline knew that Sable's wrong move had been the bait. A flash of hope to lure her in.

Eveline felt a dull sensation spreading through her stomach from where the knife had opened her. "We're done now, I think," Sable breathed, and let Eveline fall to the ground, tendrils of blood crawling like worms into the water around her.

Sickly and the guards rounded the corner and came out into a cul-de-sac. He squinted through the haze and saw Sable Levania, standing over a body while cleaning a steel blade. The man turned, and through his damp curls of black hair, Sickly could see the smile. That same, childlike smile he had worn the night he killed Kerry Adams. The knife disappeared back into the folds of Sable's tunic, the kerchief cast aside.

Sickly started forward, heedless of the world around him. Strong arms pulled him back, but he fought with all his might to run at Sable.

The assassin turned and walked off into the hissing stillness like the shadow of the Traveler himself.

Now they let Sickly go, and he ran to the frail figure already dewed with sleet. Sickly knelt down beside Eveline and felt a wave of agony rip through him at the sight of her stomach gouged open.

Her eyes found his and her head twitched in his direction. "Vel?" he asked, voice choked.

"Sickly," she whispered back, barely audible. Her chest rose and fell in shallow, rapid gasps, making the rose pendant jump.

"Please," he whispered, "I n-need you." Where was a Ten-damned doctor when you needed one?

"Sickly," she repeated, "you're not . . ." her lips moved but no sound emerged. Her breathing was beginning to slow and her green eyes no longer focused on him.

You're not.

The world around him seemed to drop away like the chasm he had felt open between them just the night before. As if he was alone in a sea of blackness, a sole soul beneath a crushing ocean of dark.

Deep inside Sickly, something broke.

"No!" Jamie was sprinting towards them from the mouth of the cul-de-sac. Seeing Sickly cradling Vel's head and staring blankly at her face, Jamie began to cry. Tears and sleet and snot ran down her face as she knelt by her best friend's body.

"Vel," her voice cracked, "I'm sorry, I'm sorry, I couldn't – we – they pinned us down and Terry and I couldn't – I'm sorry, I'm sorry I'm . . ." she continued to whisper the words as Vel's blood pumped, ever more slowly, from her body. A prayer was customary at such times. Sickly couldn't think of one, or a god that he would bother sending it to. What would be the point?

The Watch moved in, and Jamie helped the officers carefully transfer the body to a hurriedly fetched stretcher. Sickly watched the scene, as unmoved as an audience member at a bad street theater performance. Vel's sodden coat was gently removed and replaced with a warm woolen blanket. Her swords and crossbow were cast to the street. Jamie held her hand limp hand, shoulders shaking with sobs.

Sickly bent and picked up the discarded duster. It had been open at the front during her fight with Sable and his blow had not pierced it. If she had chosen to buckle it, would she have survived? No. You didn't survive when Sable decided to kill you.

Sickly wrapped the duster over one arm, picked up Vel's swords, and then walked away. "Hey!" Jamie shouted, "Where are you going?"

Sickly kept moving.

"Stop!" A watchman cried. Sickly turned. The look he gave the man made them all take a step back. Something in that dead expression and those cold eyes made them think better of calling him back.

Sickly walked into the wintry miasma, not after Sable Levania, but out, into the city.

CHAPTER 24

Sickly shed his new coat and donned Vel's duster instead, leaving the jacket on the ground for some lucky urchin to find. Then he let his feet carry him through the empty streets under the iron sky.

His feet directed him towards Murder Town, and he descended into the worst of Hambridge. He wrapped himself in his cloak and kept to the sides of streets, in the shadows of the decaying architecture.

Sickly passed buildings with dilapidated fronts and doors yawning like the mouths of toothless old women, their windows like dark and empty eyes. He passed pubs where drunken rowdy men screamed themselves hoarse and fought until the blood ran down their eyes and their knuckles cracked. He passed shops where smiling merchants enticed their victims with promises of perfection that would last as long as it took to cut a deal or a throat. He passed homeless men and women who had been beaten so badly by life that they cried out at their own shadows, laughed hysterically at nothing, or worst, stared through passersby with no expression at all.

Sickly was the eye of the storm in the gritty lives of a thousand Hambridgers. His mind registered the fear, the struggle and the pain around him, but he felt nothing. His immovable and unemotional exterior had calcified his insides.

He passed by a street fight between thieves; two rival gangs having a turf war over pickpocketing rights in an area where few people even owned trousers with pockets. From a shadow, Sickly watched as one man kicked another in the fork of his legs, smashed his nose with a pair of brass knuckles and knifed him in the back as he fell to the ground. A moment later, the killer had fallen to a pair of men with blackjacks who beat him into an unrecognizable pulp.

Sickly wandered on, sheltering his mind with horror and violence. Young girls with rouged cheeks and little clothing, even in this weather, eyed him coldly as he passed. One called out to him, and Sickly turned his eyes on her. She stepped back and hurriedly disappeared into the shadow of a doorway.

Sickly was jumped by a street gang, five thugs too poor to pay Thieves' Guild dues. They wore anything they had managed to steal, beg, and kill for. Their jackets were rent with holes, covering shirts that were barely more than rags. Their feet were clad in dirty, soaked bandages or boots that were barely more than that. Their faces were bruised and battered, their eyes small and cruel set deep in their faces. Their knives were the only parts of them that gleamed in what little light filtered through the clouds and pollution.

They didn't even ask Sickly for his purse, just attacked him. He drew the swords he had taken from Vel and blocked and parried the first wave of attacks. Then, dispassionately he began to gash their arms and legs. It was pathetically easy. They moved slowly, clumsily, and attacked without form or intention. They dropped their weapons and ran in disarray. Sickly toyed with the ring on his finger and thought about killing them. Instead, he cleaned the swords and walked on.

It was impossible to distinguish the alleys of Murder Town from the actual streets. Degeneration was the word for it. A place where trash, mud, and human life were thrown together to grind each other down. Sickly stared into a few windows and saw people crammed together in tiny, lightless buildings, stinking and filthy. As he passed, one or two turned diseased, cataract-blind eyes to follow him while the flies buzzed round their heads, waiting for the next one to die.

Sickly peered down the gap between two houses and saw piles of rags scattered across the ground. Human beings. Out of a morbid curiosity he stepped closer and gazed down at the nearest one, a woman with gaping mouth who stared up at him, so hopeless she didn't even ask for a coin. Sickly went to the next one, a man, already dead from the cold, or more likely the bottle he was still clutching in one hand. The final pile of rags was a child with dark hair and pleading eyes. It was so emaciated and frail that Sickly thought he might shatter it with a touch. It shivered in the cold, whimpering, unable even to speak.

Sickly didn't have any food, but he unwrapped the cloak from his shoulders and gently pressed it around the child. The duster alone would warm him. Its shivering gradually stopped. Sickly left his cloak still wrapped around the corpse.

You're not . . .

Not what? Sickly's legs plodded relentlessly on. What had Vel meant? Not fast enough? Not strong enough? Not brave enough? You're not good enough to fight Winderstint and Sable? What if, worst of all, she had meant 'You're not right for me'? What if she had been trying to tell him that she didn't feel the same way about him as he did for her? What if, with her last breath, she had been trying to break his heart, even as hers stopped pumping?

The uncertainty ate away at his mind like a plague worm at an apple, corrupting and infecting his trust. But at the core lay a steel certainty that could not be gnawed away. His friends were in danger from Sable and Winderstint. He would protect his friends. That was all he had left. They had ripped everything else away.

"There you are." Jamie clambered down from a rooftop and looked Sickly up and down. Her eyes were red, her face taut. "Are you done behaving like an idiot?" Sickly gave her a blank stare. "Eveline was my best friend. And they killed her. But you have to go off by yourself like a bloody fool and make us all come look for you. You risked everyone's gods-damned necks!"

"Sorry."

"Get stuffed, that was bloody stupid and you bloody well know it. It was – you're just – look, let's get back to the others." Jamie sounded as if she was trying hard not to scream at him.

"No," Sickly replied flatly. "I'm not going with you to Klodge."

"Sickly, there's something I need to tell you."

Sickly cut her off. "I know what you're going to say. You think the only way to stop this from happening again is to run away while we have the chance. You think I'm sacrificing everything for a campaign of personal revenge."

"Sickly, that's –"

"But I'm not. I'm going to protect what – who I have left. The only way to stop this is to kill Sable and Winderstint. I know it's impossible. I know it's not the smart thing to do."

"Listen, I –"

"And yes, Jamie, I know Eveline didn't sacrifice herself so that I'd throw my life away in a futile attempt at revenge."

Jamie's mouth was a taut line. Then she glared at him. "If you're not going to listen to me, fine. But you can't stop me from coming with you. I won't let them get you, too."

Sickly blinked. "No, none of you are coming with me," he stated. "No more deaths except theirs or mine. You're all too important."

"Shut up, dear. You need us, and I don't care what lie you're telling yourself about why you're going to kill them. I want revenge for Vel, too."

Sickly sighed, emotionless. "All right. Where are they?"

"Billys, Terry, and I went to look for you. We were going to meet back at the watch house at nightfall. Thumbs is safe with the Watch. He stayed to . . . take care of Eveline." Her voice caught, but it looked like she had used most of her tears up. Her fingers wound a braid of hair round and round.

Sickly's eyes burned, but no tears came.

CHAPTER 25

They arrived at the watch house on Raft Street as it was growing dark. A few watchpersons ushered them inside without even bothering to check their weapons. Extra guards had been posted along the street for the look of the thing, for all the good it would do against another ambush. The walk back to the station beside Jamie had been good for Sickly. Some of her fire had briefly warmed his icy surface, like sparks landing on a slab of ice bringing out ephemeral hues.

Though it was after nightfall, the main building was alive with activity. Constables rushed to-and-fro, sergeants barked orders, corporals frantically jotted down lists or reports, tongues sticking out with the effort of concentration. Billys, Terry, and surprisingly, Anemia, were off to one side, trying hard not to be buffeted this way and that by the relentless activity.

Sickly and Jamie made their way over, and Jamie shouted above the din, "What's going on?"

"Captain Cassidy put the station on full alert, after what happened," Billys shouted back, and because he was Billys, added, "Big showoff."

"That's Captain Showoff, to you," a voice growled. The room quieted, though watchmen still proceeded about their business.

The captain had arrived, unnoticed in the hubbub. "Mr. Dodger, I would like to have a word with you and your friends in my office."

Sickly looked into the Captain's eyes and saw . . . resignation, exhaustion, and something else, a flash of triumph so brief, Sickly wondered if he had imagined it.

"Permission to tag along, sir?"

"Granted, Corporal Cassidy."

Mr. Cassidy's office was smaller than Sickly had expected, though very tidy. A simple desk, a few chairs, and several filing cabinets took up most of the available space. The desk looked worn but the top of it was still visible – a rare thing in any profession that involved paperwork – and had a small plaque with George Cassidy's name on it.

The only thing of ornamental, or in this case probably sentimental, value in the room was a painting. It appeared to be a likeness of the captain in uniform in front of a white house next to a little girl. The Captain's nose was a little off center, and his smile and posture suggested he had swallowed his badge. At the bottom it was signed: From Nemi, To Daddy.

The captain noticed Sickly's gaze and turned to the work. For the first time that day, he allowed a careworn smile. "Anemia's work."

"Father," Anemia whispered in embarrassment, "I asked you to take it down ages ago."

"Why should I? It brings the room together," her father replied, in the tones of a man who is proud of his child's artistic talent, in spite of relentless mortification to the child herself.

"Couldn't you at least put up something more recent? I painted that when I was eight," Anemia muttered.

"Now, Mr. Dodger," The captain began. "I offer my official regrets that your friends were attacked outside this very station. On a personal level, I'm sorry about Ms. Lucrezia. I'll send a prayer to Drasilla for her soul." Sickly stood mute and mercifully unfeeling as an ice sculpture.

He was aware of the commonly held beliefs meant to paper over the chasms at times such as these. Supposedly the Traveler arrived to shepherd the deceased to the gates of the afterlife. Then Hagrippa, goddess of the netherworld, the matron of hells, heavens and poetry, would judge their deeds. Worthy souls were allowed to pass by her huge three-headed grimalkin, Tabberos, as the beast licked itself indifferently. Unworthy, or unlucky, souls were batted off the nearby ledge to atone for their wickedness and to ensure that gravity was still in effect. Prayers to patron gods were often invoked on behalf of the departed along the lines of "See here, Caestos, I know Jimmy 'Godcusser' Stainthorpe wasn't the most devout bloke, but here's a sack of coin to see he makes it somewhere adequate, eh what?"

Captain Cassidy continued in a voice as flat and colorless as a week old mug of Prout's Red Ribbon Ale. "The brass have informed me that investigation of the attack is out of our hands. A team from the Main Watch House will handle the inquiry."

"Do you think they are likely to turn anything up?" Sickly asked stonily.

"I am required to tell you that they will." Sickly ignored the unmistakable sound of the man's pencil splintering between those calloused hands.

"Some people are above the law."

The captain's voice was eerily calm as he said, "They may think so." He and Sickly shared a look.

Sickly, a man now well out on the frozen pond of equivocation, said, "Hambridge justice seems a little vertically challenged, these days."

"Then it is my job to find a Drasilla-damned stepladder."

"I wish you the best of luck," Sickly said, and he meant it. "If there's anything I can do to aid the Watch, I would be happy to."

"The Watch thanks you, Mr. Dodger. But for now, I believe you should get some rest. I regret that I cannot offer you a place here, for that would be against regulation, and I must of course adhere very strictly to letter of the law."

Yes, Sickly thought, that will be very important.

"I would also advise that you do not discuss this within the watch house."

Yes, Sickly thought again, I understand.

"Permission to accompany them, sir?" Anemia broke in, drawing sharp looks from her father and Jamie. "To ensure their safety as good citizens of Hambridge."

"While we appreciate the offer, it might not be entirely safe," Sickly tried.

"Exactly. Anemia, don't be foolish. People fear assassins for a reason. They're bloody dangerous. If something happened, I —" George Cassidy cut himself off. He and Anemia locked eyes, a master of unshakable conviction pitted against his greatest student.

"Safe? I'm a copper. And that means protecting everyone. No matter who they are or what's coming after them. Isn't that right, *captain?*" The muscles in the captain's jaw worked furiously for a few seconds as civic duty warred with paternal anxiety. But Anemia refused to give an inch, and for the first time Sickly saw the man drop his gaze first.

"Very well. Corporal Cassidy will accompany you and your friends, Mr. Dodger. If you think of anything to assist our investigations, don't hesitate to send her back to us." This compromise seemed to satisfy everyone.

"Yes, sir," Sickly said. The captain gave a small smile and ushered them out of his office. Anemia led them back to the front room before going to change out of uniform.

"They found you! Thank the Ten!" Sickly turned, stony-faced, to see Booter tracking rain into the building, two coppers on his heels.

"Yes. Where've you been?"

"Sickly, there's something I have to tell you!" Booter started.

"What." It was a statement. Booter opened his mouth but quailed as he stared into Sickly's eyes.

"I've been – I mean, er. Well, I was with Eveline. I helped the

Watch take her to the hospital." Sickly's gaze bored into the shorter man. Booter looked wretched. "We – they did the best they could. But. Oh, Sickly. I'm so sorry." Sickly nodded. He had known the outcome as soon as he saw her lying in the street. There was a long silence broken only by the bustle of those around them.

When Anemia returned Sickly led them all out of the watch house and then on a circuitous route through Hambridge. The six of them fanned out. Billys and Jamie climbed up to the rooftops, while Terry followed along stealthily at ground level, leaving Sickly, Booter and Anemia walking quickly through the streets, hoping no one would ambush them.

Sickly tensed at every noise, even though he knew he would never hear assassins coming. They had been attacked so often that his hands were practically glued to the hilts of Vel's swords. He knew it would only make him stand out. Right now, he didn't care.

The sleet had turned into an unhurried snow, as if it wanted to see the city from above before being trampled beneath the feet of its occupants. The buildup became a slurry of muddy water that soaked into their boots, froze their toes, and splashed as they walked, making silence impossible.

Not that Booter and Anemia were much good at stealth anyway. Anemia was a born copper. She had the solid, one-foot-after-another trudge that defined a watchman walking the beat. Unfortunately, this made her about as quiet as a rhino wearing galoshes stomping through a tea set.

Booter was worse. He hadn't earned the title of Thumbs for nothing.

Oh, he tried to be stealthy, Sickly would be the first to admit it, but he tried too hard. He slunk down the street, half crouched and all the more conspicuous for it. Sometimes he remembered to stay out of the streetlamps, other times to muffle his footfalls, but never both simultaneously. Once, he even tried a shoulder roll, botched it and landed on his back in a puddle. He rose, looked around awkwardly, and limped after Sickly and Anemia.

At last Sickly led them up a long drive. Jamie, Billys and Terry caught up with them soon after, still alert for danger. "Sickly!" Booter whispered. "Where are you taking us? This is where nobs live."

"We're almost there," Sickly replied. They arrived at a large door with a brass knocker, and Sickly rapped the door several times, not bothering with any secret knock nonsense, no matter how many of his friends rolled their eyes.

They waited for what seemed like hours, huddled underneath the large porch until a lantern's light illuminated the glass in the door. The door opened to reveal Mr. Stashcrumb in a faded red and white striped nightgown and sleeping cap, and all six of his dogs. The animals' eyes and teeth flickered in the lantern's light. None of the dogs growled. They didn't need to.

"I'm terribly sorry, Mr. Stashcrumb, I know it's late, but I need to take you up on your offer. My friends and I need a safe place to stay for a little while, and I'd really appreciate it if you could give us one."

"It's you is it, boyo? And with a few more than I was expecting. Thought it would be just you and that young lady. Last we met, I said to meself she is something special, no mistake."

"She was," Sickly stated, meeting the old man's eyes. Mr. Staschrumb dropped his gaze.

"Right then, in ye come, and wipe your feet! Don't want you tracking mud all over me carpets, you hear?"

They entered, a little nervously because the dogs were still giving them hungry looks; all except Sickly, whom they recognized. Spoon jumped up and put his paws on Sickly's chest, covering Sickly's mouth and chin in a deluge of sloppy dog kisses. This, more than any words or human gestures, brought Sickly back to himself. It fueled him enough to carry on a bit further, no matter what deep rivers of unthawed pain still hid beneath his façade.

The visitors cleaned their feet fastidiously on the large mat that covered most of the entrance hall, and made the mistake of breathing in. The smell was repulsive. Old fish, pipe tobacco, and unwashed clothing, not to mention the overpowering aroma of wet dog. Anemia, Booter, Jamie, and Billys gagged as they entered, but Sickly was used to it, and Terry didn't seem bothered.

The foyer was large and served as the site for leashing dogs and cleaning paws after walkies. "Follow me, and don't touch anything! Especially you!" Mr. Stashcrumb said as he jabbed a finger towards Billys.

"Me? What did I do?"

"You look suspicious, now shut up." Anemia stifled a giggle at Billys' indignation as they followed the old man through a passage to a well-furnished kitchen. He put a large kettle on an old iron stove and lit a fire. Their host then went over to a pantry and got a large tin of biscotti which he left on the kitchen table. "Don't eat all of 'em," he growled as he pried the lid off. "I'll go make up some beds." And he bustled off, lantern swinging, Crowbar and Gnosher following along behind him. Gout, Gangrene, Gouger, and Spoon stayed behind to watch the intruders closely.

"Which one of Caestos' crevices did this codger crawl out of?" Billys demanded. "And why are those mutts looking at me like that?"

"His name is Mr. Stashcrumb. He was one of my dog-walking clients. He offered to help if I was ever in trouble, and since he isn't directly connected to any of us, they probably won't think to look here. You might not want to call them mutts, by the way."

The four remaining purebred mastiffs, each nearly as tall as Billys, were giving him grumpy looks. Sickly clicked his tongue to get their attention, and rummaged in a pocket. Instantly, the dogs trotted over, tails perking at the unmistakable sound of a treat. Spoon licked hopefully at Sickly's hand, Gouger snuffled his shoes, Gangrene whined pitifully, and Gout stuck his nose in his crotch just to be sure it really was Sickly. Sickly broke the crumbling biscuit into fourths and parsimoniously passed it to each pup.

"I love biscotti," Booter said, breaking the silence, and took one, crunching away happily at the tiny wizened biscuit. Sickly raised his eyebrows, having always felt biscotti to be a bad excuse for a burnt, dried out scone that had been the runt of the litter and would never make anything of itself. He had once tried one by accident. Instantly, all the moisture in his mouth had been sucked out, his teeth cracked, and his tongue was coated in crumbs. He had then had a lie down because he felt ill.

"What we do now?" Terry asked, helping himself to the tin.

Sickly pushed the exhaustion back and focused his mind. "First we rest. We all need to recover from our injuries, but the sooner we act, the better. Tomorrow, we'll try and find exactly where Winderstint and Sable are. Then we can plan our attack. Nothing too complicated, we'll all go in quickly, during the day when they won't expect us. We'll sneak past as much as we can, and then fight the rest of the way. Questions?"

"If we sneak by and then start a fight, anyone we snuck past will hear and attack from our backs. We have to take out anyone we find along the way," Jamie said, thinking quickly.

"Nonlethal takedowns, if we can help it," Sickly decided.

"Sickly," Jamie growled, a knot forming between her eyes. "This isn't the graduation ritual. It's snuff or get snuffed. Remember what they did to Vel? Can't you at least consider killing them?"

Sickly opened his mouth, but, before he could speak, Anemia interrupted. "I'm going to pretend I didn't hear this. What you're plotting isn't assassination, it's murder!" Sickly turned on her, and she looked nervous at his cool stare.

"You volunteered for this, copper," he said, calmly. "This is not your world."

"Excuse me, Mr. Dodger, but this is exactly my world. I am, as you say, a copper. Through and through. And I won't sit idly by while you premeditate murder! I came to protect you lot, not to abet in violent crime!"

"Your father understood what needs to be done," Sickly replied, evenly.

"And so do I. I'm a copper, and murder doesn't happen on my watch. I may not have understood everything that went on between you two, but I know this: he won't do anything against the law. And neither will I." She and Sickly were staring each other down. Sickly noted, dimly that she had her father's eyes of iron.

"Sickly's right," Jamie turned her anger on Anemia, "stay out of assassin's business. We're doing what needs to be done for the greater good. Sometimes that means working outside the law."

"You sound like Sable," Billys sneered. "We may have a license to kill, but we've got rules! They don't call it the Assassin's Code for nothing." They turned on him. "I can't be the only one who remembers, right?"

Jamie glared at him. "Don't quote the Code at me, Williams Kid."

Billys continued as if she hadn't spoken. "Three tenets. One: Stay your blade from those who are innocent. Two: Be always hidden. Three: above all, never compromise that which is most sacred, that which is greater than all of us, that which is the purest virtue: Gold. We don't kill for revenge, or political gain, or for sport, or for a cause, or a belief, or out of passion. We kill for that which is most holy: Gold."

"I'm not an assassin," Sickly argued. "The Code doesn't apply to me. And Sable and Winderstint aren't bothering with it either."

"Yeah, Sickly, but we're still assassins, whether you like it or not. And I won't just throw the tenets out the window because your girlfriend got killed!" Billys snapped.

"Don't talk about Vel," Jamie growled and took a step toward the short man. But Sickly got there first, sliding as hypnotically as a serpent to within an inch of Billys' pinched face.

"Walk away, Billys," Sickly said. "Like you should have done instead of going to the watch house this morning." The blood drained from Billys' face.

"Can I interrupt?" Booter squeaked, and then choked on his dry tongue. When he had recovered, he said, "Sickly, you've been, well, cold, since Eveline died. I don't think you're thinking things through rationally." Sickly paused at his friend's words.

Though he was still looking into Billys' eyes, he no longer saw them. Or anything. He gathered all the anger and pain and let it go, returning to his icy center.

"Thank you, Booter," Sickly said calmly. "You're right, Billys, Anemia. I'm sorry about what I said." Anemia looked relieved, but Billys looked even more unnerved at this rapid turnaround.

"What?" Jamie rounded on him, eyes cold with fury. "How can you say that? Think about Vel! Think about what they did to her."

"We'll just have to find someone to pay us to assassinate Hank Winderstint." Jamie still glared at him but left it at that.

"Come off it," Billys groaned, "who's going to pay for that oily old prick to die?"

"Sounds like it's your lucky day, boyo," came a voice. They all turned to see Mr. Stashcrumb standing in the middle of the kitchen, a ghoulish grin on his lined face.

"Where did you come from?" Jamie asked in the sudden silence.

"I'll pay for Winderstint's assassination, and that, hah! lapdog of his, Sable Levania, too."

"You heard all that?" Sickly finally asked, after a stunned silence.

"Oh yes, boyo. It may have been a while since I went to the Dalton College for Men in Black, but I still remember a thing or two."

"You went to the Dalton College?" Sickly croaked.

"Yep. Graduated at the top of a very short list of one. They called me The Subtle Stiletto!" he said, proudly.

"Why?" Booter asked.

"I used to wear high heels a lot," Mr. Staschrumb said, deadpan.

Jamie shook her head. "You're lying. The Subtle Stiletto died years ago."

"'Course he did, lass. How else do ye expect to retire from being an assassin? If you're the best, you can't just say 'Well, I've had enough, been lovely, thanks for the memories, but I'm done killing.' They go after you all the time, trying to be top dog." He gave a wheezy chuckle and patted Crowbar's head. "So, I faked me own assassination."

"Didn't anyone figure it out?" Sickly probed.

"Why else do you think I live alone in a big, trap-filled house with the blood-thirstiest pack of dogs money can breed? 'Course, some figured it out, but they won't be telling anyone soon, will they, Crowbar?" Crowbar smiled. "One of them even disguised himself as a mailman! The nerve!" He chuckled again. "But as I was saying, I'll pay you lot, you included, Mr. Dodger if it makes you feel better, to kill Hank Winderstint."

"What have you got against him?"

"Oh plenty, boyo. Not least of which is that he tried to assassinate me back in the day! Me! The Subtle Stiletto! And he killed a lot of the old crowd to make room for his lackeys. They weren't friends, but you don't have to be friends with someone to share a pint," he said wistfully. "And he was an annoying little tit, to boot!" Mr. Stashcrumb spat, making them jump.

He hobbled over to a cookie jar in the shape of a bear that sat atop a cabinet and pulled it down. Opening the lid he drew out a fistful of banknotes and coins, all in large denominations from what Sickly could see. Billys' eyes bulged with anticipated possession. "Fifteen thousand Hambridge dollars to each of you what survives on completion of the assignment."

"That's a lot of money, Mr. Stashcrumb," Sickly said softly.

Behind him Billys sank to the ground at the thought of so much wealth at his fingertips.

"Money," the man repeated. "What do I need money for? I've got the house, the dogs, the silver spoons, the red carpets, and shiny tinkley chandeliers. That's the dream, innit? I've seen the dream, boyo, it's all glitter and smoke. Look at me, and tell me I'm happy."

Sickly looked at Mr. Stashcrumb. The man's face was cracked and careworn, and his voice matched. He leaned heavily on an expensive walking stick that shook slightly in a hand so thin it was nearly skeletal. Above all, his eyes were hollow and lonely. Sickly didn't say a word. "Money," Mr. Stashcrumb repeated. "It gets people dead."

"In Winderstint's case, this is enough money for him to be very dead indeed," Jamie commented, her eyes sparkling grimly. "Sir, could we each get a small advance, to equip ourselves for the assignment?"

The old man thought about it then nodded. Mr. Stashcrumb rummaged in the bear's guts like some travesty of Grandma Winterwatch's knitting bag, handed her a few bills, and then did the same for Terry.

"This is sick," Anemia whispered.

"Hey, he's paying us, right?" Billys said. "That makes it legal!"

"It doesn't make it right. How could you take a person's life for . . . for money?"

"Like the Watch hasn't ever killed anyone," Billys retorted. Anemia looked away.

By the kitchen table, Mr. Stashcrumb was offering Booter his first payment. "Go on then," he rasped. Booter was looking, if anything, even more nervous than usual when addressed directly by someone he didn't know.

"Me? Um well, the whole killing thing? Not really my style. I mean, there's all that blood and screaming and, er, I'm not really into that."

"Suit yourself, boyo," Mr. Stashcrumb, said, not unkindly.

Finally, he came up to Sickly. Sickly glanced sideways at Anemia, then shook his head.

"I'm not an assassin. I won't kill for money." Mr. Stashcrumb eyed him thoughtfully from beneath the grimy nightcap.

"Then call it a bit of a raise for a little job I'm givin' you. You're going to walk Crowbar for me."

"It's a bit late tonight, Mr. Stashcrumb."

"Boyo, I meant when you go to kill Winderstint."

CHAPTER 26

Mr. Stashcrumb's palatial house contained three guest bedrooms. The old man left them with the assurance that if anyone, especially Billys, mucked about with his possessions then he would rearm the mantraps, set the dogs on them and call the Watch. Then he would laugh.

Jamie pondered her rooming assignment with that copper, Anemia. Well, that was fine so long as she didn't get overly friendly. Jamie was not in a mood to make friends.

The washroom door opened, and Sickly emerged into the corridor. They both paused, and Jamie failed to meet his gaze. She stared instead at the floor. "I'm sorry, about earlier, dear. When I snapped at you. I thought – I mean, I wasn't thinking. I thought you were siding with them. Sickly, I'm –"

"It's all right," he said flatly. "You're – we're both just –"

She nodded. "Yeah. Vel." There was a long silence. "You're a good person, Sickly, I mean it, you're . . ." She had to tell him. Show him that he really was worth saving. The way things were going, she might not have another chance. "You're . . ."

"Thanks. Just a bit tired," Sickly cut in. Jamie bit her lip, and then nodded. Sickly brushed past her. He was not cold exactly, just horribly remote. It was as if they were calling out to each other across a blank grey ocean.

As his footsteps retreated Jamie stared at the carpet, trying not to cry. It was a rich red with gold threads woven throughout it, like the first leaves of autumn. This whole place reeked of money. And dogs.

Everything was going so wrong. First, she had mucked things up with Vel. They had put that all on hold after she'd come back, but they'd both known there was still something unsaid between them. Something that now would never be said. And Da was still sick, only now it was more dangerous than ever to look after him. Now, Sickly was slipping away from her. A lump rose in her throat. The odds of success were growing longer all the time, Drasilla knew.

There was a susurration of feet over rug. "Oh, um, sorry." She looked up to see Thumbs' expression of perpetual, pale worry looking up at her.

"About what?"

"Just that, y'know. Sorry for needing to get around you."

"You really shouldn't apologize so much."

He quailed. "Oh, right. Sorry." Jamie rolled her eyes. He was worse than Sickly, if that was possible. "Erm, thanks for, for saving me today." She raised an eyebrow. "You know, when they attacked us outside the watch house?"

Jamie paused, taken off-guard. Finally, she managed, "You're welcome, Thumbs." He winced, and she inwardly cursed. She wasn't trying to make him feel bad. That was the thing about Thumbs. He acted like a kicked puppy no matter what you said to him.

Booter's face creased, his eyes closed as if bracing himself for a surprise attack by dentists. "Could you, um, not call me Thumbs? I'm – I'm Booter."

Jamie was almost as surprised as he appeared to be. "Oh, right. Sorry about that, er, Booter."

"Uh, thanks?" He was smiling in an odd way, as if he couldn't quite believe what had just happened. Jamie was taken aback by the tiny amount of spine he had just displayed. It reminded her of something else.

"Look, I don't think I ever thanked you properly." His grin retreated behind its typical mask of hesitant worry. "For treating my wounds from that attack on my house, dear." The smile reappeared, shaky with whiplash and infrequent exposure to the outside world.

"You're, uh, you're welcome. Least I could do. Actually, I don't often get to take care of anyone. Usually I'm just in the way and need to be protected. Mostly by Sickly."

Jamie smiled back. "It's not often someone looks after me, either. Except Sickly." It was strange to be reminded that even she needed support, and stranger still that the reminder came from this tremulous little man. To her great surprise, Booter walked up and hugged her around the waist, like a child. She patted him awkwardly on the back, unsure of what to make of this. He backed away quickly, with a look of mixed worry, trust, and hope.

"Anyway, good night, Booter, dear."

"Night, J-Jamie."

Sickly lay in the unfamiliar bed, listening to Terry's snores from the double reinforced cot Stashcrumb had scrounged for him. Sickly suspected it had been forged rather than assembled and would probably outlive the world, barring destruction in a handy volcano. He should have made more efforts to include his large friend in their discussion. He should not have snapped at Billys. He should have listened to Jamie. He shouldn't have shut Booter out.

You're not . . .

He hadn't prayed for Henry Dodger as they'd put his coffin in the ground. Not to Drasilla and certainly not to Hagrippa, nor any of the others. His father would have shaken his head slightly and sighed. He would have said that the only measurable effect of heavenly appeal was to make the petitioner feel morally superior.

He did not pray for Vel now. He wasn't looking to make himself feel better. He wasn't looking to feel.

The next morning was all business. Billys appeared no worse for having been recently poisoned, and Terry had all but recovered from his wounds. Sickly envied Terry his constitution, since he had woken up with a headache, shakes, and a sore throat that made his voice sound almost as gravelly as Mr. Stashcrumb's. He revived a little over a mug of strong tea with lemon.

They made plans. They argued. Billys shouted. Jamie made logical points. Terry nodded slowly. Sickly just tried to mediate to the best of his ability. They used several pieces of paper to draw up a list of supplies they would need. When finally they had worked out something that wasn't entirely suicidal, they took a break.

Booter and Anemia went to purchase supplies. Terry and a grumbling Billys left on a scouting mission to Ponsingham Palace, Winderstint's most likely base of operations. Jamie ferried the ludicrous amount of weaponry they had at their disposal down to the basement workshop to do a weapons check. Mr. Stashcrumb had generously allowed her the use of the room, on the proviso: you break it; you get torn apart by Crowbar. Sickly gave a huge sigh and rubbed his face in his hands, trying to wake himself up.

"What about you, boyo?" Mr. Stashcrumb asked. "I'm taking these pups for their walkies. You can follow along and see how it's really done, if you like."

"Oh, no thank you, Mr. Stashrumb," Sickly replied. "I expect I'll . . . do some thinking."

"About that girl, you mean? The lass who was with you the other day?"

"No."

"Hmph."

"Does it always end up like this?"

"Does what, boyo?"

"Being an assassin. All these politicians and assassins Winderstint killed to get out of the way. All the ones who killed each other. My dad. Vel."

"Let me tell you a story, boyo. It ain't advice, because I hates people who gives other people advice. A story is all it is, all right? Right. Well, back in my salad days, or, because it was the Dalton College, my blood sausage days, I graduated. Went into business as an enterprising young assassin. I took contracts on corrupt political leaders, tyrants, despots, dictators. Thought I could change the world."

He sighed. "Well, as it happens, I did. And then it changed again, and again, and after a while I got tired of keeping up. So I faked me own assassination and settled down here. It may not be glorious, but I'm still alive. Got me dogs to keep me company. So no, not always." Sickly took a deep breath, then exhaled. The old man's rasping brogue was strangely comforting.

"Thanks for the . . . story, Mr. Stashcrumb."

Sickly wandered downstairs and found Jamie tinkering with a crossbow. "This one's being tricky. I think I fixed the psychotic dampener, which should lead to reduction in the number of hiccups experienced when priming the Findle lever, and an overall improvement of the secondary schadenfreude augmenter." Sickly raised his eyebrows, not sure he had heard correctly. "Try it out for me?" Sickly began to back away, hands raised protectively in front of him. "Just tell me if it shoots straight, while I get to work on this one," Jamie ordered.

Sickly took the bow.

He spent an hour helping Jamie fine-tune their Shling but went upstairs when he heard the door open and the sounds of happy, tired dogs. He laid the latest crossbow to be tested on the hall table and then helped Mr. Stashcrumb with the dogs.

"See here, boyo. I been thinking. I hates advice. Just hates it. But practice, now there's a thing! All this cloak and dagger talk got me thinking. I oughta pass on some of what I knows before I shuffle off and find out if I should have listened to those prayer pushers. Follow me, and I'll show you how I escaped an assassination attempt by the infamous Crow's Talon back in the day. Now, she were a dangerous one. Not like the assassins you get nowadays!"

An hour later Sickly was gasping for breath, sweat running down his chest. The old man, despite appearing frail and wizened, was surprisingly fit. No doubt it was a result of all of the morning exercise with his dogs.

He faced Sickly, wielding a small shield and a dagger. They circled for a moment before Sickly struck forward. He made a couple of false swipes before fully committing to a direct attack. Mr. Stashcrumb saw through his bluff and in a bewildering movement caught Sickly's attack on the buckler and pulled him off balance. A second later the knife was at Sickly's heart.

They backed away, and Sickly nodded his defeat. The old man then showed him exactly how to perform the blocking technique. Sickly practiced it until he had it down to the codger's satisfaction.

Mr. Stashcrumb wore a self-satisfied smile. "Just remember, boyo, that one needs the shield. A real assassin never lets himself get injured, eh? That's the whole point of being an assassin!"

Before they could begin again, a crisp knock echoed through to them. "That'll be Booter and Anemia back," Sickly panted. He wiped his sweaty palms on his pants and headed to the door, accompanied by Crowbar.

Standing on the front steps was Ulrich Munz.

"Ah, Mr. Dodger, I was hoping it would be you who –" Sickly grabbed the crossbow next to the door with one hand, and Ulrich's collar in the other. "I say, I just want to talk," the towering man protested.

"I'm done talking," Sickly stated, and jerked the surprised Ulrich down to eye level. Sickly shoved the point of the arrow under Ulrich's chin. The man's eyes bulged, and there was no trace of his usual, bone white smile. "This is for Eveline."

Sickly pulled the trigger.

But there was no answering twang of sinew, and the arrow did not drive through Ulrich's skull as Sickly had intended. Sickly smashed Ulrich across the face with the stock of the bow, sending the stunned assassin crashing to the ground. Sickly then jumped over him before Ulrich could rise and checked the bow. The safety was on. Sickly removed it and pointed the bow into Ulrich's face. Crowbar snuffled his way over, seeming to recognize Ulrich from earlier. At the dog's approach, the assassin looked even more unnerved.

"Sickly!" someone shouted. "What's going on?" Sickly paused, though his eyes never left Ulrich.

"Well," Ulrich gasped, "Mr. Dodger, I'd say you've found something to kill for."

Sickly ignored him. "This was a pretty poor assassination attempt."

"I repeat! I merely wish to parlay."

Sickly let Ulrich squirm beneath the steel point of the arrow and Crowbar's gaze for a few seconds before saying, "Fine, parlay."

"On the ground like some commoner?" Ulrich asked indignantly. Sickly gave him a look. "Oh, very well. I'm here to offer my services." His used-wagon-salesman's smile flashed for a second.

"Does that line usually work on your victims?"

Ulrich scowled. "It is not a 'line,' it is the truth. Mr. Winderstint and Mr. Levania decided my assistance was no longer required after I failed to kill you. I packed up my bags and escaped before they got the chance to 'retire' me. I had been hiding out for a few days, and was just considering my options when I saw an old man walking this hell hound," Ulrich jerked his chin toward Crowbar. "I thought to myself: Ulrich, that is Mr.

Dodger's dog. He has proven himself highly adept at escaping Mr. Winderstint's plans, why not go present myself?"

Sickly gave Ulrich a calculating look. The man's beard and moustache, which normally looked like they could perform the changing of the guard, were beginning to grow out. His untidy mane of black hair was dirty and unwashed, and he had been carrying a large bag. "Check it," Sickly said to Jamie, motioning to the bag.

Jamie did so. "Clothes, weapons, poisons, toiletries. Some water," she reported as she dug through the contents. "Standard bugout bag."

"Sorry, Mr. Munz, I still don't believe you. This is a set up," Sickly said.

"Normally, you would be right," Ulrich began, "but if it was, you would be dead. I would have stationed a sniper with a long range crossbow in that elm tree," he gestured, "and he would have put a bolt through your brain the moment you were checking the safety on your weapon."

"That's probably true, innit," Jamie allowed. "Ulrich hasn't attacked without backup yet. We would have been shot by now if this was a group attack."

"I say! I'll have you know they were just slowing me down. I would have succeeded if it wasn't for them," Ulrich protested.

"You're doing a bang-up job convincing us," Jamie said drily, and Ulrich closed his mouth.

"I still think it's a trap."

"I am not just offering my services," Ulrich added. "I offer information. You grant me protection, and I'll give it to you. But I'm not saying anything until you decide, fair's fair. Either let me up, or shoot me down."

"We do need information, dear," Jamie said unhappily. "We could use him."

After a long moment, Sickly nodded. "I know." He put the safety back on the crossbow and shouldered it. Crowbar gave him a last glare. "Come inside, Mr. Munz."

"Thank you, Mr. Dodger, and especially to you, Ms. Webb." Jamie gave a noncommittal grunt. Ulrich went in, trailed by a watchful Crowbar, but Jamie pulled Sickly aside before he could follow.

"I know you don't trust him. Neither do I, but he'll know where Winderstint is, and how he's guarded." Sickly sighed and nodded. "Guess it was lucky you had the safety on, or we'd be back at square one."

"I knew it was on."

"What?" Jamie gasped.

"I just wanted to scare him. Put him on the defensive. I guess it worked." Jamie gave Sickly an incredulous look, but Sickly was already heading in after Ulrich.

Booter and Anemia arrived five minutes later, carrying huge bags of supplies and interrupting Sickly, Jamie, and Ulrich's argument. Jamie and Sickly wanted Ulrich's information, and Ulrich wanted a bath and a shave. Sickly did a quick round of introductions. Ulrich kissed Anemia's hand when they were introduced, making Sickly fervently glad that Billys was out of the house.

Ulrich went to his bath, while everyone else unloaded the packages. After they finished, Jamie went back down to the workshop. They ate a quick lunch and brought Mr. Stashcrumb up to speed on their new guest and the plan. "Well, he better not touch anything!" Mr. Stashcrumb warned. Then he went down to a coffee shop to read a paper, play some chess, and gossip with old Mr. McCraw about what the real trouble with the Merchants' Guild was these days. Sickly decided this might make more sense when he was older.

If he lived that long.

Terry and Billys returned while Ulrich was still in the bathroom which was lucky. It gave Sickly and Jamie a chance to explain why a man who had previously attempted to kill them on numerous occasions was singing show tunes loudly and off key in the bathroom. When Billys had grudgingly agreed not to kill him on the spot, payment or no payment, he admitted that Ulrich's information would be useful.

Ulrich finally exited the bathroom in a cloud of steam, looking his old self, with his wide, white smile back on his face, and his facial hair lovingly groomed. "Let's get started. Now, what I know is highly important, and –"

"Mr. Munz," Sickly interrupted, "ground rules. You are not in charge here. I am. My decisions are final. You are here only to offer your advice and expertise when called for. If you prove troublesome in any way, you'll be on the street and probably dead by morning, and I will sleep well that night. Clear?"

Ulrich smiled again. "Transparent as a vial of Roquemine's Invisible death." He bowed a little too low. "If it please you, might I continue? Thank you."

That was the thing about Ulrich, he was dangerous and cunning, like Gangrene, or one of the other dogs, but they all paid respect to the pack master because Crowbar didn't play silly buggers. Sickly would have to remind Ulrich regularly that he was top dog. He had impressed Ulrich with his display at the front door, but that would only keep the man in place for so long.

"As you may know, the Hambridge Parliament will convene two days from now so that both the House of Peerless and the House of Uncommons can vote on a new law. The Fair Representation Reform or some such nonsense proposed by Annette Martinez. Mr. Winderstint has spent great time and assets on blocking her. He intends to strike down her law as a show of strength and to shut the merchants out of Hambridge political power. If he succeeds, it will bring the other old families in line behind him and give him the political leverage to entrench himself even further. However, it does give us an opening in which to strike."

"Interesting," Jamie mused. "With so much to worry about, he might just leave his guard down." Ulrich gave her a smile, and Sickly nodded.

"Now, Mr. Winderstint and his entourage are fortified in a private wing of Ponsingham Palace," Ulrich continued. "This gives him easy access to the new Lord's ear and the houses of parliament."

"Dat's da truth, Sickly," Terry intoned. "We saw it. Lucky his suite's got all windows round it."

"But we couldn't actually get in the Retainer's Wing of the palace. Too well guarded. Plus, they kept looking at me suspicious-like," groused Billys.

Nodding, Ulrich went on. "Yes, and palace security isn't the only thing we'll have to avoid. He's installed his own private security measures. Though he wasn't considerate enough to lend me a guide to all his traps and patrol routes, I managed to scope out a few things. You know how it is. Of course, his greatest defense is anonymity. Most of the people who are aware of his schemes are working for him. And he was quite careful to ensure that none of us knew who all his lackeys were."

Billys interrupted again. "So Ulrich, why haven't you – oh, excuse me, I meant the *other* lackeys – tried kill Winderstint?" Ulrich's smile vanished for a moment, causing Billys to smirk. "All that power in one place would be ripe for the taking. You could've leaked his plan to a noble. I bet you could've made a load of gold on a contract against Winderstint."

"Ordinarily, you would be right. But Mr. Winderstint doesn't pay in gold. He pays in property, in favors, in power. And this is only the first stage. Today, they rule Hambridge, but with Mr. Dodger's little red notebook safely in hand, they will soon control every city big enough to have been infiltrated by Hambridge spies. They are not playing for the peanuts they'll get from a local merchant."

Billys looked pacified. "Makes sense," he admitted. "Wish I could get in on that."

"Billys!" Anemia chided.

"Bradley Wells encrypted the notebook," Jamie reminded

them. "And I hid the only key. They won't be getting anything useful out of it."

Ulrich gave her another winning smile. "You have Drasilla's own cunning, Ms. Webb. But don't underestimate them. I'd wager they'll crack the code if given enough time. Power like that can be so . . . motivating.

"In any case, Mr. Winderstint's second greatest defense is that all of the most dangerous assassins are working for him. His third is obviously Mr. Levania, who guards him at all times except when he is sent off on a mission. Given those three things, our old headmaster isn't too worried about the rest of his security. That leaves half a dozen traps at the side entrances, windows, and openings into his suite, not to mention half a hundred more in the gardens outside." Booter choked, but Ulrich kept going. "He doesn't use regular palace guards inside his chambers, of course. Instead, a team of at least six shadow wardens patrols the floor, garden, and roof at any given time."

"Shadow wardens?" Anemia said, raising her eyebrows.

"Anti-assassins," Ulrich explained, smiling. "Finally, there's Hansom and Jeeves Caduceus, the assassin brothers who graduated two years ago."

"Oh, bloody hells," Billys grumbled. "Aren't they the ones who single-handedly butchered the entire class, and then threatened to take poison if they weren't allowed to both graduate? Didn't they keep complaining that there 'had' to be a graduate every year, so it would have to be both or none?"

"The very same," Ulrich replied.

"I never heard de end of dat story. What happened ta dem?" asked Terry.

"The headmaster at the time, Professor Hale, magnanimously decided to let them both win, and then shot Jeeves with a hand crossbow the moment they let their guard down."

"Hale," Terry mused, "Don't remember 'im."

"Let's just say the brothers Caduceus specialized in taking contracts against certain members of the Dalton College," Ulrich said. "In fact, they were probably the ones who killed Professor Ignacius so that Winderstint could take over as headmaster."

"We have to deal with all these: the traps, the shadow wardens, and the Caduceus brothers, before we even get to Sable." Sickly began, returning the conversation to the problem at hand. "Of all of them, I'm most worried about the shadow wardens."

Jamie nodded. "How does one counter that which counters oneself?" she asked philosophically.

"Simple," Booter said, surprising everyone. "It's what Sickly's been saying this whole time. Don't be assassins."

Billys snorted derisively. "That's the stupidest thing I've ever heard."

"Shut up, Billys," Sickly cut in, "Booter has a point. Booter, if you were trying to break into Ponsingham Palace to steal from it, how would you do it?" Booter shrank a few inches farther into his seat, fingers twisting his necklace.

"I don't know. Thieves are good at getting in to places, but I've never even heard of a place with this many traps. Sure you could disarm one or two at a time, but how does anyone go up against a wall of traps?"

"That's brilliant," Sickly breathed. "We'll turn the traps against them. No, Jamie, hear me out. Where will the shadow wardens expect us? Through windows, chimneys, and side doors. Instead, we'll walk straight in the front entrance, and while they're scrambling to get to the one place they haven't guarded, we'll set a few traps of our own. They'll never see it coming, because the traps are all supposed to be on their side."

"We'd never be able to set them up in time," Jamie argued.

"There'll be four," Sickly glanced at Ulrich, "five of us there. We'll practice setting them up on the fly beforehand."

"And what do you propose to do about our mutual classmate, Mr. Levania?" Ulrich asked lazily, though Sickly detected a hint of tension behind his words.

"It'll be five against one, if everything goes according to plan."

"Excuse me, but you'll have to do a little better than that if you want my help. No plan survives contact with the enemy, as they say. And it won't be five against one. Winderstint is an accomplished assassin himself. He won't sit back and let Mr. Levania do all the work if he thinks his life is in real danger. So, if you still want my services, you'll come up with something better than that."

"Mr. Munz, do you remember what we discussed at the beginning of this conversation?" Sickly asked, with a hint of threat.

"Mr. Dodger, I'd rather take my chances alone than face Mr. Levania and Mr. Winderstint with nothing more what you've told us." Sickly took a deep breath, then exhaled. It was early afternoon, but after everything he'd been through, it felt like midnight. He doubted a vat of tea would have curbed his exhaustion.

Jamie gave Ulrich a look. "Don't get your knickers in a twist, Munz. I've been working on a new kind of blinding powder. It not only blinds, but is also able to infiltrate every gas mask I've ever tested it on, and causes choking, burning lungs, and, if too much is inhaled, death."

"What's it made of?" Sickly asked drily, "Ground biscotti?" They looked at him. "Sorry, go on, Jamie."

"All we'd need to do, right, is refine enough of the stuff, package it as a missile weapon, and, of course, make a gas mask that can stop it, so that we aren't affected."

"An interesting proposal," Ulrich mused. "I suppose you *can* make this mask."

"Shouldn't be difficult," Jamie said, sounding a little unsure. "I just need to make a filter treated with a compound that will undergo a rapid neutralization reaction with the agents in the irritant." Ulrich brushed this away.

"That's all very well, whatever that means," he said, "but I doubt it will be enough."

"We also have Crowbar," Sickly added. Ulrich turned a long-suffering expression on Sickly.

"You don't mean the . . . the hell hound, do you?" Sickly's eyebrows rose.

"Yes, I do."

Ulrich made a small despairing noise, like a kitten being trod on. "Oh, blintz."

Sickly turned to Ulrich. "Mr. Munz, you do know that a blintz is a small pancake filled with cream or fruit, right?"

"Obviously," Ulrich sighed, still looking unhappy. "But saying 'Oh, bugger' lacks imagination and style."

"Sickly," Jamie warned, "I don't think I can make a mask for a dog in time. I don't know what the effects on him would be."

"Then we agree we'll only use your weapon if Crowbar dies or it's absolutely necessary."

"We're going up against Sable Levania, dear. By definition it will be bloody necessary," she pointed out.

"I grant you we may be able to pull this off, if we are very, very lucky," Ulrich began. "But we still have to get out of there. Mr. Winderstint's associates throughout the city will respond to any call for aid, and even if we kill Winderstint, I doubt they'll stop. They are enjoying their newfound power, and they won't give it up even if you kill the head of the operation. So, where is the exit, Mr. Dodger?"

Terry nodded gravely. "Dey'll be crawlin' outta da woodwork like . . . like . . ."

"Termites?" Booter suggested.

"No." Terry asserted. "Like . . ."

"Ants," Billys tried. "Flies? Bees?"

"Sconces!" Terry exclaimed happily. They stared at him, and he looked abashed. "For putting dem little candles in. Never know when you'll be sup-rised by a sconce."

"Yes . . . well, Terry, dear. What can we do about them? The assassins, I mean," Jamie asked.

Sickly had been mulling this over for a while, and a thought finally struck him. He turned to Anemia. "Corporal Cassidy, I think this is where you may be of assistance." She looked nervous. "Don't worry, I wouldn't ask you to do anything outside the law. In fact, quite the opposite. I don't know if there's any more you can do here, so would you kindly return to the Raft Street Station and take the captain a message?" She nodded, hesitantly. "When is the next official Watch inspection of the guilds? We'll be ready two days from now."

"Sure, I can tell him."

"I don't get it," Billys whined.

"Then let me explain."

They listened. Their eyes widened, Ulrich's smile faded, and Billys swore. Anemia's frown morphed into a diabolical grin.

"You bastard," Billys exclaimed appreciatively. "You conniving, crazy bastard."

"Thank you, Billys." Sickly said. "The one problem is that if it's going to work, we need to be completely ready by the time Parliament convenes. As Mr. Munz said, that's two days from now."

"Two days?" Booter squeaked. "I think I need to sit down."

"You is sitting down," Terry pointed out.

"Oh." Booter gripped the edges of his chair just to be sure.

"Jamie, you'll work on the masks and the blinding powder. Anemia, if there's anything else the captain needs to tell us, you're welcome back here."

"The Watch will be ready," Anemia said with iron certainty. "I still don't like the rest of it, but I'll do my part to protect this city."

"Everyone else, we're going to Mr. Stashcrumb's training room to practice working together. Booter, why don't you help us?" They all stood up from the table, and headed in their respective directions.

As Sickly was exiting the room however, he noticed that Anemia and Billys had stayed behind. He went into the hall, shut the door behind him, and pressed his ear against the door. It was too tempting not to listen in.

". . . sorry for what I said last night. About the Watch. I was out of line," Billys was saying.

"No, it hurt because it's true. Some coppers think the badge is a shield for their own crimes. And the brass at the top let the big crimes go, the ones committed by nobles and merchants. I wish there were more like my father."

"He's a bastard, but he's straight, I'll give him that. Don't tell him I said it though. He'd just better watch his back."

"We all need to watch out."

"True. But once it's all over we should celebrate! Would you like to go dancing again?"

"I'd like that. We'll have to work on your waltzing skills, though." Billys huffed and Anemia giggled. "But please, be careful."

"Aren't I always?"

"Come here, then." Sickly's eyebrows rose as he heard the unmistakable sound of two people kissing. He pulled back. He had never expected that. Of all people, of all his friends . . . Billys? He couldn't believe it.

Billys had actually been kissed by a girl. A real, live, actual girl. No matter what you did or didn't believe in, the world was full of minor miracles. Sickly's eyebrow twitched.

Yet as he walked down the corridor, a tiny, traitorous part of him hated Billys. Billys could only enjoy his moment with Anemia because Vel had sacrificed herself to protect all of them. A sacrifice she would not have needed to make if Billys hadn't goaded them into following him in the first place. Or if you had let him go alone, an even darker voice reminded him.

For the rest of the afternoon they trained in Mr. Stashcrumb's chilly but well stocked dojo. Booter puttered around trying not to get in the way, handing people dropped weapons and reloading crossbows with a look of panic. After a few bouts of sparring to warm up, they began to train their teamwork maneuvers in earnest.

Billys and Ulrich were both skilled assassins, but mostly this meant they bickered over the best way of accomplishing even the simplest of tasks. Sickly would have thought Ulrich, as one who had been part of a team of assassins before, would have had a little more self-control.

"What are you, a bricky fool? Anyone's going to see a front snap kick coming a mile away!" Ulrich shouted, red faced. Sickly chalked it up to nerves, and his experience as a leader. Unfortunately, Ulrich had only given the orders. He'd never actually had to work *with* anyone before.

"Did the Graeod give you a double helping of beard to offset your empty skull? No one can execute a Yakistani Backflip in a five foot wide corridor!" Billys screamed back. As for the others, Ulrich and Billys both tried to order Booter and Terry around, and gave only tacit respect to Sickly. Sickly reminded himself that they had another day left to sort things out.

By dinner, more energy had been expended yelling insults and provocations across the room than had been spent training. Ulrich and Billys were both hoarse, Sickly's ears were ringing, Terry's calm was damaged, and Booter had chipped a nail. Sickly ordered everyone to separate corners.

He and Terry went to the kitchen where they borrowed from their host's pantry to cook the evening's meal. Mr. Stashcrumb arrived while they were all eating, sat down grumpily, and declared he had lost his chess match that afternoon. He then relaxed back into his ground state grumbling, though to Sickly it sounded almost contented. Perhaps Mr. Stashcrumb didn't mind a full house as much as he professed.

After the meal, Terry and Booter cleared the table, and Jamie took Sickly and Ulrich down to show them her work. "I got the powder all ready, and I'm set for a final test of the mask. If I've done everything right, we should be protected. Stand back." Sickly and Ulrich backed to a far corner while Jamie tucked her long braids under a cloth, donned her headgear and a pair of treated gloves and wrapped a thick oil cloth round herself.

"Genulum protect fools and tinkerers," she muttered. Little plumes of reddish yellow dust fountained up as she undid the ties on one of the pouches. Jamie shook the hand holding the bag, and was engulfed in a small cloud of particles so fine they looked like a foul red and yellow mist.

"Jamie?" Sickly called hesitantly.

"I'm all right, I think," came the muffled reply.

"Thank goodness," Sickly breathed a sigh of relief.

"Sickly? See that crank-powered water sprinkler over there?" Jamie gestured. "Could you use it on me? The mask works fine but the dust doesn't settle for minutes unless you get it wet." Sickly found the device, which looked like an oversized water skin connected to some kind of pipe system with a crank on one side. Sickly pointed the nozzle at Jamie and began to turn the crank. Instantly, several jets of water burst forth and cut swaths through the roiling cloud of vapors surrounding Jamie. Once the dust had settled, Jamie pulled the mask off her face and dropped the dripping oil cloth. "I'd call that a success, right."

"Brilliant, Jamie," Sickly commended. "I'm glad the masks work."

"Wait just a moment, Mr. Dodger," Ulrich said, coolly. "We know that one of them works."

"Mr. Munz," Sickly said in warning tones.

"I won't trust my life to a mask that I haven't seen tested. Ms. Webb's mask works, but she could easily have made a mistake with one of the others, and who's to say she hasn't tampered with them?"

"Excuse me!" Jamie exclaimed. "Of the three of us, you're the one who's tried to do us in!"

"Jamie, he has a point. You ought to test the other masks." Jamie looked betrayed, but Sickly plowed on. "And if it will make Mr. Munz feel better, he can watch you when you test them."

"This is ridiculous." Jamie muttered. "But have it your way."

"Thank you for attending to my concerns, Mr. Dodger," Ulrich said, smiling toothily. Sickly left Ulrich and Jamie to their work on the masks and headed upstairs to make sure that Billys wasn't bullying Booter.

Having finished the weapons check, Jamie joined them for practice the next day.

Unfortunately, this meant a third person arguing with Billys and Ulrich over strategy. It had to be nerves, Sickly decided. He couldn't blame them. They were going up against the most powerful and dangerous people in the city with little more than two days of preparation. But there was no help for it. Sickly did his best to focus everyone on the overall goal without getting caught up in trivial squabbles.

Something finally seemed to click, and by the second half of the day, even Billys and Ulrich were getting along well enough to practice beside each other. All their weapons and armor were ready, courtesy of Jamie's efforts, and everything seemed to be in place for the next day's assault.

Dinner was quiet that night, as everyone was busy going over the plan in their minds, trying to think of ways it might be improved. Finally, Sickly stood up, and as everyone turned to face him, he took a deep breath. "We're going in there and we're going to kill Winderstint and Sable." They nodded expectantly, waiting for him to inspire them, to tell them it would be all right. "Well, then." Sickly turned and walked up to his room.

He closed his eyes, trying not to think about the next day because whenever he did, he feared he was going to throw up. He went over to the closet where he had hung up Vel's duster. Taking the coat in his hands he brought it to his nose and inhaled. It still smelled faintly like her, and yet he felt no grief. All he could think was how beautiful it was. A masterfully crafted assassin's garment, for all the good it had done.

"Hey." Sickly looked up to see Booter's worried face framed by his short blond hair. "How are you?"

"Fine," Sickly said mechanically. It was not even a lie.

"Me, I'm a wreck. I know you and the others have the hard job, but still, I doubt if I'll sleep tonight."

"Booter, thanks for leaving the Thieves' Guild to join us."

"I didn't have much of a choice, did I? And besides, it's not like spending last week at the guild would have been any better. Worse, probably." He looked glum in the candlelight. "After missing a whole week of classes, I bet they expelled me."

"I'm sure it'll be all right," Sickly said without conviction.

A tremor entered Booter's voice. "They've been looking for any opportunity to get rid of me, and this is it. What if they really have expelled me? The last four years of my life will have been a total waste!" Booter's face scrunched up around his eyes, which began to leak big, blobby tears. "I hate it so much! Why am I such a failure?" he choked out. Sickly gave him a hug, and Booter subsided into despairing sobs. "What'll I do?"

"We'll figure it out," Sickly said calmly.

"What if you die? Then where will I be?" Sickly's eyebrows rose. Booter gave a watery smile, "What I mean is – I'm worried for you, Sickly. I wish there was more I could do to help."

"Were you able to track down that lead I sent you out on this morning?"

Booter wrinkled his brow. "That new giant mansion off Patterlin Street? I mean, I think it's the right one."

Sickly took a moment before he responded. "If you're sure about it, and you really want to help . . ." Sickly leaned forward and whispered in Booter's ear for a moment.

Booter's eyes widened. "But, me? I can't do that, Sickly, I –"

"We'll be counting on you, Booter. You."

"Me?" He repeated, in the tones of a man singled out to read a new taxation policy to a mob of unfriendly Hambridgers. "Really me?"

"Yes, really you, Booter. You may not be able to pick a pocket, but you can avoid trouble. Remember that and be careful."

"Yeah," Booter said shakily and gripped his pendant necklace. "I'll – I'll do it. I mean, I'll try. For you, Sickly." Sickly nodded, and Booter left.

"That was interesting." Sickly turned his head sharply to see Ulrich in the doorway, head cocked to one side. "I didn't know you kept such damp company."

"Mr. Munz, I'm not in the mood."

"I didn't come to insult you." Sickly raised his eyebrows. "I heard about Ms. Lucrezia from Ms. Webb. Truly, she was the best of all of us, and I'm sorry for –"

Sickly cut him off. "Don't say you're sorry for my loss."

"I wasn't going to. I meant that she was the better assassin, though I'd never admit it to her face. The tactical advantage she would have conferred might have tipped the odds tomorrow. She even managed to injure Sable." Sickly blinked.

"Oh." It was oddly refreshing to have Eveline discussed as a warrior, rather than as a lost friend. "Yes, she probably would have tipped the battle in our – What?" he shouted, making Ulrich jump. "Did you just say she injured Sable?"

"Er, yes?" Ulrich replied a little warily.

"Why didn't you mention that?"

"I thought you knew," Ulrich retorted crossly.

"How would I have known?"

"Ah, quite right. Shards and shillings, I'll forget my own knife, next. Well, I had been given the boot earlier that morning. After I was out of the door, I skulked around the palace and happened to spot Sable returning. I could tell he had sustained damage to his torso and left leg."

"Thank you for telling me," Sickly said.

"Indeed." Ulrich grinned toothily. "Now to the business at hand. I don't trust you, or your friends." Sickly raised an eyebrow. "If it were not for the fact that Mr. Winderstint and Mr. Levania would hunt me down and kill me, I would leave you and your ragtag band of misfits to the tender mercy of the crows. As it is, I will adhere to the old adage: The best defense is a knife in the back of your enemies. I need you, but I will not be so naïve as to trust you."

"Do you have a point?" Sickly asked coolly.

"You lost the notebook because someone set you up. I think it was one of your so-called 'friends.'" Sickly turned away in disgust. "You can't see it, because you trust people, Mr. Dodger. I admire that, I really do. I freely admit that some things in life are easier if you trust your friends. One of them is getting shot in the back."

"Says the man who has been trying to do just that."

"Yes, Mr. Dodger, I'm the only one who's openly tried to kill you. That means you'll be on your guard around me. It's the ones who haven't tried to kill you yet that you need to keep an extra eye out for." Sickly's mind unwillingly recalled the eagerness in Billys' voice when Ulrich had described the power and favors offered by Winderstint. It had been his idea to go to the watch house, where the assassins were waiting in ambush. And Jamie had been out of Sickly's sight often enough in the last week, how could Sickly be sure that she hadn't been spying on him?

"I have a contingency plan," he told Ulrich. "For obvious reasons, I won't elaborate."

"I hope it isn't contingent on anyone you . . . trust," Ulrich purred.

Sickly stuck out his chin, "Yes, it is. You know why? Because I trust my friends, no matter what they do or say. You'll never understand, Mr. Munz, the power of trust." Ulrich rolled his eyes.

"I won't say I've got your back," Ulrich stated curtly, starting to go. He looked back, over his shoulder. "But I'll make sure no one else gets anywhere near it, either." Then he was gone.

Sickly sat down on the bed, suddenly exhausted. Beside him he spread Vel's coat out, and laid down next to it. "You're not . . ." he whispered. "You're not . . ." He repeated Vel's dying words over and over, wondering what she might have meant. He lay in the dark for an eternity, his thoughts spilling over one another.

What if he had arrived in time to help Vel? What if she had run, instead of fighting Sable? What if she hadn't been wounded by Ulrich and the others the night before? What if the attack outside the watch station hadn't been random chance? What if Billys hadn't made them visit Anemia? Vel would still be alive. What if?

He wished that tomorrow he and Winderstint and Sable would all die together. It was the only strong desire he had felt in days: a quick death once his task was done. He wanted it so badly, it ached inside him. He only feared that he would fail to kill Sable and Winderstint first.

When he heard Terry's massive feet on the landing, Sickly hurriedly pushed Vel's duster off onto the floor. Terry entered, bowing his head to fit through the door. He noticed the coat, picked it up, brushed it off, and hung it up in the closet. Then he went and removed some of his less comfortable protective gear for bed. He blew out the candle, and Sickly heard the cot groan under the man's weight. Sickly rolled over and tried to sleep.

After a while, Terry's voice broke through the silence. "Sickly? Could I have a drink of water?" Sickly rolled over in disbelief and stared in the direction of Terry's voice. "Please?" Sickly went and got the water and passed the glass to the expectant hand.

"There," Sickly said. Terry gulped the water down in a single huge swallow.

"Sickly?"

"Yes, big guy?"

"Can't sleep."

"Really?" he asked, sarcastically.

"Don't feel right. Feel sick."

"You're just nervous, you'll get to sleep eventually."

"How come you so sure?" Terry asked.

"Because we're going to succeed tomorrow."

"How do you know?" Terry's barrage of underhanded questions flummoxed Sickly.

"Because . . ." he struggled to think of a reason that would placate his friend. "Because Jamie is really smart, and Billys is really clever, at least when it comes to killing. Ulrich is really cunning, and you're really strong. We'll win, Terry, don't worry."

"Sickly?" The shy, deep voice came again. "You don't tink I'm very smart." Sickly bit back his automatic denial of this fact. "I know I'm not clever like you or Jamie. Everyone knows. Dey say mean fings 'cause dey tink I don't understand."

"I know, big guy," Sickly whispered.

"Dey tink I'm not a real person 'cause I'm not smart. But not you, Sickly. You treat me like a person, even dough I'm big and dumb. Dat's why you my friend." Sickly shifted uncomfortably, unable to forget all the times he had said careless little things about Terry when the man wasn't around. Terry deserved better than he got. He deserved better than Sickly as his friend. "Are you mad, Sickly?"

"No, Terry, I'm not."

And it was true. He just felt tired to his bones, alongside the deep familiar ache of the old wound on his back. Terry was silent, and Sickly felt the chasm between himself and the rest of the world widen a crack further.

CHAPTER 27

The next morning, Sickly pulled Vel's duster on without a second thought. He hadn't realized before now how well the garment fitted him, as did the ring snug around his finger. As a concession to safety, he did at least button his cloak firmly around his shoulders to prevent the casual observer picking him out of a crowd. The others dressed similarly, hiding weapons and armor beneath cloaks or dockworkers' coats. Looking at the faces around him, he knew they were on edge. He could feel tension in his own movements, but the weight of numbness prevented him categorizing the feeling as either excitement or nerves.

Together, they walked into the chill morning light. Terry hefted their bag of traps over his shoulder and followed. Outside, Sickly breathed in the scent of the derelict Hambridge dew. Mr. Stashcrumb handed Sickly the huge chain which served as a false sense of security to those who did not know Crowbar. Then the codger gave him a last kernel of wisdom. "Don't screw it up, boyo." Sickly wasn't sure whether the old man was talking to him, or Crowbar.

Doing a faultless impression of a concerned mother, Booter watched from the doorway as they descended the drive. Sickly turned to wave a farewell, which the young thief returned only half-heartedly. Then they were off into the slate-grey streets of Hambridge, headed for Tumult Hill.

As they neared the crest of the rise, a flurry of carriages, carts, and coaches bound for Ponsingham Palace forced them to the edge of the streets. Stone-faced palace guards pointedly failed to react to the tourists and hecklers critiquing their tabards. Said tabards proudly displayed the royal coat of arms, which featured a concussed-looking pig rampant on a purple field of psychedelic flowers. Above them, banners bearing the same motif flapped disconsolately under the weight of the Hambridge smog. Attendants scurried about trying not to tread on the wrong toes, while criers flagrantly fabricated titles and honors for the personages they were announcing.

Sickly and his friends fought their way through the crush, unaccustomed to a crowd that did not part for them. Their passage up the road was made easier when Crowbar began to growl. They did not dare use the rooftops for fear of being spotted either by the Royal Guard or by any of Winderstint's assassins. Sickly relied instead on his old tactic of hiding in the anonymous mass of Hambridgers. Besides, it was difficult enough handling Crowbar at ground level. At last, they struggled into sight of the palace proper, which sprawled across the crown of the hill like a contented lion.

Ponsingham Palace, built *circa* Ages-Ago by Her Grace, Lady Flagellanta Ryker, was a marvel of ancient and modern history. Since its first construction as a fort against the disgruntled Hamedic barbarian tribes who had thought they owned the land, the palace had been sieged twice, captured once, and burned down wholesale four times. The Hamedic tribes had been responsible for all said incidents, save the final fire.

Legend had it that, tired of the endless conflict, Lady Flagellanta and Warchieftess Brutitia Severa united their peoples by coming together in a sacred marriage. The following nuptial revelries resulted in the palace's final combustion and a campwide hangover that lasted until the next week. Quoth Lady Flagellanta: "Ugh, bloody hells, art there anything left? That fortress wasn't even fully paid off yet. And will someone fetcheth my knickers and a damn espresso?"

The current model stood three stories tall and was crafted of limestone blocks that could at best be called beige. Each stone had been lovingly carved by a legion of artisans to depict heraldic devices, coats of arms, and the occasional lewd bas-relief. Long windows adorned the walls of each floor, secured with curlicued lattice grates. Here and there towers sprouted from the onyx roofs and gables, looming over the city. By far the largest was Severa Tower, at the base of which a grand ingress allowed the procession of nobles, officials, merchants and retainers access to the edifice. Though it was early, the houses of parliament were already cramming themselves inside, eager to engage in the day's political debate and mud-slinging.

Terry led the way like a large snow plow, gently but inexorably shifting the crowd, allowing Sickly and the others to reach their target entrance. Sickly held tightly to Crowbar's manacle, sending a silent prayer to Caestos, patron of hounds and berserkers, to help the dog keep a lid on it until they were inside. It did make him feel a little better. At last they clustered around an unobtrusive door set into the outer wall of the eastern palace grounds, and Jamie set to work with a roll of lock picks. They bunched around her to block the crowd's view, staring resolutely towards the main gate of Severa Tower to fend off suspicion.

A moment later, Jamie squeezed Sickly's hand and they slipped one by one through the little door, shutting it behind them. They stood in a walled garden bordered on three sides by the tall wall, and by the palace itself on the fourth. Paths crisscrossed the area, separated by white trellises and empty flower beds, shielding them from view. Sickly saw no signs of life beside a few barren trees which had already dropped their leaves. The noise of the street was muffled as the door shut and partially replaced with the sound of fountains gushing.

"Traps ahead. Be on full alert," Jamie said.

"Just get on with it," Billys snapped.

Jamie led the way down a trail, as she was their best trap expert. Sickly's eyes flicked this way and that as they dodged from one point of concealment to the next. Suddenly, Jamie held up a hand, halting them. She peered up into the branches of an old oak, then climbed up the trunk and tinkered with one of the limbs. After about thirty seconds, there was a tinny clang, a spring whizzed past Billys' ear and a heavy metal object drove into the ground ahead of them.

They proceeded to the edge of the walled pathway after disarming two more traps, one of which nearly caught Terry before Ulrich stopped him, pointing to the snare at their feet. Sickly and the others, hidden by the topiary thickets, peered out at the remaining stretch of open lawn between them and the palace proper.

"Look there," Ulrich said, and pointed to a yard gnome situated in the shadow of the palace façade. He unlimbered his crossbow, loaded a blunted bolt, and fired. The bolt struck the gnome between the eyes. Instead of shattering, however, it flew backwards and released a hail of tiny darts.

"How did you know that was a trap?" Sickly asked in amazement.

"Trap? I just wanted to get rid of the vile, silly thing."

One by one they broke cover and ran to the gnome's position, flattening themselves against the wall and avoiding the windows. Sickly had been worried about Crowbar giving them away, but he needn't have bothered. The dog was as eerily quiet as ever and moved with a low-slung grace as he bounded across the lawn beside Sickly. Terry and Billys' reconnaissance combined with Ulrich's knowledge had helped them choose this spot, a little past Winderstint's apartments. This would allow them to infiltrate the palace with relatively little fear of provoking the shadow wardens too early.

They paused to survey their next move. "Now we've got to

make it to the third floor," Sickly said. Everyone nodded, except Crowbar, who relieved himself on the gnome. As they had planned, Sickly was the first one up the side of the building. Given the intricacy of the stonework, he had no difficulty finding handholds, though he did mutter an apology as he used the stone head of Lady Grisly Reiker as a footing. He reached a window on the third floor, braced one boot against the opposite side of the frame, and jimmied the window with a thin strip of steel he pulled from his boot.

Sickly pushed on the window which swung inward, and surveilled the room on the other side. It appeared to be an elaborate smoking room, currently empty given the early hour. After determining the coast was clear, he dropped silently to the thick purple and gold carpet. Now, the hard part.

"Terry, ready!" he half whispered, half shouted to his friends below.

"Right den, good doggie," Terry rumbled happily. To the complete surprise of Crowbar, Terry grabbed the dog in his enormous hands. Before Crowbar could disembowel Terry, the man crooned, "Doggy, up! Up, doggy!" and launched the mortified beast skyward. Terry's accuracy left nothing to be desired, and the mass of enraged fur flew through the window to land in a heap at Sickly's feet. Sickly quickly grabbed the dog's chain, just as Crowbar lifted himself to his feet, black eyes ablaze with the fury of an active volcano.

"I say, who goes there?" A crisp voice cut through the air, making Sickly's heart stop. Sickly turned, slowly and saw a guardswoman standing at the entrance of the room. Bugger. Based on her long O's and clipped R's and I's, the woman was probably from near Lyecastle, a distant region on the northwestern border of the Autarchic city-states. She likely didn't know every minor member of Hambridge nobility. Sickly had to hope so. Their backup plan depended on it.

"It is I," he started, "Sir Rupert Pudding, Baron of The Seventh Precinct of Puddingshire." He gripped the chain firmly to keep his hands from shaking and was strangely glad that his face betrayed none of the sheer terror mounting inside him. It was just lucky that he was wearing one of the outfits he had bought at Amos' Quality Armor and Formal Wear. If nothing else, at least he looked the part.

"Ah, sorry, sir," the guard said, sounding more friendly. "Have a . . . hang on. Why've you got a dog? Animals aren't allowed up here." Her tone hardened again.

Bugger everything. If only they had waited just one more minute, one more *bleeding* minute to hurl Crowbar up. The sentry started moving forward frowning.

A mad, wonderful idea came to him. Sickly felt like laughing manically, though his face remained locked in neutral. "Ah, but this is my seeing-eye dog. I'm er, half-blind, you see. Since the, ah, the paprika incident at my family's summer house. He helps guide me around, don't you, Scruffles?"

Crowbar growled, deep as a pit of hell and without any of the warmth.

"Oohhh," the woman said, brightening again. "I've got a cousin who's got one of them. What a good boy, eh? Again, sorry to bother you, milord. Oh, and His Grace, Lord Scoke Reiker will be opening the day's proceedings soon, if you'd like to take your seat, milord."

Sickly inclined his head with what he hoped was magisterial acknowledgment. The guard bowed and moved off the way she had been going, perpendicular to Sickly's corridor. He stifled a sigh of relief before dropping one end of a length of cord out the open window for the others to climb.

Quickly and quietly the group assembled in the room and pulled their rope up after them. Well, Sickly thought, Phase 1: Enter Ponsingham Palace hadn't gone as badly as it might have. He only hoped that Phase 2: Unleash Crowbar on Someone Else went as well.

. . .

One after another they stole out of the room and down a corridor that ran parallel to the outside of the building. Following it left, away from the guardswoman's trajectory, they soon came to a bend. Jamie, still in the lead, snuck a glance around the corner then motioned the all clear. Following her, Sickly and the others soon stood before the closed double doors that would lead to Winderstint's suite, according to Ulrich.

Sickly turned to the man. "Mr. Munz, you said most of the guards would be on the main floor, dealing with the crowds, yes?"

"I believe that to be likely, yes, Mr. Dodger."

"Well, then. Terry, say hello."

"Hullo," Terry said, dutifully.

Sickly sighed. "Break the doors down, please."

There was a pause. The doors were not blasted off their hinges.

"Terry?" he asked, and looked at the large man.

Terry looked sheepish. "I know dis was da plan, but dem's nice doors. Hand carved and all. Look at da scrimshaw! Dis ain't a door, it's a . . . a . . . a work of art!"

"Is now really the time?"

"Right. Sorry, Sickly." Terry turned and noticed a stone statue of a satyr standing on a plinth set some way along the corridor. He grasped it in one shovel-like hand, cocked his head, then with a speed Sickly would not have thought possible, impelled it head-first into the doors. The satyr smashed through the doors, sending finely carved wood splinters in every direction. A hidden row of slits above the door loosed a deadly barrage of spring-loaded blades which thudded harmlessly into the threshold, even as the doors began to list inward on their hinges. "Now dat's what I call a battering ram," Terry said happily.

Without a moment's pause, they dashed into the room beyond. Winderstint's suite was well furnished, if they could judge by this foyer. Antique furniture sat atop imported rugs and was lit by priceless lamps. The walls were hung with silver framed mirrors and portraits of ancient nobility wearing expressions ranging from stoic to suffering a pressing need for a bowel movement. Over everything, a chandelier of green Umundi crystal hung and shimmered.

They admired the grandeur for no more than a second before leaping to action. Sickly dropped Crowbar's chain and converged on Terry with the bag of traps. Sickly grabbed a handful of items, including a coil of Murderer's Wire, a steel filament so thin it was nearly invisible, perfect for garrotes, triggers, and traps.

Four doors, two on either side, and a fifth opposite them stood open and menacing. First, Sickly took a one-shot miniature Burlington crossbow and secured it to the wall of the nearest door by the simple expedient of nailing it there with a tack hammer. Glad of his gloves, he next tied one end of the wire coil to a handy gas lamp. Just as they'd practiced, Sickly unspooled the rest across the doorway and tied it to the trigger of the crossbow. Finally, he upended a leather bag full of caltrops on the threshold of the door.

Pausing for a moment, he looked around at the others.

Jamie was already finished, Terry was nearly done, but Ulrich and Billys were struggling to finish their crossbow traps. Crowbar stood resolutely in the middle of the hall contemplating with grim pleasure the optimal method for ripping out a human's jugular. Sickly made to help Billys, but Jamie's shout stopped him dead.

"Incoming!"

The first shadow warden appeared at the door Sickly had just left. Sickly turned to see a figure swathed in loose grey clothes charge through the doorway. It jumped the caltrops but failed to notice the razor thin wire, which bowed taught, triggering the tiny crossbow. A small but deadly bolt thudded into the warden's side. The attacker landed heavily, staggering. Before they could retreat however, Ulrich hurled a throwing knife, and the figure fell backward, clutching at the wound.

The second warden was more cautious, firing a crossbow bolt

into the room first. Jamie almost dodged. Luckily, the bolt glanced off her armor and buried itself in the wood of the opposite wall. Jamie returned fire with her own crossbow, but missed the snap shot.

The warden sliced through the wire trap over the doorway and ran through, only to trip over the caltrops. Jamie wasted no time in grappling the overbalanced warden, knocking her victim unconscious in a well-practiced movement.

Sickly pivoted again, trying to take stock of the situation. Before he could get his bearings, a pair of shadow wardens faded into view at the foyer's far door. One fired a crossbow through the doorway, as the other cut Terry's trap to wispy threads. The bolt narrowly missed Billys, who was forced to dive out of the way. Wary of the caltrops, they did not advance into the room.

"Take cover," Sickly yelled. He jumped over the body of the first warden and his own caltrops. Everyone dove for the doorways to avoid the crossfire.

Sickly unslung his own crossbow, removed the safety and peered out. The wardens at the end of the hall were taking turns firing their weapons through the door. Jamie and Terry had both fired their bows, missing. Sickly was about to take aim, when he was startled by a yell from Terry.

Terry staggered and fell, a bolt sticking out of his shoulder. Sickly's head whipped around to see the last two shadow wardens advancing through the front doors. The doors which Sickly and his friends had completely forgotten to trap.

Ulrich and Sickly were closest to the door and in most immediate danger from their unexpected arrivals. "Munz! Behind you!" Sickly called. Ulrich ducked, and barely avoided decapitation. The sword buried itself in the woodwork, but instead of making the mistake of trying to wrench the weapon from the wood, the anti-assassin just drew another sword.

The other warden closed in on Sickly. Sickly sighted down his bow and fired. The assassin dove aside, sneering, "Nice try, Dodger," as he rolled to his feet. The warden Sickly had been aiming at however, the one trying to kill Ulrich, gave a startled cry as Sickly's arrow hit its mark. After which Sickly could spare no more time for Ulrich.

Instead of trying to reload, Sickly tossed his weapon toward his enemy who was forced to knock it out of the way. Sickly drew a knife and hurled it. The knife hit with the hilt, bruising but not killing. "Dodger! I'm going to really, really savor this." Sickly's eyebrow quirked. Why was that voice so familiar?

The assassin pulled off the gray cloth that had concealed his visage. Hamilton Traplek's previously handsome features had been badly mauled by Crowbar's attack just days ago. Long scars covered in dark red scabs clawed their way up the left half of his face. His eye was swollen and puffy, and the corner of his mouth had been ripped and resewn with stitches. "Ah, Mr. Traplek, always a pleasure to see an old face."

Hamilton actually shrieked in rage.

Sickly leapt backward into the room and rolled behind a desk as the shadow warden cautiously entered.

"Just you bloody wait, Dodger. I'll give you and that damn dog worse before I'm done with you." Sickly heard a metallic tinkle, as of a pin being pulled from a gas canister, followed by the tell-tale hiss of escaping air. He hastily rammed a gas mask down, over his head. The world turned a shade darker thanks to the protective goggles, but his lungs labored for air through the filter.

Hamilton had disappeared. Sickly peered around frantically, looking for his enemy. A hail of needles appeared out of the smoke. Most buried themselves in the desk, but Sickly felt a sharp pain just below his mask. The stinging sensation began to spread down to his chest.

Sickly swore. His mask might protect him from gas, but it did nothing against weapons coated in poison. And while he stayed in this smoke-filled room, there was no way to take a dose of anti-venom by mouth.

"Come out, Dodger," Traplek growled. "Come out so I can flay the skin off your freak face." In spite of the grave circumstances,

Sickly rolled his eyes at the old insult about his features. With limited options, he dove back into the foyer, over his caltrops, and then pressed himself against the wall to avoid stray crossbow fire.

Hamilton was right behind him. Before Sickly could move, his classmate raised a sword to deal the final blow. "The next time Joanna and I shag, I'll be thinking of this moment."

That was when Crowbar's teeth sank into Hamilton's rear with a satisfying crunch.

Crowbar had been forced through noisy crowds he could not silence, hurled like a common Chihuahua through a window, and suffered the indignity of a demeaning pet name like 'Scruffles.' He was not some bug-eyed lap dog. He was not a mewling domestic inbred. He was the Alpha and the Omega. He was the stuff of wolves' nightmares. He. Was. Crowbar.

The assassin screeched in surprise and pain as Crowbar's jaw muscles contracted, forcing razor teeth straight through custom body armor as if it were tissue paper. The man was borne to the ground, and Crowbar went for the kill. "Oh, Ten Gods! Not that beast! Not again!" were the last words Hamilton Traplek ever screamed.

Sickly couldn't take time to be horrified by the messy noises coming from Crowbar's direction. He ripped his mask off and felt around with one hand for his bandolier of anti-venoms. His heart pounded faster than normal. His breath came in short, painful gasps. Dimly, he was aware that he was dying. He let out a strangled cry for help, but his voice sounded faint, even in his own ears. He picked a bottle at random and with shaking fingers brought it to his lips.

The cork was still on.

How funny.

He tried to raise an eyebrow but couldn't.

CHAPTER 28

Sickly awoke and gasped for breath. "Smart dog, you've got there, Mr. Dodger."

"Ulr – Mr. Munz?" Sickly asked, muzzily.

"The very same. I wouldn't be talking to you if it weren't for the hell hound. Dragged you across the line of fire to me. You were barely breathing, you had a vial of anti-venom in your hand, and I thought to myself: Ulrich, Mr. Dodger's been poisoned, sure as I breathe. Checked the needle in you, and it's lucky I did. The vial you picked would have killed you faster than the actual poison. I administered the proper antidote, of course. Now, we'd best get moving before the brothers Caduceus arrive."

"Ngh," Sickly said. He blinked at the spots still cluttering his vision. When he tried to raise his head, queasiness floored him again.

Ulrich was muttering to himself. "Has no one killed those two? Blintz this for a game of soldiers." Ulrich shouldered the bow and took aim. From the floor, Sickly frowned. Both of the wardens were behind walls, there was no way for Ulrich to see them, let alone hit them.

Ulrich's finger brushed the trigger, and the recoil sank the bow into his shoulder.

The bolt blasted a hole through the wall, leaving a crater and a quickly stifled shriek of agony.

The last shadow warden peered out from behind cover, but was forced back by a bolt from Billys, who took the opportunity to drop his Burlington and charge the door. Jamie fired her bow, keeping suppressing fire on the doorway. By the time the shadow warden looked out again, Billys had closed in.

Their weapons clashed for a few seconds, and the warden pushed Billys back. Before they could press the advantage however, Jamie leapt forward and assisted Billys in rendering the last defender unconscious.

Sickly's head was beginning to clear. He mastered his stomach, as only one subject to frequent nausea, flu, and digestive trouble could, and rose to his feet. Ulrich helped propel him forward to meet up with Jamie and Billys who were removing the bolt from Terry's shoulder and applying first aid. "Is he all right?" Sickly asked.

"We gave him some anti-venom for the poison. The armor helped of course, but those broad-heads sever a lot of blood vessels. He won't be at full strength, dear," Jamie assessed, finishing the bandaging process.

"I'm okay." Terry stated, but Sickly heard the strain in his friend's deep voice.

"Keep to the back, big guy. Take care of yourself, all right?" Sickly said.

"Touching as this is, we need to keep moving," Ulrich interrupted. "This way."

Sickly grabbed up Crowbar's chain once again. Conscious that he was in the royal palace, he used his handkerchief to wipe the worst of the gore and drool from Crowbar's jowls and stowed the befouled garment in a pocket. Then he followed Ulrich. Billys and Jamie came last, helping support Terry, whose breath caught with every step. Ulrich led them through the central door, past the bodies of the downed wardens. "I give to you, lady and gentlemen," Ulrich said, with mock theatricality, "Winderstint's office!"

They stared at the empty room, and Sickly was not alone in quirking his eyebrow at Ulrich.

"Bats and bricks," the man said, put out.

Sickly ground his teeth. Of course, it was too much to hope that Winderstint would just be waiting around for them to find him.

"Sickly, dear," Jamie began, "if we don't hurry, Winderstint will use their puppet Lord to strike down the bill that Lady Ironside is pushing through. If that happens, there won't be any political resistance left. Even if we kill him after, the assassins he's already put in place won't budge."

"What you're saying is, if we don't stop them before the final vote, nothing will," Ulrich said, with only a sliver of his usual grin. Jamie nodded. The large man cast his gaze around, and his face brightened. "A solution for finding them presents itself! All we need do is torture the location out of one of the survivors. I knew you had us leave them alive for a reason, Mr. Dodger."

"No, no torture," Sickly responded automatically. He had to think.

"See here, you're being completely unreasonable. Ms. Webb appreciates the stakes!" Sickly stared him down flatly. Ulrich shook his head in disgust. "You're a scraggy fool. When I allied with you, it was because I thought you had finally found a little steel in your spine. If you don't face reality, we'll all have a little steel in our spines, if you follow me. Give me thirty seconds with one of those wardens, and we'll have the answer."

"No," Sickly repeated.

"You're too soft, Dodger. Weak."

"Shut up, Ulrich." Everyone looked at Billys, startled. "Sickly might be soft but he isn't weak. He's done more to stop them than any of us, so shove it where the sun don't shine." The pinch-faced man turned to Sickly, his watery eyes full of confidence. Ulrich's jaw twitched under his beard, but he said nothing.

In that moment, Billys' unexpected support meant more to Sickly than he could adequately describe. "Thanks, Billys," he managed. Now if only he could live up to their expectations by deducing Winderstint's location. What had that guard said? "Lord Reiker is about to open the parliament. Winderstint and Sable would want to be there to oversee the vote, wouldn't they? Let's try to find the Lord's vestibule."

"Nice one, Sickly," Billys said, grinning. "Let's crack on, then!"

Crowbar's leash pulled Sickly onward as the dog and Ulrich led the way through Ponsingham Palace. They hurtled through corridor after corridor, slowing only at intersections to ensure no guards noticed them. Thick rugs muffled their pounding feet, and the increasing cacophony of debate covered the sound of their garments rustling past ancient suits of armor and moth eaten tapestries. Though they hastened, Ponsingham Palace was huge, and they could not throw all caution to the winds. Sable and the Caduceus Brothers were still at large.

"This is it," Ulrich hissed, suddenly, bringing them up short. The little band stood before yet another grand door. "This should be the office of His Grace. For drafting speeches and the like. There's a pulpit beyond where he can stand to address all of Ponsingham Hall. If they aren't there, we could try the vestibule on the other side." Sickly nodded.

With a deep breath of stale air, Sickly strode forward and pushed the door open.

Booter's heart raced.

Please, oh pleaseohplease let me not die. Drasilla, Genulum, anyone? Not dying right now would be really good. Also, not being seen. If they see me, they won't just kill me, they'll torture me, force me talk, and then kill me. And then they'll torture me again, probably. Oh gods. Please not that. Please, please, please not that.

But Sickly had said they were relying on him. It was up to

him, Booter Squill. No turning back, not on Sickly. Booter couldn't do that. Even in the face of torture, and death, and then more torture. Oh merciful Ten.

No! Don't think about that. Will it hurt? Of course it will, moron. That's the point of torture.

Come on, Booter, come on! He wished he could grip his pendant for luck.

Booter's hands shook. Sweat poured off him, soaking into his shirt. His shirt and the last of the oil soaked rags he was stuffing under the elaborate back porch of this Eel Park mansion. Genulum, Flame Bottler, please let me keep my eyebrows. He gritted his teeth, took a deep breath. No time to think.

Booter lit a match.

Sickly entered a large, beautifully appointed antechamber built for the Reiker's preparation before addressing the assembled members of the Hambridge parliament. Deep green velvet curtains were drawn across the windows of the left wall blocking the morning sun. The space was illuminated by dusky yellow gas lamps. Their glow washed over mahogany paneling, thick green carpet, antique tables and chairs, and several large armoires for the Lord's convenience. In pride of place before the west-facing windows was a magnificent desk, the kind fitted with a dozen puzzle locks to allow the heads of state access to myriad secret stashes of snuff.

Behind the desk sat their old headmaster, Hank Winderstint. There did not appear to be anyone else in the room. Lord Scoke Reiker and his attendants must have been in the far vestibule.

"Mr. Dodger," Winderstint said, with a wide, oily smile, "I'm amazed you and your, nyeh heh, *friends* made it here." There was no mistaking the dreadful nasal hum that passed as human speech. Both its timbre and air of superiority set Sickly's teeth on edge. "Thanks to you I have Bradley Wells' notebook. And now that you've so conveniently arrived we'll soon have you spilling your guts about the decryption key, nyeh heh." Sickly stared at him blankly. "Sable will enjoy torturing you. I will enjoy watching.

"We couldn't have done this without you. You led us right to the little spy, Adams, or whatever she called herself. Glad you two found each other, it worked out so well. For me, I mean. And speaking of finding people, did you ever find your murderer?" His crooked tooth gleamed in the yellow light. "The person who killed Bradley Wells?"

This was the man who had sowed panic and chaos throughout Hambridge, who had threatened Sickly and his friends, who had ordered so many lives to be snuffed out, including Vel's. There should have been anger. There was only cold calculation as Sickly spoke. "With respect, Professor, shut up. I don't want to talk to you, I just want to kill you."

Winderstint gave a small sigh. "Then allow me to –"

Sickly and the others didn't wait for him to finish the sentence before they opened fire.

Mr. Winderstint wasn't nailed to the back of his chair as Sickly had hoped, but he did yelp and dive for cover behind the desk.

"Kill Winderstint before Sable gets here!" Sickly commanded, cranking another bolt into his bow.

"On it, Sickly!" Billys laughed, and drew a pair of swords, starting towards Winderstint.

From somewhere behind the desk, Winderstint sneered, "Interrupting your elders, Mr. Dodger. Such impudence." His greasy visage reappeared above the desktop. "Allow me to enlighten your narrow mind one last time. The assassin who slew Bradley Wells for me was Jamie Webb."

This at last stopped them in their tracks. It was the fact that Winderstint had spoken without any trace of his usual flair or preamble. Sickly turned to Jamie, his eyebrows quirking. He noticed that she alone had not fired her crossbow at their old headmaster. She was instead standing stock still, a look of pained indecision plain upon her face. The bottom dropped out of Sickly's stomach.

Billys reacted first, turning in disbelief to Jamie. "I don't believe this, Jamie! You —"

A steel tipped bolt ripped through his chest, exactly over his heart. Sable Levania emerged from the shadows, wearing head to toe black and a gas mask. He held the killing bow in both hands. Billys looked down at the arrow which had pierced him from behind. "Oh," he said, and collapsed.

Jamie slunk down the corridor, juggling statistics. Could she win the graduation ritual? Putting down two opponents was worth a lot, but she was up against Sable, Vel, Ulrich, Joanna, and Hamilton. That would increase the variation in the distribution . . . and Roderick Gablehaus had been boasting that he'd got two already. Right up until she had dealt with him. It was the last time he would ever call her a tupenny doxy.

Merafey's salty trench, Jamie cursed. The simplest way to get high-paying contracts straight out of College was to score well on this test. Higher paying contracts meant she could pay off her student loans faster, accrue less interest. The faster she could do that, the faster she could start putting extra money aside for family. Her mind flashed to Leila's open face, huge brown eyes, and snaggle-grin, to Connall's scraped knees and bare feet, hair tangled and knotted from playing in the street. And there was no telling what would happen if Mum or 'Da took sick. She just needed one more, a third to add to her score.

Of course, all the easiest prey was gone by now.

Jamie took a breath and focused. The mansion was silent in

the way that a crouching predator was silent. There was no noise, but the danger prickled at the back of her neck.

Her ears picked up the sound of conversation.

Frowning, she crept forward to investigate, readying her weapons.

As she peered around the bend, she saw two figures. Sickly and Vel murmuring to each other. She weighed the odds. Sickly and Vel were her best friends. She could probably trust them not to attack on sight. If she could just convince them to join her, she might have a chance against the others. She stepped out. "Hello, you two."

Eveline instantly took a defensive posture, but Sickly stopped her. "How are you dears doing?" Jamie asked, trying to gauge whether Vel would attack.

"Surviving." They said together, and Vel smiled at Sickly. Jamie suppressed a grin. Vel was often as cold as Sickly's expression. It was so cute to see her fawn over him. She wondered if Sickly knew that Eveline couldn't keep her eyes off the back of his head in any class they had together. On reflection, probably not. Men were hopeless at subtlety. It was what made women better assassins on the whole.

"I marked Yesterday Sam and Roderick Gablehaus but only just escaped ambush from Sable. He's teamed up with Ulrich Munz, a strategic and unfortunately deadly combination." Jamie said, hoping that her best friend would take this as a sign of peace.

"I saw Terry go down, but the doctors got to him quick I think. Haven't seen Billys anywhere." Vel sheathed her weapon. Jamie allowed herself to relax by the shadow of a breath.

"Sable finished him with a punching dagger," she said, trying to keep a note of relish out of her voice. Billys never failed to make Jamie feel like she needed a bath, not least because of his incessantly lewd comments about her and Vel.

"Just us then?" Sickly asked, shaking her out of a reminiscence of seeing Sable take down Billys.

"Yep. Do you want to make a go of it together? I bet we'd have a chance of giving Sable some exercise," Jamie said, trying to understate her request.

Eveline's whole body tensed, a second later Jamie heard the incoming footsteps. Her body took over, dropping and rolling sideways. She heard Sickly's gasp of pain. Poor Sickly, he just didn't have the same reflexes that she and Vel had. On one knee Jamie registered Sable and Ulrich closing fast.

Her chest flooded with hot panic. No. No! Sable *and* Ulrich. Damn Thumbscale! The odds of success were dwindling with every footfall approaching them.

Eveline fired down the hall, forcing Sable and Ulrich to separate. Protecting Sickly, as always. But who to help? Sickly might be able to stall Ulrich for a moment. Jamie moved to Vel's side just as Sable detonated a smoke bomb.

"Hells," Eveline cursed. "Jamie?"

Targets in smoke? Caltrops. Jamie jumped forward to scatter a bagful of the metal spikes into the expanding smoke.

Sable struck so fast Jamie never saw it coming. Her body jerked uncontrollably, the pain was fire. Lightning made flesh. Her neck seared with pain and . . . poison! She panicked. Was it nonlethal? Was she already dying? No, please no. She had too much to protect. Protection . . . that was it! Only nonlethal doses were permitted, right? A wave of dizzying hope washed over her, or maybe the venom was already doing its work. She had to move. To take the antidote.

She was on the ground. When had she fallen? She fumbled at her belt. Thoughts hammered through her head. Odds of success dwindling. Vel above her, fighting Sable. Sickly and Ulrich obscured by smoke.

Her hands shook. She struggled to her feet. Smoke everywhere. Neck blazed. Hurt. Mum. The score. She didn't have enough. Da. Just one more.

I'm sorry. Connall. Leila.

Someone gasped.

Someone moving very close. Sickly's voice. Sickly, retreating from Ulrich. Back to her. The knife was already in her hand.

Forgive me, Sickly.

CHAPTER 30

Sickly's mind went blank. It had happened so fast. Billys had fallen with barely a gasp. Oh, gods. Billys lay sprawled on the ground, blood leaking out of him.

Ulrich started forward. "She's a bricky turncoat, Dodger! I warned you!"

Mr. Winderstint's rickety grin stretched across his face. "Mr. Levania, Ms. Webb, deal with these interlopers! My goodness, I've always wanted to say that. Oh, I've got tingles!"

Sickly's thoughts reeled. He took half a step towards Billys. The corpse was utterly still. He stopped. Focus, Sickly. He turned on Jamie. She stood, stunned, and her eyes were wide and horrified as they met his.

Ulrich charged at her but was cut off by a second crossbow bolt from Sable. "Ah, Mr. Levania. One more round, for old times' sake?" Crowbar leapt after them as the two men bore down on each other.

"Sickly, you got ta talk to her," Terry rumbled, then barreled after Winderstint to prevent his escape.

"Jamie? What's going on?" Sickly's voice felt brittle as frost on a window. He barely noticed as the crossbow dropped from his limp grasp.

"It wasn't supposed to go like this," Jamie whispered.

"Did you kill Bradley Wells?" demanded Sickly.

She licked her lips and nodded. "Yeah, I did."

"I thought you worked for Lady Fullfrigate."

"That was the codename I used for Winderstint."

"But they attacked you. They broke into your flat. You were hurt!" Sickly said, grasping for sanity. None of this could be true.

"They sent a Rose Notice with my next assignment. We staged it all, Sickly. So I could get close to you. So that you would trust me," her voice cracked with shame and sorrow.

"I did trust you!" She flinched. "But it was you who told them about the notebook after we got it from *The Daily Piccolo.*" It was as if his foundation was cracking, sending knife edges piercing through him. Vel dead. Billys dead. Jamie's lies.

"I also tipped off that thief, Lady Fingers, to steal it."

"All that time you let me chase blindly after his murderer," Sickly whispered, heart hammering. He began to yell. "You led me in circles to keep me off their trail! Off your trail!"

"I was trying to protect you!" she shouted back, the strain of the last few days boiling over. "I was trying to keep you lot out of it! That's why I hid the codes for you. So I could string Winderstint and the rest along without it looking dodgy. To give me more time to get you out of Hambridge."

"But why, Jamie? Why?" Sickly could feel the walls he had erected around himself creaking as the tide of frustration, anger, betrayal, and guilt flooded over them. He was barely aware of the fact that she was holding a loaded crossbow pointed at him.

"Because Winderstint and Sable gave me a promise."

Terry didn't understand what was happening. Billys was dead. Jamie and Sickly were angry. Terry was very sad.

But Sickly needed Terry. Needed him to stop Mr. Winderstint. Terry would do that for Sickly.

Terry raised his metal gloves. Mr. Winderstint ran away from

Terry. Mr. Winderstint threw lots of needles at him. Terry rolled aside. Mr. Winderstint had to keep Terry away. Terry was too dangerous up close. Terry had to get up close.

But the pain in his back was bad. Moving made it burn. Made him slow. Terry charged forward, but Mr. Winderstint ran away too fast. Terry needed a new tactic. "Professor Winderstint!" Mr. Winderstint faltered.

"Ah yes, Terry Andrews. Ranked nineteenth in the graduation ritual. I remember being forced to fail you out of my Political Science course for your insufferable stupidity. I suppose it proves that even a noble lineage can produce a common freak. Much like your friend, Sickly Dodger."

"Why you try ta kill me and my friends?" asked Terry.

"I'll respond in terms even you could understand. It is because you and your fellow degenerates don't fit." Mr. Winderstint threw more needles at Terry. Terry blocked them with his fists and his armor. "I have a vision, you see. A vision of power."

"When you had dis vision were you drinking heavily?"

"No you overgrown oaf! A flash of inspiration. An epiphany! Did Mr. Dodger ever question what my motives were?" Terry picked up the chair behind the desk and threw it. Mr. Winderstint dodged. The chair smashed on the wall.

"You want da power," Terry said. "You want ta control Hambridge."

"Obviously! But I also desired revenge. The Winderstint name is as old as the Reikers, from the days when the original colonizers brought civilization to the Hamedic barbarians. We had wealth! Titles!" Mr. Winderstint threw a smoke bomb at Terry's feet. Smoke went everywhere, and Terry couldn't see Mr. Winderstint.

Lucky for Terry, Mr. Winderstint was still doing a power-crazed monologue. "But it didn't last. When we fell out of favor, our ancestral lands were sold to repay our debts. Those who used to call us friend turned against us. They said Caestos had turned his sight from us. Can you imagine being born into such disgrace?"

Terry turned, trying to make out where Mr. Winderstint was going to attack next. No point in moving. Mr. Winderstint would attack as soon as Terry left the smoke. But in the smoke, Terry was safe. Terry heard things whistling by his head. Needles hit his armor. Terry crouched down so Mr. Winderstint would miss.

"I attended the Dalton College on the pittance left to us. After I lost the graduation title to that scheming Victoria Burnsbottom, I had to struggle to make a name for myself. I took any offer connected to the noble houses. Oh, how I remember the sweet revenge I wrought upon all those fools who had ground my family beneath their heels. But it wasn't enough. There were always more nobles, and more of their assassins for me to kill. Nothing had changed.

"And then it came to me. As an assassin I could only influence who got the power, but as a headmaster, I could direct the assassins to give *me* the power! At last, I will put the Winderstint family name back where it belongs! Great things are coming to Hambridge. Such a pity you lack the vision to be part of them."

Mr. Winderstint's voice was right behind him. Terry whipped around, in spite of the pain that brought tears to his eyes. Mr. Winderstint didn't expect Terry to react so fast. Terry used his gauntlets. Mr. Winderstint finally stopped talking.

"Winderstint hand-selected a group of young assassins. For our intelligence, our strategy, our abilities. Some were like him, disgraced nobles, second scions. Others already had everything, and wanted more. Hamilton and Joanna. And a few were like –"

"Like you," Sickly finished.

"Yes, Sickly, like me. Too bloody poor to pay for the Dalton College on my own! Can you understand that? No noble, no merchant, *no one* wanted to hire a common scholarship girl like me! It doesn't matter how good your class marks are, or – or how many friends you sacrifice in the graduation ritual if you don't come from the right background."

"You," he panted. "You were the one who killed me during the graduation test. Not Ulrich!"

"I needed another mark. To make the top ten." Tears were filling Jamie's eyes.

"I would have let you beat me, if you'd asked!"

"But don't you see? It wouldn't have mattered! Even in the top ten I couldn't get contracts! The only employer who didn't care about my background was Winderstint! Him and Sable. They promised change. They promised to help me. To help my family."

"What about your friends? What about us?" Sickly demanded. He was panting for breath, and his chest heaved with the emotion flooding through him.

"You weren't supposed to be involved, Sickly! We could have wrapped up the coup neatly if Bradly Wells hadn't caught on. He slipped that damn notebook past me, and brought you in against us. It's all gone wrong since then. I kept trying to tell you to run! But you were too gods-damned stubborn, innit! On your little crusade to save the city! But for who? For a bunch of nobles and merchants who wouldn't lift a finger to save my family as we starved?"

"Why didn't you tell us?" Sickly shot back.

"I tried! But I had to wait until we'd got the notebook. And it was never the right time. And then Vel died and you went round the bend. I tried to tell you that night but you cut me off!" Her body shook with emotion but her hands held the bow rock steady, aimed at his chest.

"So you were just going to lead us, your friends, into a trap and watch Sable kill us? Like he killed Billys? Like he killed Vel?"

Jamie screamed in frustration.

Shards and shillings, Ulrich cursed to himself.

Ms. Webb a traitor. Mr. Kid dead. Facing Levania with

nothing but his wits, his Schling, and a multi-murderous canine. This was going to be *fun*.

Ulrich had to hand it to her. He hadn't seen it coming. He had thought Williams Kid had the kind of temperament that lent itself to Winderstint's machinations. Ms. Webb had played the long game well, though. He could respect someone with that level of intelligence, steel, and ruthlessness.

Levania didn't bother to reload his crossbow. He drew a small handbow and fired again.

Ulrich rolled to the side, coming up on one knee. "All right, pup," he whispered to the hell hound. "I'm going to lay down some smoke. Bark if Mr. Levania comes out, or we'll both be dog meat by tomorrow. Understood?" The huge beast blinked. "I could get to like you."

"Surprised to see me again so soon, Mr. Levania?" Ulrich asked aloud, working a knife out of his leg sheathe. Behind his back, with his other hand he grasped a pouch of flash powder.

"Somewhat," said his old friend. Well, acquaintance, Ulrich amended. "I'm certainly surprised to see you taking leaves from Mr. Dodger's book."

Ulrich drew the knife back and winged it at Levania, who was forced to step aside. Even as he did so, Ulrich's other hand hurled the flash powder. He closed his eyes just as it exploded in a blinding crack of light and sound.

"A feint," Levania breathed. "Very nice."

"Another leaf out of Mr. Dodger's book," Ulrich gloated, smiling as he detonated smoke bombs at Mr. Levania's feet. Ulrich pulled the mask down over his face. He just had to hope the dog would target their common enemy.

And then, they danced. He and Mr. Levania swanned blindly through the smoke, as precise as ballet dancers, jumping and twirling at each roil in the cloud, performing pliés and leaps, crossing and weaving. They hurled knives and dropped caltrops to try to lure the other out of hiding. Twice Ulrich was nearly shot dead on the spot by errant crossbow bolts. Once he nearly forced Mr. Levania to move into a cloud of the special blinding powder. A flask of Genulum's Fire burst upon the ground. Greasy purple flames erupted from the floor, adding even more smoke to the ever worsening battle conditions.

It felt like hours, but couldn't have been more than a minute or two before Ulrich heard the bark. He turned and charged in its direction, drawing his short swords.

A slim figure wearing a gas mask appeared at the torn edges of the smoke. His quarry! Ulrich leaped, sword raised.

At the last second, Mr. Levania dove aside. Then Ulrich saw why.

Ulrich and Crowbar met in midair and fell in a snarling heap of teeth, armor, fur, and blades.

Ulrich rolled sideways and assessed the damage. It was grim.

Dog drool coated his designer body armor! The slime would take ages to get out.

As a side note he was prone and bleeding. And Mr. Levania was closing fast.

Ulrich rose to a knee and hewed at him with the sword. Mr. Levania blocked, but the dog bit into Sable's leg.

The man didn't let out a sound, just stabbed downward. Crowbar growled but didn't let go. His powerful neck and shoulders muscles bulged, and Sable was dragged off his feet. Ulrich swung, but Mr. Levania managed a hasty parry.

Enough of playing silly blintzes, Ulrich thought. He grabbed his other sack of blinding powder and poured it over all three of them.

Yellow particulate fountained everywhere. The dog stiffened, its eyes went wide, then squeezed shut. For once, Crowbar actually *whined*. He began to shake violently as the dust entered his nose, eyes and mouth. He fell to the floor, his great frame twitching weakly, and then went deathly still.

Ulrich crawled out of the cloud and stood. Pity about the dog. Not a great pity, mind you.

But Mr. Levania was down. Ulrich smiled, breathing a sigh of relief. He was about to slit Mr. Levania's neck to be certain but glanced up for a second.

Ms. Webb was drawing down on Mr. Dodger with a loaded crossbow.

Oh, blintz, Ulrich thought, and started forward.

Motion caught his eye. Ulrich turned to see Mr. Levania rising from the yellow cloud, picking up his weapons. It hadn't penetrated the man's mask.

Oh, *shite*.

Ulrich's grin vanished.

CHAPTER 31

"That powder isn't really blinding powder!" Jamie explained, her voice shaky. She and Sickly stood in a corner of the room, an eye in the storm of battle unfolding around them. "It's a formula I mixed up to put you all into a deep sleep! I was going to knock you all out and make it look like I'd killed you. I was going to tamper with your masks, but Ulrich's paranoia mucked that up, too. I could have smuggled you out of the city. I could have saved you, Sickly!"

"But not Vel?"

The blood drained from Jamie's dark cheeks. "That wasn't supposed to happen. I tried to bring her in to help fix Hambridge with me, but she – she didn't understand! She acted like everyone was supposed to be out for themselves. She didn't understand that you've got to help family. You've got to help those who can't help themselves.

"Hamilton and Joanna and Vel were buying new houses and coaches and body armor. Me? I was saving every penny! Food for mum's table. School for Connall and Leila. Medicine for 'Da. My father is dying, Sickly! River Lung. There's nothing I can do but buy him the next antidote. And every day the debts got worse and there wasn't – I didn't know what else to do!"

"I asked about your dad, remember? You could have opened up then," Sickly pointed out.

"What was I supposed to say? He's dying but don't trouble yourself over it? You were pretty quick to tell me I could sort it on my own."

"Jamie, if you'd just asked – Vel and I would have helped! We have money!"

"You have no idea what it's like, being poor, Sickly. You're just like them. With your family fortune to put you through school, right? I didn't want your pity, or your money. I didn't need it! I found a way to pull *myself* up. A way to save my family on my own. And change Hambridge for the better! And it was all going so well until you got in the way!"

"So that's why you let Sable kill Vel?" His words hit their mark.

"Stop it!" she shrieked.

"Because she got in your way?" Sickly pressed on, doggedly. She was the one who had been leading him in circles. The reason he was in this place. The reason the world was so upside down and Vel was dead. He considered the swords at his side. He could continue to verbally spar with her, goad her into dropping her guard. Then a few steps forward and he would be within striking range. Feint left, draw the swords, and cut her down. Avenge Vel and Billys.

"I didn't want her to die! Vel was my best friend, Sickly. I never wanted –"

"Never wanted what? To betray us? We're your friends, Jamie. You were *my* family. I've been trying to protect you and Booter and Vel and Terry and Billys this whole gods-damned time! Don't you think I would have done anything to help you?"

"Then why can't you understand why I did this to help my family? Mine and all the others like them." Jamie's eyes were dark with pain and frustration and fear.

Sickly thought back to his walk through Murktown. Bodies jammed together, living in their own filth and the pollution that had made Hambridge great. Children dying of cold and disease while hospital administrators pandered to bruised nobles. People killing each other over pocket change a banker wouldn't bother to pick up if he found it lying in the street. Street walkers ready to sell themselves for the price of another meal.

All while he, Sickly, had walked the dogs of the idle rich and played at being a detective.

A great roar erupted from Ponsingham Hall. The assembled peerage was rallying support and opposition for the vote. "Please, Sickly," Jamie begged. "I've come so far for this. If I don't do this now, all of it will have been worthless. Why can't you just step aside?"

Sickly walked forward slowly, arms at his side, yet he had no intention of attacking. He could feel the rage dissipating, leaving a cold, deep sorrow in its wake. Sorrow for this woman. His friend. His family. He would never hurt her. He stopped with barely an arm length between them, the point of the crossbow arrow digging into the armor over his thin chest. They had asked what he would kill for. No one had asked what he would die for.

"If you think it will make the difference," he said, "then I trust you. We do this your way."

"I'm so sorry," she said, "I'm sorry for everything. For Vel." He bit back his own automatic apology, a reflex honed over his years of failures in the eyes of his father. She didn't need to hear how sorry he was that he hadn't reached out, that he hadn't made the effort to understand her struggle and pain. Instead, he said what he always wished his father had told him.

"I forgive you." It was true. Sometimes when the mad dog slipped the leash all you could do was hurl yourself forward and try to save whatever was left. You couldn't always make the best decision. You couldn't always save everyone, no matter how hard you wanted to play the hero. Sometimes you had to just go home. Sickly had to hope so. Because if not, the ghosts of Billys and Vel would haunt him forever. Jamie's amber eyes were full.

"Well done, Ms. Webb," oozed the headmaster. He had reappeared from the clouds of smoke that now filled the anteroom. He was sporting a few bruises and cuts from his encounter with Terry, but their large friend was nowhere in sight. Flames glinted in his crooked smile. "Mr. Levania will finish off that oaf, Andrews and then we can remake Hambridge according to my dream. We can rule the city today, my dear. I'm sure your, aheh, family will be so proud of your efforts. And this is only the beginning! All you need do is get Dodger to give up the location of the encryption keys."

Jamie swallowed looking back and forth. Sickly braced himself. He was terribly aware of the pressure on his sternum from the arrow's fiery tip. Jamie could shoot him and pretend he had already given up the location of the ciphers. His ears were full of a peculiar ringing. It felt as though the tide of his blood was beating heavily through his head. His vision focused down to Jamie's face. Her eyes.

"I understand," Winderstint said with oily placation, "don't worry. Sable can, of course, take care of the messy parts of getting Dodger to talk. Just think of how rich you're about to become."

The world paused.

Jamie lowered her weapon. "He doesn't know where they are."

"What are you saying, girl?" Winderstint's voice snapped like a whip as he glared at the lowered bow. His voice abruptly lost much of its unctuous slither. "I hope you are not forcing me to question your loyalty? Think about who took you in after all other employers had rejected you. Who ignored your background. Who recognized your worth from the beginning."

"You did," Jamie breathed.

She raised her arm and grasped Sickly's shoulder. Their eyes locked on one another. And at last he felt the chasm between himself and the world, the walls around his core, fall. The tears came, welling up and pouring down his cheeks. Billys and Vel, maybe even Terry, were dead. But Jamie was still here.

"Hambridge needs to change, Sickly. But not like this." She glanced to Winderstint. "I hid those codes."

Their old headmaster looked on in growing disgust and fury. "You what? But you . . . I see," he hissed, voice dangerously low. "After everything I've given you. You silly girl. This is precisely why your kind can't be trusted. I should never have relied upon a dirty little gutter-rat like you. You'll hang as a traitor. But first I'll get those codes. And if you don't cooperate, I'll track down your family and stamp them out like the vermin you all are."

Sickly and Jamie turned, their eyes flashing. Jamie pointed the bow at Winderstint. Sickly drew Vel's butterfly swords.

"Not so fast!" he laughed, reaching for a torch sconce in the wall beside him. "I'll let the Caduceus brothers deal with you!" The sconce rotated and a hidden panel slid open, revealing a secret passage.

"No!" Hansom yelled, his eyes wide with panic and fear.

"It can't be," his brother, Jeeves, breathed in horror.

Before them, the inferno that had once been their new luxury mansion roared with heat and flame. "Why?" Hansom sobbed, in the voice of a father mourning the sudden, violent loss of a newborn child.

"If only we had been warned sooner," Jeeves said, solemnly. "It might have been prevented."

"Whoever did this will pay!" Hansom growled, fury blazing through the grief. He unsheathed a dagger. "Hear me, Merafey, Sea Witch! I swear," he drew the knife across his palm, "an oath upon this blood! An oath that I shall find whatever worm did this!"

Jeeves grabbed the dagger from his brother. "Oi! Me too! By all your devils and torments, Merafey, I so swear!" he snarled, cutting his own palm. Vengeful blood welled from between their fingers, dropping like fire to the scorched ground.

"Hang on then," Hansom said, suddenly. "Weren't we supposed to be somewhere?"

"Relax Hansom, it's not like Lord Winderstint really needs us."

A block away, Booter ran as fast as his scrawny legs could carry him.

"Strange, that usually works," Winderstint mused, genuinely puzzled.

Jamie pulled the trigger. The bow recoiled and the arrow flew towards its target. But a dark shape was already moving at blinding speed. It struck Winderstint in the side, knocking him down a split second before the bolt found its mark.

Sable stood from his crouch, helping the prone man to his feet. "Excellent timing, Mr. Levania," Winderstint said, voice shaky. "Status?"

"I incapacitated the other intruders but was forced to come to your rescue before confirming them as fatalities." Sable was staring at Sickly and Jamie. His mask perched above his head, ready to be rammed down in a second if Sickly tried to go for the sleeping powder. His noble features were as usual composed into a look of innocent interest. One of his gloved hands held a knife while the other flicked a spot of ash off his armor.

"Well done! Unfortunately, it appears our own Ms. Webb has been playing both sides of the field. The answer to the notebook quandary has been under our noses all along. Be sure to take her alive, though I have no more need of Dodger or the others. With this tidied up, the doors to every nation state will be –"

"Sir, we should deal with . . . Mr. Dodger before he tries anything stupid." Sable stated, still examining Jamie with his calculating stare. He hefted his weapon.

"Ah, yes, quite right. I nearly got carried away again. Must be those two semesters of drama I took."

Damn, Sickly had been hoping that Winderstint would give them a few moments to think of a plan. Against both Sable and

Winderstint they didn't stand a chance. But Sable had paused. He still hadn't decided about Jamie. Maybe they didn't need to fight?

"Sable," Sickly said, not exactly sure where he was going. "You once asked me if I had been to Murktown." Sable hesitated again, and Sickly pounced on the opening. "I've seen it now. Death and disease and decay. People killing each other over money they don't have. I watched a child die in front of me." The man stood stock still.

"After you've killed me, I want you to think about something. I want you to think about those nobles and merchants and bankers you killed. They weren't in charge of Hambridge when that child died. You were, Sable."

"Are you trying to goad me, Mr. Dodger? It won't work," Sable replied coolly.

"Kill him," Winderstint ordered. The assassin's knife was poised, burning in the light of distant flames.

"That's right," Jamie added. Sable's eyes flicked back and forth between her and Sickly. "Where exactly is the difference you promised me? My mum still starves herself so my brother and sister can eat. My da's still dying. Our neighbors still can't find honest work. This city's no different than it was."

Sable sighed. "Remember, this city is still not under our control, Ms. Webb. Today we can change that fact. Tomorrow, we can begin to save it."

"And how exactly are you going to do that?" Sickly inquired.

"The world is divided, Mr. Dodger, between rich and poor. There is no changing that fact. But no matter their wealth or background, everyone is a slave to currency. A gleaming trap that keeps merchants, peasants, and nobles alike chasing our tails day in and day out. As the privileged elite, it is our duty to awaken from this hopeless fantasy to guide our society along a path that will benefit everyone. The Bricquébécois have a phrase, *noblesse oblige*. Literally, the nobility shall oblige. If they fail to do so, we shall slay them until a more enlightened group arises in their place." The muscles in Sable's arm coiled like a dog ready to tear into Sickly's throat.

"So this is your great contribution to Hambridge? Kill people off until things get better? Sable, who can you murder to cure the sick? Who can you assassinate to end violence?"

"Stop listening to him, Levania," Winderstint snapped, but Sable continued to stare down Sickly and Jamie.

"As an assassin I can kill those who would impede progress. And as a noble I can donate to institutions that take care of the needy. My family has sponsored the Charity Barnsforth Loving Hospital for generations. We've also funded the Alchemists' Guild to research new cures and installed one of our own, Simon Digby, as the Head Alchemist."

Jamie let out a bark of laughter. Her face was a mixture of disgust and frustration, though she smiled humorlessly. "Charity Barnsforth? You mean the same place where I tried to get my Da treated for River Lung? Where they see patients based on who can pay the most? Oh, yeah, and don't think I don't know about Digby. He tripled the price of that bloody curative as soon as took over the alchemists."

"She's right, Sable. The hospital didn't even bother to treat me until I told them about my family name."

Sable regarded them both, the knife still poised to strike. Winderstint huffed with impatience. "Really, Levania. I don't know how you can be hesitating. All hospitals operate that way, it's simply the price of business. And Digby's decision to raise the price of Beaupierre's was a stroke of outright brilliance from Caestos himself! Think of how much money it made. For the cause, of course. Now, I really must insist we stop arguing morality and do what's right. Dodger threatens our power, and Ms. Webb must reveal those codes."

Winderstint unsheathed a knife and made to step towards them.

The man shrieked once in agony and toppled sideways. Sable withdrew the knife from the falling man's back and cleaned it on a black handkerchief. Sickly's heart lurched. It was the same knife that had stabbed Kerry Adams. The same knife that had cut out Vel's breath.

"The gleaming trap has claimed so many," Sable opined, still cleaning his blade. "Thank you for helping me realize that our philosophical differences were too great for collaboration to continue. Still, it illustrates my point rather well, don't you think? This is why we need a benevolent, awakened ruling class. To prevent men like him corrupting our efforts to save the poor. Mr. Dodger, now that you have witnessed the suffering in this city, perhaps you would reconsider your motives. Would you like to dedicate your ingenuity towards a real cause?"

Sickly paused. Was Sable really trying to recruit him? The man's tone was always so honest, so intellectual, it was difficult to gauge his sincerity. Could it be that easy?

Then Sickly thought about Sable's actions. The piles of bodies he had left in his wake while Hambridge's people continued to suffer. The manner in which he so easily lumped everyone beneath him into a single group. He fought to save people, yet refused to see anyone beyond the scope of their social class. All while he took the power and entitlement of his birth as his right. Sickly quirked an eyebrow. "I would consider it, Sable. I'm dedicating myself to helping Jamie."

Sable allowed a slight frown to mar his brow. "Her family will, of course, be looked after. Ms. Webb, will you rededicate yourself towards making Hambridge a better place?"

"You just don't get it, do you?" Jamie said wonderingly. "The fact that Winderstint and Digby and all the rest were willing to bend people like me over a barrel for a little extra coin? There is no such thing as *noblesse oblige*. The only obligation nobs see is to themselves, innit? The only way to make real change is for everyone to be equal. To put everyone on even footing. To give everyone the same opportunities from the start."

"Your naiveté is charming but puerile. No one can be equal,

and therefore the strong must protect society. Can you truly not comprehend this?" He looked into their faces.

"If you're not willing to listen to people, how are you going to save them?" Sickly retorted.

The man shook his head. "I see. Then an assassin will save this city alone."

Sable struck, but Sickly was ready for it.

He raised his twin swords and parried Sable's thrust, forcing Sable back. Jamie stepped up in the wake of the lunge, keeping Sable on the defensive. Together, they matched Sable blow for blow. When Jamie struck, Sickly moved to parry Sable's response. When Sickly was forced to retreat, Jamie leapt to enfilade their enemy, covering him. They coordinated to flank Sable, working in unison to hound the assassin from both sides.

Sickly used every trick he knew, every attack and counterattack Mr. Stashcrumb and the professors at the Dalton College had taught him, dodging, feinting, and riposting.

Vel and Crowbar had wounded Sable. They exploited these weaknesses at every opportunity, striking hardest on Sable's weakened side, and constantly retreating so that Sable would have to use his injured leg as much as possible.

But they were fighting a losing battle. No matter how quickly Jamie struck, Sable was always a hair faster. No matter where Sickly retreated, Sable always followed. No matter what feint they tried, Sable always managed to block and counterattack. Sickly's arms burned hotter and hotter as the seconds dragged on for an eternity of panic and adrenaline. Sable disarmed him, but he managed to draw a dagger. Sickly's hands cramped around its sweaty hilt, his thin arms shook, sweat streamed from his brow, and his armor and clothing stuck to his skin.

At last, he shifted his foot just wrong, and he stumbled. Jamie was pushed back by a ferocious set of strikes, knocking into him. By the time he looked up, he saw – nothing. Sable had disappeared into the thickening smoke. He and Jamie leaned on each other, back to back, waiting for the inevitable, fatal strike.

Then, rupturing the silence, another great roar issued from Ponsingham Hall. In a daze, Sickly realized that someone must be calling for the vote. They were nearly out of time. Jamie cursed and he knew she must be thinking the same thing.

"Change of tactics, dear," she gasped. "Got to stop their puppet." Sickly nodded, too winded to even speak. "I'll do it. You won't have to kill anyone. Just keep Sable off my back."

"I will," he managed, still waiting to be picked off soundlessly. The seconds stretched long. Sickly closed his eyes, trying to master his ragged breathing, to slow his heaving chest. He listened for all he was worth, tried to sense the shifting air currents wafting over his sweat-soaked skin. Where would the perfect assassin strike from?

Sickly moved involuntarily as he realized the answer, just as Sable dropped from above. Sickly barely escaped the scything knife as it kissed the air behind his neck. Jamie was not as lucky. Sable's kick connected with her leg and there was a terrible crack. She screamed, half falling to the floor.

Without a second to consider a better plan, Sickly hurled himself at Sable's back, catching the man in a manic grapple. "Go, Jamie!" Sickly shouted.

With Sable momentarily trapped, Jamie escaped the melee and forced herself into a limping trot, her broken leg slowing her progress. "Ah, clever," Sable breathed, cool voice betraying nothing of his injuries or the exertions of the fight. "Forcing me to expose myself or risk losing the vulnerable Lord." He reached a gloved hand up to Sickly's arm, about to break his hold.

In a daze, Sickly was stunned by how pristine Sable's gloves were. He had always kept himself immaculately clean, even during training exercises. Billys had made fun of him for it behind his back.

Calmly, Sable contorted under Sickly's shaking arms, simultaneously breaking the hold and flooring Sickly so hard the wind was knocked out of him. Sable's knife flashed downward, and Sickly managed to roll aside so that it scraped across his armor.

He was playing for time, just long enough for Jamie to cross this impossibly large office.

Sable kicked him hard in the stomach. Still on the ground, Sickly folded with the pain of the blow, coughing weakly with whatever air was left to him. Quick as a serpent, Sable stood and reached for his handbow, leveling it at Jamie's retreating back. Perhaps he thought he could find the codes himself, or perhaps he was beyond caring about Winderstint's plans of dominating the other cities, Sickly didn't know. "I really thought she understood," Sable continued, with that childlike frankness of his. "Such a waste of potential."

The man who had casually slain men and women for his cause took measured aim at the woman he claimed to be fighting for. The arms that had embraced and lowered Kerry Adams' lifeless body angled in perfect unison to direct the bow's aim. The hands that had fired an ugly, foot-long shaft of oak through Billys' heart held the weapon. The fingers that had guided the knife gently through Vel's gut now caressed the trigger. The tip of the bolt hung weightless in the air, and upon it rode Jamie's future. Her hopes, her desires, her fears, and her love glinted in the steel tip.

Sable never hesitated.

And then Sickly clapped a hand over Sable's mouth. A hand containing the handkerchief soaked in dog drool and gore he had used to wipe Crowbar's maw earlier that day.

Sable stiffened in surprise as he fired. The shot missed Jamie's head by inches, burying itself in the wall beyond her. With a roil of smoke, Jamie disappeared into the next room, hunting Lord Scoke Reiker.

Sable was having problems. Sickly had never heard anything but cool indifference in his voice, but now the man was making a mewling, gagging cough that sounded horribly organic. Sable flailed, sending Sickly crashing back to the floor. He scrambled away as Sable spat and wiped frantically at his mouth.

"You're a germophobe," Sickly breathed as the man hacked

and cursed. "That's why you keep yourself so tidy. You're afraid to get dirt on you." Sickly stood, clutching his dagger with one hand and his kicked ribs with the other. The pain was making him lightheaded.

"Is that what you think?" Sable rasped. Sickly's eyes widened. He hadn't expected Sable to recover this quickly. "That I couldn't ignore a little filth? In *my* profession?" The assassin regained both his feet and his knife. Sickly was so very, very dead.

"Ignore it? Maybe. But that's your problem, Sable. It's beneath you. Just like Jamie, right? How can you help someone without being able to reach out to them?"

Sickly had trained hard to understand the strange mechanisms underlying facial expressions in his vain attempts to emulate them. At his words, Sable's face twitched briefly. The tiniest flicker of doubt in his righteous certainty.

"It changes nothing. You will die. Ms. Webb will die. The city will be saved."

Sable charged Sickly. Sickly watched the blade coming towards his gut and read the barest imperfection in his enemy's lethal movement. A single window of opportunity opened. Sickly's training took over, bringing him to a fighting stance. His left arm moved, caught Sable's right hand with the knife and drove it down into Sickly's own leg. Pain exploded from the deep wound, but Sickly barely felt it.

Sable's eyes widened, but Sickly was still moving. He pivoted, forcing Sable off balance and tugging him closer while at the same time bringing his own dagger upward. With the unstoppable weight of momentum it tore through cloth and armor and meat, sliding up under Sable's ribs.

"But you –" Sable whispered, his body stiffening around the piece of hard metal. "Why would you?" He was still staring at the injury he had inflicted on Sickly, uncomprehending. The perfect assassin never let himself get injured, Mr. Stashcrumb had said as he drilled the maneuver into his pupil. Of course, Sickly was far from perfect.

Sable stared into Sickly's eyes. "You don't kill people . . ." His voice was not just thick with pain, but shock. For the first time, Sable Levania had misjudged an opponent.

"I found what – who – I will kill for," Sickly whispered, calm as ice in Sable's ear. "You will never touch one of my friends again."

There was something new in Sable Levania's eyes. Something that had never shown itself in the light of the world.

Fear.

Sable was terrified of death. He didn't understand it. He dealt it to others. It was not something that he ever thought of suffering.

Sickly saw Sable's fear and felt no pity.

He wrenched the knife out and slid it across Sable's throat.

Hank Winderstint crawled across the floor of his office. His legs had stopped hurting. Other parts of him screamed and bled, but everything below the waist was simply numb. He hadn't been this wounded since . . . well, he had never been this wounded. He had seen this kind of wound. He had even inflicted it on some of his victims. Taken pleasure at the thought of them bleeding out slowly, knowing there was no hope.

Now, he was terrified.

"Please, please," he mumbled, "Someone. Anyone. Help me!" He dragged himself forward another pace, not knowing why. It was a bodily reflex to escape the pain.

A shadow, like Drasilla's night, fell upon him. His vision was going. He looked up through hazy clouds of smoke or blurriness to see a massive figure.

"Mr. Winderstint," rumbled a low voice.

"Mr. Andrews?" he coughed weakly. "Do something. I – I order you –"

"Do not speak to me dat way." The voice came dangerously low.

"I'm sorry!" Hank wheezed, "Please! Help! Can't you s-see I'm dying?"

"You are not a good person."

"I know," Hank begged. "I – I've done terrible things, I know it. You're right. Mr. Dodger was right. I can see that now. Really, I can!"

"Sickly is a good person. He likes ta help people."

"Yes!" Hank gasped, "He is!"

"Not like you." There was a pause. "Not like me." A huge hand descended.

Winderstint tried to scream.

Sable fell silently backwards.

Sickly dropped to his good knee as nausea rolled over him. Before he could master himself, he vomited all over the carpet.

It wasn't very heroic, but Sickly was still unfortunately well suited to his name. The pain in his left leg was like a bar of red hot iron gouging through his awareness. He collapsed to the floor as a huge shape loomed out of the smoke.

"Sickly!" cried Terry. "You are hurt." The man reached out to him with bloody fingers.

Sickly tried to focus, "We should . . . leave. There's a fire?"

"We are going now, yes." Terry helped him to his feet just as Jamie reappeared, limping towards them with an antique sword as a makeshift crutch.

"Sickly, you won't believe it, Lord Reiker is dead!"

Sickly nodded, saddened at the thought of his friend committing another killing.

"It wasn't me!" she added. "He was just lying there in his vestibule. Someone did for him and his guards, quick and clean like. An assassin. No one's noticed, by the looks of it. Bloody parliament is still in session even with this racket." She gestured at the battlefield.

"What?" Sickly murmured. This was too much. His head was so hazy. At least his leg didn't hurt so badly now.

"Hang on a minute," Jamie gasped, staring first at Sable's corpse, then at the dagger in Sickly's leg. "You didn't!"

He nodded.

Her words were tinged with awe. "Bloody hells. How?"

"He was going to hunt you down. So I stopped him."

Jamie gaped, then shut her mouth and nodded. There was something new in her tawny eyes. Respect? Fear? Sickly's head swam. "We need to get you out of here. Leave the knife in there for now though, dear. You need a professional."

"I say, what the bootlicking barnacles is going on here?" Ulrich had arrived, groggy and pale from blood loss. Despite this, he pulled one of his short swords on Jamie.

"Come on, Mr. Munts, dere will be no fighting now. We are all friends." Sickly slumped again, but Terry picked him up in his great arms, mindful of the knife. "We all need ta go now." Terry's voice was so warm and rumbly, like deep sea bubbles, Sickly thought dazedly.

"Blintz it, Andrews, how can you even move with those injuries?" Then there was motion, and after an eternity of agonizing jarring, sun broke upon Sickly's face.

Behind them, Ponsingham Palace had begun to belch oily black clouds of smoke, trailing screams and the wail of alarm claxons.

The houses of parliament shifted in comfortable bickering. A minor mishap like a fire in the palace and the assassination of a callow Lord Reiker wasn't enough to derail the momentum of centuries of court procedure. After measures of brandy had been doled out by servers, the minor clamor had easily settled back down to affable naysaying and name calling. The only concession they had made to the circumstances was to reopen the floor to debate for an additional hour.

The Trade Minister was just finishing a stirring speech directed against Lady Runcible. "And that is why your objections are nothing more than slander, you warthog-faced prune!"

Half the hall clapped lazily while the other made dire threats against the personage of the Trade Minister.

At last it was time for the vote. But without Lord Scoke Reiker to rally the old families against the Fair Representation Reform their bloc was confused. The fractious lords and ladies lacked a clear leader to guide the arm of their power.

Annette Martinez smiled to herself. Her daughter, Joanna, had at last done something right.

CHAPTER 32

Sickly swam through the muggy fog that was the womb to consciousness. Sensation followed soon after, and unfortunately, most of it was pain. It felt as if he had been rolled down a mountain of fist-sized gravel. Worst, his left thigh sang an aria of operatic agony. Not to mention he had a headache fit to drop a mule.

In spite of it all, he opened his eyes. Above him was a pristine, white ceiling. He inhaled and coughed on the smell of antiseptic, rubbing alcohol, and the kind of cheap cigarettes smoked by hospital nurses who light up just beneath 'NO SMOKING' signs. Waves of nausea and dizziness rolled over him in turns. He wasn't sure if this was due to his injuries, or his poor constitution. Probably both.

Memories struck like a sledgehammer.

The arrow punching through Billys' chest, his mouth opening in a little gasp. Jamie limping through the smoke as Sable took aim at the back of her head. Vel, lying motionless in the sleet stricken street, eyes pale as the Hambridge sky.

And, again, Sickly cried.

He cried for Billys, who would never dance again, and who would never be with Anemia Cassidy. He cried for Jamie, who had wanted so badly to protect her own family and couldn't tell anyone. And he cried for Vel, who had trusted Sickly more than any of them, enough to give him her life, and who would never know that Sickly, for his friends' sake, had become a killer.

The memory of shoving the knife home burned as brightly as the pain in his left leg. The feel of the steel passing neatly through the soft flesh of Sable's stomach. The brief resistance of the body armor followed by the involuntary stiffening of the man's musculature. The barest hint of drag as the knife opened his throat. The look of fear in his eyes as Sickly had ended him.

Sickly rolled on to his side and vomited into the bucket set conveniently by his bed.

It wasn't just the sensations or the thought of the death on his hands. It was how easy it had been. That he had not felt a thing at the time. Only the cool logic that Sable had to be stopped. Perhaps, he thought in growing horror, that was how Sable had justified to himself each life he had taken. It barely mattered that now he felt remorse for Sable. For the man who had killed so many of his friends. The man who had wanted to make a difference.

Sickly's vomiting episode made Terry jerk awake. The big man sat forward in a nearby chair, rubbing his eyes with two fists the size of bread loaves. "You are awake. I am glad."

"What happened?" he croaked. His throat was raw and scratchy. Terry handed him a glass of water.

"We carried you out of da palace before dey found us. Da par-lament was a success. Da House of Peerless tried ta fill a buster, but da House of Uncommons passed da law. While dat was happening, we took you all to da Hambridge Hospital. You very nearly died," Terry explained, as if this was a proud achievement on Sickly's part. "And you will never guess who it was dat stitched you up." Sickly frowned. No, indeed, he hadn't a clue.

A shock of yellow hair peered around the white curtain that was the far wall of the room. "Er, hullo, Sickly."

"Booter? What are you doing here?" Sickly asked in amazement.

"I, er, work here," Booter mumbled, stepping farther into Sickly's view and blushing to the roots of his hair.

"B-but you're a thief," Sickly said, stupidly. "You work at the Thieves' Guild, don't you?"

"Trouble is, when you're the worst thief in the world, you don't exactly have a lot of pocket money. Or even actual money, to pay for tuition and the like. So, I've been working the night-shift here, at the Hambridge Hospital, to put myself through Thieves' School. Or I was, but the Thieves' Guild suspended me indefinitely as of yesterday." Booter looked resigned but not unhappy. "Now I just work here."

"Don't you need some kind of special, uh, surgeon training?"

"Well, yeah, but the night classes aren't too hard," Booter explained, "and I got a fair amount of practice at the last couple of your Dalton school graduation tests. I'm still technically a nurse, y'know," he added, modestly. "I just help the surgeons, handing them forceps and gauze and sandwiches."

"Since when?" Sickly asked, feeling stunned.

"A bit more than three years, which is roughly the exact amount of time since mum and dad cut me off and told me they didn't want a son who couldn't support himself."

"That's – Booter, I'm so sorry! Three years, and you never told me?"

"Well, you were busy, and it never seemed important." Booter's voice trailed off apologetically.

"So . . . so you saved me?" Sickly said, slowly. He looked down at the neat bandaging around his leg and the numerous other gashes he had sustained at the hands of Winderstint's assassins. "You mended this? But you said you worked as a surgeon's assistant."

"Well, as it turns out, none of the other surgeons wanted to operate on you, in case something went wrong and you got angry about malpractice. On account of you being an assassin, and all."

"Malpractice? Do you mean they think I'd litigate them? Assassins don't usually bother suing, do they?"

"I believe that *was* the crux of their apprehension, yes. So, I volunteered. They told me what to do, and how to do it. But I was the one that did the stitches. I do hope everything's all right," he glanced worriedly at Sickly's leg. "You aren't going to sue me, are you? Or do anything . . . worse?"

Sickly coughed and raised his eyebrows. "Sue you? Booter, if I didn't feel like I was going to throw up, I'd hug you for a week straight!" His eyebrow quirked. "You may not have a thief's fingers, but it looks as though you certainly have a surgeon's thumbs!" Booter blushed at this abundance of praise. "What about you, Terry? And what about Mr. Munz?" Sickly asked.

"Ulrich's still in the intensive care unit, but I reckon he'll be all right. Too arrogant to die, that one," Booter said, admiringly.

"And I am okay, too." Terry rumbled, from his chair, sounding content. "Da wounds were not so bad, you and da doggy were not too heavy for me to carry out of da fire." The hairs on Sickly's neck prickled, his memories of the trip out of Ponsingham Palace were fuzzy . . .

"Oh Ten, you don't mean – surely you don't mean you carried out Crowbar, too?" Terry beamed, and Sickly sank back into his pillows.

Booter piped up, "Dr. Septic had him put in the veterinary wing. So far, he has tried to kill three nurses, a vet, and eat the cage we locked him in. We think that means he's going to be all right." His smile sagged. "More's the pity."

"And . . . and Jamie?" Sickly asked, suddenly worried about her absence.

"I'm fine, dear," said Jamie, who had been standing well back from the group. Her leg was splinted, but otherwise she seemed no worse for wear.

"She and Terry stuck with you the whole time," Booter added.

Sickly and Jamie regarded each other for a moment, and again the chasm of fear and distrust that had separated them threatened to reopen. Then she limped to his bedside and put her arms around him. "Thank you, Sickly. Thank you for showing me who – what Winderstint was. An entitled nob with more ego than brains. He wouldn't've saved a drowning orphan if he couldn't turn a profit off it."

He squeezed her back. So much pain and death could have been avoided if they had opened up to one another sooner. But in the end, they had fought Winderstint and Sable side by side. "Thanks for trusting me. Even though I am a nob."

They broke apart and she grinned wryly. "Yeah, but at least you admit it, dear." He raised his eyebrows at the warmth in her tone. "But seriously, I think I always knew he was a wanker. Winderstint, I mean. It was just really easy to get caught up in the dream. And it was enough gold to make it simple to look the other way when things got bad. And, of course, Sable kept talking about making things better. He really thought he was making a difference."

"So did I," Sickly reminded her. "I thought I was saving Hambridge."

"Me too, dear. That's the thing about philosophy, innit? Tough to say who or what has an effect or what backlash it might cause. All I know is I'm not going to stop fighting, yeah?"

"How's your father?" Sickly asked as Jamie went to sit on Terry's bench.

Jamie shrugged, stretching out her leg gingerly. She looked too worn out to muster anything more solid than that. "He's all right. Stable, I guess you doctor types would say," she murmured glancing at Booter. "That tonic, Beaupierre's, is the real thing, innit. Even if it is bloody expensive thanks to Digby and the Alchemists' Guild."

"Jamie, if there's anything I can do, I –" Sickly began.

"We can talk about it later," she said, flicking a coil of black braid over her shoulder dismissively. "But I promise to let you know when." She gave a guilty smile.

An awkward silence descended upon them. A silence broken

as someone tried to knock on the curtain, failed, and said, "Er, knock, knock."

"Who is it?" Terry queried.

"Corporal Anemia Cassidy," came the reply.

"Corporal Anemone Cassidy who?" Terry responded, dutifully.

"Come in," Sickly called quickly. Anemia's head of dark hair appeared between the curtains. Sickly could see from here that her grey eyes were red-rimmed, but that her face was stoic.

"Captain Cassidy of the Raft Street Watch sent me to inform you," and she coughed, staring at a point just above Sickly's left ear, "that: 'Those bloody fools who turned the city into a damn assassin warzone free-for-all are damn well under arrest.' His words, not mine. But as you are currently hospitalized and unfit for the cells, he sent me to watch over you here."

"I see," Sickly said. "Would it be within your purview, Corporal Cassidy, to explain what Captain Cassidy meant when he said a 'damn assassin warzone'?" Anemia sighed, and with the exhalation shed much of her formality. She put her helmet under one arm and sat next to Terry. Booter perched on the edge of Sickly's bed.

"We performed our inspection of the guilds and sent officers round to all guild offices taken over by assassins, like you suggested, Mr. Dodger. During our inspection the assassins, oh pardon me, the *officials* began receiving messages about something important. But they couldn't leave during an official Watch inspection since that would've been grounds for arrest.

"Next, Lord Scoke Reiker was found assassinated during the parliamentary procedures. Apparently there was also a fire, which is currently being investigated. So far, the bodies of Mr. Winderstint, several of the men and women known collectively as shadow wardens, and the assassins Sable Levania, and," her voice faltered for the first time, "Williams Kid, were found dead of the fire, or fire-related accidents."

Sickly swallowed words of comfort he knew would be hollow.

Nothing he said would make her, or anyone else, feel better, least of all himself.

"In the hours that followed, it seems that all the assassins working for Winderstint turned on each other and plunged the rooftops of the city into a bloodbath. Unfortunately, the late Commander of the City Watch, Hannabelle Merc, was slain in the fighting. Deputy Commander Wilhelmina Vorchimbeau issued general orders to keep the peace.

"The officers of the Watch have been forced to keep the populace indoors for fear of flying daggers, crossbow bolts, poison gas, explosions, and anything else you crazy basta- er, citizens use to kill each other. But assassins killing each other is strictly legal, under Hambridge law, so we aren't able to do anything about it, except wait for it to die down. Literally." She let out a breath. "What I don't understand is . . . why?" Anemia gave Sickly one of the Cassidy clan's penetrating stares.

"Because they are, and always will be, assassins." Sickly said simply. "Winderstint kept them in line with promises of greater power and the sense that they had a strong leader. As soon as he and Sable were dead, they turned on each other. Assassins aren't meant to work together. That was Winderstint's mistake. He thought he could organize a force of solo-killers into an army. Looks like he was wrong."

"You mean to say," Booter interjected, "there was no danger of Winderstint taking everything over?"

Jamie shook her head. "Oh, yes there bloody was. Between him and Sable, they had enough fear and respect to keep the others in line. I saw it firsthand. But without him, I reckon they went back to being your run-of-the-mill assassins."

Sickly nodded, and continued. "And all of them, being assassins, feared each other. I'm guessing that's why they went straight to backstabbing. They couldn't trust one another. And they needed to reestablish hierarchy. Like dogs, you know, but with knives. I guess this means we should start reaching out to the remaining spies, though they'll be tough to track down."

"No dey won't." Terry stated. He was smiling to himself. They stared, and he pulled from his pocket a battered, red notebook. "I took dis from Mr. Winderstint at da big fancy palace. It will help."

"Wow, big guy," Sickly breathed, astounded. "Smart thinking." Terry beamed. "When Parliament finally elects a new Foreign Minister we can pass it on properly. It's over at last," Sickly said. But even as he said it, their smiles began to fade, and his eyebrows lowered. A grim silence perched over the room.

"I miss Evline," said Terry quietly. "And Billys."

"It's just so hard," Anemia whispered, her voice choked. Sickly felt his own throat constrict in sympathy. "How do you move on, knowing that they . . . that they won't come back?"

"I don't know," Sickly said. Now that the fight was over there was little to distract him from the pain of knowing two of his closest friends had been ripped away so easily. It was like losing his father all over again. It wasn't just the tragedy of their deaths. It was the ache of all the lost opportunities that he could have shared with them, had things been different.

Terry put a gigantic arm around Anemia's shoulders. She stiffened at first, surprised by his gesture. Then she buried her face against his chest, and her shoulders began to shake. Jamie laid a hand on Terry's other shoulder. Booter tentatively took Sickly's hand in his own and squeezed. Somehow it eased the weight on Sickly's thin chest.

After a moment of silence, Booter coughed and fidgeted with his necklace. "Actually, there's, um, something I've been meaning to tell you." Sickly quirked an eyebrow.

It was at that point they were interrupted by a commotion from the room beyond the curtains. A number of voices were approaching their bed space. A few sounded indignant or harassed, but one cut through the chatter and set Sickly's heart lurching.

"If he's awake, I'm going to see him. Get your bloody hands off me or you'll lose them!" The curtain shielding his bed was thrown wide, revealing a pair of frustrated hospital attendants and a figure in a hospital gown with a mess of wavy red hair.

"Oi!" Booter yelled, in a remarkable imitation of a mother bear defending her cubs. "I did not tell you it was okay to walk from the women's ward all the way here! I told you to stay in bed or you'd reopen your wounds!"

"Well that's all right then, innit? See, m'fine!" said Eveline Lucrezia, as she shuffled on slipper-shod feet to the end of Sickly's bed. Her stomach and arm were both heavily bandaged.

"You. Are. Not. Fine!" Booter intoned, staring her down so severely that Vel dropped her gaze and sat apologetically on Sickly's bed. The other nurses left in a huff.

There was a moment of silence long enough for a colony of moths to make quite cozy homes in the open mouths of Sickly, Jamie, and Terry.

Jamie gave a little shriek of disbelief. "What in Hagrippa's hells?"

"How?" Sickly croaked.

Booter reddened. "Well, after Sable stabbed her and you went a bit daft, Jamie, Billys, and Terry went looking for you. Then, like I said earlier, me and the guards took her to the Hambridge Hospital. I gave her first aid on the way, and we were lucky it was so nearby. I convinced Dr. Septic, the Chair of Surgery, to try to operate on her. I helped out and just sort of hoped for the best. When the worst was over, I went back to the station."

"But – but," Sickly stammered, dumbfounded, his heart was pounding and he felt shaky with joy. "Why didn't you tell me?"

Booter's face darkened. "When you thought Eveline was dead, you got . . . scary. You went sort of, cold, y'know? I figured the only way for us to beat Winderstint and Sable was if you were still like that. I'm sorry, Sickly, I lied to you." He looked down, shamefaced.

"That was very clever of you," Sickly said, after a while. "You're certainly full of surprises today." Booter blushed again. Sickly wasn't sure how he felt about it, being used as a stone cold killer. It had worked, certainly, but he didn't like the idea that his emotions, pale as they might be, could be turned off like a switch. "Vel, you're going to be okay, right?"

"'Course I am," Vel said. Her laugh quickly faded into a wince.

"No humor!" Booter snapped. "No laughing or you really will bust a gut."

Jamie rushed to Vel's side and grasped her hand. "Eveline," Jamie breathed. "I thought you were dead. I thought I let them kill you." Vel's brow wrinkled in confusion. Slowly and awkwardly, Jamie explained how she had been working on both sides to secure information for Winderstint while also trying to protect her friends from the coup.

"So that's what you were going on about at Le Hibou Maigre," Vel said. She looked troubled. "All right then. But when we've both recovered, we're going to have a nice long chat, luv." Jamie nodded, her expression contrite. "And then right after that, I'm taking you shopping."

"I'd love to, dear, but I can't really –" Jamie began.

"I said that *I* am taking *you* shopping, luv," Vel clarified severely. "And then we are going to work on getting you a new job. We'll find you something that pays well and doesn't lead to the palace burning up and endangering our friends. I expect there'll be lots of jobs for assassins opening up, what with the blood bath and all." Jamie nodded, looking much happier. She and Vel hugged gingerly.

"Yeah, and I'm going to find a way to make a difference. A real difference. From the ground up." Jamie looked round and met each of their gazes. They nodded back.

After a long moment Terry said, "I still don't get what happened to da Ca-doo-see-us brothers? Why didn't dey kill us?" They all looked to Sickly.

"The first night at Mr. Staschcrumb's house, we came up with the plan to fight Winderstint. But I knew it wasn't enough, so the night before our attack, I came up with one last thing we could try. Booter?"

"Sickly and me figured their new mansion was pretty precious to them. So, I worked out where it was in Eel Park and I . . . well, I burnt it down." There was stunned silence.

"They must have got a message about a fire in their neighborhood, so they left to protect their home and call the Guild of Firefighters." Sickly finished. The tension cracked like pair of mahogany doors under Terry's assault, and they broke into laughter. Sickly twitched his eyebrows.

Finally, Vel turned to Sickly, her face becoming more serious. "I'm proud of you, y'know? Booter told me you were the one who killed Sable." Sickly dropped his gaze, unable to meet her eyes. "What's wrong?" she pressed.

"When you died – or when I thought you died, you said something to me. You said: Sickly, you're not . . . What did you mean? I'm not what? Not good enough?"

"Of course not, you idiot," she said, and punched him on the arm. "I was trying to tell you that you were right. You're not an assassin." A wave of relief swept over Sickly.

"You're right, I'm not. But I am a killer."

"I guess so," she said, her eyes thoughtful. He wasn't sure how to react to that. He had assumed she would have been proud of him. Henry Dodger probably would have been proud of his son. Certainly, Sickly was grateful to have paid the price to save his friends. That didn't mean he was sure what taking a life had cost him.

"What happens now?" Booter asked.

"I for one am going back to walking dogs," Sickly decided. Other things could wait. Vel groaned. "But I'm thinking of doing something else. Something on the side. I'm thinking I might solve assassination cases, the ones that aren't legal. Like a police detective, but for assassins. Like Kerry Adams said. A watcher who watches the killers who watch the watchers. Or something like that. Anyway, I reckon I might start a business. I could be Sickly Dodger: Assassin Hunter."

"That's terrible," Vel scoffed. Sickly rolled his eyes.

"Fine, what do you think I am?"

"Mad, but that goes without saying."

"Wait!" Booter exclaimed, "You could be: The Sickly Dodger!"

Jamie snorted. "Come off it, Booter, he needs a clever title, and that isn't artful at all!"

A figure picked its way across thick velvet carpeting. Getting past the Watch barricades had been simple, getting past the traps littering the grounds less so.

Luckily, the fire had been contained rapidly and had barely singed the great desk Winderstint had briefly used. During the renovations, it had been moved to a wing of the palace now used primarily for storage of artifacts and things the royal family didn't wish to display to its guests. The figure quietly passed by iron maidens, displays of torture instruments, and heirloom pottery piranhas.

It approached the desk.

The figure smiled, tapped at a side panel here and here, then there. A tiny lever clicked, a crack appeared in the desk, and the figure dug its nails into it, opening a tiny door.

The safe behind the secret door had no lock, just a series of intricate sliding panels and steel rods. The figure paused, disarmed a poison needle set to kill unwanted visitors, and considered the lock. Then, deftly, it slid panels and pivoted rods until there was another soft click. The safe door opened.

The Thief made a satisfied noise and slipped the leather briefcase beneath a cloak.

The River Ham oozed its way through the troughs and channels of the big city. The marketplaces bustled. A thief escaped a pair of cursing coppers by taking the Bridge of Snails at a dead run, knowing that city ordinance required officers to cross at the pace of the bridge's slowest user to prevent gastropod related accidents.

To the tourists who bought postcards featuring portrayals of the most famous serial killers of Murktown and miniature replicas of Ponsingham Palace (Complete with Figure Jumping from Severa Tower!) it was business as usual in Hambridge. It was indisputably the greatest city every built and anyone who said different would be bored to insanity by the city's Guild of Historians and Plausible Inaccuracy.

A group of five enormous mastiffs picked their way down the grimy streets of Hambridge in the wake of a sixth, larger mongrel. Behind these beasts a figure ambled slowly along, walking with a cane and a slight limp.

It hadn't always been this way. The city had been shaken during the events surrounding the assassinations of Lord Timothy and Lord Scoke Reiker. Change was in the air and, more importantly, in the little bits of dried and pressed tree mulch covered in ink which passed between smiling merchants in exchange for inert metals.

Passing through a particularly busy intersection, the limping figure fought a knitted wool cap more securely over his head.

"Outta the way, kiddo!" A young man with calloused hands and a scar puckering his upper lip barged past.

The cane swung up to tap the boy's shoulder. Reflexively, he grabbed a knife from his belt where it had been concealed by his frayed coat. "M'not playin' around, cully. You – oh, gods, not again!" The hard lines of his face scrunched into a look of pure terror as the six dogs converged around him.

"I'm not a kiddo, sir," said Sickly. The boy sank to his knees, a pleading look in his eyes. "Nor am I the kind to kick a man when he's down." The boy flinched and put a pair of protective hands over his groin. "Ah, I see you've met my friend, Mr. Stashcrumb. Well, I'm not him. I'm just a killer." Sickly's face was expression-less. The boy's eyes went wider, if that were possible.

"But mostly I prefer the term 'dog-walker.' Shove off then, if you know what's good for you." The boy bolted through the opening the dogs had left for him. The small crowd which had gathered applauded.

Sickly doffed his cap, the Dodger family signet ring on his finger catching the light as he did so. Then he moseyed up the road.

"Something new's coming," he said to the dogs.

He could feel it in the ache of his leg.

Lars Konrad Mooresmith grew up rambling with a brother and a dog over the rolling hills of the Inland Northwest of the United States. He spent most of college with his nose in a book, preferably action packed fantasy or sci-fi, but looked up one day to find he had graduated with a degree in neuroscience. Going to graduate school was a no-brainer, and he now spends most of his time poking that mysterious tangle of neurons called the central nervous system to see what makes memories tick. He currently lives in the Greater Boston area juggling graduate work, writing, punning and sleep.

He also writes poetry ranging from humorous to darkly incisive, enjoys hobby lock picking, painting, 3D printing, and swords and sorcery role playing games.

For more information and content, please visit
mooresmithbooks.com
or follow L.K. on Twitter @LKMooresmith

www.ingramcontent.com/pod-product-compliance
Lightning Source LLC
Chambersburg PA
CBHW030829110726
47900CB00006B/1808